Dear Readers,

This book is part of a new editio
stories about the Gibson family. It
I hope you like them as much as I
this one for each book, sharing some of what was going on
behind the scenes when I wrote the stories. It's brought back
a lot of lovely memories.

I'd spent all of Book 4 (*Hallam Square*) making Annie's
second and much older husband ill enough to die gently. Now,
in Book 5, the time had come to bite the bullet and kill him
off.

Oh, how I wept as I wrote the first chapter of *Spinners
Lake*! My husband came home to find me with swollen red
eyes and rushed across to put his arms round me. 'What's
wrong?'

'I've killed Frederick Hallam,' I replied, sobbing some
more.

Yes, my secret is out now, readers. Whenever I write a sad
bit, I cry. If my husband finds me looking as if I've been
crying, he always asks, 'Who did you kill today?' It's become
a joke in my family.

Of course, as the story continued, an attractive woman like
Annie was bound to find another husband. I wanted this one
to be very different from Frederick.

And then this was the time of the American Civil War,
which cut off supplies of cotton to Lancashire. This left mill
workers starving, literally, because there was no welfare state
in those days. Of course Annie wouldn't let her workers starve,
so she started a project to give them employment.

I often get asked if I'm going to write another book about
Annie. No, I'm not. Most definitely not. If I did, I might have

to kill her and I couldn't bear to do that! But I did continue her brother Mark's story in *A Pennyworth of Sunshine* and *Twopenny Rainbows*. And I did use the cotton famine background again in *Farewell to Lancashire*.

Happy reading!

Anna Jacobs

ANNA JACOBS

Spinners Lake

The Gibson Family Saga:
Book Five

HODDER

First published in Great Britain in paperback in 1997
By Hodder & Stoughton
An Hachette UK company

This paperback edition published in 2015
by Hodder & Stoughton

I

A CIP catalogue record for this title is available
from the British Library

Paperback ISBN 978 1 473 61716 2
eBook ISBN 978 1 444 71444 9

Typeset in Plantin Light by Palimpsest Book Production Limited,
Falkirk, Stirlingshire
Printed and bound by Clays Ltd, St Ives plc

Hodder & Stoughton policy is to use papers that are natural, renewable
and recyclable products and made from wood grown in sustainable
forests. The logging and manufacturing processes are expected to
conform to the environmental regulations of the country of origin.

Hodder & Stoughton Ltd
Carmelite House
50 Victoria Embankment
London EC4Y 0DZ

www.hodder.co.uk

To David again, with so much love.
You're the best husband a writer could have –
Reader and astute critic of my tales,
Patient when my mind is 'elsewhere',
Good at cooking,
And even sharing my love for the Mikado!
What more could anyone want of a spouse and friend?

John Gibson
(1798)
m(1)
Lucy Woolley (1799–1830)

Annie	Tom	Lizzie	Mark	Luke
(1820)	(1822)	(1825)	(1834)	(1835)
m(1)	m Marianne			
Charlie	Lewis			
Ashworth	(1828–1851)			
(1800–1844)	m (2) Rossie			
	Liddelow			
	1859			
William	(1823)			
(1838)				

m(2)
Fredrick
Hallam**   **Frederick Hallam
(1798)   m(1) Christine Ramsby (1800–1845)

Oliver	James	Mildred	Beatrice
(1821–1843)	(1822)	(1823)	(1826–1859)
	m Judith	m Peter	
		Jemmings	

m(2) Annie Gibson

Tamsin	Edgar
b. 1850	b. 1852

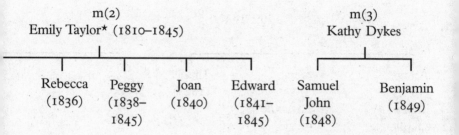

m(2)
Emily Taylor* (1810–1845)

m(3)
Kathy Dykes

Rebecca (1836)

Peggy (1838–1845)

Joan (1840)

Edward (1841–1845)

Samuel John (1848)

Benjamin (1849)

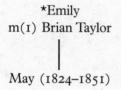

*Emily
m(1) Brian Taylor

May (1824–1851)

m(2) John Gibson

FAMILY TREES AT 1860

Contents

Contents

1860

I

Bilsden: July 1860

Frederick Hallam stared longingly out of the window. The gardens were magnificent with a summer's wealth of flowers – and for the past two weeks, he had not even been able to walk outside to smell them without help.

'We could get you a bath-chair,' Annie suggested, knowing how much her husband longed to go out into the fresh air.

'No!' His voice was harsh, but it softened as he added, 'I'm weakening fast, love, but I won't be wheeled around in an invalid chair.' He knew it was foolish, but he could not bear the thought of her seeing him like that. It would be the ultimate indignity. He held up one hand to still the protest he knew she would make. She had been so brave about his long illness, his lass had. 'Don't say you haven't noticed how quickly I tire now, how I pant for breath if I walk even a few paces. We agreed not to lie to one another.'

She could only nod. All Frederick's family and friends had noticed, of course they had, and worried to one another, but Jeremy Lewis said nothing more could be done to help her husband and Jeremy was the best doctor in town, as well as a close friend. Frederick's heart was failing fast. One day soon it would simply stop beating. Riches couldn't buy you health.

'As far as I'm concerned,' Frederick went on, his voice steady, 'I'd prefer to die now, while you can still remember me as a man, not a helpless wreck.' For a moment, on that last phrase, his voice was bitter, then he fought and regained control of it, as he had kept control of himself all through his long illness.

3

'Don't say such things!' Annie walked slowly across the room to the sofa and sat down as close to him as she could.

He put his arm round her shoulders. At forty, she was still young and vibrant, her glorious auburn hair only lightly threaded with silver and her skin fresh and unlined, except for a few faint wrinkles at the corners of her eyes and mouth. He could not imagine her old, somehow. But he was old. At sixty-two, he looked a decade more than his years. And he hated it! Hated most of all not being able to pleasure his younger wife, and hated too the indignity of having to be carried upstairs at night.

'When I'm gone,' he said in her ear, 'don't waste your time grieving for me, Annie-girl. Get on with living!'

'Don't say—'

'Shh! I mean it. Our marriage has been the best thing in my whole life. I've never loved anyone as I love you, never been so happy. But because I care so much about you, I don't want you moping around for years in widow's weeds and I don't want Tamsin and Edgar wasting their childhood grieving for me, either. Promise me that you'll get on with living afterwards! *Promise!*'

She nodded, frightened by the urgency in his voice. 'I promise, love.'

His arm tightened for a moment, then he leaned back his head and said quietly, 'It's time to tell the children. I want to do it myself, one at a time. Will you send Tamsin down?'

'But, Frederick—'

He gave her a wry smile. 'No buts. Do this for me, please.'

Annie went upstairs, but had to stop briefly in their bedroom to pull herself together and wipe away the tears that would fall. At the schoolroom door, she took a deep breath and walked in. Elizabeth MacNaughton, more a friend than a governess by now, looked up and smiled, then the smile faded as she saw Annie's expression.

'Can I see Tamsin for a few minutes?'

Tamsin bounded to her feet, always eager to leave her studies.

She was too active and wilful to sit still for long, and only a clever woman like Elizabeth could have persuaded her to attend to her lessons.

Annie led the way back to their bedroom. 'Your father wants to see you in the library, Tamsin. Wait!' She tried to find the words to prepare her daughter, but could only say, 'Listen to him carefully and think before you speak, love. It's not good news. He's not at all well. But if he can bear what is to come, so must you, or you'll make it worse for him.'

The child looked puzzled, but when her mother said nothing else, walked slowly downstairs. After a moment's hesitation, Annie followed, to wait quietly in the hall, ready to offer comfort or to restrain this difficult daughter of hers if she flew into a rage. Annie would not have ventured to predict which it would be. She tried hard, but had trouble understanding her only daughter.

In the event. Frederick did this job as well as he had done everything else in his life and the children emerged, one after the other, white and shaken, but quiet. Edgar hugged his mother then rushed upstairs to weep in his governess's arms, but Tamsin said not a word, just went and shut herself in her room. She refused to come down to dinner or to open the door to anyone until the following morning. And Frederick gave orders that no one was to disturb her.

At dawn the next day, Annie woke and slid out of bed quietly so as not to waken her husband. She turned to look at him, seeing how shallowly he was breathing, his chest barely lifting beneath the covers. He had been so tired yesterday after his interviews with the children. His complexion had been grey-tinged, though his mouth had still been drawn into that thin determined line that was so much a part of him. And she had heard him tossing and turning during the night. Let him sleep as long as he wished this morning.

Dressing quickly without her maid's help, she went along to her studio, intending to work on some dress designs for the ladies' dress salon she still owned, though she had not worked there since she got married, of course.

But today the ideas would not come. She could only sit and stare out of the window as the dawn colour faded from the sky above the moors. In the end, she took a piece of art paper and bent her head over it, sketching the lake and the gardener's boy who was carefully watering the flower beds nearby. It had been such a beautiful summer! But after a while, she screwed up the piece of paper and put the pencil down. She could not draw, only sit remembering the conversation with Frederick the evening before. Not long now. They both knew it.

As the hall clock chimed seven-thirty, she went quietly back to the bedroom to check whether he was awake yet. It was not like him to stay in bed so long. He needed little sleep nowadays and was usually awake before she was.

Something about the stillness of the figure in the bed alerted her before she got to his side. There was no movement of the covers now, no rise and fall of his chest. She could not speak, only drop to her knees by the side of her beloved husband and stroke his cheek. 'I'm glad,' she said fiercely, 'glad you got your wish, glad you died before you grew worse.'

And she was. So she used that feeling to keep the grief at bay. It felt as if there was a bottomless well ready to open up inside her, but she would not allow herself to fall into it. Not yet, anyway. For now she had to carry out his last wishes, see him laid to rest in peace, see that everything else was done as he had planned.

But how would she cope afterwards? He had been her best friend, as well as her husband. She could not think how she would face life without him.

Summer rain fell softly on the little Lancashire mill town as Frederick Hallam's funeral cortege wound its way down Ridge Hill towards the church. Even heaven was weeping, one woman said fancifully, to see such a good man pass away. And no one contradicted her. The streets were lined with his workpeople, mourning a good master, standing silently in the rain to pay him their last respects in the only way they could.

'We s'all not find another like him,' one man said to another.

'No. He weren't soft, but he were a fair master, an' he paid a fair wage, too – well, as fair as a master will ever pay. Unlike some on 'em. I've been a Hallam's man all my life, an' proud of it.'

'What'll happen t'mill now, do you think?'

'I don't know. That little lad of his is too young to take over, an' his other son lives over Leeds way. He hasn't set foot in the mill since he were a lad, that James hasn't. He's a starched-up sort, an' allus were. Takes after his mother. Looks down his nose at common folk. The Mester never did that. No, never in his life.'

'D'you think the family will sell the mill now?'

'Eh, I hope not. It wouldn't be Bilsden without Hallam's. It were the first of the mills, an' it's still the biggest.'

Annie Hallam, born Annie Gibson, was sitting in the first carriage with her children. All four people were clad in unrelieved black. She looked across at her eldest child, William, who was now twentytwo, and managed a brief twist of the lips that some might have called a smile.

He nodded back, wishing his mother would let go and weep. She hadn't – well, not that anyone had seen – since she'd discovered three days ago that Frederick had died in his sleep. She had just set about organising things, looking grim, tense, and somehow smaller than usual. Her eyes had not been red-rimmed, just burning with a fierce green glow that said, to him who knew her so well at least, that his mother was living on her nerves.

Annie was thinking of the afternoon to come. There would be another confrontation with James Hallam, she was sure. He had arrived with his wife and children the day Frederick died, in response to Annie's telegram, and had immediately tried to take over at Ridge House. He was only two years

7

younger than she was, but he looked years older. And acted it, too.

She scowled, remembering how he had tried to treat her as he treated his own wife, as if she were a lesser being, incapable of understanding anything more than her house and children. When Judith married him, she had been a determined, confident woman, but that had gradually changed. Now, she only voiced opinions approved by her husband, obeyed his orders in all things and exerted no authority except over her home and two children. And they were quiet docile creatures, too, in Annie's opinion, seeming afraid to open their mouths in front of their parents.

Well, she thought, I soon put James straight about the fact that I'm still in charge here. He must have guessed that Frederick's left Ridge House to me, for the children's sake. James will be a bit more careful how he acts with me next time, I think.

Frederick's daughter, Mildred, had been nearly as trouble-some as her brother, though for different reasons. She had arrived from London the day after her father's death, with her husband, Peter Jemmings, and her younger daughter, Phillipa. The older daughter, Rosemary, had married recently and was already in an 'interesting condition', so had not attended.

Mildred, too, had started giving orders to the servants within an hour of arriving, orders that contradicted those of their mistress. Mildred had never forgotten how the house had been run in her mother's day, apparently, and believed she had a right to change things, now that her father was dead. Annie's lips tightened at the memory of their short, sharp quarrel about that. Her servants were too loyal to obey anyone else and the housekeeper had referred the contradictory orders to her, to Mildred's fury.

Annie had not deigned to argue with her step-daughter, but had simply stated her intention of continuing to run her own home as she always had. 'And if you don't like it, then you can leave!' she had wound up, before walking out of the room and leaving Mildred to exchange very uncomplimentary views with her husband about her father's second wife.

The complaints continued, however, every time Annie was with her visitors. It was as if they were deliberately trying to make life difficult for her.

When Mildred sat down to dinner, she glared at her step-mother and fired another salvo. 'My dear Annie, your brother tells me that you intend some of the workpeople to sit inside the church with their betters at the funeral!'

Annie clutched her knife and fork tightly in case she gave way to the impulse to hurl them at her step-daughter. 'It was your father's express wish,' she said, articulating each word carefully.

From the other side of the table, William frowned at Mildred and then looked at his mother. His loving expression was nearly Annie's undoing.

'Pah!' James Hallam got everyone's attention, but it was Annie he was looking at, making no attempt to hide his scorn. 'That's bad enough, though it's typical of Father – but to let one of the operatives act as pall bearer is unconscionable! Isn't it enough to have the Manager of the mill as one? Matt Peters can perfectly well represent the workpeople, if that's what you're trying to do.'

Mildred nodded vigorously. 'And it's my husband's right to act as pall bearer.'

Beside her, Peter Jemmings stirred uneasily. He didn't care if he wasn't involved, but his wife had wept and raged about the insult. On and on. Heavens, why did men need wives? Life would be so much easier without them.

'It's an insult to my father's memory,' Mildred continued the attack, colour high, head nodding vigorously in support of her statement. 'I can't believe that you're doing this to us, Annie.'

But Frederick himself had chosen the pall bearers and Annie was merely following his wishes. Only they would not believe that. She stood up, pushing her chair back so abruptly that it fell over. 'I'll be back in a minute.' She marched out, fumbled in the desk in the library and returned with a piece of paper, which she slapped down in front of James. 'These are the notes your father made about his wishes.'

He read it, then breathed deeply and read it again. 'I see.' His voice was chill and curt.

'I hope you do.'

Mildred stretched out one hand imperatively and James passed the piece of paper to her. She tutted under her breath as she studied it. 'Whatever can he have been thinking of?'

'Father was thinking of the people who have made this family's wealth, the people who have toiled and sometimes given their lives in service to the Hallams!' William snapped, unable to keep quiet a moment longer. 'And I, for one, honour him for that.' He had loved and respected his step-father.

Even Annie was surprised when her quiet elder son joined in the argument so emphatically. But grateful for his support. Very grateful. He had grown into a solid dependable sort of man, her William had.

Now, sitting in the carriage, trying to find the strength to face the funeral itself, she looked across at Tamsin and then down at Edgar, sitting close by her side. They were both fighting against tears. She saw William squeeze Tamsin's hand and felt Edgar's hand creep into hers. There was nothing she could do to make it easier for them. Everyone had to learn that life was uncertain. In this world, at least. Unlike her father and William, who were devoted Methodists, Annie was not sure about the next world, not at all sure if there was life after death.

After the funeral, Annie lingered by the grave, not wanting to leave Frederick alone there in the large plot his father had had laid out many years previously.

She was aware that people were standing staring at her, but she wanted a little more time with her husband. As a shadow fell across her, she sighed and looked up. Why could they not leave her alone?

'You should come away now, Step-mother.' James offered her his arm with a little imperative shake.

She needed a minute or two on her own, needed it quite desperately. 'No. I'll stay here for a while, I think.'

'But there will be people to receive up at the house! Your duty is there.'

'I'm sure Mildred will be more than happy to greet them in my place.'

He spoke with weary patience, certain that his time to take charge had come, that she was now about to betray the normal weakness of her sex. 'And we have arranged to have the will read, don't forget, Step-mother.'

'I'll be home within the hour. The will-reading can wait until then. Send the carriage back for me.' She saw William looking across at her and made a shooing gesture with her hand, looking meaningfully at Tamsin and Edgar. William nodded and led his half-brother and -sister away, speaking to them gently, one arm around each child's shoulders.

James muttered something beneath his breath, but left.

Annie sighed in relief. How could her Frederick have fathered a son like James?

When everyone had gone, she found a bench and nodded to the grave diggers to continue filling in the hole. She sat quietly with her hands clasped in her lap, watching them. Beside that mass of disturbed earth was Thomas Hallam's grave, the marble monument still the largest in the churchyard of St Mark's. Frederick wanted nothing but a simple headstone and that was what she had ordered, causing yet another quarrel with James and Mildred.

'All the memorial I need will be in the memories of those who have loved me,' Frederick had said quietly one day. 'And in the square they named after me. I'm so pleased about that.'

She nodded now. Hallam Square. How happy it had made

Frederick when the Town Council named the new square after him! What a glorious day that had been.

She sat on, feeling the quietness with relief, feeling her tiredness, too. There was only the sound of the grave diggers shovelling the earth and the pattering of light rain on her umbrella. It was not cold, not even very wet. When the will was read, James and Mildred would be even more furious. Frederick had explained to her exactly how he had left things, and she was dreading the moment when his wishes were revealed.

Annie wasn't even sure if she was happy about it herself. Frederick had placed a heavy burden of responsibility on her shoulders. She sometimes thought she'd had more than her share of responsibility in her forty years.

She suddenly became aware of a figure standing beside her and turned, sighing in relief to see her father.

'Are you all right, lass?' John Gibson had been watching for a few minutes.

'Yes.' She gestured to the seat beside her and he sat down, as unconcerned about the rain as she was herself.

'It's hard to lose a spouse,' he said in his slow quiet voice.

She nodded. He should know. He had lost two wives. Her mother had died when Annie was ten, and her step-mother when she was twenty-five. His third wife, Kathy, was younger than she was. But now, Annie realised with surprise, she had lost two husbands. Her first, Charlie Ashworth, had been a slow-witted man, incapable of fathering a child or being a true husband. He had married her to give her child a name after she had been raped at the age of seventeen. And so William bore Charlie's surname and remembered him fondly, too, for Charlie had been a kindly man. Though of course William knew the truth about himself now.

She realised that her father was waiting patiently for her to finish her thoughts and gave him a half-smile.

'Are you all right, lass? Really?'

'Yes. I was just needing a bit of quiet, Dad. The house seems to be so full of Hallams.'

'Aye. And they're a pushy pair, those two.'

Not until the grave diggers had finished did she stand up, then she plucked a white rose from those cascading over the side wall of the churchyard and dropped it on the grave. I'll be back, she promised Frederick silently. Often.

She turned to her father. 'Will you come up to the house with me for the will-reading, Dad?'

John nodded. 'Kathy's taken the two lads home, but when I saw you stopping behind, I thought you might need me.'

'Oh, I do!'

'An' the others have gone up to Ridge House already.' He was speaking now of the children of Emily, his second wife. 'Mester Pennybody said they were wanted, that they were mentioned in the will. Our Luke went with William, an' Rebecca was with Simon, of course. Joanie went with them.' It had taken John Gibson a while to get used to calling Simon, Lord Darrington, by his first name, but since his future son-in-law was not one to play off the airs and graces, John had gradually grown accustomed to him, as he had once had to grow accustomed to Annie's marrying the master he had worked for most of his life.

'I wonder what Mark is doing now?' she said.

'Eh, if I could just hear that he's safe, I'd not care what he were doing,' said John. For Mark had run away the previous year, rather than marry Nelly Burns, the girl he had got pregnant, and John had blamed himself ever since for threatening to disown his son if he did not marry her. John still felt that a man should give his name to his childer, but at least Mark had made provision for the babby. They had heard nothing of the lad since the night he left and the anxiety was preying on his father's mind. And by now even John, who never judged anyone else harshly, felt that Nelly was a spiteful fool of a wench. Not worthy of his Mark. Not worthy at all.

Annie and her father sat together in silence as the carriage horses, still wearing their black ribbons and plumes, clopped slowly up the hill to Ridge House. Groups of people were lingering on the streets, in spite of the dampness of the day, for the mill had been closed out of respect. Some of the men raised their hats to the carriage as it passed and the women nodded their heads.

Annie knew them all by name, for she had been working in the mill for a while now, acting for Frederick. 'They won't like the will, James and Mildred won't,' she said abruptly. 'They'll cause a fuss.'

'They mun just fuss, then. If it's what Frederick wanted, that's good enough for me an' it should be good enough for them, too. A man has a right to leave his possessions as he wishes.'

Two people had stood by the churchyard gates to watch the funeral and had stayed on afterwards when they saw that Annie Hallam and John Gibson had not left with the others. Harry Pickering, a heavy-featured young man who worked in the office of the Bilsden Gas Company, turned to his sister, Maddie. 'Didn't make old bones, did he, for all his money?'

She sighed. 'I don't know why you wanted to come today. Funerals always make me feel down!'

'I wanted to show respect. And I wanted us to be seen showing respect.'

She gave a cackle of laughter, not as loud as her usual shrieks of mirth but loud enough that he put a hand across her mouth and hissed, 'Shush, you fool!'

When he had removed the hand, she hunched her shoulders against the cold. 'Didn't Joanie look funny? I don't think black suits her.'

'It doesn't matter whether black suits her or not. It's a sign of respect.' He had waved at just the right moment to catch Joanie's attention and her expression had brightened briefly at the sight of her two friends – which was the main reason he'd come here today. But to his delight, John Gibson had noticed him and Maddie as well, and had nodded his head to them.

'We can go now,' Harry said. 'We've done as I wanted.' Better than he had hoped, for John Gibson had acknowledged him. He wanted the old man to think well of them. Harry had every intention of worming his way into John Gibson's good books over the next few months.

When she got back to the house, Annie gave her cloak to a tearstained maid, then moved among the guests, accepting their condolences and murmuring responses which were as polite-sounding as they were meaningless.

Her children, together with James's, had retired to the school-room in Elizabeth MacNaughton's charge. Tamsin was under strict orders not to quarrel with the other children and had declared scornfully that she'd be happy not even to speak to them, so silly were they.

Edgar had said nothing. After his first outburst, the boy had held his grief about his father too tightly inside himself and that was worrying his mother.

After a while, James bustled up to Annie, looking swollen with importance, as if he had grown taller and plumper on the drive up the hill. 'The family needs to move towards the library now, Stepmother.' He opened his mouth to issue the order.

'No!' Annie's voice came out sharply. To her, it didn't even sound like her own voice.

He stared at her, surprised by her white face, the burning unhappy light in her eyes. At least she had truly loved his father, he thought. But then another thought followed. Well, she's been well paid to love him. I've never been able to understand his marrying a woman like her, a woman from the Rows. James intended to see as little as possible of her, now that his father was dead. His half-brother and -sister seemed more her children than his father's, anyway. Gibsons rather than Hallams.

'I'm still capable of managing my own household, James, as I told you when you arrived.' Annie's voice was quieter now, but her eyes were flaring a challenge at him.

He did not reply for a minute or two, not wanting to lose

control of himself on such an important day: the day he came into his inheritance as eldest son. He didn't approve of women like her, he thought, not for the first time, scowling at his step-mother. A line from a poem which he had once read had stuck in his mind: '*Man to command and woman to obey; All else confusion.*' Tennyson. And so true.

His eyes flickered to his own wife. Even Judith had needed moulding to his ways after they married. Women should not even try to think for themselves. Their brains were not capable of logic. His step-mother, with her businesses and the opinions she didn't hesitate to express, was an embarrassment to him, an outrage against nature. 'I was merely trying to save you the tr—' he began.

She cut him off sharply, her voice carrying all too clearly and making him hiss in annoyance. 'Then don't. Don't try to save me anything, James. This is my house and I'm still mistress of it.'

'Ah.' He nodded as if what she had said confirmed a suspicion. 'Father has left you the house, then. We were afraid he might.'

'Father's in his dotage,' Mildred had commented, and she'd been right.

Annie turned away abruptly, hating the cupidity in James's eyes, hating most of all his blurred resemblance to Frederick. Around her were people who really mourned her husband, who deeply regretted his passing. She left her step-son without a word of apology and went to speak to them instead, for it soothed something inside her to hear the genuine regret in their voices.

Nearly an hour passed before Annie had found time to speak to everyone who had been invited to the funeral. After the encounter with her, James retired to the bay window, with his wife, sister and brother-in-law in attendance, and made no further attempt to talk to the other guests.

But she was conscious of his eyes on her all the time. The expression in them was cold and disapproving, and Judith, beside him, kept eyeing her husband anxiously, as if a little afraid of his temper.

Well, let him stare, Annie thought. What do I care about him? Carrying out Frederick's wishes is all I care about now. And she would do that whatever it cost her. Whatever!

2

Ridge House

Annie nodded farewell to the last guest and turned to face her next ordeal. The lawyer had asked some of her own family to stay for the reading of the will and she was glad of that. Tom's wife, Rosie, nodded to her from across the room and Annie gave a tiny nod of response. She liked Rosie and was glad that her brother had married again.

The only persons present now who were not Hallams or Gibsons were Matt Peters, Manager of the mill, and Rebecca Gibson's fiancé, Simon, Lord Darrington, together with the two lawyers, Jonas Pennybody and his son, Hamish.

Annie glanced through the doors of the library and saw Jonas Pennybody shuffling through some papers on the table, setting them out in precise piles. He was looking old and frail nowadays, but had insisted on presiding at the will reading of his most important client. Behind him Hamish hovered, ready to help his father who had now mostly retired from active participation in the firm.

Matt Peters was waiting just inside the library door. He, too, had grown up in the Rows, in Salem Street, a few doors away from Annie, and at one time the two of them had been engaged. Until Fred Coxton raped her. Then Matt had turned away, broken their engagement, left her to fend for herself. But she did not hold that against him now. There was no point in holding on to grudges. Life was too short for that.

And Matt had done well by Frederick, who had seen promise in him as a child and had trained him carefully, later promoting him to help run the mill.

Annie had come to realise that she would not have been happy with Matt, though at the time he had been the sun in her sky. He was now married to a cousin of Frederick's first wife and, like most men, seemed to dominate his family and home. Time and again she had seen poor Jane subordinate her wishes to his, change her plans, even her opinions. Annie would never have stood for that and Frederick would not have asked it of her. Strange how things often worked out for the best, though life was hard at times and you could not always understand where it was leading you.

She realised that she was prevaricating so cleared her throat loudly and waited for a moment as all eyes turned towards her. 'We'll go into the library now, shall we?'

Before James could make a move, William stepped forward to offer his mother his arm and together they led the way into the room that had always been Frederick's favourite, with a scowling James and his wife pressing on their heels. Annie squeezed William's hand. 'Thank you. I'll be all right now.' She indicated a chair and he sat down, leaving her to wait at the front of the room alone, head held high.

'If you'll sit there, James.' She indicated a place. 'And Mildred here.' She saw that James had a sour, suspicious expression on his face as he took the seat indicated.

Mildred looked around the room rather complacently as she followed her brother and Judith to the front row. She did not doubt that this day would see her a rich woman, and that was all she cared about. The prospect had put dear Peter in such a good mood. She looked sideways at him. Yes, he was definitely in a good mood today. Not that he was glad about poor Father's death, no, of course not. But there would be compensations, there was no denying that. She wiped her eyes, though there were no tears in them, flourishing a black-edged lace handkerchief and sighing loudly.

When everyone was seated, Annie turned to the lawyer. 'Mr Pennybody?'

He stood up and tugged at his old-fashioned high collar,

making the flat bow of his necktie a little crooked. 'Ahem. We are gathered here today to—'

While the introductory phrases were being spoken, Annie sat back, relieved to let someone else deal with things for a while. It was hard to concentrate, for she had not slept much the previous night, but she didn't feel tired now, just light-headed. And wary. She had been dreading today. But at least the funeral was over now and she hadn't made a fool of herself at it. Only when she was alone would she allow herself to give way to her grief, she had decided, for if she once started weeping, she knew she wouldn't be able to stop.

Mr Pennybody paused and took a deep breath. 'Although my late client was a rich man, the will is very straightforward. I have had full copies made for the principal family legatees, so I shall just, with your agreement, summarise Frederick Hallam's wishes today.'

There was a ripple of sound as most people leaned forward attentively.

Mr Pennybody took a deep breath. He, too, had been dreading this moment. He loathed it when people made a fuss about how things had been left and there was sure to be a fuss today. 'To his eldest surviving son, James Stephen Hallam, my client leaves a ten per cent share in the mill and other businesses, together with certain specified items from Mr Hallam's personal jewellery as mementoes, and—'

'What!' James stood up, anger radiating from him. He had expected the major share of everything. It was his right. He was the eldest son.

'Please wait until I have finished, Mr Hallam.' Jonas frowned over the top of his spectacles.

James snapped his lips closed, but his eyes sought those of Annie and his glare promised trouble thereafter. Beside him, Judith gazed down at her clasped hands, which were trembling slightly.

'To my daughter, Mildred Rosemary Jemmings, née Hallam, I leave a ten per cent share in the various businesses and all her mother's jewellery.'

Mildred's lips trembled and she looked quickly sideways at her husband. This wasn't nearly as much as they'd expected and she could see how displeased he was. Her eyes filled with tears. Dear Peter had had some trouble with his investments lately. She didn't understand what exactly, but she knew he had been hoping for a quarter share of her father's estate. Well, she too had been expecting more. Like her brother, she turned a reproachful look on Annie.

Jonas Pennybody stopped summarising and read from the will itself. He wanted Frederick's words to bring the next point home. '"The shares of the said James Stephen and Mildred Rosemary in Hallam's Mill are to be held in trust under the direct control of my wife Annie, as principal legatee. They may not be sold to anyone but members of the immediate family, and then only with her permission. The shares in the other businesses may be sold to any suitable purchaser, but again only with my wife's agreement and at a time convenient to her."'

'No!' James was back on his feet, utterly furious now. Rarely did he allow his temper to boil over in public, but when he did, his family quailed before him. Judith was sitting bolt upright beside him, one black-gloved hand raised to her mouth, the other stretched out as if to pull him back. But she let it drop. James had been so irascible since his father's death that she was a little nervous of trying to stop him doing anything today.

'Mr Hallam, please!' The lawyer tried in vain to make himself heard as James shouted at Annie and Peter Jemmings joined in, with their two wives bleating a chorus of dismay behind them.

John Gibson put an arm round Annie. His daughter shouldn't have to face this on top of her loss. Money didn't make for happiness with some folk; it just made for more greed.

William, angry on his mother's behalf, stood up. He was a huge muscular man who towered over everyone else in the room. 'Be quiet!' he roared. And as the voices faltered and faded, he added cuttingly, 'Have you no respect for my step-father's wishes?'

'Your mother has cheated me and mine out of our inheritance! Taken advantage of a foolish old man,' James added, taking a step in Annie's direction, one clenched fist half raised.

'It's a damned shame!' Peter Jemmings echoed. 'Not of sound mind, if you ask me. The will should be overset.'

'My mother has never cheated anyone in her life,' William declared, moving forward until he was standing between the two men and Annie. 'And if you ever say anything else like that, I'll be happy to discuss it with you in the garden.' There was no mistaking his meaning.

Peter moved backwards hastily, but James stood toe to toe with William. 'I have not finished and I intend to say my piece, and I don't see why I should wait any longer to do so.' He glared at Annie and opened his mouth to speak.

John Gibson had moved to his eldest daughter's side and it was he who interrupted this time, raising his own voice to the tone which carried clearly to every corner of the Methodist Chapel at which he was a favoured lay preacher. 'Shame upon you for creating a fuss at such a moment, James Hallam. Shame, I say!' He watched James's mouth drop open and Peter Jemmings take another step backwards. 'I pray the Lord to bring a little sense into your heads and a little seemliness to this sad occasion.'

Tom, who had stood up to intervene, sat down again, eyes gleaming with approval. His father might have spent most of his life working in Hallam's Mill, but at that moment he had an air of immense dignity, before which even James Hallam hesitated.

For a moment, all hung in the balance, then James threw himself down in his chair, shaking his wife's hand off his arm when she tried to whisper something soothing to him.

At the front of the room, Jonas Pennybody waited for his heart to stop thumping, rustling his papers while the two angry men settled down. Then, into a silence pregnant with emotion – not, alas, an unusual occurrence at will-readings – he read out the rest of the provisions.

To Frederick's beloved daughter Tamsin and his equally beloved son Edgar, there were annuities of two hundred pounds per annum, payable from the age of twenty-one. Not until their mother died or decided to give them a share in the mill would they be entitled to receive more.

The two children were sitting a little way back, near their Uncle Tom, and their presence was another thing which had annoyed James and Judith, whose own children were always kept firmly out of sight in the schoolroom.

'That means we'll eventually get more than James,' Tamsin said in satisfaction. She did not like her half-brother. 'When Mother dies.'

Edgar punched her in the arm. 'Don't you dare talk like that!' he hissed, surprising them both, for he was usually content to stay in his sister's shadow. 'I hope Mother never dies. And I don't care about the money.'

'I didn't mean that,' she whispered, shamefaced. 'You know I didn't.'

Rosie leaned across to shush them.

Minor bequests included an annuity of two hundred pounds per annum to Frederick's step-son, William Ashworth, so that he could afford the time to find his own way in life. Even James, peering jealously sideways, could not doubt by the sheer surprise on William's face that Annie's son had known nothing of this.

Other Gibsons were mentioned. For Mark there was a watch: 'Since I have every confidence in Mark's ability to do well for himself.' For Luke, Rebecca and Joanie there was two hundred pounds apiece.

Joanie sat with mouth agape. It had never even occurred to her that Frederick would have left her anything. She had never had much to do with him and had thought him scornful of her. But for once, she had received just as much as Rebecca. Two hundred pounds! she thought. It seemed like a fortune. Why, I can buy that blue velvet for a new dress now. She missed the rest of the bequests, lost in plans for spending her money.

To Matt Peters, both Manager and friend, there was a three

per cent share in the mill, which brought his holding up to
five per cent. Again, this could only be sold to a member of
the family.

Matt nodded once, then bent his head to hide his elation.
Frederick had hinted that there would be something and he
had kept his word. Matt had said nothing of his hopes to Jane,
who was sitting beside him as quietly as always.

Then, at the next words, both of them jerked upright.

'And to my relative, Jane Peters, an annuity of fifty pounds
a year, paid from the mill profits, for her own use and pleasure
entirely.'

Jane swallowed hard, knowing Matt would not like her to
weep in public or draw any attention to herself. But she did
glance at him quickly and he nodded approval as he squeezed
her hand.

Finally, each servant at Ridge House was mentioned by
name and left a sum of money in gratitude for and in propor-
tion to the years of faithful service they had given to Frederick.
By the time that part had been read out, Mrs Jarred and the
maids she supervised were sobbing in the back row and Nat
Jervis, the head gardener, was knuckling his eyes.

'He were the best of masters,' he whispered to Mrs Jarred.
'The best. I s'll miss him sorely.'

Finally, to Annie, went Frederick Hallam's eternal gratitude
for the happy years of their marriage – not only as his wife,
but also the best friend a man could have had – and the residue
of the estate to use entirely at her discretion. He had also left
her a personal letter with a further small request, which
Mr Pennybody was to deliver to her in nine months' time.

'In short,' Jonas Pennybody wound up, feeling the need to
say it loudly and clearly to James and Mildred Hallam, 'my
client has left his wife everything else of which he stood
possessed: the mill, a good many other businesses, some large,
some small, and this house. I have lists ready,' he added quickly,
catching James Hallam's eye. 'These goods and properties are
for Mrs Hallam's absolute use during her lifetime, whether she

remarries again or not, then at least a quarter share each of what remains is to be given to Tamsin and Edgar Hallam – more if Mrs Hallam sees fit. Mr Hallam expressed his absolute confidence in his wife's capacity to manage the various businesses on behalf of her children.'

Peter Jemmings muttered, 'Disgusting!' quite distinctly. James growled in his throat and started to get up.

Jonas Pennybody thought a great deal of Annie Gibson, whom he'd known since long before she married Frederick Hallam, so he looked over his spectacles and said icily, not troubling to hide his disdain, 'I have not quite finished, Mr Hallam.'

For a moment, all hung in the balance, then Simon, Lord Darrington, sitting quietly beside his fiancée, Rebecca Gibson, stood up. 'Keep your disappointment and greed to yourself, Hallam! And have some respect for your father's widow.' He swivelled round. 'And I wouldn't want to hear that word on your lips again, Jemmings.'

James folded his arms, threw a glance of pure hatred at Annie and then turned back to the lawyer. Jemmings blew his nose loudly to hide his embarrassment at being rebuked by a peer of the realm. Though what sort of a nobleman would get engaged to a girl from the Rows, he did not know. What was it about these Gibson women? The widow wasn't bad-looking, if you liked red hair, which he didn't, but her sisters were pretty ordinary, if you asked him, not to mention scraggy.

Annie just sat with bowed head, ignoring them all. It was aching now and felt so heavy. Widow, she thought. That's what I am now, Frederick's widow.

'Mr Hallam wished this statement to be spoken aloud after the reading of the will.' Jonas Pennybody unfolded a piece of paper, cleared his throat and read Frederick's final words to his older children.

I am aware that my son James and my daughter Mildred will consider themselves unfairly treated by this will. I therefore wish to remind them of the sums of money disbursed by me on their behalf during my lifetime, especially the buying of a partnership in a legal practice and a house for James, and a substantial dowry plus buying of a house in trust for Mildred and her heirs.

Should either Mildred or James decide to contest the will, then their legacies are revoked in toto, and will be gifted instead to the town of Bilsden in the form of a trust to fund projects to beautify the town.

I would further remind James and Mildred that my second wife Annie has my full confidence as a businesswoman, and that she and I have shared a great love. No man could have asked for a better wife. I will expect them to respect that.

Suddenly tears started running down Annie's cheeks for the first time in public since Frederick's death and she made a muffled sound of pain as she dabbed at her eyes with a black-edged handkerchief. Even in his will, Frederick's chief thought had been to protect her.

John Gibson put his arm around his daughter's shaking shoulders, worried to see her looking so ill. At each interruption to the will-reading, she seemed to have grown paler, her face so white now that he did not know what to do to help her.

For a moment, Annie leaned against her father, then she smeared away the tears and stood up. Everyone in the room was looking at her as she moved towards James, standing facing him. 'You shall not deny your father his last wishes. You shall not.' Her voice was husky and her green eyes looked half-blind with tears and far too large for her pinched white face.

For a moment longer she stared defiantly at her step-son, then the fierceness left her face, she gasped and crumpled slowly to the ground, supported by her wide black silk skirts. Her father rushed to grab hold of her before she could hit her head on anything, and William pushed forward to take his mother's unconscious body from his grandfather.

He swept her up in his arms, with Tamsin darting forward to hold the crinoline skirts down. 'Get out of my way, you!'

he threw at James as he carried his mother across to the door. 'She's borne enough this past year. You can keep your greed and your spite to yourself.'

And so ferocious was the expression on William's normally gentle face that James and everyone else moved back to let him pass. Edgar ran after them.

It was left to John Gibson to speak the last words. 'I should think shame to behave as you two have done! That's where the shame is today!' He, too, walked from the room, leaving James to go forward to the table and harangue the elderly lawyer, before snatching his copy of the will.

'You can be sure that I'll contest this. My father was clearly of unsound mind at the last.'

Simon Darrington stepped forward. 'I was one of the witnesses, Hallam. As was the doctor, Jeremy Lewis. You'll have trouble proving that.' His voice rang with scorn. 'You'd have trouble proving it, anyway. Only two months ago, your father took part in the ceremony to name the new square. The whole town can bear witness that he was of sound mind then, and his will is of earlier date than that.'

Then he turned his back on James and offered his arm to Rebecca, leading her out of the room in silence. The rest of the Gibsons followed, equally tight-lipped, with Joanie clinging to Luke's arm and keeping her eyes down.

3

Ridge House: Late July 1860

During the night, Annie stirred, then blinked around in the dim light from a shaded lamp. She could not for a moment think where she was. 'What—' She tried to sit up.

Rebecca, dozing in a chair nearby, was awake immediately. 'Annie?' She knelt by the bed and clasped her sister's hand. 'Don't try to get up, love.'

'What happened?' Annie felt dazed and so weak she could hardly lift her head. 'How can it be night already?'

'You fainted just after the will had been read. Dr Lewis said it wasn't surprising, because you'd been living on your nerves for a long time.'

'Oh.' The realisation that Frederick was dead hit Annie again, as it kept hitting her every time she woke. Tears filled her eyes. She put one hand up to wipe them away, but more followed, till suddenly she was sobbing in Rebecca's arms, on and on, all the tears she had held back for so long coming out in harsh, painful spurts.

When she had stopped weeping, Annie lay back and let Rebecca wash her face. 'I don't know what came over me. I don't usually . . .' She sighed. What did it matter? What did anything matter now?

For the next few days, she just lay there in bed. Her lethargy and lack of interest in anything worried her family greatly, because no one had ever seen her in such a state. Their Annie was more likely to nag folk or order them around than ignore them. They met in hushed groups to worry about it, but could not think what to do.

'It's about time,' Jeremy insisted, when Rebecca took the

family's worries to him. 'Do nothing. Your sister's mind is forcing her body to give it the rest she desperately needs. She'll come out of this phase presently. Just see that she eats regularly and that nothing disturbs her.'

'I'll do my best.' But Rebecca was having a lot of trouble keeping the peace, for James and his wife had refused to leave Ridge House, insisting that while Annie was ill, they were needed to look after things. If they tried to push their way into Annie's bedroom, they'd have to do that over her dead body, vowed Rebecca, but they didn't. However, they'd dropped all semblance of cordiality towards the Gibsons since Frederick's death and James made no bones about his resentment of the will. Judith followed her husband's lead, as usual.

Even William, normally so equable in temperament, had had sharp words with James several times since the day of the funeral. For several days, he had not been into Manchester to the Mission to the inner-city poor where he worked, feeling he should be at hand, in case of more trouble, in case his mother needed him.

Mildred and Peter Jemmings had returned to London with their younger daughter the day after the funeral, saying they had engagements which they preferred not to break, but Peter was still stating that the will should be challenged. It was James who held him back, for as a lawyer he was much more circumspect. He did not even mention the will openly, but he did go into Manchester a couple of times and came back looking furious.

None of the Gibsons could understand why James and Judith were staying on at Ridge House and Tom, at least, was all for telling them to leave. Surely they didn't expect Annie to be permanently ill? Surely they didn't think she would just hand the business over to James to manage after what Frederick had said in his will?

But Rebecca gradually realised that they did expect just that, from the remarks James made about women's capabilities to understand business and finance. He seemed to think that

Annie's collapse proved she could not manage on her own. And the longer she stayed in bed, the more confident he became.

Rebecca had to bite her tongue several times not to quarrel with him, but as she told Simon, 'It won't do Annie any good, and anyway he's a bigot. He doesn't listen to other people's opinions. So I'd be wasting my breath.' She raised her eyes and her love for Simon shone in them. 'Unlike you, love. You're always courteous to everyone you meet.' A smile crossed her face briefly. 'Winnie thinks you're absolutely wonderful and boasts of her acquaintance with you.'

'She's a real character, your Winnie is. I wish I had a few maids like her at home to cheer me up, but my new servants are all very meek and obsequious. I can't wait to have you there with me. I'm sure you'll bring life to the house.'

'You do understand that I can't go on with our wedding plans while Annie needs me?'

She looked so anxious, so adorable, that he had to kiss her before he replied, 'Of course I understand. It's one of the things I admire most about you Gibsons – the way you look after one another. I hope we can raise our children to feel the same.'

Which made her blush and then he had to kiss her again.

The meetings with Simon were the only bright spots in Rebecca's life. Even when James was out, Judith made a point of interfering whenever she could. Since her own children had been brought to Bilsden to attend the funeral, she had an excuse for spending a lot of time in the schoolroom, as she took a personal interest in their education. Already she and Elizabeth had had words over disciplinary methods and the subject matter being taught. Judith was genuinely horrified that neither Tamsin nor Edgar could recite the Kings and Queens of England, with all their dates, or the countries of Europe with their capitals and main rivers. She was even more horrified that Tamsin refused point-blank to attempt any needlework and could not recite passages from the Bible.

Judith also poked her nose into the kitchen and upset Mrs Lumbley, the cook; she had sharp words with Mrs Jarred, the housekeeper, on the subject of the upstairs maid's duties with regard to visiting children and she scolded Winnie about her continual grumbling and weeping. That resulted in Winnie, who genuinely mourned her master, throwing an unprecedented fit of hysterics and having to be calmed down by Mrs Jarred.

Annie heard the sounds of the various altercations, but turned away and commented fretfully that the noise was making her head ache. Only in the evenings did she rouse herself a little when Tamsin and Edgar came to say goodnight to her before they went to bed, for she could see how worried her son was. 'I just need some rest,' she said to him every evening, as he stood clutching her hand, reluctant to leave. 'I'm very, very tired, love. Try to be good for Miss MacNaughton.'

'It's one thing being good for Miss MacNaughton,' Tamsin grumbled to her brother on their way back to the schoolroom – James and Judith refused to allow the children to dine downstairs, so Tamsin, Edgar and their governess, too, had been relegated to eating their meals upstairs – 'but it's another thing to be good for Judith.'

'I don't like her,' Edgar whispered, after a hasty glance round to make sure she wasn't hovering nearby.

'Neither do I. And if she slaps you again, I'll throw something at her. Mother never slaps us. And she wouldn't let anyone else do so, either. When she's better I'm going to tell her about Judith, but Rebecca says we mustn't upset her now.' She frowned. It seemed to her that Judith actually enjoyed 'chastising' the children; their cousins were absolutely terrified of their mother and her cane. And Judith seemed in turn to be afraid of her husband. How could that be? Tamsin's father had loved his wife dearly, and she him. And her grandparents were the same. Why were James and Judith so different? It was all very puzzling to a girl just beginning to contemplate the relationships around her as she approached womanhood.

As well as going into Manchester, James went to the mill several times and insisted on poking his nose into everything there. 'I might be only a minor shareholder, but I intend to make sure things are run efficiently here,' he snapped when Matt Peters queried his presence. 'And kindly remember that I am the head of the Hallam family now!'

Although James had no power to make Matt change anything, his mere presence caused ill feeling. The office and yard staff did not like the way he treated them, and when he scolded them about their sloppy, old-fashioned ways and even about the way they dressed, they became surly and uncommunicative. The operatives in the mill itself were equally unimpressed and did not like the way he expected them to kow-tow to him. Kow-towing wasn't a characteristic much prized by Lancashire folk and they did not hesitate to answer him back sharply when he made daft comments that showed how little he knew.

When he threatened them with dismissal, one man spat at his feet. 'The Mester didn't leave the mill to you, so how can you dismiss us, eh? Just tell me that.'

A woman's voice called from the back of the crowd that had gathered, 'Go home, Master James. Tha knows nowt about cotton.'

There was a chorus of approval from the people who had gathered around them, and even some laughter, but when James swung round, he could not tell where the original voice had come from.

'The Mester must be turning in his grave,' the same woman said to another when he had left.

'The Missus will deal with that one when she gets better,' her companion retorted. 'You'll see. Mr Peters says she's not ill, just tired an' needing a rest.'

'So am I tired!' But she didn't grudge the Missus her rest, for they'd all watched the Mester fade slowly away, and they'd all seen how much his wife loved him. 'Life's hard sometimes,' she sighed.

'Life's hard all the time,' her friend said grimly, thinking of the eight children she had to find food for each day.

The millworkers continued to ask Matt daily for news of 'the Missus' and to behave as they saw fit once away from work. Judith might wince when she saw the women walking about the town, arm-in-arm and often shrieking with laughter, but there was a life and vigour to them that Frederick had always loved. 'I'm proud of my fellow Lancastrians,' he'd said to Annie once. 'They don't hesitate to tell me what they think. And I learn a lot from that.'

But since Annie continued to lie in bed, drifting in and out of sleep, Judith's interference continued unchecked and the household of Ridge House grew more and more unhappy.

'It makes you wonder if she played him false,' Winnie muttered one evening in the servants' sitting room.

Peggy stared at her. 'Who played who false?'

'The first Mrs Hallam. The way Mr James is behaving, makes you wonder if she played the master false.'

'You should call him Mr Hallam now,' Peggy corrected, 'not Mr James.'

'That was the Master's name and this one doesn't deserve it.' Winnie wiped another tear away. 'No, this one's like a cuckoo in the nest, he is that.'

Peggy gave it a moment's thought, then shook her head. 'No, he looks too like his father.'

'Yes, he does, but he doesn't act like him, does he? I think the Master would be sad to see all this, and if *that woman* runs her fingers along my mantelpieces again, I'm giving notice. I was dusting mantelpieces before she was born. Does she think I don't know my job?'

Peggy murmured something soothing and exchanged amused glances with Hazel, the under-housemaid. Winnie would never give notice and everyone knew that. She was a fixture in the Hallam household by now. Why, it'd break her heart to leave. Well, come to that, Peggy was happy at Ridge House, too, and had expected to spend the rest of her life there, confident of being cared for in her old age. But if James Hallam and his tight-mouthed wife moved in permanently, as *that woman* had been hinting they might, Peggy would give notice. It was as simple as that.

As Winnie's sniffles continued, Peggy tried to change the subject to something more cheerful. 'It was nice of the Master to leave us the money, wasn't it? I've put mine in the Savings Bank. What have you done with yours?'

'Mind your own business. But it was nice of him, very nice.' Winnie had not yet decided what to do with her twenty pounds, but had sewn it into her best petticoat while she considered the matter. The thought of it was as comforting as the coins felt, banging against her legs as she walked to church. Tears trickled down her face now. 'We'll never get another master like him. Never!' She had been saying that ever since the funeral.

'Now, don't you start again!' Peggy said hastily. Really. Winnie was wallowing in her misery. 'Mrs Hallam needs all our support till *they* have gone back where they belong.' And that thought, at least, seemed to make Winnie pull herself together.

One morning, ten days after the funeral, Annie seemed to Rebecca, who was still in close attendance, to be a little better. There was nothing very definite, just a more relaxed look to her sister's face, a little colour in her cheeks, and the fact that she ate some of the lavish breakfast sent up by Cook without having to be nagged.

Afterwards, Annie lay back against the pile of soft feather pillows and looked up at Rebecca. 'I haven't thanked you properly, have I, love?'

'For what?'

'Just for being here. And what about your own wedding? You've had to postpone it twice now.'

'We can wait.' Rebecca smiled at her sister. Yes, Annie was definitely better today. 'We've all been so worried about you,' she admitted. 'Dad's come up to the house every evening after work. And William hasn't gone into Manchester for days now.'

Annie stretched and sighed. 'I was more tired than I realised. It must have been all—'

Suddenly, there was a shrill scream from upstairs.

'That's Tamsin.' Annie jerked upright in bed.

Another scream was followed by a muddle of voices shouting and footsteps moving to and fro on the floor above their heads, as well as furniture being overturned.

Rebecca went to open the bedroom door and they saw William run past them on his way up to the schoolroom. When she turned round, Annie was already throwing off the covers and reaching for her dressing gown.

'Should you?'

Annie thrust her arm into one sleeve. 'I most certainly should. I want to find out what's happening to make my daughter scream like that.'

Upstairs, William found Judith, spots of high colour in each sallow cheek, clutching a cane with one hand and Tamsin with the other. Even as he stared in horror, the cane descended on Tamsin's shoulders. The child was shrieking and struggling, and there was no sign of Elizabeth MacNaughton or Edgar.

Tamsin suddenly noticed her half-brother and shouted his name at the top of her voice. 'William! William!' She would have run across to him, but Judith was a strong woman, well used to handling children, and did not let go of her husband's half-sister whom she considered a spoiled brat, more than overdue for a caning.

'What's going on here?' William demanded. 'Let go of Tamsin at once!'

'Mind your own business, young man, and leave the children to me!' Judith snapped. She swished the cane again and caught Tamsin a glancing blow across the arm.

William growled in anger as Tamsin yelped in pain and kicked out at her tormentor. The girl was unable to reach Judith through her thick layers of petticoats or to pull free, so she gave up the attempt and shouted desperately, 'William, never mind me! Go and rescue Edgar!'

But he went first to the woman who was, he supposed, a sort of step-sister to him, and pulled from her hand the cane that was poised for another blow. 'We don't beat children in our family.' He snapped the cane in his strong hands and then broke the pieces again, the anger which cruelty always raised in him needing further action.

'Well, you should beat this one,' panted Judith, struggling desperately to hold the girl, feeling a little nervous as he loomed over her, but fairly sure that William would not manhandle a lady of her age.

Tamsin seized her moment and twisted out of Judith's grip, tugging at William's hand. 'She's shut Edgar in the cupboard in his bedroom and you know how terrified he is of the dark. He can't breathe in it! Come *on* !'

'What!' William turned to follow her at once, forgetting everything but his little half-brother. They all worried about Edgar's fear of the dark and how breathless he got sometimes, so much so that he had to struggle for each breath.

Judith stood with hands on hips and watched them go, anger painting a mottled and unlovely flush on her cheeks. After a moment, a small smile twisted her thin lips as she fingered the little brass key in her pocket. William Ashworth would have trouble letting that spoilt brat out of the wardrobe without this. She glared at her own two children, who had retreated to a corner, and hissed, 'Get back to your work at once! I'll hear you recite that poem later and it had better be correct.'

'Yes, Mama.'

Once inside her own room on the floor below, she locked the door. If necessary, she would stay there until James came back from the mill, but she wasn't giving up the wardrobe key. She would not have children defying her! Any children. Tamsin and Edgar were going to learn that once and for all.

In Edgar's bedroom, Elizabeth was crouched on the floor by the huge mahogany wardrobe, talking soothingly to the boy locked inside it. 'I'm still here, Edgar. Try to keep calm. I won't let anything happen to you.'

But from inside the cupboard there came no response, only the sound of someone wheezing for breath, gasping and choking. On and on it went.

Tamsin ran across to press her mouth against the gap between the wardrobe doors and call out, 'William's here with me. We're going to let you out, Edgar! You'll be all right now.'

But he was too upset to hear her. The sound of choking and gasping continued, interspersed with little mews of panic.

'Thank heavens you're here, William!' Elizabeth stood up. 'Did you get the key off her? She wouldn't give it to me.'

'Judith Hallam has the key?'

'Yes.' Tears were running down Elizabeth's cheeks. 'I've never heard Edgar sound so bad. Please, William, go and take the key from her – by force if necessary.'

He shook his head and rage welled up within him again. He did not intend to wait another minute to rescue his little brother. Besides, he'd guess that that woman would have locked herself in her bedroom by now. 'Stand back!' He raised his voice. 'Edgar, I'm going to break down the door.'

'W-What?' Another long wheezing choke cut off the boy's attempt to speak.

Elizabeth did not try to dissuade William, but pulled Tamsin to one side, her face grim. The past week had been dreadful, but she would never have expected even Judith Hallam to go this far.

Just as Annie appeared in the doorway, William took hold of one of the wardrobe doors. As she stood gaping in amazement, he shook it a bit to test it, then put one foot against the other door and pulled with all his might. His face grew red and the effort of pulling made him groan deep in his throat, but suddenly the wood split and the handle pulled away from the central upright with a great cracking sound. He slammed the door aside.

Tamsin dived forward before anyone else could get to Edgar,

who was doubled up in a ball on the floor. 'It's all right now,' she said very loudly. 'It's all right, Edgar. Calm down, please!' She put her arms round him and pulled him out of the wardrobe.

Her voice seemed to penetrate his brain, where before he had been impervious to everything but the struggle to breathe. Annie, who had been going to speak, closed her mouth and watched.

'See, you're out now. And William's going to open the window. He'll let in lots of nice fresh air. You'll soon be breathing easily.' Tamsin made a flapping motion at her older brother with one hand, then went back to cuddling Edgar.

William went across to the window and flung it wide open.

With Rebecca's arm round her in support, because she was still wobbly on her feet, Annie moved forward and fell to her knees beside her two children. 'I'm here, too, Edgar.'

He looked up and held out one arm to her, but still could not catch his breath properly.

It took a few minutes, but between them, she and Tamsin got him calmed down and gradually the boy's desperate struggle to breathe eased. As colour returned to his face, his first word was, 'Mother!' But he kept hold of Tamsin as well.

'I'm feeling a lot better now, Edgar, you know,' Annie said, keeping her voice as calm as she could. 'Soon we'll be able to go for walks around the garden together and up on the moors perhaps.' She hugged him and caught hold of Tamsin's free hand even as she turned her head towards William. 'Send for Dr Lewis, please. And Rebecca, will you go and find my maid? I need to get dressed.'

When their footsteps had faded away, she helped Tamsin coax the boy into bed. Only when he was lying there peacefully, propped high on the pillows, did Annie speak again. 'Will you stay with Edgar, Tamsin, while I talk to Miss MacNaughton about what happened? Elizabeth, I'm a bit weak. I need someone to help me back to my bedroom.'

Tamsin nodded. There was a livid weal across her cheek,

Annie noticed, and another mark across the back of her hand. What had been happening?

At the door, she stopped. 'Tamsin, you were wonderful. Your father would have been extremely pleased with how you helped Edgar. So would your grandfather. I'm so proud of you.'

Tamsin's eyes filled with tears of pleasure, but she just nodded again and gave Edgar's hand a little squeeze. Rarely did her mother give her such unstinted praise.

'You'll – come back – soon?' Edgar begged as she went out of the room.

'Of course I will.' Annie stopped again to smile at him. 'But I need to get dressed now.'

'Promise you'll come back.'

'I promise.'

'And you won't – you won't let *her* – come here?' He looked fearfully over his mother's shoulder.

'Who?'

It was Tamsin who answered, her voice bitter and sounding suddenly very grown-up. 'Judith Hallam, our dear half-sister. She shut Edgar in the cupboard, though I told her what would happen.' She fingered her cheek and a scowl darkened her face. 'And she caned me for impertinence.'

Had the world gone mad? Annie wondered. Why would Judith Hallam attack two grieving children? What on earth had been going on in her house for the last few days? 'I won't let her come near either of you again, I promise you. Nor shall anyone cane you again.' Then she turned and allowed Elizabeth to help her to her bedroom. On the way, she had to stop and lean against the wall for a moment, for she felt very dizzy. 'I'm a bit weak, I'm afraid.'

'Come back to bed.'

'No. I'm not going back to bed.' The world still seemed to be wavering around her, so Annie closed her eyes till it stopped. 'I just need to rest for a minute. And I need you to tell me what's been happening. Everything.'

She might look a bit frail, but to Elizabeth's delight Annie was speaking in her old tone of voice again. 'Mrs James Hallam decided to interfere in the schoolroom. It seems she has very different ideas of how children should be brought up and prides herself on her views and methods. She also decided that Tamsin should call her "Aunt Judith" because she feels it wrong for a child to address her by her first name, even if that child is her own husband's half-sister. Of course, Tamsin refused to do that.

'Then, this morning Mrs James,' without thinking, Elizabeth was using the name the servants had given their visitor, for there was only one Mrs Hallam, as far as they were all concerned, and that was Annie, 'sent me down to fetch some books from the library and told me to get a cup of tea and not come back for half an hour or so. But I couldn't settle.' She grimaced. 'It was so unlike her that I crept upstairs again and when I found she had shut Edgar in the cupboard, I stayed with him.' Elizabeth looked at Annie, pleading for understanding. 'I could hardly refuse to obey her direct orders, could I? Oh, but I wish I had.'

'You were in a difficult position. But from now on, if I'm not there, you're in absolute charge of the children, and you'll be disobeying *my* orders if you let anyone else interfere.'

Elizabeth nodded, then confided in disgust, 'It's Mrs James's favourite punishment for her own children, apparently, locking them in cupboards, though she's fond of wielding the cane, too, from the things they've let drop. She wouldn't listen to Tamsin trying to explain that since his father died, Edgar is far more terrified of the dark than before. Even when he started to wheeze – oh, Annie, it hurt me to hear him! – she wouldn't give us the key. She seemed to enjoy having the power to torment him! And when Tamsin shouted at her, she produced the cane and said it was about time Tamsin learned a few manners, too. I think when Edgar heard his sister screaming, he panicked completely. They're very close, those two.'

As Annie leaned against the wall, she heard Tamsin's clear voice from upstairs reassuring her brother. Downstairs a clock struck the half hour. Somewhere Winnie was humming as she went about her work, as only Winnie could hum, tunelessly, droning on and on. All the ordinary noises of her home. Annie suddenly realised how very much she loved it. No, she had not lost everything when Frederick died. She still had her children and her home.

William came back upstairs and stood waiting for his mother's attention. 'I've sent for Dr Lewis.' After a short pause, he added in a low angry voice, 'Neither you nor Grandfather ever needed to cane any of us.'

'She canes her own children regularly,' Elizabeth told him quietly. 'They're terrified of her.' Then she looked at Annie in concern. 'You're still looking very pale. We need to get you back in bed.'

Annie shook her head. 'No. I'm going to get dressed, after which I'm going to take great pleasure in sending James and his wife packing.' She was swaying on her feet, but her face was set in its old firm expression.

William didn't ask permission, just picked her up. 'Let me carry you back to your bedroom, then, Mother. You're in no fit state to be getting up, but I agree that we need you there to drive out the enemy.' He grinned at her, looking so like a gigantic schoolboy that she pulled his head down and planted a kiss on his cheek.

'And should the James Hallams make any protest,' he said firmly, 'or refuse to leave, I'll take enormous pleasure in throwing them out bodily.'

He was surprised at how angry he still felt. I'm a Christian. I'm supposed to forgive them that trespass against me, he thought, but I'll find it hard to forgive Judith – or anyone else who hurts young children. And yet, in that moment, he also became aware that he was now ready to train for the ministry.

Annie clung to him as he walked easily along the corridor and into her bedroom, amazed that she, who was only just over five foot tall, should have produced this young giant.

Elizabeth held open the door of the bedroom for them.

'You perhaps ought to know something else, Annie. James has been to the mill several times!'

Annie scowled. 'Oh, has he? Well, I shall be very angry with Matt if he's paid any attention to the man. James doesn't know the first thing about cotton.' But I do, she realised suddenly. Frederick made very sure of that by using me as a messenger between himself and Matt. Oh, Frederick, was there anything you didn't think of? Aloud she merely said, 'It'll be the last time James tries to interfere in our mill, or his wife in our house, I promise you.'

As William set her gently on the bed, she said fretfully, 'Oh, how annoying it is to be so weak! I don't know how Frederick bore it patiently for so long!'

It was the first time since the funeral that she'd managed to say his name, or even think about him, without weeping help-lessly. She looked at William. 'Will you wait outside, please, and then help me downstairs when I'm dressed?'

'Should you?'

'I have to. Only I have the power to tell them to go away.'

'You're not seeing him on your own!' he insisted.

She reached out one hand to pat his cheek. 'No. I'll let you guard me, love.'

He bent to kiss her. 'One always guards one's treasures.' And was not surprised when tears came into her eyes.

After a short rest, she waited for James in the library, drawing strength from the memories of Frederick that would always be associated with this, her favourite room. Judith remained upstairs, not coming out for luncheon even.

When James's loud voice sounded in the hall, William went out to intercept him. 'My mother's waiting for you in the library. She'd like to speak to you.'

'After I've changed.'

'Now.'

'Don't you threaten me, young man!'

William's voice sounded as if he were forcing the words through a mouth full of gravel. 'My mother is waiting.'

Annie smiled as she heard James come clumping across the hall. It was as if he always made the most noise he could as he walked. When the door opened, she leaned back in her big armchair and studied him. Not even half the man his father had been. And was developing quite a paunch lately. A good trencherman, James.

'I'd like you and Judith to leave,' she said without preamble.

'Step-mother, you should not have left your bed.'

She ignored that. 'As soon as possible, James. I think you'll have time to catch a train from Manchester to Leeds this afternoon.'

He reddened and glared at her. 'Are you throwing me out of my father's house?'

'I am, indeed.'

'May one ask why?'

'Because you've outstayed your welcome. And because Judith dared,' Annie's voice grew suddenly sharp, 'to ill-treat my children. We do not cane children in this house, nor do we lock them in cupboards.'

'It might be better if you did. I tell you to your face, Step-mother, that you are spoiling those two.'

Exhaustion made her sag back in the chair, but a singularly sweet smile curved her lips. 'Good. I want to spoil them. They deserve to be happy. Now, you'd better go and pack, James. My servants are at your disposal to expedite matters.'

'I have no intention of leaving in such haste. What will it look like?'

William took a step forward and Annie held him back with one gesture of her hand. 'Go now, James, for Frederick's sake, before I say something I'll regret.'

He opened his mouth to speak, then something in her steady gaze made him close it again. 'Very well, if you're sure you're recovered enough to manage without us.'

When he had gone stamping upstairs, she let her head roll back against the chair, feeling utterly drained and boneless. 'By the time he gets to Manchester, he'll probably have convinced

43

himself that he stayed merely to help me, at great inconvenience to himself and is glad to get away.' Her voice trailed off.

'You did well,' William told her, 'but now you'd better go back to bed.' And knew how tired she was when she didn't raise a single objection as he picked her up.

4

Manchester: August 1860

In August, William's beloved mentor, Alan Robins, died suddenly. One minute he was helping an old woman to hobble inside the converted warehouse where his Mission was situated, the next he was lying on the ground and she was screeching for help.

William came running outside and dropped to his knees.

Alan's eyes were open and for a moment he looked bewildered, then he managed to focus on his young helper. 'It's good we've got time to say farewell, lad.'

His voice was so faint that William had to bend over to hear it.

A frail old hand sought for the strong young one. 'It's been such a joy to know you.'

'It's not – we must send for a doctor—'

The white head shook and with a smile of sheer happiness, Alan squeezed William's hand. 'What could a doctor do? My Maker is calling me now and I'm glad to go. So very glad.'

It was a moment before William could speak, then he bent his head to kiss the paper-thin skin of his beloved mentor's cheek, the man who had helped him finish growing from a lad to a man. 'I shall miss you so much.'

'No. You'll be too busy.'

William frowned at him. 'What do you mean?'

'It's time for you to go and train.' Alan paused for a moment to gather the last dregs of his strength together. 'You're ready for the ministry now, William.'

'Are you sure?'

'Don't you know it, feel it inside you?'

For a moment the younger man stared at him, then he nodded his head. 'Yes. Yes, I do.'

'I've already written a letter to my old friend in Didsbury about you.' Alan gave the ghost of a chuckle at the surprise on William's face. 'I grew up with Jerome Bersall's father. The world was much smaller then, somehow.' Another pause to gather enough energy to speak, then, 'I've loved you like a son, William. Now you can carry on where I leave off. Go out and share that love you carry within you. This world needs it.' He sighed and closed his eyes.

William leaned forward. Alan was still breathing, so William picked him up and carried him inside, calling, 'Will you go and fetch his granddaughter, Bill?' For Bill Midgeley had come to work and live at the Mission lately, to help Alan with the tasks he was no longer strong enough to do himself, and to keep an eye on him at night. Bill thanked the Lord every day for the chance meeting with the young fellow who bore the same name as himself. It had been the saving of him after his wife's death and losing his job.

'I'll be as quick as I can.'

Alan opened his eyes. 'I'll wait for her,' he said in that fading thread of a voice. 'Stay with me, William.'

So when she came, it was to find her grandfather still alive, though only just, and still clasping William's hand. As she knelt by the bed, he seemed to sense her presence, for he opened his eyes and smiled at her.

'Oh, Grandfather.' She took hold of his other hand.

'You've been a good lass to me and I thank you.'

She sniffed away a tear and nodded.

Suddenly Alan Robins's face was transformed, seeming full of light and so radiant with love that it was a wonder to see it. 'I'm ready, Lord,' he called out in a voice which sounded loud and strong. He raised himself a little in the bed. Then the light faded from his face and he sank back with a sigh. It was a moment before the watchers realised that he was gone.

She looked across at William and behind him Bill. 'How can

our family ever thank you for helping him in his last years? Before you joined him here, we were so worried about him. He never looked after himself.'

'It was an honour,' William said. 'And he taught me so much.'

Behind him, Bill nodded. He could not have forced a word out through the tears that clogged his throat.

By the end of the week, Alan Robins had been buried with love and quiet dignity. As well as family and friends, a crowd of poor people had made their way to the church on foot to say their own farewells. When the will was read afterwards, William found that Alan had left him his watch and had already made arrangements for the small Methodist church nearby to take over his Mission to the poor.

'What shall you do now?' Alan's granddaughter asked afterwards.

'I've been to Didsbury and asked to train as a Minister.'

'I'm sure they'll accept you.'

'They have done already. Your grandfather wrote to them when he felt himself weakening. They thought very highly of him, you know, even though he wasn't of the same denomination.'

As he came out of the house, William found Bill Midgely waiting for him. He had a responsibility to the man who had laboured so hard with them for so little money.

'What's going to happen now, William lad?'

'I'm going to Didsbury to train.'

Bill's face fell, but he quickly tried to hide it.

'Would you be willing to come and live in Bilsden now? I'm sure we can find you a job there.'

In fact, John Gibson had said only a few days ago that he'd have to take someone on at the junk yard. 'I shall take my time finding a chap, though,' he had added. 'I s'll want someone honest and hard-working. Strong, too.'

Bill gaped at William now. 'Dost mean that?'

'Of course I do.'

He nodded once and seized William's hand to pump it vigorously. 'Then I'll come. And I'll work right hard for you, too. I'll not let you down.'

'I knew that already, or I'd not have offered. Let's go and get your things from the Mission. I'm sure my grandfather will give you a bed until you can find some lodgings for yourself.'

'My brother and his wife will be glad I don't have to go and live with them again. But I should like to go and see him, to tell him where I'll be.'

'Then we'll take a cab and call there on the way.'

When William got home that night, he had left Bill at his grandfather's. As he had expected, the two men had taken to one another immediately and John had nodded his approval when William suggested taking Bill on at the junk yard.

'I don't know owt about junk,' Bill felt bound to tell him.

'Then you can learn my ways from the start,' John replied with a chuckle. 'For I'm a bit set in how I like to do things by now.' Luke was beginning to tease him about that, but if a man who had turned sixty could not do things as he liked, who could? And by that age, you'd found out a thing or two, so maybe your ways weren't all that stupid.

As he entered Ridge House, William let out a gruff sound of relief at being home and his mother's voice called from above him, 'How did the funeral go?'

He looked up towards the landing. 'It went well. There was a big crowd from the Mission.' He fumbled in his pocket and held out Alan's watch to show her. 'He left me this. I'll always treasure it.'

Annie reached the bottom of the stairs and took the watch in her hand for a moment. 'It was a kind thought. I know you'll treasure it.' She gave it back and reached up to pat his cheek. 'You look exhausted.'

'I am. But you look as lovely as ever, Mother.' She did. She was her old self again.

Annie twirled round to show off her dress. 'It's my day for callers. I have to look fashionable.'

'I like the touches of white.'

'Yes. Unrelieved black can be so gloomy. But this is not the time to talk of clothes. You'll miss Mr Robins.'

'Yes.' Suddenly the time was right to tell her. 'Could I talk to you? About my future?'

'Why don't you change your clothes and then join me in the library?'

'I'd rather say it straight away.'

For a moment, fear ran through her. Say it? What did he mean, say it? Something was wrong. Then she looked up at her huge son and saw the steadfastness in his gaze. No, not wrong exactly. But it was important from the look on his face. 'Very well.' She linked her arm in his and they walked into the library together.

When she was seated, he stood in front of the fireplace and said, 'You must have realised that I have a calling.'

So it has come, she thought. 'Yes.'

'I've been to Didsbury this week. They've accepted me for training. They're very pleased with the work I've been doing, think it gives me a good background. And the lay preaching, of course. Alan wrote to them just before he died. He knew Jerome Bersall's father. I start there in September.' He looked down, not avoiding her eyes but rather looking into himself. 'It was easy somehow,' he said quietly. 'Alan was right. It was time.' He raised his eyes and for a moment humour glinted in them. 'And it'll not take as long for me as it does for others, because I'm already well-educated. They train you according to need, you see, not according to the calendar.'

She could not smile. But she could not gainsay him, either.

'The education I've had wouldn't have been enough,' he added, 'if I didn't have a true calling. That is the most important thing of all.'

'So you'll become a Methodist Minister.'

'Yes. You don't mind?'

Her voice was sharp. 'Of course I mind! I mind very much! But it's what you want, so how can I stop you? And at least, with Frederick's legacy, I'll know you won't starve, however poorly you're paid.'

He stared at her, tolerant in his happiness. Always, for her, it came down to money. She wasn't greedy for it, but needed the security that money brought. He acknowledged, as he had done many times before, that she must have been terrified when she found she was with child at the age of seventeen. He had seen other lasses in the same predicament. But few of them had her inner strength. None of them would have won through the dark times to do what she had done – build up a good life for herself and all her family, too.

'You're a wonderful woman,' he said quietly. Then he smiled. 'And one day, I'll make you proud of me.'

Annie could not think what to say to that, so she just began to scold him about sitting around in wet clothes. 'Go up and change at once. You'll be nobody's Minister if you die of a chill.'

When he had gone, she sat staring blindly into the fire. It was not what she wanted for him, but it was what he wanted, and that must be her comfort. She sighed. At a time like this, she missed Frederick quite desperately. She had no one to talk to now, no special person of her own. It could be very lonely.

5

Ireland: August 1860

In a cottage on his father's estate, Carraford, Tian Gilchrist stepped back from the head and shoulders portrait he had just finished painting and nodded slowly. Yes, it was finished. And he was not sure whether he was glad or sorry about that.

He walked to and fro in front of it, nodding. He had caught her exactly – not just her physical appearance, but her dauntless spirit. Her head was flung back, her eyes challenging the world. It was his best work, though it had been the most painful to do. What he really wanted was Annie herself – not a portrait, but a warm loving woman in his arms. It had been three months since he'd seen her and his longing for her had not faded, not in the slightest. Every woman he'd met since he left Bilsden seemed pale and uninteresting by comparison. Would he ever be able to forget her?

Sighing, he looked at the photograph which he had purloined from Ridge House before he left and which he had used to guide him in the painting. 'Oh, hell, I wish we'd met when we were both young and heart-free,' he muttered. But he and Annie hadn't met until long after she married Frederick Hallam, and Tian had rarely seen such love as those two shared. So he had finished painting the family portrait Frederick wanted so much and had then left without painting a full-length portrait of Mrs Hallam in all her mature glory as had been agreed. He had explained why to the man he had grown to like and respect, had had one last meeting with Annie to tell her that he would always be ready to help her in any way he could, then had gone back to London.

He had intended to drown himself in good Irish whiskey till

her memory faded, but alcohol had done no good. She was with him, waking and sleeping, sober and drunk: Annie laughing, Annie frowning in thought, Annie turning her head to look at something which had caught her interest. But the most poignant memory was Annie clinging to him when he saved her from plunging to her death after a frenzied attack by Beatrice, Frederick's youngest child by his first wife. Beatrice had died in the attack, but he, Tian, had saved Annie.

No, he decided, you could not lose the memory of a woman like that in drink. In the end, after several sleepless nights, it came to him that what he needed to do was paint a portrait of her, get her out of his system. Maybe then he could get on with his life. Maybe.

In London, he had made several attempts to paint, but the light there was as dull and lifeless as his soul. 'I need to go home,' he acknowledged aloud one day.

So he had come back to the rambling family home, hugged his parents, caught up with his brothers and sisters and their families, and had wallowed for a time in the love he did have. Then he had grown restless, driven to do that painting. Only he had found he couldn't paint Annie when he was living in the big house. There were too many people between him and his memories, too many people 'just taking a peep' or raising their voices to shout or sing nearby. He had not realised before how noisy his family were.

'Can I have the use of Molloy's cottage for a couple of weeks?' he asked his father one day. 'It's been empty for a while.'

'What in heaven's name for? Are you not comfortable here in the big house? You've got your old room back and the attic to paint in.'

'I want to paint something special. And I need some time alone to do it. Without people peering over my shoulder all the time.'

Seamus Gilchrist cocked an eye. 'Who is she?'

Tian froze. 'What do you mean?'

'You haven't looked at a woman since you got back and not only is that not like you, for you used to be the divil of a flirt, but goodness knows, your mother's tossed enough of 'em at you.'

'Ma's been tossing women at me for years. Usually ugly ones with money.'

His father grinned. 'And you've been tossing them back. And you'd better not let her hear you callin' her "Ma", either. Anyway, Sarry said you'd met someone in England, said you were in love. She's usually right about you.'

'Well, Sarry should just mind her own business, then!' The silence between them lasted too long. Tian looked across at his father and felt the tears rise to his eyes. Damn! He could never fool his da. 'She's married,' he admitted. 'And her husband's a lovely man. She'd as soon leave him as I would fly to the moon. So I came away.'

His father nodded. 'Quite right, too. I'll tell your mother to stop the match-making, then. Not that it'd ever have done any good with you. I told her that, too. You've always been a stubborn lad, always gone your own way.'

Tian knew to what his father was referring. 'I have to paint. And I'm making a living at it now. Not a good living. Not yet. But Miles Correnaud, my London agent, thinks things will improve steadily as I get better known.'

'And have you sent him many paintings lately?' his father asked.

There was no fooling old Seamus. Tian shook his head. 'No. I can't do anything till I've got Annie out of my mind.'

'Annie, is it?'

Annoyance surged through Tian. He had not meant to reveal her name, not meant to reveal anything about her. But it was always like that with his father. Those silences were masterly. You blurted out something to fill them when they ran on for too long. And Seamus just smiled as he watched and waited, patient as ever, picking up crumbs of information and fitting them together into neat little pictures.

Now, alone in the cottage, Tian studied the finished portrait and knew it was the best thing he'd ever done.

He heard a sound outside and looked through the window. Sarry was strolling down from the big house, singing at the top of her voice, looking happy and relaxed. At sixteen, she was growing into an attractive lass. Not beautiful, no, she'd never be that, but she had charm, Sarry did, and that was just as good as beauty to his mind. It lasted better, too. His mother was the same and folk still spoke of her as 'a fine woman'.

'What's brought you down to the end of the garden?' he called out through the open window.

Sarry waved a thick envelope at him. 'This came for you. From Lancashire. Pa thought you'd like to have it at once.'

He stood still for a moment as hope bloomed briefly and faded just as quickly. Lancashire! The only people he knew in Lancashire were the Hallams. But Annie wouldn't leave Frederick. Perhaps Hallam was going to try again to persuade him to paint her portrait. The old man had been rather set on it, and no wonder with a lovely wife like that. Throwing down the palette, Tian grabbed a piece of rag and started wiping his hands as he walked through into the main room of the cottage.

Sarry held the envelope out, a teasing smile on her face, and as he tossed the rag on the table and reached for the letter, she pulled it out of his way. 'Tell me who it's from and I'll give it you!'

He grunted and lurched forward, pinning her between the table and the settle. Before she could even exclaim, he had the letter out of her hand and was pushing her towards the door.

'Will you not let me make us a cup of tea?' she protested.

'Another time. Just leave me alone to read my letter.' He slammed the door shut and slid the little-used bolt into its rusty catch to make sure that Sarry couldn't get inside again. He didn't want anyone near him when he read the letter, didn't want anyone seeing the emotions on his face.

Sarry tried the door, frowned to find it locked, then kicked it and called through the window, 'And you didn't even say thank you, you mean pig!'

'Thank you. Now go away!'

Not until he had seen her walk back across the meadow did Tian open the letter. To his disappointment it wasn't from Annie, or even from Frederick, but from a lawyer called Jonas Pennybody.

We regret to inform you that our client, Mr Frederick Hallam, died two weeks ago. He has left the enclosed letter for you, and has asked that you tell no one of its contents until at least a year after his death. He has also left you a small legacy of a hundred pounds to express his gratitude for the family portrait you painted, which gave him great pleasure in his last months of life.

Enclosed was the letter from Frederick Hallam. Tian turned it over once or twice in his hands, for some reason reluctant to open it. 'Money couldn't buy you extra time,' he whispered. 'You poor sod. You didn't make old bones, did you? And Annie,' he drew in a sudden sharp breath, 'she's a widow now.' But she'd be a grieving widow. 'Oh, hell, nothing's really changed!' he said and tore open the envelope with such force that he ripped off the top corner of the letter and had to hold the two pieces together to read it.

Dear Tian,

You will perhaps find this a strange letter, but I hope you will give my request thorough consideration.

When you receive this, I shall be dead. I have enjoyed my life and cannot complain. The only thing I haven't done in the past year or two, which I wanted very much to do, was have a large, full-length portrait painted of my wife.

I wonder if you would reconsider now and accept the commission to paint it? I am well aware of why you left and agree that it was the right thing to do at the time. I do not think Annie will be ready to contemplate sitting for you for a while, but maybe if you left it until about a year after my death, you could then approach her?

*I've written another letter to her, explaining that it is still
my wish to have her portrait painted. That letter is not to be
given to her until nine months after my death. I don't think
she'll deny me my last wish, but if she doesn't contact you,
then I ask you to contact her and show her this letter. Push
her into doing it, if need be.*

*And, Tian, if the attraction between the two of you flares
again, then know you will have my blessing upon it. I don't
want my lovely girl to spend the rest of her life alone.*

*Annie will have a heavy burden to bear for a while. I've
left the major part of my estate to her and she will be responsible for running my businesses. If the troubles in the United
States escalate, then we could see war across the Atlantic, and
a shortage of cotton for Lancashire – though no doubt the
authorities will do something quickly to remedy that. Trade
often moves governments to action when simple justice doesn't.*

*In conclusion, I wish you every success in life and every
happiness, too. You have a great talent for painting portraits,
Tian Gilchrist.*

Yours very sincerely,
Frederick Hallam

Tian read the letter slowly through again. 'That's a measure of
the man,' he said, wiping a tear from his eye and not ashamed
of it, either. 'Even when he's facing his own death, he's still
thinking of her. It's a lot to live up to.' But he knew he was
going to try.

He walked across to put the letter on the mantelpiece, but
could not settle. A few minutes later, he had to come in and
read it again. 'But will she let me paint her portrait?' he
asked aloud. 'Will she allow me back into her life?'

For he knew, and he realised that Frederick Hallam had
known, too, that his feelings for Annie went very deep. He
had walked away from her once. He doubted he could do it again.

'A year!' he said exultantly. 'In nine months' time, she'll
get his letter. Three months after that, I'll write to her. And

meanwhile,' he looked round the small cottage with a grimace, 'I'm damned if I'll sit here moping. I've always wanted to see America. And now's the time to do it, before any trouble starts.'

He would frame the portrait first, though, then leave it with his father. He went back into the next room to stare at it and say quietly, 'I love you, Annie Hallam. You're a fever in my blood.'

A couple of weeks later, Tian walked along the docks at Liverpool, his stride free and easy, followed by a porter with a hand trolley. He had brought one bag of clothing and personal necessities, and two bags of drawing and painting materials, which were much more important to him. He had also brought the photograph of Annie and the preliminary sketch he had made for the portrait. He could not bear to be without something to remind him of her.

He found his ship, an auxilliary of the Inman Line. It was screw-driven by a steam engine, but ran mainly under sail. It looked funny to him, as hybrids often do, but as long as it got him across the Atlantic safely, what did that matter? Maybe one day they'd be able to dispense with sails entirely, though how they'd carry enough coal for long voyages, he didn't know.

When booking his passage, he had found to his amazement that the line ran a fortnightly service across the Atlantic, with places being taken mainly by emigrants to America. Six guineas a head for most of the four hundred passengers, who didn't travel in the comfort he was paying extra for. Why, if things went on like this, with faster ways of getting around, then ordinary people would start to travel the world just for the pleasure of it. As he was doing now. As the rich had always done, the lucky devils.

Feeling excited, he dumped his things in the cabin he was to share with two other gentlemen, neither of whom had yet arrived, then went back to stand at the rail, watching folk embark. What he saw sent him hurrying to the cabin again to fetch his sketching materials.

For the next two hours, he forgot about unpacking and waved away the steward's suggestion that he might like a cup of tea. He stood at the rail, his pencil flying, covering sheet after sheet of his precious paper with sketches full of the agonies of par ting. Unlike him, these people were leaving for ever. Unlike him, most of those boarding the ship would be travelling steerage, crammed together below decks. Homesickness was written on their faces and they often had screaming children dragging beside them. With the family groups was the occasional sad-eyed older person, but most folk were young. A few of the men looked happy and excited, but the rest looked apprehensive or even downright miserable.

Only when the sailors started making preparations to cast off did Tian stir and realise how stiff he was.

'You've caught them to the life,' said a voice behind him and he turned to find a portly gentleman watching him.

Tian shrugged and grinned. 'Thanks.' He didn't care whether strangers watched him work or not. It was only family who got under your skin and stopped you from concentrating. All he had really cared about for most of his life had been his painting and his drawing, and finding interesting new subjects. Well, he'd fallen lucky now. He had not expected to be so fascinated by his fellow passengers, but he had, he realised with a surge of exultation, all the makings for a large painting, one which might even make his name.

'I hope I've caught them to the life,' he acknowledged to the stranger. 'But this is only the first step. I'm going to make a painting of that scene one day. A big painting.'

'Come and sip a farewell brandy with me and tell me about it,' his companion suggested.

'Not this time. My mind's too full of these.' Tian indicated his sketches.

'Another time, then. My name's Brownsby. Thaddeus Brownsby. Of New York City.'

'Tian Gilchrist. Artist. From Ireland originally.'

'Emigrating?'

'No. Just going for a visit. I have a year or so to while away before an important engagement.'

Brownsby nodded. 'You couldn't be whiling it away in a better place, my friend. Let me tell you, New York is like no other place on earth. Bursting with life and enterprise. Just bursting. Are you sure you won't change your mind about that drink?'

Tian realised how his arm was aching and that his mind was too full of the pictures he'd seen to do anything else for a while but leave them to settle. 'Oh, why not? Very civil of you, sir.'

He did not realise then that in accepting the invitation not only was he making a good friend, but he was also making a decision which would have ramifications for the rest of his life – and would nearly ruin it, too.

6

Bilsden: September 1860

During the few weeks which followed the abrupt departure of James Hallam and his family from Bilsden, the thing that gave Annie the most comfort as she tried to make a new way of life for herself was the family portrait. She would stand in front of it in the library and feel connected to her husband. In the painting, she could see the continuity, herself and William, herself and Frederick, a union resulting in Tamsin and Edgar.

Inevitably, she thought about the artist once or twice as well. Tian Gilchrist had done a wonderful job on the portrait. He was a talented painter and a very warm person. Look how kind he had been to the children. What was he doing with himself now? She had never forgotten how he had saved her life, never stopped being grateful, for he had put his own life at risk to do so. She still had the card with his address on, but would never get in touch with him. She had her family and that was enough. The Gibsons had always stuck together and they always would.

Unlike the Hallams. How could a man like Frederick have had such dreadful children? Oliver had died young, a spendthrift gambler. James was still trying to take over Frederick's legacy to her, bombarding her with letters and demands for information about their mutual inheritance. He also kept sending cur t demands directly to Matt at the mill. Did he really think Matt wouldn't pass them on to her! She told the Manager to ignore them and tried to do the same, but they made her angry.

Peter Jemmings had written once or twice as well 'on my dear wife's behalf' to ask about returns on the 'investment' and also about selling some of the smaller businesses 'to realise some capital for more important investments'. He seemed mollified when she and Matt sold one or two of the smaller concerns and sent him and James their share of the proceeds.

Inevitably, when thinking about Frederick's children, Annie could not help remembering Beatrice. Always a moody, difficult person, she had blamed Annie for alienating her from her father, though in truth it was her own spiteful and outrageous behaviour on her wedding day which had done that.

She had made several attempts on Annie's life, which had at first seemed like accidents, then one day had followed her stepmother and some friends across the moors, disguised as an old woman, and pushed Annie over a cliff. It was sheer luck that there was a ledge just below them when they both fell, and that Annie had lodged on it, while Beatrice had fallen to her death.

And afterwards, Annie had lain there frozen with terror, unable to move. It was Tian Gilchrist who had climbed down to the ledge, at some risk to himself, and had coaxed her, terrified though she was of heights, back up the slope – coaxed her by the use of Frederick's name, which showed how well Tian understood her. It was the second time the artist had saved her life, for he had been there at a crucial moment in London, too.

She wished him well, but unfortunately could not help remembering sometimes how attracted she had been to him, both in London and back in Bilsden. She always blushed and felt guilty at the memory. Just a physical need, she always assured herself. But she knew it had been more than a physical need on Tian's side, knew that he had fallen deeply in love with her. That was why he had not stayed to paint her portrait, as Frederick had wanted. It was the only one of Frederick's final wishes that had not been met and she regretted that now. Everything else he had expressed a desire for, she had managed to do or get for him.

'I miss you,' she always said to the portrait last thing at night before going up to the big empty bedroom. And she seemed to hear his voice whisper, 'I miss you, too, Annie-girl,' in reply.

As the weeks passed she began to worry about Edgar, who had experienced several more of the breathless attacks, for no reason that anyone could tell, and who could not even go into the mill without starting to wheeze in the dusty atmosphere. To take his mind off his father's death, she had tried to start him working there on Saturday mornings, as she had started Tamsin at a similar age. To her it seemed right, even for rich children, to learn that money was earned, not a God-given right. But they had had to stop Edgar's visits to the mill because of the wheezing, so instead he now went to help his grandfather and Bill Midgely at the junk yard every Saturday and seemed happy enough working in the fresh air there.

That was another sort of continuity, for William, too, had spent a lot of time with his grandfather as a child. Indeed, John Gibson had been the major father-figure in William's life. Frederick himself had admitted that, always saying with a wry smile that he had been too wrapped up in the mother to give his step-son all the attention he needed.

'But the lad could do worse than model himself on John Gibson,' he had inevitably added. 'Salt of the earth, your father is.'

Annie knew that, but wished her father had not inculcated William quite so deeply with his own religious beliefs.

When she asked Jeremy Lewis to examine Edgar, he said that apart from the breathless attacks, the boy was in fine shape. 'There's nothing we can do about them, Annie. We've all seen people wheezing like this,' he said gently. 'Sometimes they grow out of it, but more often the weakness remains with them for the rest of their lives.'

'But it only got bad in the past year or so. Why?'

'Who can tell?' There was so much he didn't understand about human bodies, hard as he tried to learn, to keep pace with modern discoveries.

'But you think he might grow out of it?' she pressed.

Who was he to deny her hope? If you prophesied a gloomy outcome, he was sure that it was more likely to happen. 'He might. Some do. But most don't. It's in the Lord's hands, not ours, Annie, whether the attacks will stop as Edgar grows up. Just keep him away from things which upset him and let him grow up happily, without worrying him about it. The more he worries, the worse he'll become. I'm sure of that, at least.'

So she had pushed that concern to the back of her mind for the time being, and it was not hard to do, because she was so busy learning to run Frederick's businesses. For all the knowledge she had gained about cotton during the past year or two under his guidance, she still had more to learn.

Annie now went to the mill two or three times a week to confer with Matt Peters, and sometimes he came up to the house, but not often. Matt was a good manager, Frederick had always said, so long as there was someone else to take the final decisions for him. Annie did just that. She brought her brother Tom into it sometimes as well. He had helped her and Matt decide which of the smaller businesses to sell, in order partly to pay out James and Mildred.

Tom had bought one or two of the businesses himself, though he had insisted the Pennybodys value them, so that no one could accuse him later of profiting unfairly from his brother-in-law's death. They all knew who he was thinking about when he said that.

On one particular visit to the mill, Annie found Matt worrying about whether to buy some more made-up cotton goods.

'Mr Hallam bought quite extensively just before he died,' he told her. 'He said you couldn't lose at that price, so long as you stored them carefully. And cotton goods have fallen even lower in price lately. Mr Hallam didn't think they would go much lower, but they have. There's a huge oversupply, you see.'

'If you believe we ought to—'

'Well, we should certainly think about it. I'm sure the over-supply won't last. Some of the smaller mills are in trouble already, I hear, with the low prices. Mr Hallam always said there were too many mills and he prophesied that the worst-run ones would not last the pace. And we do have plenty of storage down near the River Rows since Hallam Square was rebuilt. Mr Hallam always kept an eye open for a useful piece of property and he owns – I mean, *you own* – several warehouses.'

'Mmm.' She nodded, encouraging him to continue.

'Mind you, that new millowner who took over at Yerslow's – Leaseby he's called – has offered to buy one of the warehouses – quite pressing about it, he's been. But Mr Hallam wouldn't have sold it to him, I'm quite sure of that. Mr Hallam didn't like selling property. And besides, he didn't take to Leaseby. Said the man was a trickster.'

'Mmm,' Annie prompted again.

Matt was talking more to himself. 'And if we buy cheap cotton goods, that warehouse would be ideal for storing them. We can offer Leaseby the smaller warehouse in Blackworth Street to rent. It'll be enough for his needs now.' He frowned. 'I don't really like the man, either. I agree with Mr Hallam on that. Leaseby's a bit careless of his workers' safety, too. You can't stop accidents, of course, but you can take care and you can help those who are injured.' As Hallam's always did. 'Your husband would have had words with Leaseby about that last accident, but I don't feel I have the authority to do so.'

Nor I, thought Annie, with a sigh. No millowner would listen to a woman, even if she was a millowner herself. Frederick was missed for all sorts of things in the town, large and small. The operatives still talked of him with great affection. To them, he would always be 'the Mester'.

She brought her attention back to the matter at hand, listening carefully, letting Matt run on in a gentle monologue, as was his way. He would have been horrified to know that she usually based her decisions on what he told her, for he seemed to think Frederick had left her with some special understanding of how things stood. Prompted by a nod or two from her, however, Matt could be guided into presenting all the arguments for and against a decision, and admitting his own preferences. And the clinching argument to both of them was still what Frederick Hallam would have done.

'Well, from what you're telling me, I think we should buy more cotton goods,' she said at last. 'After all, Frederick must have thought the prices would rise again one day.'

Matt nodded. 'Yes. But,' he hesitated, 'we don't want to leave ourselves short of reserves.'

'We have quite a generous reserve fund.'

'We'll have to dip into it, though, if we buy.' He sighed, his expression anxious. 'I feel, well, responsible for you now. And I worry about taking risks, even the smallest.'

'I'm responsible for myself, Matt, and always have been.'

He looked at her, really looked for once, as man to woman, not subordinate to owner. 'Do you ever wonder what would have happened if we'd married, Annie?'

She responded instantly, her voice crisp. She did not intend to encourage such fantasies. 'We'd have made each other very unhappy. You like to rule the roost. I like to make my own decisions. No, Jane is the ideal wife for you.'

'Yes, I suppose so.'

She thought it better to change the subject. 'And it's your own money you're risking, too, nowadays, Matt. You have a five per cent share in the mill.'

He tried not to smile, but it was there in the curve of his lips, the gleam in his eyes. He took great pride and happiness in his role in life. A man fulfilled, Matt Peters. He'd come a long way from Salem Street. They all had. But he would go no further.

Would Annie go any further? Or had she, too, settled into a pattern that would go on until she died? Somehow, she did not like the idea of that. Somehow, she wanted to find a few more challenges to face. Maybe, when Tamsin and Edgar were older, the three of them could travel, see something of the world. She brought herself back to the present. Inexperienced as she was in cotton matters, she could not afford to let her attention wander.

'So, we're agreed?' she prompted. 'You'll buy more cotton goods as cheaply as you can. And we'll store them in the river warehouse.'

'Yes.'

When she came out of the mill, Annie dismissed the carriage, feeling like a walk. It was one of those crisp autumn days which absolutely begged you to take advantage of the sun's fading warmth before winter crept upon you. She stood for a moment as the carriage rumbled away, deciding where to go. She could visit several people and be sure of a welcome. Her step-mother Kathy at Netherhouse Cottage. Her childhood friend Ellie, Matt's sister, now Jeremy Lewis's wife. Her new sister-in-law Rosie, who seemed very happy to be back in Bilsden after her latest concert.

She did love this town, Annie thought, smiling around her, so what did it matter if she stayed here for the rest of her life? It wasn't the prettiest place on earth, but she knew every street corner in it. She had played along the Rows as a child. Had run her second business, an exclusive ladies' dress salon, in the High Street. And had then moved up to the top of Ridge Hill when she married Frederick. And every time she walked round Hallam Square, she felt proud that it was named for her late husband. That had made him so happy, too.

In the end, she decided to visit Tom at the Emporium, for the two of them were still involved in one or two other businesses not connected with the mill. She had a share in the Emporium in her own right and, with Rebecca's help, kept an eye on the drapery and haberdashery departments there. Which reminded her, she had better start thinking of a replacement for Rebecca. She had intended to find one before now. She didn't want to give her sister any reason to delay her wedding again, so the matter was urgent now.

'You're looking better, but you're still a bit thin,' Tom said, as he showed her upstairs to his office, blunt as only a brother could be. 'You're working too hard, my girl.'

'I have a lot to learn, Tom. There don't seem to be enough hours in the day for all I need to do.'

'Well, even you have to stop and eat. Will you come and have dinner with Rosie and me one evening next week? To

christen the new house. Those damned painters have finished
at last.'

'I—' So far she had refused all evening social invitations,
even from her family, but she couldn't go on doing that. 'All
right. But just a quiet family night, hmm?' For you never knew
whom you would meet at Tom and Rosie's nowadays. Rosie
knew all sorts of people, and when her friends came to
Manchester, other musicians and artistes of all sorts, she often
invited them over to Bilsden, a mere half-hour away on the
train. Rosie got on well with all the family, being a particular
favourite of Simon Darrington, who adored her voice. And the
Bilsden gentry were rather proud of having such a famous
singer resident in their town.

'Of course, dear Miss Lidoni isn't like the usual theatrical
person,' one lady had informed Annie. 'She's a very special sort
of singer, isn't she? One who deals only with the gentry and
nobility.'

Annie had hidden her amusement. If the ladies of Bilsden
knew that Rosie had been born Rosie Liddelow in the narrow
alleys and courts of Claters End, now knocked down for health
reasons – if they knew that Rosie's drunken mother had died
in a brawl, leaving the child's upbringing to her grandmother
– if they knew she had performed first in the singing room at
the Shepherd's Rest public house in the Rows, where she was
also a barmaid, then they might not have been quite so enthusiastic about their dear Miss Lidoni. But no one who had known
her before seemed to have recognised her. And that was probably a good thing.

'How is the new house?' she asked, for she knew there was
still a lot to be done.

'Coming on well.' Tom rolled his eyes. 'Though Rosie's still
spending money like it grows on trees.' He could not hide his
pride in that, for he had worked hard to get where he was
today.

'I'm looking forward to seeing it.'

After Annie left Tom, she went to stroll round Hallam Square.

A worthy monument to Frederick, this, she thought as she walked round it twice, nodding to acquaintances and enjoying the play of the water in the central fountain and the brightness of the flowers in the beds around it. His good taste showed in the clean harmonious lines of the buildings, as well as in the fountain itself, which he had gifted to the town. And since his death, the Council had kept it all very nice. He would have been pleased about that.

As she turned back along High Street, she admitted to herself that she was enjoying the walk, enjoying the fresh air and sunshine. A pang of guilt shot through her. Then she remembered Frederick's words and stood stock still. He was right. She must get on with living now. Not forget him, never that, but get on with the rest of her life. She had a mill to run, businesses to supervise, children to bring up.

She had a large and loving family, too. She would not get married again. No one could ever take Frederick's place. But she intended to lead a very full life.

And anyway, grieving and wearing black wouldn't bring him back. Nothing would. He was there in her heart, though, would always be there. And in that painting.

That evening, Mary Benworth wasn't feeling well and since there had been no customers for an hour, she closed the salon early. Although the sun was getting quite low in the sky, Joanie Gibson was in no hurry to go home and she dawdled along, turning on a whim towards Hallam Park, named after Frederick's father. It was almost deserted but that suited her mood, so she wandered around the flower beds, watching the light breeze lifting the first fallen leaves and stirring the yellowing leaves still hanging on the branches.

The man standing under the trees didn't notice her at first. He had just had another row with his father and had stormed out of the house. Anger was still surging through him. It couldn't go on. His father and brothers might be satisfied to spend all their spare time on religion, but he wasn't. There must be more to life. There must! And he would not be bullied into spending most of Sunday in the small chapel folk called Redemption House. He hated it.

When the young woman with the sulky face sat down on one of the benches, he watched her for a moment and a wry smile replaced the frown on his face. She looked as fed up as he felt, poor lass. On a whim he strolled across. 'Mind if I join you?'

She nearly jumped out of her skin. 'Oh! You startled me.'

He didn't wait for her agreement, but sat down beside her on the bench. 'How are you keeping, then, Joanie Gibson?'

She shrugged. 'All right.' Then she scowled again. 'No, I'm not. I'm fed up, if you must know. Fed up to the teeth.'

'Oh? What of? I thought you Gibsons were all perfect.'

'Hah! Well, our Rebecca is. She can't do anything wrong, our Rebecca can't. I'll be glad when she gets wed, I will that!'

'What's upset you today?'

'Everything. My dad treating me like a child. An' going to chapel. I'm sick to death of going to chapel. He wants me to go to a Biblereading class on Thursday evenings now. But I'm not.' She hadn't told her father that yet, though. When he looked disappointed, you usually wound up doing as he wanted, whatever your own feelings.

Her companion made a scornful noise in his throat. 'Aye, well, my father's a deal worse than yours, I reckon. I'm sick to death of him. And of Redemption House. It's a bloody sight worse than your chapel, believe me! I reckon my father's lot make up half the sins they confess to, for a meeker herd of sheep you'll never find.' And his father never confessed to his own sins, which were real enough. Cheating poor folk out of their pence, usury, sharp practice, bullying. The Burns family were good at all those.

'They sing loudly enough at your chapel,' she volunteered, beginning to cheer up.

'Too bloody loudly.'

'You shouldn't swear in front of me, Bart. It's not nice.'

'Aye, you're right. I'm sorry, lass.' For a moment, Bart Burns just sat there, staring down at his clasped hands, then he stood up. 'Well, I'll leave you with your thoughts, Miss Gibson.'

She didn't know what made her say it and blushed at her own daring. 'Don't go! It's nice havin' someone to talk to.'

'Are you sure? Your family and mine don't exactly like one another. They'd not be happy to see you sitting here with me.'

'Hah! Who cares about them?'

He smiled and sat down. 'Not me, that's for sure.'

For the next hour, they sat and talked about themselves and their hopes, unburdening themselves as only the young can. Neither was able to talk freely at home and as the daylight faded gently into dusk, it seemed to encourage confidences.

Only when the station clock, which was now used to set the time for Bilsden folk, rang out the hour, did Joanie realise how long they had been there. 'Oh, my goodness! I should have been home half an hour ago.' She smiled at him cheekily. 'They'll have a search party out.'

'They're right to care about you. Young lasses can get into trouble, an' it's them as pays, not the fellows.'

She knew he was talking about his sister and reached out to touch his hand fleetingly. 'She's all right now, isn't she? Nelly, I mean.'

He stared at her, a long sombre look. 'No. She's not all right. She's unhappy.'

'Doesn't her husband treat her right?'

'Oh, he's kind enough. Not strict enough for my father's taste, but I'm glad about that. It's not him. It's just – not what she wanted. I think she really cared for your Mark.' As much as Nelly was able to care for anyone other than herself.

Joanie made a soft sound of comfort. 'Maybe she'll be better after the baby's born.'

'Maybe. I doubt it. How is your brother?'

'We don't know. We haven't heard from him.'

By unspoken agreement, they began walking towards the

park gates. There, Joanie stopped. 'I suppose we'd better not walk out of here together.'

'No. That'd never do.'

She moved a few steps away, then turned. 'It was nice talkin' to you, though, Bart.'

'Aye, it was.' He watched her walk briskly along the street. She was a nice lass, Joanie Gibson. She didn't have her sisters' good looks, but she always made him feel protective, somehow, with her faint air of unhappiness. And he liked her voice, too. Gentle, it was, with a little gurgle of laughter running through it when she was amused.

'Pity,' he said aloud as he walked away in the other direction. But what it was that was a pity, he didn't articulate, even to himself. And he soon forgot her as he neared his home. Even for his mother's sake, Bart Burns wasn't staying there much longer.

7

Bilsden: October 1860

When Annie got back to Ridge House, she found a visitor waiting for her. 'Why, Simon! How nice to see you!'

'You're looking well, Annie.'

She smiled and went to clasp his hand for a moment. She had grown very fond of her future brother-in-law. 'Do come into the library.'

He followed her and, after a perceptible hesitation, took the chair Frederick had always sat in when she pointed to it. 'Your people thought you might be back soon, so I took the liberty of waiting.'

She could guess what he had come about, but let him get round to it in his own time.

His voice was gentle. 'How are things, Annie?'

She shrugged. 'As well as can be expected.'

He fidgeted with the edge of his sleeve. 'You can probably guess why I'm here?'

'Yes.'

'I want to marry Rebecca now, not wait and wait.'

He stood and began pacing up and down the room, a tall thin man with an attractive face, for all its long bony nose. Annie could see why Rebecca had fallen in love with him. He might be a Darrington, but he was kind and caring, nothing like the rest of his family.

'She says it wouldn't be fair to you for her to get married yet,' he went on, 'but Annie, I don't want any further delays. I love her and I want to make her my wife.'

'There's no reason at all why you shouldn't get married now.

And so I shall tell Rebecca. It's just a question of making the arrangements.'

He clasped her hand for a moment. 'Thank you. Let's keep it simple, then, so that it can be done very quickly. I don't want a fancy society wedding, anyway. I hate them. I just want a few of the people I like around me, which is mainly your family and one or two old friends from London.'

'When exactly do you want to get married, then?'

'Tomorrow, if I could.' He sighed, running one hand through his dark hair, making it even untidier than it had been before.

She didn't allow herself to smile, but she could see exactly why he didn't enjoy fashionable life in London. Not for Simon Darrington the elaborate back parting and side hair carefully brushed forward of fashion-conscious young men. (How silly some of them looked, too, with a bush of teased hair standing out behind each ear!) He wore his dark locks short and his only concession to modern fashions was his neat moustache, which did, she admitted, suit his lean face.

Even Frederick had considered growing a moustache, but she had persuaded him not to. He wouldn't have been her Frederick with a moustache or whiskers or beard. 'Oh, sorry! My mind was wandering, I'm afraid.' It did that a lot recently. She missed having someone to talk to, so she'd started talking to herself, inside her head.

'I said I'd like to marry your sister tomorrow, but more realistically, just as soon as can be arranged.'

'Why not?'

His face lit up. 'You don't mind?'

'I'm also presuming you'll want to come back here to Ridge House after the wedding and so I'm repeating my offer to hold the reception here for you.' Her step-mother, Kathy, would not be able to cope with such a thing at Netherhouse Cottage.

Suddenly Simon was hugging her, forgetting all protocol and etiquette, behaving like a young man in love, not a lord.

'Oh, Annie! You're a wonderful woman. Even now, you can think of others, help them.'

For a moment, she leaned against his hard masculine body, remembering the feel of a man with surprise and longing, then she pulled away and managed a half-smile. 'Well, I have one stipulation to make. I do think you should consider inviting more of the Bilsden gentry to the wedding than you had on your first guest list, Simon. If you do mean to make your life here, that is.'

He pulled a face. 'Do we really need to?'

'It's a small town. You'll be seeing these people regularly for the rest of your life. So don't offend them now.' Frederick had taught her that when she grew impatient with the social niceties of paying calls upon other ladies.

'Oh, well, all right. If you think so. Could you draw up another list for us, then? And help us arrange it all as quickly as possible? Surely we don't need to wait longer than a week or two?'

'Yes, of course I'll help. But I think we should plan for a month from now.' She saw his mouth opening to protest and said firmly, 'We really will need that much time to make our preparations.'

He sighed and shrugged his acceptance.

'And would you like me to talk to Rebecca for you, explain to her that I don't want you to delay the wedding because of me?'

'Please.' He was beaming at her now. 'Thank you so much, Annie.'

She heard him in the distance, whistling happily as he rode his horse back down the drive. She tried to feel glad for him and Rebecca, and she was glad, of course she was, but she could not help feeling a twinge of jealousy as well. And she could not help remembering the feel of a man's arms around her. She had not thought she would miss Frederick's touch quite so much. He had not been able to make love to her for a while before he died, but he had cuddled her and loved her

74

and shown her in a thousand small ways how much he cared about her.

She flicked a tear away from one cheek and took a few deep breaths. Pangs of grief struck you from time to time. But you couldn't give way to it. You just had to get on with things.

At first, Rebecca was angry that Simon had gone to Annie behind her back. 'I told him not to go upsetting you.'

'He hasn't upset me,' Annie lied. 'And I think it's more than time you and he married. Third time lucky, eh? We won't let anything stop us this time.'

'But you still need me at the salon.'

'I'll find someone else and persuade Mary to do more downstairs. Or maybe I'll even sell the place.' For she had completely lost interest in it now and she had enough on her plate with the mill and Frederick's other businesses.

Rebecca gasped. 'Sell it!'

'Why not?' It was the first time Annie had thought of it seriously, the first time she had realised that her interest in the salon had faded completely, but it made sense. 'Now, are you all set to move in at the Hall?'

Rebecca took a deep breath. 'Well, to tell you the truth, Annie, I'm a bit – a bit nervous of the servants there. They'll think I'm so young and inexperienced. And I am!'

'Come and spend a few days here working with Mrs Jarred, then we'll get her to help you choose a new housekeeper. You must find someone you like and respect, someone who'll work with you, not undermine your authority. In large houses, servants take their tone from both mistress and housekeeper.'

And she should know, Annie thought, for she'd once been a maidservant herself. Goodness, was it really twenty-eight years since a frightened little girl from the Rows had cried herself to sleep in the attic bedroom at Park House? And Annabelle Lewis, her first mistress, was long dead, while the doctor had remarried, this time happily to Ellie, Matt's sister and Annie's best friend from childhood.

Rebecca's voice made her start. 'Are you all right, Annie?'

'Oh, sorry! I'm doing it again, aren't I? I keep wandering off into my memories. I can't think what's got into me lately.' She clasped her sister's hand and said very firmly, 'Look, life's too uncertain, Rebecca. Don't waste any of your precious time. Marry Simon now, and be happy.' She laughed. 'Well, marry him as soon as we can arrange the wedding, anyway. And if you think you can get out of having Tamsin as bridesmaid, you don't know your niece. She's been planning her dress ever since you got engaged.'

One month later, a small, select group of Bilsden dignitaries assembled at St Mark's to watch Rebecca Gibson marry Simon, Lord Darrington. And to Martin Leaseby's chagrin, the Leasebys were not among the guests. It only added fuel to his anger with Annie Hallam for not selling him the warehouse. He would, he decided, as he read the guest list in the *Bilsden Gazette*, make that upstart bitch pay for how she'd treated him.

He'd found out about her, growing up in the Rows and marrying that old idiot Ashworth years ago to give her bastard a name. She was no better than the rest of them, for all her fancy ways. And he'd get back at Matt Peters, too, upon whose advice she'd surely acted. Fobbing him off with a lease on that small warehouse in Blackworth Street when he needed a warehouse of his own! He was still too new to Bilsden to see his way clearly, but Martin Leaseby hadn't got where he was by taking such insults lying down. As the bloody high and mighty Hallams and Gibsons would find out one day.

One or two other people were not exactly delighted about the wedding. Simon's step-mother, Lady Lavinia, was one of these, but she had decided to grace the occasion with her presence all the same. She might shudder at the thought of being connected to such a common person as this Rebecca Gibson, but she did not intend to give gossips in London or Lancashire a field day by declining to attend. She wrote that she was bringing Sir Anselm Maybeere with her to lend his support and hoped this would be acceptable.

'I reckon he'll be the next husband,' Simon said to Rebecca when he showed her the letter of acceptance from his step-mother. 'She's been seen a lot with him during the past year or two. In fact, I'd expected her to snaffle him before this, but maybe he's not in as much of a hurry as she is to marry again. They say his first wife was an absolute shrew.'

But when his step-mother arrived in Bilsden, she was wearing an engagement ring, a huge diamond surrounded by rubies, and she informed Simon, with a rather smug smile, that she too was soon to be married.

'I wish you happy, then, Step-mother.' He turned and shook Sir Anselm's hand. 'And you, too, sir, of course. I'm delighted about the news.' In more ways than one. The marriage would release him from the burden of his step-mother's extravagance, which paid no heed to the impoverished state of the family purse or the size of the jointure to which she was actually entitled.

The fact that her ladyship would be attending made Rebecca even more nervous than before and on the day itself she scarcely knew what to do with herself as she waited to be driven to church. She was satisfied enough with her appearance, thanks to Annie's talent for design and Kathy's talent for arranging hair. She was wearing a simple dress of white silk, with a huge crinoline in the latest pyramid shape, with all the fullness at the bottom. The separate bodice was made high at the neck, with pagoda sleeves under which silk muslin *engageantes* were tightly gathered into delicate lace frills at the wrist. On her head, she wore a wealth of artificial orange blossom.

'Eh, it's a silly fashion, that skirt is,' said John Gibson as he and his daughter waited for the carriage to take them to St Mark's. 'I can't get close enough to give you a proper hug.'

She tried to smile at him, but could not manage more than a twitch of the lips.

'Nervous?' he asked gently.

She nodded.

'Don't you love him?'

She stared at her father. This was the last question she would have expected. Her whole family knew very well how much she loved Simon. 'Of course I do.'

'Then stop worrying about the fuss you have to go through to get wed. Think of how much you love him instead.'

'It's his step-mother who frightens me,' Rebecca admitted. 'She looks down her nose at me, I know she does.'

'That's up to her. But you're Simon's choice.'

And that phrase really did comfort Rebecca as she walked down the aisle of St Mark's on her father's arm, feeling horribly exposed in front of all these people. *She* was Simon's choice, not some high-bred young lady from London. And when he smiled at her as she stood beside him, her fears fled.

I love you, he mouthed.

And I love you, she mouthed back.

Behind Rebecca, Tamsin stood looking down complacently at her own dress. A shorter child's skirt which came only to midcalf, but it, too, was of white silk and it was trimmed with her favourite green ribbons. Real silk, she thought, smiling blissfully. And my Cousin Lucy is only wearing muslin. Even Tamsin's pantaloons were trimmed in deep lace frills. She peered down at them, and stroked a knot of ribbon on her skirt, then a warning hiss from her mother in the pew at her side made her stop doing that and stand very still.

Next to Tamsin, Joanie sighed. She had agreed to act as her sister's bridesmaid, but felt as out of place here as a fish in a tree. She felt sure all the other guests were mocking her behind her back, for she didn't know how to talk fancy like they did. What's more, Annie had made the bridesmaids' dresses too plain, with only a bit of green ribbon to trim them. Nothing was too good for Rebecca, but she, Joanie, had to make do with the plainest of silk and only a measly bit of trimming.

And her hair was falling down already. For the millionth time, she wondered why Rebecca had been gifted with dark wavy hair, which could easily be styled in many ways, while

Joanie's hair was only a pale, faded-looking brown, so fine that you could do nothing with it. She scowled at the ground, wishing they had let her invite her friend Maddie today. She'd have felt much better with someone of her own there. The two of them would have had a grand time at the reception, laughing at the way Lady Lavinia spoke and the way that fat old man she was engaged to tried to hide the fact that he was deaf in one ear.

She'd seen Maddie waiting outside the church with her brother Harry as she came in, and the two of them had smiled at her, ignoring the bride and the other fancy folk. For a moment, Joanie had felt warm inside. She did have some good friends, friends who really cared about her, who knew how nervous she was feeling today. Oh, if only Maddie were here with her now! And Harry, too, of course. He was quite nice, but a bit solemn for Joanie's taste and she didn't admire men who were so – so chunky. She banished him from her mind, as she usually did.

When she got married, she'd make sure she had a livelier wedding. This one might just as well have been a funeral, so quiet was it. Maddie was right when she said Joanie's two sisters were snobs. They were. Annie and Rebecca both. And they needn't expect her to marry a boring old rich man like they had! (To Joanie, Simon's thirty-four years made him well past his youth.) Or even a boring middle-aged one. She was going to marry someone who was both good-looking and fun to be with. But she was in no hurry. It was more fun to be single, more fun to knock around with Maddie and flirt with the lads in the park.

Then she smiled. No one knew about her new friend, though, not even Maddie. Bart wasn't like the other lads. He was quiet and he listened to her and he was rather good-looking, too. Tall and strong. Of course, nothing could come of it, but she enjoyed talking to him, enjoyed just being with him. And she wasn't going to tell anyone about him. It was her special secret.

After the wedding, at Ridge House, Lady Lavinia and her fiancé condescended to be gracious to the other guests until Tom, who was having none of Sir Anselm's condescension, answered a patronising remark very sharply. After that the couple kept themselves mostly to themselves, exchanging occasional scornful comments about the other guests.

They were not the only ones feeling critical. The few others who had come up from London were pleasant enough, Tom decided, but a bit colourless. In fact, if truth be told, he found weddings a huge bore. It was best the way he and Rosie had done it, just gone and got wed on a special licence, with only young Albert and Rosie's manager, Stephen Harris, as witnesses.

As the inevitable speeches were made, Rebecca sucked in her breath in near disbelief as she first heard herself called Lady Darrington. At the sound of the same phrase, Joanie's scowl came back with a vengeance.

'What the hell's got into our Joanie today?' Tom asked Luke in a quiet moment.

'Jealousy.'

'Ah, she's a silly piece, that one.'

'She's still our sister.'

Tom let our a sniff of disgust and changed the subject. He had better things to talk about than Joanie. 'How's that cottage of yours going? Got it finished yet?'

Luke's gentle face was lit up by a beam of sheer delight. 'Yes. And it's very comfortable.' His smile faded. 'I'm moving in next week, whatever Kathy says.'

'She doesn't want you to leave home, then?'

'No. She likes a house full of people. But I'm twenty-five, a man grown, and I'm more than ready to go. Nor I shan't miss the fusses and frets that our Joanie's been causing lately. Like I said, she's jealous of our Rebecca and doesn't mind who knows it.'

'Well, Rebecca won't be there any more after today.'

'But Joanie will.' Luke shook his head. He tried so hard to be patient with his youngest sister, but even his patience had worn thin lately. 'She's so contrary! And I don't like those friends of hers, those Pickerings.'

Tom shrugged. 'It's her choice who she pals on with.'

'And a bad one, too. I don't think much of Harry Pickering, for all he's so pleasant to everyone. His smile doesn't reach his eyes.'

Tom stared at Luke in surprise. It was very unlike his brother to be critical of anyone. Then he shrugged and changed the subject. He had had enough talk about Joanie to last him the rest of the year. 'It's about time *you* found yourself a wife,' he pointed out. 'Who's going to look after your cottage and cook your meals?'

Luke shrugged. 'I'm not bad at cookin' the plain stuff myself. But I will get someone in to clean the house and do my washing.' He smiled. 'And if I can't be bothered to cook, I'll go down to our Mark's chop house. Maud's running it as well as ever. No, Tom, it'll be years before I marry. I've got too much to do getting my market garden established.'

Tom dug him in the ribs. 'I thought you weren't infected with the family desire to make money.'

'I'm not. But I want to grow so many things.' Luke's eyes went all dreamy. 'And I can afford to have a hothouse built now, thanks to Frederick's generosity.'

They were both silent for a moment or two, then, 'I miss him,' Tom admitted.

'So do I. And Annie hasn't looked truly happy since he died.'

'What did you expect?'

They both turned to look at their eldest sister. They owed everything to her, and there was nothing they would not have done for her, but more than that, they loved her deeply. They were close, as only people who have gone through hard times together could be. But they were only Annie's brothers. Frederick had been both lover and friend. They could not replace him.

'Do you think she'll ever marry again?' Tom asked.

Luke shook his head. 'Shouldn't think so. After all, she's forty now.'

'Hey! Forty's not that old!' Tom growled, giving his brother a mock punch in the arm. He was thirty-eight himself.

'It is for women.'

'Well, she doesn't look forty. Even in those dreary black clothes. I wish she'd stop wearing them.'

Harry made his sister wait around until the wedding party came out of church and it worked out as he had planned. Joanie's face brightened at the sight of them and he was pleased at that.

Neither of them saw a young man who was walking down the street stop to watch the wedding party. He looked at the richly clad group rather scornfully until he saw Joanie, standing by herself to one side, looking unhappy and ill-at-ease, then his expression softened.

That poor lass isn't enjoying herself, he thought. He wished he could go over and tease her, cheer her up. They'd met once or twice in the park now and each time he'd enjoyed her company. He stood watching for longer than he had intended. He didn't know why she attracted him, because she wasn't exactly pretty, but she did. A lost soul in the midst of the almighty Gibson family, that one. Just as he was a lost soul in his own family. He scowled at the thought. He'd had enough of his father and a bellyful of Redemption House, too. The time was coming closer when he'd just up and leave. Then see how they'd miss him. He was better than any of them at buying and selling, and they all knew it, too, though his father would never admit it.

A smile creased his dark face for just a minute. Well, his father didn't know everything. He didn't know how much money his youngest son had in the Savings Bank, money he'd kept back from the market sales. It wasn't stealing to take a fair wage, since his father didn't pay his sons more than a pittance.

With a final pitying look at Joanie as she was helped into a carriage, Bart started walking down the hill again. One day! he told himself. One fine day he'd go his own way in life. And the only one he'd miss would be his mother – though not as much as she'd miss him. How had a warm, loving woman like her come to marry a mean, vicious fellow like his father?

Outside the church, Maddie nudged her brother. 'Can we go now, Harry?' Her voice was sulky. Joanie might think that her dress was plain, but Maddie envied her the silk and the important role in such a big wedding.

Harry nodded. 'Aye.' Now that Joanie had been driven away, there was no benefit to be gained from lingering.

As they walked back home, Maddie glanced sideways at her brother. He looked well pleased with himself. 'Why did you want to go today? I mean, we had to stand outside like everyone else, for all we're Joanie's friends.'

'I wanted her to know we care about her. She was nervous, you know. She doesn't fit in with those fine relatives of hers.'

'Who'd want to fit in with such toffee-nosed bores!' Maddie scoffed.

'I would. And I'll do it one day, too.'

She stopped dead in her tracks, mouth open in shock. 'What do you mean? How will you ever have to fit in with nobs like that?'

'I mean that whoever marries dear little Joanie will be under the wing of the Gibson clan. They'll make sure she has a nice house, and they'll also make sure that her husband earns a decent living. They're like that, the Gibsons are.'

Maddie's mouth fell open. 'You mean, you want to marry Joanie?'

He nodded.

'But I thought it was Rebecca you fancied?'

He shrugged. 'I did, but she's out of my reach now.' He looked sideways at his sister and decided not to favour her with the rest of his plans. He placed no reliance upon the silly bitch keeping secrets, or even being tactful. 'Joanie's a taking little thing,' he said, trying to sound warm about the girl. Unfortunately, she was the last of the Gibson girls of this generation, so he had no choice. He'd failed once with Rebecca, but he didn't intend to fail again. He'd make very sure of that. This time he'd take any steps necessary to ensure that both she and her family wanted to see her married to him. Any steps he had to.

'And anyway,' he added, choosing his words carefully, 'Joanie's more fun than Rebecca, as well as being your friend. There's only you and me left now. So I reckon I need to make sure you get on with my wife.' Their parents had died a while ago, and then a year or two after that, the aunt they lived with had also died, leaving them nothing but a collection of worm-eaten furniture. They'd stayed on in the house she had rented for years, but Harry wanted more than that out of life.

Maddie was still staring at him, her mouth half-open. Then she beamed at him. 'That'd be grand, that would. I'd like to have Joanie for my sister-in-law.'

'Don't you go saying anything to her.' He let his features settle into a sad, wistful expression that he'd practised carefully in front of the mirror. 'Maybe she won't fancy me. I'm not a good-looking chap like that lord of Rebecca's.'

She stopped again to study him. 'Hmm. You could do something with your hair, you know, grow it a bit longer, to be more fashionable. And you could smarten up your clothes. Joanie likes a well-dressed man.'

It was his turn to be surprised. He had not credited Maddie with the intelligence to be of much help to him. ''Mmm. I'll think about that. Thanks.'

For the rest of the walk home they were silent, both thinking hard, and Harry was careful to keep the wistful expression on his face. Even his sister was not to know how indifferent he really felt to young Joanie's charms. It was time to do something now. He didn't want to lose his last chance of moving up in the world honestly. He didn't intend to stay a clerk in the Bilsden Gas Company all his life. By heck, he didn't!

8

Bilsden: Christmas 1860

By Christmas, Annie felt she had a reasonable grasp of all the Hallam business interests, minor and major, though they were not making quite as much profit now as when Frederick had been there to share his wisdom and experience with Matt. Well, that was only to be expected. And how much money did you need to make, anyway? Her life was more than comfortable.

She also felt enough her old self to invite her family up to Ridge House for Christmas dinner. As she was finishing getting dressed, Tamsin came into the bedroom and sprawled on the bed. 'Do you have to wear black all the time, Mother?'

Annie turned to stare into the mirror above the fireplace, seeing herself and, behind her, her daughter. 'It's expected. And I have got some touches of lilac piping now.'

'I still don't like it. The black keeps reminding me of Father.' Tamsin was scowling at the bed.

Annie watched her, feeling for the child's pain. Tamsin hated to show any weakness or grief in public, but Annie was sure that her daughter still wept for her father sometimes. 'I don't like it either, love, but believe me, it'd cause a scandal in town if I didn't wear black for at least a year.'

Tamsin fiddled with the counterpane. 'People are silly. What you wear doesn't change how you feel inside.'

'No, I agree. Only you can know that. Or those who love you can sometimes guess.' When Tamsin didn't volunteer any more remarks, Annie changed the subject, 'Is Edgar ready?'

'He's downstairs with William.' Tamsin went across to stare out of the window. 'Sometimes, he seems such a little boy, even if he is as tall as me.' Edgar's height advantage was an irritation to her.

'You're going to be short like me, I think. Edgar takes after his father.'

Tamsin gave an exaggerated sigh.

Annie looked at her. Tamsin had been so good since her father's death, but lately she had seemed restless, ready to take offence at the slightest provocation, her voice louder, sharper. She needed company other than her gentle little brother, girls of her own age to play with. But other mothers were a bit wary of a girl who went to the mill each Saturday and worked there alongside who knew what rough types, even if she was Frederick Hallam's daughter. One or two had ventured to comment to Annie that perhaps it was a mistake sending a girl of Tamsin's delicate years to work in the mill. She had soon set them right. The Hallam money came in the first place from cotton. It was only right that the Hallam children should know something about the mill.

Tamsin swung round and stared down at the lace-trimmed pantaloons showing beneath her full skirt. The latter was short enough to reveal the fashionable striped stockings and neat black patent house shoes she was wearing. She pointed her toes to get a better view of her shoes, concentrating on them as if her life depended on knowing every curve and wrinkle of the gleaming leather.

Annie realised that a confidence was brewing.

'Prue Leaseby says her father and mother think it's wrong for a girl like me to work in the mill.' She raised her eyes and looked straight at her mother, a very level, adult look. 'My father didn't think it wrong. And you don't, either. So I told her to leave me alone, to go and play with her dollies.'

Annie bit her lip. She could just imagine Tamsin saying that. The child had a very cutting tone sometimes.

'I like working in the mill, Mother. It's my favourite thing to do. Besides, it's our family mill. And when I grow up, I'm going to work there all the time like Mr Peters does. I don't care if other girls don't. It's our mill, so I can do as I please there. And Father's will said I'll own part of it one day, so no one will be able to stop me. Though I hope it doesn't become mine for ages.' Her voice became gruff. 'I – I don't want you to die as well.'

Past experience told Annie not to deny Tamsin this hope of working in the mill when she grew up. She didn't want her daughter walking round like a thundercloud on Christmas Day. Joanie would be bad enough. That girl hadn't had a good word for anyone in her family since Rebecca's wedding and had worn even Kathy's love and patience thin. 'We'll have to see how you feel about the mill when you grow up, then. People change, you know.'

'I shan't,' Tamsin said confidently. 'Besides, it makes Edgar wheeze if he goes into the mill. So he can't work there. That only leaves me, doesn't it?'

A chill of premonition ran down Annie's spine, but she pushed it away. No, she told herself, Edgar will get better. Jeremy said some people do. She did not repeat Jeremy's words to Tamsin, and did not allow herself to doubt them either.

Tamsin clutched her hand suddenly. 'You won't stop me working in the mill, will you, Mother?'

'Of course not. If it's what you want.'

Tamsin sighed in relief, then cocked one ear. Outside, there was the sound of footsteps on the gravel drive. She ran over to the window. 'They're here. Come on!' Grabbing her mother's hand, she dragged her downstairs, still child enough to enjoy family parties and to be looking forward to getting some presents.

Annie followed more slowly, glad that her daughter was beginning to confide in her. When Frederick was alive, the girl had clung to her father, speaking mainly to him about her problems and worries. Now, she seemed lost sometimes. Annie felt the same, but couldn't let it show.

Winnie, smiling broadly, let John and Kathy Gibson into the hall. They were carrying string bags of parcels and brought a breath of icy air with them, but they looked happy and rosy-cheeked. They were followed by Joanie, with her thundercloud expression, then Samuel John and Benjamin, looking aloof and bored, as only boys on the verge of manhood can when forced to associate with their families.

Goodness! Annie thought. Samuel John's as tall as I am now.

William and Edgar came out of the front parlour, to join in the chorus of welcomes, and Winnie hovered in the background, still beaming at 'her' family and not moving until Luke came in through the back door of the hall, set his hands on her plump waist and moved her aside to an exclamation of 'Mr Luke!' in which delight and mock reproof were mingled.

He was still working part-time with Nat Jervis, the head gardener at Ridge House. All the women servants thought the world of him. Never too busy to lend you a hand moving something heavy. Always a pleasant word. It was a difficult balance to tread for the owner's brother, but he had managed it. Even today he had insisted on taking his share of the work before changing his clothes in Nat's cottage behind the big house.

I must find time to go and see how Luke's getting on in that cottage of his, Annie decided. Tom says he's got it all nice now. She sat down next to Kathy and chatted for a while, then spoke to her father. She was missing Frederick quite dreadfully today, but tried to keep a smile on her face.

It was a relief when Tom and his family arrived for she had to go and greet them, accept their wishes for a happy festive season and get them settled. The secret was to keep busy, she told herself, take an interest in the others. But it was hard.

It was Tom who started them all playing games, Tom who badgered Annie into joining in, Tom who stopped Tamsin quarrelling with Samuel John, as she often did. But even Tom could not get Joanie to join them and when he tried to pull her forward, she burst into tears and retreated to the library.

'Eh, I don't know what's got into that lass lately,' John said.

'Best leave her be,' Kathy whispered. 'I think she's a bit jealous of our Rebecca and Simon.' She smiled across the room at her son-in-law, who had just arrived and with whom she now felt completely at ease, lord or not.

Later, when the meal was over and things had quietened down, Annie noticed Rosie's son. Young Albert usually hovered quietly on the fringes of everything at such gatherings, not unwilling to join in but showing the diffidence of a stranger who was not used to large families. The children did not know that he was Tom's natural son, so the others treated him as a complete outsider. Tom said that Albert got on all right with Lucy, David and Richard at home, but Annie sometimes wondered. He was too polite for a lad his age. Too knowing. Now, he and Tamsin were arguing together over the chess board and for once, both looked to be enjoying themselves. She was glad to see them together. Albert would be a good influence on her wild daughter.

Annie kept the final surprise until they had opened their presents and everyone was sitting replete in the large front parlour. Then she clapped her hands together to gain their attention. 'I have a piece of good news to share with you.'

Everyone turned to look at her as she went over to the mantelpiece and took down the letter. 'This came a few days ago. For all of us. It says on the outside that Dad has to read it aloud on Christmas Day if it arrives in time.' She had been itching to tear it open ever since, but had forced herself to do as Mark wanted. For of course she had recognised the handwriting immediately.

'What is it?' John took it from her, pulling his pince-nez from his top pocket. Lately he had admitted that he could not see to read without their help, but he refused to get some proper spectacles made, saying they'd make him look like an old fellow if he walked around with them on all the time. When he saw the handwriting, his mouth dropped open and the paper in his hand began to tremble violently. 'It's from our Mark.'

'Oh, John!' Kathy rushed to clutch his arm and stare at the piece of paper.

Annie passed her father a paper knife and John slit open the envelope with great care, spreading out the single sheet of paper inside, smoothing it carefully, putting off the reading as if a little afraid of what he might find.

'Well, read it to us, then, Dad!' Tom urged. 'It's about time that young devil wrote and said what he's been up to. He must know we'd be worried sick about him.'

Luke watched them, smiling. He'd already had a letter from the brother to whom he was closest, and he knew what this one would contain. He was glad now that Mark hadn't married Nelly Burns. He had written straight back to tell him that Nelly had borne him a daughter in early September, and that her new husband, Timothy Hill, had written a stiff note to the Gibsons to say that mother and baby were 'doing as well as can be expected'. Whatever that might mean.

'I'll read it aloud, shall I?' John said, then his face twisted for a moment and he looked at Annie. 'Eh, no, you read it, lass. I can't.' He smeared away the moisture that was gathering in his eyes.

Annie took the paper.

Dear Father and everyone,

I hope you're well and that you've found it in your hearts to forgive me now. I was sorry to leave you all so suddenly, but it seemed the only thing to do.

I took ship to Australia, which I've always had a fancy to visit. The voyage wasn't very comfortable, but we got here safely in the end. I made one or two friends on board and have kept with them since.

I brought some goods out with me, which I've sold at a decent profit, so I'm well enough for money. There's plenty of work here for anyone as wants it, and I'm making out all right, but I'm not sure yet what sort of business I want to run, or where exactly I want to settle.

It's such a big country and the towns so far apart. You wouldn't believe how empty the land looks, or how hot and dusty it gets in the summer.

If you've forgiven me, Dad, I'd really like to hear from you. In fact, I'd like to hear from all of you. Letters from home are a great treat out here.

I'll end by wishing you the very best for 1861. May you all prosper, but more important, may you be happy.

Your loving son who hopes he has been forgiven, and who will be back in Bilsden one day.

Mark

John was not even trying to hide his tears, but they were mingled with smiles. 'Eh, I shall have to write to him, I shall that. Not that I write a good letter, but he won't mind that, I'm sure.' John had learned to read and write late in life, courtesy of the Methodist Chapel's men's reading classes, and writing still did not come easily to him.

'You're forgiven him now, then, Dad?' Annie asked softly.

'Of course I have, love. It were arrogant of me to tell him what to do with his life. Arrogant. Though I'm still sorry we shan't know our grandchild by that lass.' He looked round the room. 'Give over staring at me, you lot. If a man can't cry at the lost sheep returned to the fold, when can he cry?'

That evening, when he got home to his little cottage at the end of Hey Lane, Luke stared around. What a difference from Annie's place! He frowned. It wasn't just the size of the cottage, though, it was the lack of a woman's touch. And he really would have to find someone to clean for him.

The next day, he bumped into his surly neighbour Ted Gorton, who nodded and would have passed on, but Luke suddenly realised that Ted knew everyone around here. 'Er – I was wondering if you could help me, Mr Gorton?'

'Oh?' It was more of a grunt of irritation than an invitation to continue.

'Yes. I'm looking for a woman to come and clean for me a couple of times a week, do my washing, too.' He didn't like to take it home to Kathy because he wanted to be absolutely independent. It was a need he had, somehow.

'How much will you pay her?'

'Sixpence an hour.'

'My wife could come in and help.'

Luke was startled. He'd hardly seen anything of Mrs Gorton, who seemed very shy. 'Are you sure she won't mind?'

'Aye. A bit of extra brass allus comes in useful. When d'ye want her?'

Luke ran a hand through his hair. 'Well, as soon as possible. It's in a bit of a mess. I've been too busy working outside. And building my hothouse.'

'She'll be down within the hour.' Ted started walking away, then turned. 'But you'll pay her wages to me.'

Luke watched him go. He was not sure that this was a good thing to do. Few people except his drinking cronies had a good word to say for Ted Gorton, who worked hard enough but who also apparently spent a lot of time in the small public house at Hey End. Luke had called in there once or twice for an ale and met some of the locals, farmers with smallholdings, struggling to make a decent living, or farmworkers from the bigger places. Nat Jervis liked to drink there occasionally, too, with a cousin who lived nearby.

Luke was not exactly a regular, because he was not a drinker, but his face was known now, and it didn't hurt to be on nodding terms with your neighbours. But would it be sensible to employ one of them? He wasn't sure. He would just have to see how having Mrs Gorton clean for him worked out. It was too late to change his mind now without giving offence.

In the shabby farmhouse at the junction of Hey Lane and the main road, two children were huddled in a corner of their bedroom, trying to cover their ears as their dad thumped their mam again. They could hear her involuntary gasps, but she did not cry out. She never did.

'Why does he hit her?' four-year-old Tess sobbed.

'I don't know,' Adam whispered back. He scowled into the darkness. At six he was too small to help. But when he grew up, he'd stop his dad hitting her. He would. It wasn't fair.

As the thuds and gasps continued, they clung to one another and wept. Silently. As they always did.

1861

9

Bilsden: January 1861

The year that was to usher in a period of great hardship for the folk of Lancashire started with a shock for Annie and the Gibsons. One afternoon Winnie, bristling with suppressed excitement, came to find her mistress.

'You have a visitor, ma'am.'

'Oh, who?'

Winnie's voice went down to a sibilant whisper. 'He won't say.'

Annie stared at her elderly parlourmaid in surprise. 'Then I won't see him.'

Winnie looked round, as if she suspected someone might be lurking under the sofa, and moved closer to her mistress, still speaking in a lowered voice. 'He says it's urgent. And – and I think I recognise him, ma'am.'

'Oh? Are you sure?'

Winnie nodded her head up and down vigorously, looking like a hen pecking at some grain. She was enjoying a rare moment of superiority. 'It's that Timothy Hill, ma'am. The one as married Nelly Burns. He lives over Todmorden way.'

Her face told Annie that she understood exactly why the man who had married Nelly would be of interest to the Gibsons. Well, servants always did know what was going on. Annie remembered that from her own days in Dr Lewis's household.

'He lives near my cousin,' Winnie continued, 'so I've seen him around the streets when I've gone over to visit her. I'm sure it's him.'

Annie felt apprehension trickle down her spine. She still

missed Mark and wished desperately that he had not gone away. But Nelly's brothers had beaten him so badly for getting their sister into trouble and had declared that they would be satisfied with nothing less than marriage. Any other family would have accepted the generous allowance Mark had offered to the mother of his unborn child, but not the Burns family.

The father, known in the town as Bible Burns, because he quoted from the holy book so often, had also seemed to relish the opportunity to get at John Gibson through his son's misdemeanour, for both men were lay preachers in their own churches and on Burns's side, at least, there was a great deal of jealousy of a man who was greatly respected in Bilsden – as Lemuel Burns himself was not.

In the end Mark had run away rather than marry Nelly or cause further trouble for his family. Even then, with his daughter's good name at stake, it had been touch and go whether Lemuel Burns would agree to keep quiet about the child that Mark had fathered on her. But the thought of the money Mark had arranged for her support had won the day and Mr Burns had not only agreed to keep quiet, but had found a distant relative willing to marry 'the sinner'.

Annie took a deep breath and squared her shoulders. 'You'd better show Mr Hill in, then. And, Winnie – thank you for your help. Will you add to your kindness by not saying anything about this to the other servants?'

'I'm always happy to help, ma'am.' Winnie puffed her way out of the sitting-room self-importantly and a minute later showed in a visitor, a young working man of earnest demeanour, who seemed very stiff and uncertain of himself.

'Thank you for seeing me, Mrs Hallam.' He looked over his shoulder, checking that Winnie had left.

'You said the matter was urgent?'

'Yes.' He fiddled with his shirt cuff, then swallowed audibly and looked across at her. 'I'm Nelly's husband. Timothy Hill. Well, I *was* Nelly's husband.'

'What do you mean by "was"?' She had noticed the black

band round his sleeve, but had not thought it concerned Nelly. Surely . . . She cut short the thought and waited for him to explain.

'Nelly died, Mrs Hallam, nearly a week ago now.'

'Nelly! But how? What happened?'

'Something went wrong,' he flushed, 'inside her. She hadn't been well since the baby was born. We had the doctor to her, but he said there was nothing he could do. It was just – just women's trouble.'

'I'm sorry.'

'I don't think Nelly cared by then. She – she hadn't been happy since the baby was born. She didn't take to it. Or to me. And she didn't get on with my mother, either.' He looked Annie directly in the eyes for the first time. 'I was sorry in the end that I'd agreed to marry her. Money doesn't bring peace to a house. Or happiness.'

What did you say to that? From her one meeting with Nelly Burns, Annie could not imagine that spiteful, ignorant girl ever being happy. But still, it was sad when people died so young. 'Um – how is the baby?'

He sighed and wrung his hands, staring at the carpet, now avoiding Annie's eyes again. 'The baby's well enough.' Then he looked up and burst into another rush of speech. 'It's a little girl. We called her Faith. My mother's had the raising of her so far. Nelly wouldn't even pick her up except to feed her. And my mother isn't young any more. She says,' another audible gulp of breath, 'she says you Gibsons should take the child and look after her now.'

'But – it isn't known that the child is Mark's, and anyway, he's in Australia.'

Timothy Hill was almost twitching with the discomfort of this interview. 'Well, I'm afraid it's you or the Burns family, because my mother refuses point-blank to look after the child any more.' He heaved a great sigh. 'I know you've been paying us to look after her, but my mother hasn't taken to poor little Faith and – and anyway, she wants to remarry herself.'

He paused for a moment, then said in a rush, 'Mrs Hallam, I know my Uncle Burns is a God-fearing man, but he's very harsh in his ways. When Nelly came to me, well, quite frankly she had been beaten black and blue, and he advised me to do the same to her. He even seemed proud of how he'd hurt her. He said the devil must be driven from her.' He shook his head. 'I'm a Christian man myself, but I don't believe in beating anyone. Not like that. So I came to you first. Please take the child because if you don't, he will.' He sucked in a breath and added, in a harsh, strangled voice, 'I just can't find it in my heart to rear her as my daughter. Not now. I'm sorry.'

'Very well.' Put like that, what choice was there? Annie had taken a great dislike to the whole Burns family herself, the three sons who'd beaten Mark up and most especially the father. Though what she would do with a baby, or how she would explain little Faith's presence at Ridge House, she didn't know.

Timothy Hill's face cleared. 'Oh, thank goodness! I'll go and fetch her in.'

'You mean – today? Now?'

'Yes. I can't keep taking time off work, so my mother said to bring Faith over to Bilsden with me today. She came too, to help me carry the things.' And had made a great fuss about the journey, her first on a train, nearly driving him mad. 'She's waiting outside the gates with the child. If you hadn't taken Faith, we'd have had to go on to my Uncle Burns's house. We've brought all the baby things with us.'

Annie was thinking furiously. She could not imagine the Burns family accepting this easily. They might try to take the child themselves. 'I'll need you to sign a statement that you did not father the child and that, to the best of your knowledge, my brother Mark did. Also that you relinquish her completely and utterly into my hands.'

He looked at her through narrowed eyes and then nodded slowly. 'If you think it necessary.'

'I do. Given your uncle's nature.'

'Yes. Perhaps you're right.'

'Go and fetch your mother and the baby, then, Mr Hill. They must be frozen waiting outside on a day like this.' She rang the bell for Winnie and ordered tea, then went across to a small escritoire, dipped her pen in the silver-topped ink bottle and began to write quickly, pausing to indicate that the Hills should sit down when a goggling Winnie showed them in again, and then turning back to the document she was drawing up.

The Gibson curse! she thought angrily as her steel nib spluttered across the paper. The men of her family found it all too easy to father children and could not seem to resist any opportunity. Tom joked about it, but she just hoped that her William wouldn't suffer from the same strong sexual urges that had made her father marry three times and sire eleven children, of whom nine were still living. Even the third time, he had already got Kathy pregnant before they married.

And if it hadn't been for Annie's help, her father's second family would all have grown up in poverty. She had brought them to live with her at Netherhouse Cottage and between them, she and Tom had seen all their half-brothers and -sisters provided with the skills necessary to earn a decent living.

But she was getting tired of pulling her family out of trouble. Very tired. Frederick was the only one who had seemed to understand that. He had told her to leave them to manage for themselves now. But how could she? And how could she have refused to take little Faith today?

Within the hour, Timothy Hill had taken his awed mother away, after signing the paper which Annie had hurriedly drafted. Because William was out, it had been witnessed by Mrs Jarred, the housekeeper, and Elizabeth MacNaughton. Winnie, the only other servant to have any clear idea of what had happened, had since been brimming with smug self-importance that was a severe trial to the other servants, but although she regularly dropped hints of her involvement in secret family doings, she never betrayed exactly what these doings were.

Within minutes of the Hills' departure, the garden lad was

carrying urgent messages down the hill into Bilsden, one to Annie's father and Kathy, and another to her brother Tom.

When Kathy and John arrived, the baby, who was now four and a half months old, was lying on the sofa, hungry, grizzling and chewing at her tiny fist. She had refused the warmed milk Annie had tried to feed her. Clearly she had never used a cup. Timothy's mother had said that a neighbour with milk to spare had been feeding the infant ever since her mother sickened. And that was another thing, Annie thought in irritation. They'd have to find a wet nurse!

Kathy forgot everything when she saw the baby, for she adored children. 'Eeh, Annie, who's this?' She took little Faith in her arms without waiting for an answer and began to rock her to and fro instinctively. 'You poor little mite. Are you hungry, then? Has your mammy left you all alone?'

Annie could think of no way to soften the news. 'Dad, Kathy, this is Mark's child. Poor Nelly died last week. They – the Hills – don't want to keep her.'

'Oh, hell!' Tom had just come in and overheard Annie's speech. 'I thought we were shut of this bundle of trouble.' He went across to hug Annie, then peered at the baby cuddled in Kathy's arms and rolled his eyes. 'She's a real Gibson! My Lucy looked just like that at her age.'

'I've agreed that we'll keep her, Tom.'

'What!'

'It was us or the Burns family.'

'Ah.'

No need to explain that to any of them.

'She's a bonny little thing,' John said, tickling the baby's chin with his thumb.

Tom ignored the child. He had jumped to the same conclusion as Annie had. 'Have you got a legal document to say she's yours? If not, we'll soon have Burns knocking on the door, out of sheer bloody spite. I wouldn't give a canary to that bast—' He saw his father's disapproving glance and hastily amended that to, 'Er, to that fellow Burns, let alone a baby.'

'I got Mr Hill to sign something, but I'm not sure it's enough. It's on the mantelpiece. Will you see Mr Pennybody for me, Tom? Show it to him? Tell him what's happened?'

'Yes. Leave that to me. And I'll stop making the payments, too.' He stared down at the child, now cooing up at Kathy, who had worked her usual magic. There wasn't a child born who wouldn't respond to their gentle step-mother. 'What the hell are we going to do with it?'

'Not "it", her!' Kathy reproved him. 'Your niece.'

Tom ignored that and groaned. 'Don't our sins come back to haunt us?'

'I'll have to hire a wet nurse, I suppose,' Annie worried. 'And turn one of the second-floor rooms into a nursery. Maybe Dr Lewis will know of someone who can feed her.'

John Gibson was still by his wife's side, studying this unknown grandchild and making soft noises at her. 'You don't sound all that pleased, Annie love.'

'Well, I'm not. I've enough on my plate with the mill and other things since Frederick died. The last thing I need is another child to bring up.'

For once, Kathy didn't seek her husband's approval. 'Then let us take her.' She looked sideways at John and was not surprised when he beamed his agreement.

There was silence in the room.

'You know, that might be the best thing,' Tom said slowly.

'But we can't ask you to—' Annie began.

'You didn't,' John said. 'But I did ask the Lord how I could make up for my harshness with our Mark. And now He's shown me the way.' He was punctuating his remarks with further tickles, which had the baby chuckling and blowing bubbles at him. 'Eh, she's a right pretty little thing, she is that.'

'And I know a lass from chapel who's just lost her babby,' Kathy added softly. 'I'm sure Mary Lucas will feed this one for us. They never thrive the same on cow's milk.'

Annie watched in amazement. Faith had already nestled down as if she knew that she had come home, and Kathy's face was luminous with love. Annie loved her own children, of course she did, but she had never had this capacity to live for others as her step-mother did. Or this delight in babies. What a pity Jeremy Lewis had forbidden Kathy to have any more children! She was a born mother.

'What shall you tell people?' Tom asked. 'We don't want them to know the truth.'

John frowned. 'Nay, I don't like to tell lies.'

'It'll be the child who'll suffer if you tell the truth,' Tom pointed out.

'Why don't you just say she's a relative's child,' Annie suggested, 'orphaned unexpectedly? That's not completely untrue.'

John looked at his wife. 'What do you think, lass?'

'I think Tom's right,' she said, her voice pleading. 'We don't want the child to pay for our Mark's sins, do we, John love?'

'No. I suppose not.' A mischievous grin creased his face. 'Hah! I'm looking forward to seeing our Lally's face when we turn up with young madam here.' His resemblance to Tom and every one of his grandchildren was very marked when he grinned like that, for all his sixty-two years.

'She'll love Faith as much as we do,' Kathy declared. Lally had started working for her and John as a general maid, paid for by Annie, when John's second family were younger, and now, at twentyfive, she was more like a daughter of the family than a servant. And for all Kathy's excellent cooking, Lally was still as scrawny as she had always been.

'And the Burns family?' Annie wondered aloud. 'Do you think they'll keep quiet about Faith's parentage?'

Tom's grin emphasised his resemblance to his father. 'Well, as it happens, I came across a little piece of information about Bible Burns's business dealings, which would do that upright citizen considerable harm were it to come out. I'll go and see him myself and discuss things. I'll enjoy that.'

Annie nodded in approval.

'And if you have any sense,' he added, 'you'll not let him

near the child. That man spreads misery round him everywhere he goes. And his sons are turning into right bullies, for all their Christian upbringing. The younger one isn't as bad, more the quiet surly type, if you ask me, but the other two don't mind using their fists and feet. No turning the other cheek for them! If me and some others hadn't got together about how things were going at the market, the Burns family would be running the place now and demanding payment from the other traders for the privilege of protecting them.'

Tom took his position as one of Bilsden's leading businessmen very seriously, and had great pride in his honesty and good name. He had been a rough lad and once had got in with a bad crowd, nearly causing a split between him and Annie. When she had saved him from trouble he had promised her that he would never do anything dishonest again and had joked that folk would one day call him 'Honest Tom'. Just before he ran away, Mark had once called his brother that in public for a joke, and it had caught on. He was now known in the whole town by that nickname.

'I don't like to think of you threatening Mr Burns,' John worried.

'Then don't think about it, Dad. Just leave that side of things to me.' Tom exchanged long-suffering glances with his sister. They knew how impractical their father could be when the Lord moved him to a course of action or when it was a question of morals.

'Nor I don't like to think of telling lies about the child,' John added.

Kathy laid her free arm on her husband's. 'For her sake, John,' she repeated. 'Let's just say she's the child of a relative.'

There was a moment's silence while he wrestled with his conscience, then, 'Oh, all right. But only for the child's sake.'

Kathy turned to Annie. 'We'd better go now, I reckon. We need to get this young lady something to fill her little belly.' The two of them refused the offer of the carriage for such a short distance and, with Kathy carrying Faith and John holding the bundle of baby clothes, they set off briskly, both beaming down at the child as if they had just been given a precious treasure.

Annie looked at Tom. 'What next?'

He shook his head. 'Who the hell knows? Just wait till I write to our Mark, though!'

When Joanie met her new friend in the park, she was smiling for a change and didn't notice the black band on his arm.

'You look pretty when you're happy,' he said softly.

For a moment, she froze, as if his words had taken her by surprise. Then she gave him one of her flirtatious looks. 'Do I?'

He took hold of her arm and shook it a little. 'But you don't look pretty when you try to flirt with me. Don't do that, Joanie. It makes you look cheap.'

She flushed and tears came into her eyes. She would have stood up and run away, but his hand was still on her arm.

'Eh, I'm sorry, lass.' And for all the size of him, his voice was gentle, and his fingers were gentle, too, as they wiped away a tear. 'I didn't mean to spoil your happiness, love. What was making you smile?'

'I don't know as I should tell you, Bart.'

'Go on!'

'Well, it's little Faith. She's come to live with us.' Joanie's expression softened again. 'An' she's a right little love, too. So small and soft and—'

'Our Nelly's baby?' he asked harshly.

She suddenly realised that he had lost his only sister. 'Oh, I'm sorry. I was forgetting. Oh, Bart, how cruel of me!'

He shook his head and stared down numbly at his hands. He had had another row with his father last night. His father had gone on and on about 'the wages of sin'. Well, in Bart's opinion, poor Nelly had only done what most folk did. She'd wanted a bit of happiness in her life, instead of the eternal talk of repentance and sin, and he couldn't blame her. 'I'm glad the baby's gone to your lot!' he said suddenly, his voice harsh. 'Right glad!'

'Is it so bad at your house?'

'Bad?' He blew out a puff of angry air. 'It's hell on earth.'

'Then why do you stay? You're a man. You could leave any time you liked.'

'I earn my bread with my family. I'm not ready to set up on my own yet. When I am, I'll leave, don't you worry.'

'Oh.'

'Shall you miss me if I go away from Bilsden, Joanie?'

She just sat there, staring blindly at him, then she said in a small surprised voice. 'Yes. I shall.' She didn't try to hide her feelings, or the tears that came into her eyes at the thought of losing her special friend.

He didn't pretend not to see how she felt about him. 'You'll be better off with someone else, Joanie. With our families allus at loggerheads, we'd have no hope of being happy. No hope at all. We should stop seeing one another, we really should.' After a pause, he said quietly, 'If we had any sense at all.'

Another short silence wove itself round them, then she shook her head and whispered, 'I don't think I have much sense, then, Bart.'

He took her hand in his and raised it to his lips. 'Nor do I, love. Nor do I.' But what this added complication in his life would mean, he didn't dare think.

10

New York: Autumn and Winter 1860–1

Tian Gilchrist was fascinated by New York. When they disembarked, his new friend Thaddeus Brownsby would not take no for an answer but swept him off home in the family carriage, which had been waiting at the docks. He introduced Tian to his family as: 'An up and coming young artist from the old country. Have we got a room for him, Mother?'

His wife, a plump, overdressed woman, was clearly used to her husband's sudden enthusiasms. 'An artist. How nice!' she said, in a comfortable drawling voice. 'I'll put him in the second-floor front. How did your business in England go, dear?'

'Well. Very well.' Thaddeus had been winding up the estate of a distant relative, of whose existence he'd been totally unaware before the lawyers sent a man to track him down as the only living descendant. It wasn't a rich inheritance for a man of substance like him, he'd told Tian, but it made a nice bit extra to settle on his daughters. 'The boys will make their own way in the world, after all.'

Tian had already been made aware that the Brownsbys had two daughters of marriageable age and two slightly older sons, one already married, the other engaged: 'To an Irskine. The iron family, you know.' The young men proved to be as engrossed in making money as their father was and Tian found it almost impossible to hold a real conversation with them, for he had no interest in profits and percentages, and knew none of the people whose names they tossed to and fro, while they knew nothing about art or Europe. At first, they showed a faint interest in the fact that he had been to London and Paris, but that soon fizzled out.

Mrs Brownsby, whose interests were purely domestic, made sure her guest was comfortable, fed him huge meals and seemed happy to sit and listen to what everyone else said. The older daughter, Dorothy Brownsby, was involved in a lively social life with her particular circle of friends, and her father nodded approval as she mentioned some of the people she'd been spending time with recently. Since she had inherited her mother's cosy prettiness and her father's shrewdness, she instantly summed up Tian as not rich enough for husband material, so although she was polite to him, it was in a distant, disinterested way.

The younger daughter, Evelyn Brownsby, was known to her family and friends as Lyn. She was just eighteen, plumply pretty and ripe for falling in love, which she promptly did with Tian, to his intense embarrassment. Whenever they were together, she sat with her eyes on him, blushing and sighing when he spoke to her and generally embarrassing him by her attentions.

After a few days of this, Thaddeus summoned his guest into the big book-lined study at the back of the ground floor and said with the bluntness for which he was famous, 'I didn't count on my Lyn taking such a shine to you. We're going to have to find you somewhere else to live, young fellow.'

Tian sighed with relief. Already he was feeling smothered by their hospitality, was tired of rich meals and money-centred conversation, and had been wondering how to escape from the velvet prison without giving offence. 'Believe me, I've done nothing to encourage her, sir.'

'Oh, I can see that. You'd have been out on your ear imme-diately if you had.' Thaddeus pursed his lips and studied his guest. 'You're still hankering after that woman in England, aren't you?'

Tian nodded. One night on the boat he had drunk too much of Mr Brownsby's fine cognac and confided more than he'd meant to. 'Yes, sir. And always will be.'

'Good, good. I like to see constancy in a young man. Anyhow, back to my Lyn: I've taken the liberty of finding you some rooms.' He let out a snort of laughter. 'Or at least my assistant, Igor Dalowski, has found them. Genuine,' he pronounced it gee-newwine, 'artist's studio. Not in a good residential area, but I'm told you artists like to live in these run-down places. We thought you'd prefer it to a lodging house, because Igor tells me his landlady has so many rules that if her cooking weren't so good, he'd move out tomorrow. He doesn't think many landladies would put up with a mess of paints and such.'

'No, Right. Well, thank you sir, but—' Tian had been going to say that he'd prefer to choose his own studio, but Thaddeus waved one hand, dismissing any objections.

'Igor knows New York. At least come and see what he's found.' He cocked an inquiring eyebrow and seemed pleased when a bemused Tian nodded agreement, thinking that he could, after all, find himself another place if this one wasn't to his taste.

'Be obliged if you'd get ready now,' the older man consulted a large gold watch which hung across his prominent belly, 'and we'll go check things out right away. Yessir. Genuine artist's studio.'

Thaddeus took his guest to the apartment personally and showed him round, only glancing at his watch a couple of times, to check that he wasn't late for his next appointment. He was always, it seemed to Tian, in a hurry to do at least a dozen things, all of them no doubt profitable, but it didn't make him a restful companion.

'Hudson Street,' Thaddeus said as he puffed his way up two flights of stairs. At the top, he produced a large key and turned it with a flourish. Tian stood in the middle of the long, bright room, then walked up and down it, nodding happily. It would make an excellent studio and from the paint stains on the floor in the area underneath the skylight, had obviously been used as such before. It also pleased him that the long room had two high, narrow windows which looked down on to the street. 'Your Mr Dalowski has chosen well.'

'Wouldn't employ him if he weren't a smart young fellow,' Thaddeus said complacently. 'Secret of a successful business is to find good people to work for you and then keep them on their toes. Yessir.'

In addition to the long room, which would have to serve as living room as well as studio, the apartment contained a small kitchen and an adequate bedroom with a delightful view of a brick wall one yard away. Tian pulled a face at it, but it was only a bedroom, after all.

On the same floor there was a bathroom, which all the tenants shared, a tiny, very modern place, with running hot water and a huge claw-footed bath. The Americans seemed much more concerned with such amenities than the Irish or English, Tian had decided, after experiencing the luxuries of the Brownsby household, such as hot air constantly circulating to all the rooms from a furnace in the cellar through a series of ducts, and also a shower room as well as a bathroom. Mrs Brownsby had pulled a face at the shower, another of her husband's enthusiasms, but Tian had tried the novelty for himself and found it invigorating. Which was more than he could say for their heating system, for that made the rooms far too hot for his taste.

The kitchen in the apartment had a table and three chairs, plus a wooden workbench and a tall, narrow pantry cupboard. It just about merited the name kitchen, for it had a tap and sink and a small cast-iron stove standing on tiles, whose top could be used for cooking and which also served to heat the whole suite of rooms.

Thaddeus saw him frowning at the stove. 'That's important,' he lectured gently. 'Not for cooking. You'll probably want to eat out. Young fellows don't usually cook for themselves. But our winters can be hard, with snow and blizzards, and I wouldn't like to see you freeze to death.' He smiled and allowed himself a small joke, a thing he only did with people from whom he did not expect to make a financial profit: 'Well, not until after you've painted a portrait of me and my family, so make sure you stoke that stove up well each night. There's a wood store in the back yard. Now, I'll ask around and work out a fair price to give you for the portrait. I can tell that you've no head for business and that agent of yours can't help you from London.'

Tian blinked. As soon stop a runaway train engine as Thaddeus Brownsby when he had set his mind on something. 'Thank you, sir. I shall be happy to paint your family's portrait. And I'd like to say that I'm delighted with this place and,' he added truthfully, 'that I continue to be extremely grateful to you.'

'Oh, it does me good to be seen as a patron of the arts,' Thaddeus replied, with the frankness that never ceased to surprise Tian. 'And you're the first artist fellow to whom I've taken a shine. I won't support a fancy boy, no matter how well he paints. Nor will I support a loafer. I'll get you some other commissions, after our portrait, if you like. If it turns out well, of course.'

Tian frowned. 'I was hoping to travel a bit later. See some more of your country.'

Thaddeus shook his head. 'Better not. Bad time to go travelling. Not only winter, but there's a war brewing.'

Tian had heard no more of the trouble in America since Frederick's letter. 'Are you sure?'

'Yep. Brother against brother,' Thaddeus said sombrely. 'Us Northerners against the Southern states.'

'I didn't realise things were that bad.'

Thaddeus just nodded again and sighed.

'Look, sir, could you spare a little time to explain it to me? I'd heard there'd been disagreements between North and South, but I hadn't realised that anything like civil war was in the offing.'

Thaddeus looked at his watch, made a swift mental calculation and said crisply, 'I can tell you the main problems, as I see them. After that, you'll only have to keep your eyes and ears open as you walk around town and you'll hear all the arguments for and against.'

Something else occurred to Tian. 'But – why did no one at your house say anything about it?'

'My wife's a gentle soul, talk of war upsets her, so I told everyone to keep off the topic when she's around.' Thaddeus settled down on one of Tian's hard wooden chairs and began to explain, occasionally waggling one plump finger for emphasis. 'The Southern states use Negro slaves. We Northerners ain't that fond of slavery. Your government abolished it a good many years ago, I believe?'

'1833,' Tian agreed promptly. His schooling had involved a lot of learning dates and had bored him silly, but they came in useful sometimes.

'See what I mean. Nearly thirty years ago. Slavery just ain't modern! When I was in the old country, sorting out my cousin's affairs, I felt downright embarrassed when folks mentioned it. That book, *Uncle Tom's Cabin*, has made a lot of people aware of the problem. I've always prided myself on living in the land of the free. Slaves ain't free.'

He stabbed his forefinger towards Tian. 'Of course, it ain't just the slavery. No, sir! We wouldn't go to war over a few blacks. There are one or two other things involved. Important things. Our ancestors fought to set up the Union and we aim to keep it that way. If some of those bull-headed cotton planters have their way, the Union will break up.

'And there are some business principles involved which affect your country, too. Those damned Southerners are too cocky about their cotton monopoly. We use their cotton in the North, of course, but we don't intend to be held to ransom over it, and your friends in Lancashire had better look to their supplies, too. If anything happens to the South, they'll have trouble finding the raw material they need. I b'lieve they get most of their cotton from America. Three-quarters, or so I'm told. And the stuff produced elsewhere is of a poorer quality. So there's a lot at stake.'

He looked at his watch and stood up. 'Don't take my word for anything, though. Go out into the streets and listen. Read the newspapers. You'll soon learn a thing or two. But it's no time to go off travelling round the country, young man, you can take my word for that.'

Tian decided to reserve judgement. He had not come all this way just to stay in New York, however exciting the city.

Thaddeus exited as briskly as he did everything else, calling out his goodbyes as he clattered down the stairs, promising to return soon and also to send his assistant over the next day to see that Tian was all right. 'I'll send the carriage back for you when it's taken me to my office. Go back and get your things. You might as well move in here at once. And you must come and dine with me at my club, Thursday. You'll hear a lot more there about the troubles in the South than you will in my house.'

Later, when he had unpacked his things, Tian went out for a stroll along the street, which absolutely teemed with life. Opposite his new home, in a narrow building two windows wide and four storeys high, was a business which announced its existence on three huge, white boards, whose bright red letters, two foot high, stated: PRINTER. CARD AND JOB. D.H. PEAKE AND SONS. Between it and the next building was an alley barely wide enough for one person to go down.

On the other side of the alley was a small terraced building, whose ground-floor shop announced itself as a DRUG BROKER, whatever that might be. Above it was another big sign saying CARPENTER. These Americans seemed eager to brandish what they were doing at everyone. A couple of the carpenter's men were taking the air at an open door on the first floor, which had no balcony. They lounged there, seeming careless of the twelve-foot drop to the boardwalk below. Tian smiled. Those boardwalks still looked strange to him: rows of thick planks which formed a kind of pavement, raising the pedestrians above the level of the street.

He chuckled as it suddenly occurred to him that perhaps he should get a big sign made saying: ARTIST. FINE FAMILY PORTRAITS PAINTED. He could hang it on the outside wall under his windows.

As he strolled along, he found people everywhere, loitering to gossip, pushing their way along the boardwalks, or standing at the doors of their premises. He was entranced. 'I'm going to love it here!' he said aloud. 'Love it.' He had definitely done the right thing by coming to America, war or no war. He had been feeling restless ever since he left Lancashire, needing something to take his mind off Annie. And he would look into the question of travelling around a bit, whatever Thaddeus said.

But next summer he would be back in England again, fulfilling Frederick Hallam's last request – if Annie would allow him to paint her, that was. No, he decided, thinking of Thaddeus Brownsby, who went straight for whatever he wanted and forced it to happen. No, not *if* Annie would allow him. He would make her listen to him, use the portrait as an excuse to spend some time with her, and then – he did not even dare think beyond that. Not yet.

Before he made any further plans, he needed to see if feeling still flared instantly between himself and Annie. He nodded as he felt his whole body react to the mere thought of her. He was pretty sure the attraction would still be there. Even loving Frederick so deeply, she had responded to Tian before. He would never have wished the man dead, but now that he was, Tian intended to court Annie. The American way, if necessary.

Within weeks, Tian had got to know a wide range of people in New York, and had bought himself some much warmer winter clothes. He had never had trouble making friends and the Americans seemed more open and responsive than their English counterparts. More independent in attitude, too. He found people from every country in Europe and loved to listen to the different accents as they fumbled with their English. He would speak to anyone and everyone whom he met in the streets, in the shops, in the small eating places where he was learning about so many different types of food.

The only thing that continued to trouble him was the unrest brewing between North and South. He had seen the trouble caused by religious differences in his own country, and also caused by the English landlords who still owned an unfairly large share of Ireland. He had seen anger flare between brother and brother, between neighbour and neighbour, and would not wish it upon anyone, least of all these happy, energetic people.

Of course, there were plenty of Irish to be met. New York was full of them: poor Irish, struggling to survive, affluent men who'd made good, new lives for themselves, and a few who were obviously corrupt. Tian made a friend or two but they interested him less than other people he met and he could not spend a lot of time with them because, to his amazement, he found himself loaded with commissions to paint portraits. Hell, he was making more money than he ever had in his life before.

He painted the Brownsby family soon after moving into his apartment, and was pleased with what he produced. They all took the time to pose for him, self-conscious at first until he got them talking. Lyn was a bit of a problem because she used the opportunity to try to flirt with him, in spite of her mother's presence at each of the sittings.

The final portrait showed Thaddeus and his family in all their wealth, with fine clothes, rich furniture in the background, gold watch chains prominent. They clearly relished their position in the world. And yet, the portrait also suggested their warmth and friendliness, their solidarity as a family against the rest of the world.

When he showed the finished work to Thaddeus, that hard-nosed businessman unashamedly mopped his eyes and blew his nose several times. 'I thought you were good from those sketches I saw on the boat, but you're a damn' sight better than good. When I tell my friends about you, I'll tell them I paid you triple what I did, so don't you let on any different. And don't forget to ask for more money from now on.'

'But, sir—'

Thaddeus poked a finger in Tian's chest. 'On second thoughts, we'll refer them to Igor. He's wanting to set up a few little schemes of his own. If you pay him ten per cent of what you get, he'll more than earn it, for he'll get you treble what you could get yourself. All right?'

Tian nodded, happy to stay away from the business aspects.

And when he saw that his friend was right, that he could get as many commissions as he wanted, he abandoned the idea of travelling and abandoned the idea of leisure, too, setting himself to make as much money as possible while he was in New York. He had never painted so quickly. And yet, he felt he gave his customers good value for their money and they seemed pleased with what he produced. Energy was flowing through him. Now, he could go back to Annie with a little something behind him. Not the sort of money she would possess, but enough to maintain his independence, at least.

By Christmas, Tian had the problem of deciding what to do with the money he was accumulating, for after associating with Thaddeus, he had come to realise that he should not leave it lying idle, but set it to work to make more.

'What shall I do with the money I'm earning?' he asked one evening in the club to which he was now regularly invited by his friend.

His host looked at him, eyes narrowed. 'How much you got?'

Tian told him.

Thaddeus refrained from saying that this was chicken feed to a man like him, because he really liked the young artist, and believed in encouraging young men to act prudently. 'You're not spending much, I reckon,' he decided, after doing a few mental sums. That was another point in Tian's favour.

'I'm not extravagant. And anyway, I'm working too hard to spend even half of what I earn.'

Thaddeus frowned at him. 'Hmm. Leave it to me. I'll think of something.'

'Nothing too risky,' Tian pleaded. 'It's the first time I've ever had money to spare and I don't want to go back to her emptyhanded.'

A few minutes later, Thaddeus stopped talking in mid-sentence and smiled at Tian. 'I'm beginning to get an idea about what to do with your money. Yes, sir. You just leave it to me, my friend.' He waggled one finger. 'Though you may not have your money back in time for your return to England. But you can safely leave it in my hands, I promise you. And it will increase. Considerably.'

'I never doubted that, sir. I have absolute faith in your business acumen.'

Thaddeus was moved to shake his young friend's hand vigorously. No compliment could have pleased him more.

But even an artist dedicated to earning as much money as possible could not paint without light. Tian spent every daylight hour painting, but as soon as the cold winter light failed each afternoon, he turned to domestic chores: shopping, taking his laundry out to the Chinese family a few streets away, deciding where to eat that night. And planning future works, sketching out the things he would paint when he got back home to Britain.

He never went out without a sketch pad and became quite a well-known figure in the district. People grew used to having him there, a quiet presence scratching away with charcoal or pencil at the side of a gaslit café. The talk buzzing around him would range over many things, but two subjects kept cropping up again and again: slavery – the Southern states and their stubborn refusal to end it – and the sanctity of the Union, and whether it would come to an outright war. Some said it was inevitable. Some said it could never happen. Not brother against brother.

But if it did come to war, all the people Tian met were utterly certain that the North and the anti-slavery forces would win, and win quickly, for they had right on their side. And, by hell, if they had to go down South and fight to prove that, then so they would!

One fine January day he was strolling in a small park when he came across a gentleman, clearly in a towering rage, slashing away at some leafless shrubs with a walking stick and muttering to himself. Tian would have passed on, but the man caught sight of him and nodded curtly.

He touched his hat in return. 'Good day to you, my friend. I hope that whatever's upset you soon passes.'

'You're takin' a risk, suh, talking to a pariah like me!'

That was enough to make Tian stop. 'Pariah?'

'Yes, suh. I'm one of those damned Southerners and it's just been made very plain to me that I'm not welcome in my hotel any longer.'

He had a challenging look on his face, clearly expecting Tian to move on. Instead, he stopped and held out his hand. 'Tian Gilchrist. I'm Irish, so I'm afraid I'm not involved in your American disagreements. But I have to confess that I've been dying to hear the other side of the argument.'

A hand was stuck out in return and the man pumped Tian's hand. 'Then I'm pleased to meet you, suh, dee-lighted, in fact. Because there are two sides to every question. The name's Darcy Langland. Of Black Oaks plantation, South Virginia.'

His accent intrigued Tian. It was like nothing he'd ever heard before. Lazy-sounding vowels, drawling intonation. 'May I invite you to take a drink with me?' he offered. 'It's getting quite cold and I'd welcome a cup of coffee.' He'd grown quite used to the American habit of drinking coffee, where at home he would have drunk tea at this time of day. 'And I'd be very pleased to listen to your side of the argument, for you're the first Southerner I've ever met.'

'I'd like nothing better than to accept your invitation, but I have to find somewhere to stay tonight. My ship doesn't leave until tomorrow morning, you see. And why that damned hotel had to tell me to get out today, I don't know. One more night was all I needed. But apparently some other guest complained about my presence, someone they don't wish to offend.' He let his stick drop. 'I came out here to work off my temper,' he confessed. 'But it's more than time I found me another room.'

'You're welcome to use my couch for the night,' Tian offered impulsively.

His hand was seized and pumped hard again. 'Suh, you are a gentleman.'

'I'm not sure everyone would agree with you. I'm actually an artist. And Irish.'

'Hah! What made you emigrate then?'

'I didn't emigrate.' A lot of people mistakenly assumed that. 'I came to America for a visit only.' Tian shivered. The sun had been shining, but with no warmth, and now that it was setting, the wind seemed twice as cold. 'Where's your luggage?'

'Still in the damned hotel lobby – I hope. I told them if anything went missing, they'd be branded thieves as well as fools.'

It was still there. The man behind the desk avoided his former guest's eyes as he instructed the porter to carry it out to the cab. The other guests sitting in the lobby stopped talking to watch him leave.

Tian waited outside, as they had arranged, because he could not afford to be recognised and accused of being a Southern sympathiser. He did not intend to risk losing any commissions. He got into the cab round the next corner.

When they stopped in Hudson Street, Darcy said gruffly, 'I'll not talk as we go up to your rooms. Contrary to popular belief, they can't recognise a Southerner from mere appearance. No use settin' your neighbours' backs up.'

'Thank you. I appreciate that.'

While Darcy was using the bathroom, Tian went along the street to his favourite eating house and ordered a meal to be sent round to his rooms, a common service round here which had both delighted and amazed him when he first encountered it.

After the meal the two men talked until well after midnight, with Darcy trying to explain just why the cotton planters had to have their slaves.

'I can see why you need them economically,' Tian said in the end, 'but I'm afraid that, morally, I still find slavery repugnant.'

'*Uncle Tom's Cabin* did us a great disservice.' Darcy's voice was bitter. 'We do not all ill-treat our slaves, suh. Some of my house slaves are from families which have been with us since my grandfather's time. I think very highly of them, I promise you. Bring the doctor in if they're sick, teach the children to read and write, allow them their own church. And if I did give them their freedom, they would not know what to do with it. They'd be lost, like a pet bird that you'd freed from his cage.'

'We'll have to agree to disagree on that.'

There was silence, then both men yawned.

'Well,' Darcy said, rubbing his forehead as if it ached. 'I'm afraid if I don't lie down now, I'll fall down.'

In the morning, the two men exchanged addresses, then Darcy shook Tian's hand. 'If you're ever in Virginia . . .'

'And if you're ever in Ireland . . .'

New York: February to March 1861

It wasn't until February that Tian bothered to ask Thaddeus what had happened to his money.

Thaddeus leaned back in his chair, looking smug and steepling his hands above his generous belly. 'I've doubled it for you. Were you wanting it back now or would you like me to double it again?'

Tian beamed and shook his benefactor's head. 'No, I don't require it at the moment. My needs are very simple. In fact, I'll soon have some more money to invest, if you would be so kind as to help me? I've just received a small inheritance from an elderly aunt whom I can't even remember.' His father had written to say that poor Moira had always liked him best of all the brats.

'How much?'

'Only a couple of thousand pounds.' But to Tian, who had nothing of his own but what he had earned and saved, it seemed like a lot. 'I asked my father to send a bank draft, so that I could set the money to work here.' He shrugged. 'It won't increase half as well in Ireland, I'm afraid.'

Thaddeus looked at him fondly. He didn't say that this was another paltry amount, but instead was flattered to think that Tian trusted him with his whole wordly wealth. And besides, his acquaintance with this artist had been even more useful than he'd expected. He regularly invited Tian to parties at his house and Tian, understanding exactly why the older man was doing it and happy to make some return for all the help Thaddeus had given him since his arrival in New York, always turned up and played the slightly wild but still respectable Irish artist for him.

Tian also found that it was well received if he dropped the information casually that he had been born to a landowning, if impoverished, family of ancient lineage. For people who trumpeted their belief in equality so loudly, some of Thaddeus's acquaintances were distinctly snobbish about birth and breeding.

When he heard one well-connected older lady say grudgingly to her friend that a man who patronised the arts, as Mr Brownsby did, could not be just the crass businessman they had thought, Tian chuckled to himself and passed the titbit on to Thaddeus.

'Now, we're getting somewhere!' he said gleefully. 'My Eva will get an invitation yet.'

Tian did not ask to what and Thaddeus did not enlighten him.

The only fly in the ointment was Lyn, who was still besotted with the artist.

I shall have to do something about that girl, Thaddeus decided, scowling as he watched his fool of a daughter trying to flirt with an unresponsive Tian at one function. He's not encouraging her, but she's gotten downright wilful lately! He did not like wilful women, especially in his own family.

That evening, when the guests had left, he gave his daughter a scolding and was amazed when she turned on him, something none of his other children had ever done.

'You don't understand, Father! I love Tian. And nothing you can do will make me stop loving him!'

Thaddeus Brownsby gaped at her for a moment and then snapped, 'But he doesn't love you. How can you make such a darn' idiot of yourself?'

She flushed. 'How do you know he doesn't love me? You haven't given us a chance.'

Thaddeus hummed and hawed, not wanting to betray his young friend's secret.

She clasped her hands to her breast, her eyes huge with horror. 'You didn't – you didn't ask him? Oh, tell me you didn't!'

Thaddeus thumped the flat of his hand down on the table,

making his wife's ornaments jiggle about like wild things. 'Of course I discussed it with him. What sort of a father would I be if I didn't look after my children's interests?'

Tears were rolling down her face now, but she was angry enough to shout through them, 'I hate you! You've spoiled everything!'

'Saved you from making a fool of yourself, more like.' He turned to his wife. 'And I'll expect you, Eva, to keep a much closer eye on this young lady in future. If she can't behave herself, she'll have to go to my sister's till Mr Gilchrist has gone back to Ireland. I'm not having her getting the family a bad name. Or herself. Running after a penniless artist, indeed! What's the world coming to?' He glared at his daughter. 'It is going to stop. Now. You hear me?'

In floods of tears, Lyn rushed up to her room. Lying on her bed, she felt waves of shame and then of longing course through her. Tian was so handsome, so very handsome. In the end she turned over to lie on her back, staring at the ceiling and listening to the rest of the house settle down for the night. When someone tapped on her bedroom door, she yelled, 'Go away!' breathing a sigh of relief when the person did just that.

For a long time she just lay there, then got up and began to undress. 'I'll not stop seeing him,' she muttered, tossing her petticoats into a corner. 'And I'll make him love me!' she added, dragging a hairbrush through her long, brown hair. 'I will!' she promised her reflection in the mirror. Her resemblance to her father was very strong at that moment.

In Hudson Street, Tian was also lying awake. Lyn's behaviour was getting beyond a joke. At first, it had amused and flattered him, but now he was beginning to feel really worried about it. He needed Thaddeus's goodwill to make the most of the money he was earning. And besides, he liked the man. He really did. He felt he had made a friend for life and one day, maybe, would bring Annie across the ocean as well, to meet the Brownsby family. She had never been anywhere outside England. He would enjoy showing her the world, taking her away from her cares and responsibilities for a time. He sighed at the thought of her. It had been exciting to come to New York. And profitable. But he had spent long enough in exile and was now counting the days until he could return.

The next time they had dinner together at the club, Thaddeus said casually, 'By the way, that was a good portrait you did of my friend Horburn's young wife. He showed it to me yesterday. He's very pleased with it.'

'I'm pleased with it, too.'

'She looks kinda sad, mind, but pretty as all damn. And some people do have sad faces, don't they? Not much you can do about that if you want to get a good likeness.'

Tian did not say that the young wife, who had married an arrogant old boor for his money, was probably going to look sad for the rest of her life. Seeing Mrs Horburn had only emphasised to him the fact that money had to come second. If you wanted to find happiness, you had to follow your love. This was the only period of his life where he intended to devote himself so intensively to earning money, to painting the rich people who clamoured for his services since he was this year's fad in certain New York circles. For the rest of the time, he would go back to enjoying life, the way he always had.

And the money was all because of Annie. He had no intention of trying to compete with Frederick Hallam's wealth, could not have done even if he'd wanted. But he would not go back to her penniless. And later, if things turned out as he hoped, he must always be able to earn enough for his own needs.

She's got to have me, he told himself as the days passed and the time for his departure grew nearer. I'll make her!

And his eyes would turn to the sketch of Annie and the photograph of her he'd filched from Ridge House. They hung prominently on one wall and he talked to the damned things when he grew homesick, which he could not help doing sometimes in what was, after all, an alien land, for all its friendliness. He said good night to the sketch and photograph, smiled at them in the morning after he'd fumbled in the darkness for his gas lights, and shared with 'Annie' his disapproval of such extreme cold as he shivered his way across to the stove to build up the fire.

One fine day in late February, when snow was still lying on the ground but the streets and sidewalks had mostly been cleared, Lyn evaded her mother while they were out shopping together and took a cab to Hudson Street. She had to see Tian, she just had to! She would make him understand that she didn't care what her father said, that her love for him was much more important than anything else in the whole world. Last time he had come to the house, her mother had kept her out of his way, and when her mother was busy, one or the other of her brothers had stayed close to her. So she had not been able to do more than nod to him. Now, she just *had* to talk to him.

She bounced up the stairs, her heart pounding in anticipation, and knocked on the door.

When Tian opened it, he first gaped at her, then folded his arms, blocking the doorway. 'What are you doing here, Lyn?'

It wasn't the greeting she had hoped for. 'I wanted to see you. Aren't you going to invite me in, Tian Gilchrist?' She smiled at him, noting the way his hair needed cutting, the smear of blue paint on one cheek.

He did not move. 'Do your father or mother know you're here?'

'No, of course not. But I had to—'

'Then I'll call you a cab and you can go right home again.' His expression softened. 'Please, Lyn. Just go away and don't come back. Do as your parents wish.'

Her anger returned full force. She had felt angry a lot lately. With a sudden push that took him by surprise she won her way into his apartment. He had to chase her across it and catch hold of her arm, or she'd have gone right into his bedroom. When he caught her, she turned and twined her arms round his neck. 'Don't you like me, Tian? I like you. A lot.' She was blushing, but determined to make her feelings plain to him.

He tried to disentangle her arms. 'For heaven's sake, Lyn, stop it!'

She clung to him even more tightly. 'Aren't I pretty enough for you?'

With a sinking heart, Tian realised that nothing but the baldest of truths would stop her. 'Come and sit down, then. We have to talk.' There was an icy wind blowing up the stairs, but he left the door open and she didn't even seem to notice it.

She sat down, resting her elbows on the table and putting her chin on her clasped hands. Her eyes were devouring him.

'You seem to think,' he said carefully, still trying to phrase it tactfully, 'that you—'

'That I've fallen in love with you.' Her face went even redder, but she was no less determined.

He thumped the table, feeling the last of his patience and selfcontrol trickling away. What this spoiled young woman needed was a good spanking. 'Have you no shame, coming here like this?' If Sarry had behaved in such a way, his mother would have died of horror and he had a good idea that Mrs Brownsby was out of the same mould.

'Where you're concerned, Tian, no. I have no time to be – to be reticent. You'll be leaving New York in a month or two, so we have to get this settled before then.' She leaned forward, her eyes luminous with love. 'Tian, I know I'm a rich man's daughter, and that makes you hesitate, but Father will come round, once he sees that we're serious and that we—'

His voice was harsh and he made no attempt to hide behind polite phrases. 'But we're not serious, Lyn. We're not at all serious. There is nothing whatsoever between us. In fact, I'm in love with someone else, someone in England. And I hope to marry her when I get back.'

'What!' She sat upright, her mouth open in shock. 'But you never said anything about – about anyone else. You never said a word.'

'Your father knows. And he also knows that I have no desire to marry you.'

'But – who is it?'

'None of your business.'

'You can't really love her or you wouldn't have left her for so long.'

'I do love her and I always will.' A glow came into his eyes at the very thought of Annie. Involuntarily, he turned to look at the sketch and photograph on the wall.

Lyn saw where he was looking and turned round. She did not move for a moment, because if she had, she'd have rushed across and pulled them from the wall. She'd have torn them into little pieces and thrown them into the stove. 'Is that her?' she asked unnecessarily, her hands clenched into fists in her lap.

He nodded. 'Yes, that's her.'

'But she's *old*!'

He laughed. 'Old? Annie? She'll never be old if she lives to be a hundred.'

It was the laughter that made Lyn furious, though she tried to hide it. How dare he laugh at her and treat her like this? She stood up, feeling pain so strong, she wanted to curl up into a ball. 'And you never said a word. Not in all this time.'

'She's still in mourning for her husband. It wouldn't be right to bandy her name about.'

Lyn hardly heard him. 'It's all your fault! You've let me . . .' sobs escaped her '. . . you've let me make a fool of myself. I'll never forgive you for that. Never!'

'I haven't encouraged you in any way. You rushed in head-long, greedy for what you wanted – you thought of yourself and no one else – and you wouldn't listen to your father, wouldn't even see the truth, that I didn't want you and have never given you any reason to think I did.'

A cough in the doorway to the apartment brought both their heads round and sent another wave of scarlet to Lyn's face.

'Your mother sent me to fetch you, Miss Brownsby,' Igor

said. 'Your father is out or he'd have come himself, I'm sure.' His eyes met Tian's and both men shook their heads in a silent admission of sympathy for one another. Clearly Igor had over-heard what Lyn was saying.

'Please tell Mr Brownsby that I'm sorry this happened and that it was none of my choosing,' Tian said quietly, walking towards the door.

'I'm sure he understands that.' Igor reached out to grasp Lyn's arm as she tried to sweep past him.

'Let go of me!'

'No.' Better to offend her than allow her to escape again.

Tian felt sorry for the embarrassed girl. 'Perhaps you can tell your employer also that I think Miss Brownsby now under-stands about my feelings for the lady back in England. I don't think she will give us any more trouble of this sort. It was just a – a misunderstanding.'

Tears were running down Lyn's cheeks now. 'I hate you!' she said to Tian in a low, throbbing voice. 'I hate you with all my heart.'

'I'm sorry for that. I've done nothing to deserve either your love or your hatred.'

Igor moved towards the stairs, still holding her. At the top, he stopped. 'I nearly forgot, I have another commission for you. I'll come round this evening to tell you about it.' Only then did he lead a still sobbing Lyn down the stairs, not letting go of her for a moment.

When the street door had slammed shut behind them, Tian let out his breath in a long whoosh, hesitated, then went across to the cupboard. He rarely drank, but if there was ever a time for a glass of good Irish whiskey, it was now. 'Stupid damned girl!' he muttered as he let its warmth trickle down his throat. 'Stupid, stupid girl!'

That evening at the Brownsby residence there was a royal row, with Lyn screaming and sobbing, her mother weeping quietly into a handkerchief and her father yelling and laying down the law in no uncertain manner. For a time it hung in the balance as to whether the girl would be sent to her aunt's farm in disgrace, but the vehemence with which she declared her hatred of Tian Gilchrist won her a reprieve.

It would have been better for him if she had been sent away, for she was one who held tight to a grudge, imaginary or otherwise.

12

Bilsden: March 1861

After the poor harvest of 1860, the price of bread rose and soon after Christmas Annie found herself at odds with the Bilsden Poor Law Relief Committee about the terms upon which assistance was to be offered to the needy. No money was to be given, just vouchers which entitled recipients to food. That would not have worried her, but the vouchers were from two particular shops, both of which were known for the poor quality of their wares.

She could only conclude that the owners of the two shops, gentlemen whom she would not have received at Ridge House, had bribed some of the Committee. How else could people like them have been chosen? She fretted and fumed over this and, in the end, took her worries down the hill to her father. 'What am I to do?'

'I don't see what you can do, love.'

'But just think of those poor people being cheated!'

'You can't help everyone, love.'

'If Frederick were alive, he'd have stopped the Relief Committee behaving so shabbily.'

'Aye, I grant you that. But he's not alive. If he were, a few of those chaps wouldn't be on the Committee at all. They're as mean as muck and sly with it.' He clicked his tongue in exasperation and after a moment added sadly, 'We've got a provident fund at the chapel, but that's only for our own people, of course. I worry about them others, I do that.'

'So do I. And I'm not having Hallam's people at the beck and call of that – that group of cheats on the Relief Committee! How will sick people get better on such poor fare as those shops provide?' She beat her clenched fist on her chair arm. 'What do those stupid men even know of what it's like to be poor, really poor?'

'Not much,' he agreed, watching her carefully and hiding a smile. He was glad to see her getting angry about something, looking more herself again. The Lord had brought his poor lass some tribulations, but she had borne them well and overcome most of them. She was a fighter, his Annie was. Like her mother. He smiled a little at the memory of his Lucy. She'd been a lovely woman, but heaven help anyone who got on the wrong side of her. 'Do you have many sick folk at Hallam's?' He knew there was a fever going round.

'Too many. Either our workers or their families. We try to help them all, but Jeremy Lewis says the town needs to improve both its water supply and its waste-disposal system if people are to stay in better health. What was adequate when the town was smaller isn't good enough now. Goodness, I can't believe how this place has grown in the past ten years!' She sighed and her words trailed off again, but there were frown lines on her forehead and her father could see that she was still very worried.

He sat quietly, giving her time to think. Since Frederick's death, she had started bringing her worries to him, not because she needed his help – well, what power did he have in this town? – but just because she needed to talk to someone. And he was happy to spend time with her, very happy. Kathy always kept the lads away when Annie needed to talk to her old dad. He was proud that his lass still turned to him. It made up a bit for the years when he'd had to pay most of his attention to Emily and his second family, leaving Annie and Tom to manage for themselves.

'Have you talked to our William about it?' he asked as the silence dragged on.

She shook her head and looked at him in surprise.

John sighed. She seemed to find it hard to confide in William, perhaps because he was her son, though the lad was very experienced in helping the poor. Lad! He was twenty-two now and well on the way to becoming a Minister. John had a young friend who was also training for the ministry at Didsbury, and Fred had said that the folk there were well pleased with William's progress, that he was an example to them all. William had never said a word about how well he was doing. The lad was singularly without conceit or pride in himself.

'What were you thinking of doing about it all, then, lass?' he probed gently, seeing that Annie was looking at him.

'I was thinking of setting up my own relief committee for Hallam's people. Do you think that's silly? Matt Peters does. His main concern is what it would cost. But we make our money because of the people who work for us, so I think we have a duty to look after them when they're in trouble.' She had puzzled this through in the long hours of the many sleepless nights which were engraving lines of deep-down tiredness on her face. She still missed Frederick's warm body beside her in the bed, still turned to reach out for him sometimes in the mornings. But most of all, she missed his companionship.

'Well then, love, you go ahead and set up your own committee. A master should look after his workfolk.'

'Only I'm not a master. Not really.' She was chewing on one fingertip, as she did sometimes when she was thinking hard. 'And I don't have the time to do it all myself. I still have the businesses to run.' What Frederick had done easily took her so much longer.

John took a sudden decision to interfere, something he rarely did. 'Why don't you ask William to come and help you? I'm sure they'd give him leave from Didsbury.'

'Do you really think he could help?'

'I'm certain of it.'

'I don't know.' She pulled a face and then confessed, 'I never thought a son of mine would become a Minister. I – I still think of him as a boy. And I shouldn't, should I?'

He looked at her, the rebuke clear on his face. 'You almost sound as if you disapprove of his calling.'

She couldn't lie to her father. 'Well, it wouldn't have been my first choice for him.'

'You should be proud of him, Annie. Very proud. He's young still, but he's a good man and will be devoting his life to the Lord's work.'

She bit off the scornful words that had leaped to the tip of her tongue. She'd wanted William to do well for himself financially, not become a Methodist Minister. Now, thanks to Frederick's bequest, her son was independent enough to do as he pleased. It was the one thing she and her husband had not quite seen eye to eye on: the future of her beloved first-born.

'Ask William to help you,' John urged again as the silence lengthened. 'He'll jump at the chance.'

So after dinner the following Saturday, since William was home for the weekend, Annie went up to kiss Edgar and Tamsin good night, then asked her elder son to join her in the library, which had become her particular refuge since Frederick's death.

'Your grandfather suggested I talk to you.' She hesitated, not quite knowing how to broach the matter. 'I don't like what the Bilsden Poor Law Relief Committee is doing, so I want to set up our own relief scheme for the folk who work for Hallam's. Dad thought you might be interested in helping me organise it?'

His face lit up – such a clear open face, his innate honesty shining through, his skin clear, his auburn hair neatly combed back and his eyes very blue and guileless. She thought suddenly, How could I have expected someone with a face like that to go into business? Every feeling he has is mirrored on his face. And it was at that moment that the pain she felt about his decision began to dissolve: not all at once, but little by little. Without thinking, she reached out to take his hand and pat it. 'Well?'

He frowned. 'I'd love to, but I don't know whether I can, Mother. I've still got to spend some time at Didsbury.' He grimaced. 'I'm a bit beyond the studies there – well, to tell you the truth, I know more than some of the masters. But they have to be very sure about my theological grounding and I do still need to talk about – about – things.' A Minister had to deal with such important aspects of life and death. He must be very sure of his own beliefs before he was fit to help others.

Guilt shot through her. She hadn't really talked to him about his studies and she should have done. In fact, she'd neglected William since Frederick's death. 'If there's any way you can help, I'd be grateful. You know how hard some folk are finding things this winter, and the fever leaves them so weak. Well, some of them are always in trouble, of course, but it's worse this year, what with the bad harvest and the price of bread being higher than usual.' She gave an angry sniff. 'The Bilsden Relief Committee is only giving vouchers for Leaseby's and Marshall's.'

William grunted. 'I'd heard about that. It's shameful.'

'Yes. I've spoken to the Committee and been told to mind my own business – very politely, of course. So I thought I'd do something myself. Just for our own folk and their families, you understand.'

His anger vanished and he beamed at her. 'You're such a good woman, Mother!'

'Me?'

He nodded. 'You. Where would our family be without your help? I've always been proud of you. Always.'

Tears came into her eyes at this unexpected compliment.

He looked across at the family portrait, to give her time to recover. 'And if you want me to help, well, I'd love to, Mother. Hmm.' He sat fiddling with the chair arm. 'Let me talk to Jerome Bersall at Didsbury about it.'

'If they let you come, do you think you could organise it?'

He looked surprised. 'Of course I could. The only problem would be fitting it in with my studies.'

She blinked in surprise. He looked so large and confident as he spoke. It was hard sometimes to believe she had produced this gentle giant. Hard, too, to believe he could be Fred Coxton's son.

'Leave it to me, Mother. I'll have a word with Jerome as soon as I get back to Didsbury.' He leaned forward to take her hand. 'Now, can we talk about you? You look so tired. You've been working far too hard since Father died.'

'Well, I couldn't turn the businesses over to James, could I? For a man who so prides himself on being a good Christian, he's very harsh in his dealings with those he calls "the lower classes".' She scowled, James continued to plague her, sending letters regularly, full of impertinent questions about what she was doing, and insisting on a monthly accounting as if he thought she was trying to cheat him. And what he and Mildred would say to this latest venture, which would decrease their profits slightly, she didn't know. But she'd deal with that when she had to.

Watching her, seeing the lines of sadness and deep tiredness on her face, William could not help wishing Frederick had not left her with so many responsibilities, or that she had married a younger man, who would not have left her alone like this. But, he told himself firmly, the Lord had chosen her to bear the burdens, so there had to be some reason for that, something that only she could do. He wished she cared more about religion, that she could find some solace in its teachings. But she didn't. And it was not for a son to try to guide his mother in things like that. Well, he couldn't do it with his mother, anyway. It took a very special person to manage her, someone like Frederick Hallam.

The next day, in the early afternoon, William borrowed his mother's carriage and went out to Collett House to discuss the matter with Saul Hinchcliffe, his old tutor. Then he came back and went to talk to Nathaniel Bell, whom the congregation at the chapel still called 'the new Minister', even after four years. When he returned to Didsbury on the Monday, he had his request thought out and ready to put to Jerome Bersall, and he felt hopeful of success. If things went as he hoped, he would come back to Bilsden the following weekend to discuss it with his mother and, hopefully, to lighten her load.

But he was back sooner, on the Wednesday to be precise, striding into Ridge House, looking huge and exuberantly alive. 'Where's my mother, Winnie?'

'Down at the mill.' With the familiarity of an old employee, she added, 'What are you doing back here, Mr William? I hope you're not in any trouble.'

'Now, why should you think I'd be in trouble, Winnie? I'm twentytwo, not twelve, you know.' He spoke gently, but very firmly.

She flushed, not knowing what to say. It was hard sometimes to realise that the young folk had grown up. She stared up at him. Where did all the years go? It seemed only a short time ago that this young man had been an eager lad and not much longer since she had been a girl herself.

'I'll just leave my bag here and go down to the mill, then.' But at the front door, he stopped and came back. 'No. Better not.' There would be no privacy at the mill.

From upstairs, someone cried, 'I told you it was our William's voice!' Tamsin clattered down the stairs and threw herself at him, and Edgar was not far behind. Elizabeth walked down the stairs more slowly, but she, too, was smiling at the man below her.

From the rear of the hall, Winnie watched the governess, as she had watched before. She's fond of him, there's no doubt about that, she thought. Poor lass! He doesn't really notice her. Not in that way. When she went back to the servants' quarters, she didn't say anything to the others about her suspicions. She liked Miss MacNaughton and understood what it was like to love someone in vain. Oh, yes she did, though she'd never told anyone about it. Mind you, William had never looked at the governess in that way, or Winnie would have noticed. She prided herself on noticing everything important about her family.

But Winnie was wrong. William *had* noticed Elizabeth in the way a man notices an attractive woman. He had admired the way her dark hair curled softly back from her face, and even though she wore it in a bun, he had remembered what it had looked like spread across her shoulders as he had seen her on that night long ago when she had helped his mother nurse Frederick. William also liked the fact that Elizabeth was tall, that she had beautiful, honest eyes, that she looked straight at you when she talked. He couldn't abide young women who simpered and tried to flirt with him. He didn't oblige them there. He couldn't. He wouldn't know how to begin flirting, even if he wanted.

But he had not thought beyond the pleasure he took in Elizabeth's company. Well, not until he went away to Didsbury and found, to his surprise, that he missed her. In some ways he was late in maturing, he supposed. Mark had been interested in 'the lasses' from the time he was sixteen. With Luke, you couldn't really tell. He kept his deepest feelings to himself. But an attraction to Elizabeth MacNaughton was stirring in William now, as well as giving him physical feelings of which he was rather ashamed. He hadn't done anything about them – Good heavens, no! – but they were there. And so was she. Too often for his peace of mind.

Across the town, at the upper end of Hey Lane, Luke stood in his kitchen staring at Amy Gorton, whose face bore yet another bruise. It was very obvious that her husband beat her regularly, but why he should do this when she was such a quiet, hard-working woman, Luke didn't know. Nor did he know how to help her.

'Are you all right?' he asked gently.

'I'm fine, thank you, Mr Gibson.' Amy's voice was calm and emotionless, but her little daughter, Tess, was huddled close to her, clutching her skirts, and the child's face was tear-stained.

'You look very pale. Are you – well?'

'Well enough. And I haven't time to chat, Mr Gibson, if I'm to do your cleaning and get back in time to make Ted's dinner.'

'No, Of course not. Sorry.' She obviously didn't want to discuss whatever was wrong, or even to have it noticed. But he couldn't help noticing the bruises. Or the anxiety as she looked down at Tess.

The following week, Amy seemed even worse than usual, swaying on her feet as she started to gather the dirty crockery together. This time the child also bore a bruise on her face. Luke felt something inside him tighten and grow angry at the sight of that. He knelt down to speak to Tess and she flinched back as he reached out to touch the bruise.

'Nay, I'm not going to hurt you, love,' he said soothingly. 'How did you hurt your face?'

Before Amy could stop her, the child said, 'My dad hit me.'

Luke looked reproachfully at Mrs Gorton. How could she let the man beat such a small child? Then he saw the expression on her face: the desperation, and the shame. 'Why don't we all sit down and have a cup of tea, eh? I'm still thirsty.' He was swinging the kettle over the open fire as he spoke. When he turned round, he saw how the child was eyeing the half-eaten loaf on the table. Surely she couldn't be hungry? 'Would you like a jam buttie, Tess?' he asked on impulse.

Amy Gorton opened her mouth to say no, then closed it again. Her daughter was hungry. They both were.

'Do you like plum jam?' Luke asked, still speaking to the child.

She nodded solemnly and took a step forward to watch him cutting a thick slice for her. When he'd buttered it, he spread the dark red jam thickly, cut it in two and put it on a plate. He reached out to lift her on to a stool, but she flinched away with a gasp of terror so he looked at her mother. 'You lift her up, eh?'

Amy Gorton nodded.

Luke busied himself cutting two more slices. He set one in front of the woman and took one for himself, though he wasn't really hungry.

'No, thank you!' she said in a tight, high voice.

'Please take it!' he begged. 'It's not often I have guests. It gets a bit lonely here sometimes. I have more appetite when I can share a meal with my friends.'

Amy hesitated, knowing he was saying this to make it easier

for her to forget her pride, but the sweet smell of the jam won over her dignity and she nodded, sitting down next to her daughter. 'It's very nice jam,' she said, eating slowly.

Tess's slice disappeared so quickly that Luke made another jam buttie for the child and tried not to notice that the mother was looking down at her own plate with tears of shame in her eyes. 'I often went hungry myself as a child,' he said quietly. 'I know what it's like. Please let me help.'

Amy tried to stop crying, afraid her daughter would say something to her husband when she got back, and Luke distracted the child by talking gently to her. 'Why don't you go outside and play with Rufus?' he asked. She adored his lop-eared dog, seeming to have no fear, although Rufus was a large creature. He was very gentle with children, though, or Luke would never have kept him. If the weather was fine, Tess often spent time playing outside while her mother cleaned the house.

Left alone with Luke, Amy gulped and tried to wipe the tears from her eyes. 'I'm s-sorry.'

'Don't be. Is there any way I can help?'

She shook her head, desolate, hopeless, her voice unnaturally high. 'No. No one can.'

He fell silent. She was right. No one could come between husband and wife, or stop a man chastising his family at will. But some men went beyond reason and he had suspected for a while that Ted Gorton was one of them.

'He's never hit the children before,' Amy whispered. 'I can stand it for myself, but when he hit Tess, I felt sick to my soul.' And Ted had enjoyed seeing how much more it hurt to see the children beaten than it did when he beat her. She was beginning to feel quite terrified of how far he would go.

'I wish—' began Luke, then broke off. He had no right to interfere. No right at all. Instead, he asked, 'Does he often keep you hungry?'

Her head was bent and shame was making her cheeks as scarlet as they had been pale before. 'He does lately. He – he's started drinking rather heavily. He takes all the money.'

'Then I should pay you personally for what you do here.'

She shook her head. 'It'd make him worse. And he'd just take it off me, anyway.'

'Well, I can make sure you and young Tess get something to eat.' He saw her opening her mouth to protest and said angrily, 'Don't try to stop me! I told you – I know what it's like. My mother used to drink, too, and hit me. It wasn't until she died and we went to live with my sister Annie that I knew what it was like to have a full stomach every day and clean, warm clothing. Please let me help! It would make me feel very happy.'

She looked at him through tear-filled eyes. 'You're a good man, Luke Gibson.'

He looked at her. She would be pretty if she were not so white and thin and weary-looking. Something stirred within him, but it was to be a while before he realised that it was the first flutter of love.

From then onwards, he made sure that he always had a meal ready for them on Fridays when they came to clean. And when Tess and her brother Adam came over to play with Rufus, he was able to slip them the odd buttie, which he knew would make Amy feel better. Kathy had once slipped food to him and the other children of John and Emily Gibson, when they all lived in Salem Street.

But try as he might, Luke could not think how to help Amy Gorton and her two children. Feeding her once a week didn't stop the bruises, didn't make her any less pale and anxious. And after she had been on Fridays, after he had seen the fresh bruises on her and the children, the worry of it would keep him awake at night. Worry, and that other thing, that fluttering feeling he got whenever she was nearby. She was such a small, gentle creature. She did not deserve this.

13

Bilsden: March to April 1861

As William worked on Annie's project, organising some of her operatives into a committee and co-ordinating the help offered, sometimes reluctantly on Matt's part, by Hallam's, news came from America that South Carolina and the other six Southern states seceded from the Union and formed the Confederate States of America. Annie would not even have noticed it, but Matt pointed it out to her in the newspaper.

'That's not good news, Mrs Hallam, not good news at all.' He'd always addressed her formally since their one short talk about the past, as if that helped him to see her as Mrs Hallam, widow of his patron, not Annie Gibson, the girl he had once courted.

Annie tried to push thoughts of the problems across the Atlantic Ocean to the back of her mind, but her father and William kept discussing the latest news earnestly, and even Tom had started taking an interest, so that just wasn't possible.

Matt continued to be very worried about the supply of cotton. 'I know we're well stocked at the moment,' he told her one day, 'but what happens when that's all gone? We get most of our cotton from the South. What will happen if our supplies are interrupted? What shall we do with our people? It'll cause great hardship in the town if we have to lay them off.'

'The supplies won't be interrupted, surely – or at least not for long. People in the Southern states will still have to eat, and for that they have to sell their produce. And we in Britain are not at odds with them, so why should they stop selling to us?'

His expression did not lighten. 'I'm not so sure that the supplies will get through, or at least not enough of them. Some men at the Exchange in Manchester – men who know a thing or two – are saying it'll soon come to an outright civil war in America, and if there's fighting and battles, then supplies are bound to be interrupted for quite a while. And prices will rise if that happens. Then how will we make our profits?'

She was shocked by that idea. 'Do you think it will come to an outright war? Surely not, Matt? Brother couldn't fight brother.' She couldn't imagine Tom trying to kill Mark and Luke, or William trying to kill Edgar. Thank goodness her own sons would not be involved! Then she felt guilty for thinking that. Other mothers' sons would be involved and would die, too. She forced her attention back to Matt.

'Well, I don't think it'll be as bad as some people say, Mrs Hallam. I mean, this is the nineteenth century, after all. Modern nations don't start civil wars nowadays. They just – just posture and threaten. But . . .' His voice tailed away.

'But what?'

'Mr Hallam was a member of the Cotton Supply Association right from the start. It was founded in 1857 to look for other sources of cotton, if you remember. Mr Hallam said it wasn't good business practice to buy nearly all your raw material from one country, and that always fretted him. Always.' Matt shook his head. 'We used to disagree about it. I mean, no one else in the world grows the right sort of cotton, or enough of it either, so what choice do we have? And the Association has not managed to find other suppliers, nor has it influenced the Government as it once hoped to. Even Mr Hallam said its members were fumbling around like a bunch of blind men, with their pamphlets and grants of cotton seed.'

Matt paused to smile reflectively. 'He used to get so angry with them. What use is it giving poor farmers in other countries seed, he used to ask, if they don't know what to do with it and can't read the pamphlets that tell them?' His smile faded. 'But he said the members of the Association were the only ones with enough sense to try to do something about the problem, so he kept up our membership. And so have I. On Hallam's behalf.'

'Oh.' Annie hadn't really thought about all this. She sometimes worried that there were just too many things for her to learn about since Frederick's death, for her children continued to grieve and to need a lot of attention, and they came before everything else.

'So you see,' Matt continued, determined to ensure that she was fully informed, 'we have no alternative but to buy a lot of Middling Uplands from America. Indian and Syrian cotton are short-stapled varieties. We're spinners of fine yarns. We can't use the short staples.' Then he saw how worried she was and said firmly, 'But perhaps people are being overly pessimistic. This trouble in America will die down after a while, surely it will. Well as I said you may be right: a modern nation wouldn't go to war, not a civil war!'

He convinced neither of them.

This idea that it couldn't come to a war seemed to be a common opinion, but as Annie continued to think about it, she remembered troubles all over Europe in the forties and fifties. There was no guarantee that being a modern nation made you avoid war. No guarantee at all.

In early March, Mr Pennybody Senior sent a little note to Ridge House, a note he had written himself in his shaky, old-fashioned italic script. He begged the favour of an appointment with Mrs Hallam on a matter of importance concerning her late husband's estate.

She stared at the note in puzzlement. What could he mean? They had settled all the bequests a while ago. But if Mr Pennybody wanted to see her, she was always available. He had helped her long ago when she was still struggling to find her feet financially, years before she met Frederick, and she had nothing but warm feelings for the old lawyer. She sent him an invitation to come and see her, and he arrived in state in his son's carriage.

Knowing his love of formality, Annie received him in the library, dressed in rustling black taffeta and wearing the pearls that Frederick had given her on one of their wedding anniversaries.

Jonas bowed over her hand. He was looking very frail now, his skin paper-thin and his eyes full of that kindly light that shines from some people at the very end of their lives. 'You look as beautiful as ever, Mrs Hallam, if you'll allow an old man to say so.'

She inclined her head. 'Thank you for the compliment. Now do, please, sit down. Shall I ring for some tea?'

'That would be very pleasant, but perhaps after we have settled our business?'

She was intrigued. What new business could they have? And why had Jonas Pennybody come to speak to her? Lately, it had been Hamish with whom she had dealt, not his father, for Jonas did not work long hours in the business nowadays.

He cleared his throat, hesitating, then said quietly, 'I was asked by your late husband to give you this letter nine months after his death.' He produced an envelope from inside his jacket and handed it to her with a bow, then got up and walked across to stare out of the window, so that she could read it in some sort of privacy.

She held the envelope in a hand that began to shake as she recognised Frederick's writing. She was managing, coping with her new life, but to hear from Frederick now would upset her greatly. She knew that. Somehow, she didn't want to open the letter.

When there was no sound of the envelope being torn open, Mr Pennybody turned to look at her, concerned at how pale she had become. 'Perhaps you might prefer to read this alone, my dear Mrs Hallam, so I'll wait for you in the hall.'

She shook her head and stood up to tug the bellpull. 'I wouldn't dream of asking you to wait in the hall. Ah, Winnie, could you please show Mr Pennybody to my sitting-room and take him some tea?'

'Yes, ma'am. This way, if you please, sir.'

Jonas glanced at his hostess and saw that her hand was still trembling and that her eyes were over-bright. He tried to think of something comforting to say, but could not, so left without another word.

When she was alone, Annie sat down on the sofa and stared at the envelope, trying to find the courage to open it. She traced her name with the tip of one finger and a sob escaped her. In the end, knowing that whatever he had written about must have been important to him, she went to find a paper knife. She could not bear to tear the envelope open. For some strange reason, it was important to her to keep her name intact.

She spread out the sheet of paper and began to read the final message she would ever receive from her beloved husband.

> *My dearest Annie*
>
> *It's hard to write this letter, knowing I shall be dead when you read it and knowing how it will hurt you. But I have one thing left undone that I'd still like you to undertake for me. Will you, my dear girl?*

Annie groaned and scrubbed her eyes with her handkerchief. It was a moment before she could continue reading.

> *I very much wanted Mr Gilchrist to paint that portrait of you. It was not possible at the time, but do you know, Annie-girl, I still hanker after it. He made such a good job of the family portrait that . . .*

She stared up at the painting, which until now had greatly comforted her, but her sight was blurred by tears and all she saw were colours and shapes. It was memory which supplied the details. And Tian Gilchrist had done a good job. Everyone loved that portrait.

> *. . . I don't want any other painter to tackle this task.*
>
> *I've arranged for a letter stating my wishes to be sent to*

146

Mr Gilchrist a month after my death, so he will already know about this. I've asked him to get in touch with you about a year after my death. That way, we shall not scandalise the gossips and you will have time to recover a little before you read this, as well as time to consider my request carefully before you see Mr Gilchrist again.

Please do this for me, my love. I know it's irrational, but I want our children and other descendants always to remember how beautiful you are, even though I know that one day you, too, will grow old as we all do.

For the rest, I want you to be happy, my dearest girl. Don't waste your life grieving, but remember me with affection and go on living. No wife could have made a husband happier than you have made me. And if you ever wish to remarry, know it will be with my blessing. People were not meant to live alone, and much as they love you, our children will grow up and leave home.

All my love, as ever
Frederick

By this time, she was sobbing aloud, her eyes quite blind with tears. She did not hear the door open and Tamsin rush in, followed by Edgar.

'Mother! Mother, what's wrong? We were in the hall and we heard you crying.' It was unheard of for Annie to weep like this and both children tugged at her, Tamsin kneeling in front of her, Edgar sitting on the couch, pressing himself against her.

For a few moments she could not speak, just rock to and fro, her arms around them. At the door, Elizabeth lingered for a moment, then went out and closed it softly behind her. They had been going out for a walk when the children heard their mother's sobs. She had no idea what had upset Annie so, but she was sure that if anyone could, the children would comfort her. A governess had no place with them at this moment.

There were disadvantages to a great love, she decided, as

she walked slowly upstairs. Then she blushed and looked guiltily around, for she had loved a certain man for several years now, a younger man who would never look at a woman like her. She felt a deep sympathy with her employer, who was also a friend, for she knew that you could not stop loving someone, however hard you tried. Even death did not stop love.

After a few minutes, Annie realised that both children were weeping with her, although they didn't yet know what had upset her so, and she made a great effort to stop sobbing.

'What's the matter, Mother?' Edgar asked, clutching her hand.

Annie wondered whether to show them the letter, then decided that she would do so. 'Your father left a letter for me, which Mr Pennybody has just brought, and – and it reminded me of him. That's what upset me.' She handed it to Tamsin. 'You two may like to read it, so that you'll understand what he's asking of me.'

Edgar got up to peer at the letter with his sister, reading just as quickly as she did, for he was a better student. When they had finished, they looked up at the family portrait.

'You will do as Father asked, won't you, Mother?' Tamsin said. 'If anything happened to you, it'd be so comfor ting to have a portrait of you.'

'But I'm in the family portrait. You already have a portrait of me.'

'That's not the same. And it's not what Father wanted. Say you'll do it for him?'

Annie's voice was husky. 'Of course I will. How could I ever deny your father his last wish?'

There was silence, but both children reached out to touch her, to squeeze her hand, to pat her arm.

'But I don't want you to marry again,' Tamsin added, her voice tight and angry. 'Promise me you'll never marry again. I don't want anyone trying to take the place of Father.'

Annie opened her mouth, then closed it. After a minute, seeing Tamsin still looking expectantly at her, she just said, 'I can't even imagine wanting to remarry, love.'

Tamsin's bottom lip was jutting out. 'You haven't promised.'

Edgar stared at them both. 'But Father said he'd be happy for her to remarry. So why should she promise you that she won't?'

Annie said nothing, because for some unknown reason she didn't want to make that promise, and that puzzled her. After all, she had vowed to herself never to remarry.

'And it'll be nice to see Mr Gilchrist again,' Edgar said, cheering up suddenly. 'He can help me with my drawing. I'm having trouble with perspective, and Miss MacNaughton is not a very good artist, I'm afraid, Mother. But I'd like to learn to draw properly.'

So when Mr Pennybody was shown back into the library by Winnie, he found Annie taking tea with her children, all three of them suspiciously red about the eyes but quite ready to accept his suggestion that in the late spring he should contact Mr Gilchrist.

'Do you have his address?' Edgar asked. 'Because if not, I do. He gave it to me before he left, in case we ever needed his help.'

'I have it, too,' Tamsin said.

Annie stared at them in surprise. Tian had given her the address, so why had he felt he needed to give it to her children as well? Then she realised that he must have guessed that Frederick had not long to live. He had wanted to help her. He was a kind man. A lot of people had been kind to her. But no one could replace Frederick.

In March, the Duchess of Kent, Queen Victoria's mother, died and the nation grieved for their Queen's loss. Out of respect, Bilsden Town Council ordered a black wreath to be hung on the door of the Council offices. Many other businesses followed suit, even the Emporium – though Annie privately thought it was a waste of time.

Kathy took a great interest in the preparations for the royal funeral and studied the reports in the *Bilsden Gazette* with great attention, reading them aloud to John when he came home from the junk yard at night, slowly and laboriously, for like him she had learned to read late in life. Annie could not understand this obsession with royalty, but Kathy had a picture of the Queen hanging prominently in her parlour and knew all about each of Her Majesty's nine children. Though even Kathy thought nine princes and princesses were enough and hoped that little Princess Beatrice would be the last of Her Majesty's family.

In the same month, a man called Abraham Lincoln gave his inaugural address as President of the United States, an address in which he declared that the Union of States was perpetual and the Confederate States were acting illegally in forming a separate group.

When this news was reported in the national newspapers, it made Matt feel better about the question of cotton supplies. 'I daresay Mr Lincoln will sort it all out now,' he told Annie. 'He sounds to be a sensible sort of man. After all, as we have said before, the planters need the money their cotton brings them. How else will they live?'

On April the twelfth, however, the Confederate forces fired on the Union garrison at Fort Sumter and President Lincoln proclaimed a blockade of the Southern ports.

When this news filtered through to England, Matt became gloomy again. 'Let's hope we can ride out the shortages until this is settled.'

'The trouble can't go on for long, surely?' Annie asked.

'We don't know how long this – this rebellion will last.' Since President Lincoln's speech, Matt had persisted in referring to the war as a 'rebellion'.

'Then go and see if you can buy some more cotton.' She had been thinking about that lately.

He looked at her and nodded his approval. 'Yes. I think we should increase our stocks. How much should we spend?'

She was impatient with him, still upset by Frederick's letter.

'You know as well as I do how we stand financially. Use your own judgement.'

He stared at her in undisguised horror.

'Matt, I have absolute trust in you.'

'But—'

She walked out of the room, an action she was later to regret, an action which was later to give her some of the most anxious days she had ever spent.

14

New York: April to May 1861

In April, on the other side of the Atlantic, Tian spent several days working on a letter to Annie, a letter which would, he hoped, persuade her to agree to her husband's request for a portrait. He changed the letter several times, and it grew longer with each rewrite. What he really wanted to do was tell her how much he missed her and how he thought about her constantly, ridiculous as that might seem for someone who had never really been part of her life.

Then, one morning, he realised suddenly that his best strategy was simply to sound businesslike; that a more personal approach would probably bring an instant refusal to see him. With a sigh, he destroyed his other letters and wrote a brief note saying that he had been informed of her husband's wish to have a portrait of her painted and that, as he would be returning to England in the late summer, he would contact her then. That would prepare the way without making her suspicious of his motives.

Once the letter was despatched, he felt happier, as if he had at last begun his campaign to win her. That night he had a drink with a few friends he had made in the district and mentally toasted Annie every time he lifted his glass. He was not a heavy drinker and in fact had a poor head for alcohol, but he greatly enjoyed the conviviality of such evenings. His exile was almost over, he thought, as he walked home through the darkness, whistling softly. He said it aloud, 'Almost over.' Soon he would see her again.

When news came that the South had begun hostilities on the twelfth with their attack on Fort Sumter, Tian decided that he had better return to Europe immediately, while he could still find a ship. Nothing, absolutely nothing, was going to keep him from Annie's side. With a much lighter heart, he began selling off the possessions he had inevitably acquired and making preparations to leave New York.

By that time, the city was full of men from the nearby country-side, come up to town to enlist, sometimes whole companies of local militia arriving together to of fer their services in the war that was fast approaching. He saw them standing on the sidewalks, gaping around at the sights, and wondered, with a quick grin, if he had been so obviously a newcomer the year before.

Just as he had his sailing date settled and had completed all his painting obligations, however, Igor Dalowski came to him with an urgent request for one last portrait. 'They're willing to pay a great deal,' he coaxed, 'and there's a ship leaving in a week's time on which you can travel. The troubles with the South are not going to stop that ship leaving, I'm sure.'

So Tian fought a quick battle between his desire to see Annie again and his desire to maximise the amount of money he would take back from America. And the money won. After all, a week would make little difference to his plans now.

But in that week, President Lincoln proclaimed a blockade of the Southern ports. War fervour rose to an instant crescendo, with men lining up at recruiting offices to sign on and fight for the twin goals of freedom for the Southern slaves and the preservation of the Union of States.

Tian saw the lines of men and some of them called out to him to join them as he walked past. 'I'm only a visitor to your country,' he called back, 'but I wish you well.'

He worked rapidly to finish the additional portrait in time to take the next ship to England, still living in the apartment, which was half-empty. He ate in a nearby café in the evening, or bought some bread and cold meat to take home. He had never been a fussy eater.

Two evenings before he was to leave, he stopped for a drink with his friends after his evening meal, feeling like a little company. The bar was full of rowdy men, singing and boasting that they would enlist the next day, or the next week at the latest, and one group merged with another, until it seemed that everyone in the bar was united.

'Got to do it soon,' some of the strangers kept telling everyone. 'Got to go and damn' well enlist. The war will be over by Christmas. We don't want to miss it.'

At their urging, Tian had a drink with them, then another. He tried to leave and was persuaded to have just one more drink to victory for the North. It would definitely be his last. But as he set his glass down, the room began to spin around him. He could not understand what was wrong. Three glasses of beer shouldn't affect him like this. Perhaps he was ill. Perhaps . . . He struggled to stay upright, trying to ask his friends for help in getting home, but the blackness rushed up to swallow him.

When he awoke the next morning, he was lying under a single blanket on a bare straw mattress in a long room full of other men snoring or twitching about on similarly primitive beds. At the door, a man in military uniform was bellowing at them to: 'Get up, you lazy scum! Do you think we'll beat the Confederates by lying in bed like this!' His voice had a strong tinge of an Irish accent and he was wearing an army uniform, a sergeant's uniform.

Tian sat up, groaning as his head began to thump and ache. The light hurt his eyes and more yelling from the man at the door assaulted his ears, making him wince involuntarily.

The man next to him pulled him to his feet. 'Come on! You can't stay in bed.'

'Where the hell are we?' Tian asked, utterly bewildered.

'At the recruiting office. We went and knocked them up last night, so that we could enlist, and they insisted we stay on here after we'd signed the papers.'

Tian froze where he stood. 'I didn't enlist!'

The man grinned. 'No, I enlisted you. The young lady paid

me well to do it. Thanks to her generosity, I was able to leave my wife with enough money to manage on for months.' He fumbled in his pocket and produced a crumpled letter. 'Here. She said to give you this.' He beamed at Tian and clapped him on the shoulder in a comradely way. 'She said you'd been wanting to enlist for a while, but had feared to worry your old mother. Well, now she's done it for you and your mother will soon come round.'

The military tyrant was still shouting and dragging men off their beds at the other end of the long hut, so Tian tore open the letter.

Dear Mr Gilchrist

You've done well out of your stay in New York. Now see if you do as well in the army. You've broken my heart, after leading me on, and I hope I'm now breaking yours. Your lady in England won't even know what's happened to you. She'll soon find another fellow. You would have done better with me.

Lyn Brownsby

Tian clutched the letter, reading and re-reading it, unable to believe what it said. How could she have done this to him? Then a rough hand shook his shoulder and a voice began to roar at him to bloody well get ready, to gather his things together and go stand by the door with the others.

He looked up, anger still simmering in him and disbelief making him think slowly. 'There's – there's been a mistake.'

The sergeant rolled his eyes. 'Half of them say that when they sober up. No mistake. You signed up as a soldier and a soldier you're going to be from now on, fellow.'

'But I can *prove* that I've been tricked into it,' Tian insisted.

The sergeant shrugged. 'Prove away. You're in the army now, however you got here, and your country needs you to fight those Southern scum.'

'But I'm not even an American!' Tian insisted. 'I'm only a visitor to New York.'

'Then you'll see more than you bargained for, won't you, on your little visit. Now, go and join the bloody line.'

Tian walked across the room, feeling a sense of unreality, as if he were trapped in a nightmare. He found himself next to the man who had taken him to the recruitment office and was received with a beaming smile. The anger that was making him seriously consider punching the fellow's face died down a little. This man was as much a dupe of Lyn Brownsby as he was. And a mere sergeant couldn't do much to remedy matters. No, the thing to do was to wait until he could find an officer, then put the matter to him as one gentleman to another. He folded the letter and put it carefully into his jacket with Frederick's letter, which he carried around as a lucky piece, then walked along behind the others. He climbed into the wagon that would take him to the training camp, sitting numb and silent in the midst of the excited men.

Bitterness coursed through him as they rattled along the streets and then along country roads. Bitterness filled him every minute of the next few days. But he tried to think things through very carefully. If he made a fuss now, he would get nowhere. He had to wait, to take orders, start training. He had to fill the interminable days with military activities he had never sought.

All the time Tian was being issued with his equipment, he kept telling himself that this was all a mistake, that it could not possibly go on for more than a few days at the most. His new trousers were too short, the flannel shirts were coarse and poorly made, one too large at the neck, one with the right arm longer than the left. The overcoat was in dark-coloured wool – some shade between black and navy – heavy and uncomfortable to wear in the warmer weather they were now experiencing.

He had been provided with a knapsack to hold his spare clothing, toilet articles and personal items. Only he didn't have any personal items, apart from the two letters, just the clothes he had been wearing when tricked into enlisting. He had a little money, the change from his pockets, but didn't spend it like the others on food from the hucksters who hung around the training camp, many of them young children selling things their mothers had baked. He kept his money safe and grimly made do with the food provided free by the army, dreadful food, such as he had seen the poor eating back in Ireland. The only thing you could say for it was that it was plentiful.

A group of ladies visited the camp and graciously gave each man a sewing kit which they had put together with their own fair hands. Tian accepted this, saying nothing as he watched them speak graciously to the group of specially selected men who had been ordered to 'talk nicely to the ladies'. Tian had begged off that duty and the sergeant must have been in a good mood that day, for he had allowed it.

Tian was also now the owner of two woollen blankets and an oiled ground cloth. They were folded and strapped around the top and sides of the new knapsack, which by that time was pretty heavy, about twenty pounds in total, he estimated. How the hell could anyone fight with that on his back?

A smaller haversack, worn slung across the chest, carried his personal food rations and eating utensils, and there was a canteen on a leather strap for carrying water. Each item seemed to weigh him down further, to tie him more permanently to the army. How he kept control of his simmering anger and outrage he never knew afterwards, but he did. He had to. He had to appear reasonable, stay out of trouble. For Annie.

Some of the other recruits, like him, were already very familiar with firearms and helped the others, the 'city boys', to learn the drills that might one day save their own lives and take those of their enemies. Tian wondered many times as he did so if he ever could shoot to kill. He had shot game many times, but a man – he seriously doubted that he could kill a man, except perhaps in self-defence. And even then, he would hope not to have to kill.

Eventually, he received word that the commanding officer of the training camp, one Captain Greeshall, with whom he had sought an interview several days previously, would spare him ten minutes. Relief made him close his eyes, then he began to get ready. He had Phil Graham, the man who had tricked him and who had somehow since become a friend, standing ready outside the office, ready to bear witness. He had the letter from Lyn. They would, they *must*, release him now. Hope surged up in him and the sunlight seemed suddenly bright, the day cheerful, as he walked across the parade ground.

The captain listened attentively as soon as it became clear that he was dealing with another gentleman. He called in Phil Graham and questioned him, and read the letter through twice. Then he sighed and handed it back to Tian. 'I believe you, Gilchrist, I definitely believe you, but there's nothing I can do about it. We have a war on our hands. There are no mechanisms for releasing those who have been tricked into enlisting. Once you're in the army, you're in to stay – at least until the end of the war. I'm sorry.'

The room spun around Tian and for a moment he had to lean on the edge of the desk. 'But—'

'I repeat: there's nothing I can do. But you're a gentleman – if you wish to apply to become an officer, I'll certainly support your application for that. It would make your life easier, at least.'

Tian could not move, only continue to stare at him in horror. He was desperately hunting for some solution, something to end this nightmare. Once he was dismissed from this room, it would be too late. This was his one chance. 'Could you,' he asked as he saw the officer's fingers start tapping impatiently on the desk, 'allow me to write one letter and make sure it gets to Mr Thaddeus Brownsby in New York? There are people expecting me in New York, others waiting for me in England. At least let me tell them I'm alive.'

The captain nodded, relieved that Gilchrist was taking his answer like the gentleman he clearly was. 'Very well. My clerk will let you have a sheet of paper. I'll see that the letter gets there. I'll want to read it myself first, though.'

But as the weeks passed, Tian heard nothing from Thaddeus Brownsby and slowly his last hope of rescue, the hope he had clung to in spite of everything, began to fade. The letter must have gone astray. He was trapped here, trapped in a war that was not his. He could be killed in America and no one would know. Not his family. Not his friends. And most of all not Annie. What would she think when she didn't hear from him again? Would she care? Would she worry?

After due consideration he applied to become an officer, in the faint hope that then he might have more freedom, for he had none now. But he heard nothing about that, either. The men in this camp were as closely guarded as prisoners in a gaol. If the sergeant and other non-commissioned officers weren't watching them, then they were shut up in the barracks, watching each other.

Tian endured the training because there was nothing else he could do. Punishment was harsh for those who slacked or infringed the rules. He saw no point in suffering physically as well as mentally. So although his muscles groaned and his hands grew callused, he obeyed orders, moving here, moving there, as ordered.

His body became fitter than it had ever been before. He made friends with the men who shared his training, the men with whom he was soon to be sent to war.

But his nights were filled with dark despair, with dreams of Annie, always just out of his reach, and sometimes with plans to revenge himself upon Lyn Brownsby. He had never thought he could hate a woman like this, but he did, he hated her with a passion.

Then, as is often the case, two things happened to Tian on the same day. He received word that he had been accepted and would soon be trained as an officer, and he received a visit from Thaddeus Brownsby.

The captain allowed the two men to use one side of his office for a fairly private conversation, while he continued to work at his desk.

For once, Thaddeus seemed reluctant to talk, fiddling with

his watch chain, then he sighed and looked straight at Tian. 'I don't know how to apologise for my daughter's behaviour, indeed I don't.'

Tian shrugged slightly and waited.

'She's been sent to the country to stay with her aunt until she comes to her senses.' Anger filled his face. 'She still defies me, still says she doesn't care, that she's glad about what she did to you! How could a daughter of mine have behaved in such an unprincipled way? My wife and I are both deeply ashamed of her. Deeply.'

Again, Tian just shrugged slightly and waited.

'I'd have come to see you sooner, but I was chasing people, trying to work out how best to help you.' Thaddeus started running his finger round an inkwell. 'And what it comes down to is – there's no way I can get you out.'

His weeks in the army had taught Tian enough self-control so that he only asked, 'Are you sure?'

Thaddeus nodded. 'I'm afraid so.'

Tian shaded his face with his hand, near to tears. The minute he had heard that a Mr Brownsby was here to see him, he had started to hope again. Now he felt he had been kicked in the guts.

Thaddeus leaned closer and patted him on the shoulder, whispering, 'So I had a talk with Igor. Come a little closer and start sobbing.'

Tian leaned forward until his head was nearly touching that of the older man and faked a few sobs.

'You'll have to decide whether you want to take a big risk,' Thaddeus whispered, 'for the only way we can help is to find a way for you to escape. Trouble is, if they recapture you, you'll be shot as a deserter.'

Tian sucked in air. 'Hell and damnation!' He saw the captain looking at them suspiciously and feigned another sob. 'Hell and damnation!' he repeated brokenly.

Thaddeus patted his shoulder again and said loudly. 'There, there, lad.' Then he whispered, 'I think you should just see out the war here, lad. The risks are too great.'

'No!' Tian's voice was low and fierce. 'Not if there's any other way. People say that the war will only last for a few months, but I don't believe that. This is a big country. Too big to settle something so quickly. It takes time for armies to get around.'

The older man was looking down at the inkwell again, avoiding Tian's eyes. 'You're probably right. But if you were caught . . .'

'I'll take my chance. Can you arrange for me to escape?'

'Igor thinks he can. It'll take a while, though. You'll have to be ready to drop everything when you get word, just drop everything and run. So if there's anything you treasure, make sure you keep it on your person.'

Across the room, the captain cleared his throat. 'Sorry, but that's all the time I can allow you. Gilchrist has things to do. Dismissed, Gilchrist.'

Tian stood up and saluted. He nodded farewell to Thaddeus and left, marching smartly out of the office. He had a thousand questions still unanswered, but if this captain said 'Jump', you jumped. There were militia groups where the officers were still elected, where orders could be debated, but this captain was regular army and he ran the training centre accordingly.

Late that afternoon, as Tian was making his way back to the dormitory to wash his hands before supper, he encountered the captain taking the air.

'A moment, Gilchrist.'

'Yes, sir.'

'Your friend seemed very upset that there was no way to get you out of the army.'

'Yes, sir.'

'Let's hope he doesn't get any ideas about helping you to escape.'

Tian looked at him, not having to feign surprise. What had made Greeshall suspect that? 'Why would Mr Brownsby do that?'

'We had a drink together afterwards. He's very ashamed that it was his daughter who got you in this predicament.'

'Well, that's not really his fault.'

'He seems to feel responsible.'

'There's nothing any of us can do about it now, sir. I've become reconciled to that, though I will admit I'm not happy about it. But at least Mr Brownsby will let my family know where I am. I was very worried about them.'

'Are you reconciled enough to take a commission?'

Tian did not intend to let the captain suspect how deep was his desire to escape. He managed a smile and tried to inject some pleasure into his voice. 'Yes, I am, sir. In fact, I think that would make this whole affair much more acceptable to me. After all, I am a gentleman.'

'I'd heard you were an artist before you joined, and doing quite well at it.'

'That, too.' Had Thaddeus told the captain about that? What had got into the man to spout off his mouth? He was usually so shrewd. Had he not seen how astute Captain Greeshall was? Or was Thaddeus trying to make sure Tian never got an opportunity to escape, so that he wouldn't have to feel guilty if things went wrong?

Captain Greeshall nodded. 'Well then, that's decided. Get your things packed and report to my office with all your kit at eight o'clock in the morning. We'll send you off to officer training camp.' He paused then added, 'You'll be too busy there even to think of escaping. And it's even further away from New York.'

Tian could only gape at him. What had made him take this attitude?

'And just to be sure you understand the exact situation – I'll make sure your superiors are warned that an escape attempt might be a possibility.'

'I think that's unfair, sir. I've made no attempt to escape.'

'No, and you'd better not. Maybe I'm just getting suspicious in my old age.' The captain turned to leave, then swung round again. 'Oh, and I'm getting forgetful, too. Mr Brownsby left you this.' He held out a small purse. 'He felt you might be short of money. He said to tell you he has your things from the apartment safely stored.'

'Thank you, sir. I *am* short of money. And I'm glad to hear that my things are safe.' Tian walked away, hoping he had convinced the captain that he was resigned to staying in the army, but not at all sure.

He found it hard to sleep that night. He was being sent to another camp. Thaddeus might not know where he was, so escape might not even be a possibility. Hell! What a mess this was! He fluffed up his pillow, straightened his blankets, but whatever he did, he could not get comfortable. Annie seemed so far away. Would it be years before he saw her again? And would Lyn Brownsby be right? Would Annie have remarried by then? No, he could not let himself believe that, he could not. He had to hold on to some hope.

15

Bilsden: April 1861

Annie opened the letter, wondering who could be writing to her from America. She gasped in shock as she read the signature at the bottom. Had Mr Pennybody written to Tian Gilchrist to say that he'd given her Frederick's letter about the portrait, or was this just a coincidence?

She read and re-read the letter, puzzled by its terseness. This was not the tone she'd have expected from him, given the fact that he'd professed to have fallen in love with her. Was that because he regretted it? Or because he had met someone else?

Amazement held her motionless as she realised that she did not like the idea of Tian's meeting someone else, kissing and holding someone else, looking at another woman with that warm admiring gaze. 'How stupid!' she muttered. 'As if it matters to me now. It's just vanity!'

That evening at dinner she mentioned the letter to her children, trying to sound as if it didn't matter very much. 'He – er – says he'll be back in England around June or July and he'll get in touch with us then about the portrait.'

Two faces lit up.

'Oh, good!' said Edgar. 'I've so much I want to ask Tian.'

Annie blinked in surprise at how delighted her son sounded. Then she realised something else. 'Since when have you been calling him "Tian"?' she inquired sharply.

'Oh, he asked me to when he was doing the portrait. Just in private, you know. We got to be good friends. Sometimes he even let me watch him paint, but he said I wasn't to tell anyone else, as usually he doesn't like people watching while he works.'

'Oh.' Annie didn't know what to say to that.

'Well, he used to tell *me* about his family,' Tamsin volunteered. 'He's got a sister called Sarry, you know. She's the youngest. She's sixteen. No, she'll be seventeen now, won't she? And he told me about Ireland, too. I'd love to go and see it one day. We never go anywhere except stupid old Blackpool and Auntie Lizzie's boarding house with Grandma and Grandad. Why, I haven't even been to London!'

Elizabeth said nothing, just sat and watched Annie, noting the way the colour came and went in her cheeks as the children discussed Tian Gilchrist. He was a lovely man, as polite to a governess as to the lady of the house, but – was it possible that Annie was attracted to him? Surely not! She had been so much in love with her husband. But Frederick Hallam was dead now, and Annie was still a beautiful woman, still young enough to need a man.

Elizabeth did not feel it her place to make any comment on the possible visit of Mr Gilchrist, but could not help wondering about Annie's reactions. She looked sideways at William to see if he had noticed anything, but he was concentrating on his food. A smile softened her face. He was such a hearty eater.

He looked up, as if he had felt her gaze, and smiled back, that sunny, open smile which always made her heart twist. As they fell into conversation, she forgot Annie completely. She loved hearing about what William had been doing. How wonderful to spend your time really making a difference to people's lives! She had done what she could while her father was alive, helping the poor in his parish, but it had not been on the scale of William Ashworth's efforts. The man seemed tireless, and yet he always had time to talk to the children – and their governess.

The following Sunday, Joanie stared out of the parlour window of Netherhouse Cottage, and pulled a face when she saw that Maddie had brought her brother with her again. Joanie was fed up of Harry Pickering tagging along on all their outings, fed up of the sight of him. And she was beginning to suspect why he came. If Maddie was match-making, she could just stop, and so Joanie would tell her next time they were alone together.

Her gaze turned back to the man walking along the street and a scowl wrinkled her brow as she studied him. Hah! She wouldn't marry someone like him, not in a million years. It wasn't that she disliked him – no, he could be quite good company in his own way. It was just that she didn't fancy him. Not at all. His face was all lumpy, and he had thick lips. And his hair was getting thin on top – well, he was nearly thirty. Quite old. And he was very solidly built. He would probably grow fat as he got older. Joanie didn't like fat, bald, old men. She liked younger men with dark eyes and curly hair. She gasped and banished the image quickly. That particular young man was not for her.

On a sudden thought, she rushed into the kitchen. 'Samuel John, Maddie's just going to knock on the door. Will you answer it and tell her I'm not feeling well and can't go for a walk today?'

'You usually can't wait to go out with her.'

'Well, she's brought her brother along with her again, and I'm fed up of him.'

'What'll you give me if I do?'

'A penny.'

'Twopence.'

She glared at him. 'Honestly, do you think I'm made of money?' Then there was a knock on the front door and she said hastily, 'Oh, all right. Twopence.'

She listened, covering her mouth with one hand to hold the giggles back as Samuel John glibly explained that his sister wasn't feeling well. How cleverly he told the lies! He was a dark horse, her young half-brother was. You never knew what he was thinking.

When he'd shut the front door, she rushed along to the parlour again and peered through the net curtains to watch her friends walk away. 'Serve you right, Maddie Pickering!' she muttered. 'If people see me out with your Harry all the time, they'll think him an' me are courting.'

For a few minutes Joanie dawdled about in the parlour. Her father and mother had taken little Faith for a walk up the hill to Tom's, for his children adored the baby. After a while, she turned and went over to the fireplace, glaring at herself in the overmantel mirror. She was all dressed up – she turned to admire the new dress – and wanted to go out. Kathy didn't like her going out on her own, but Kathy wouldn't know. No sooner had she come to that conclusion than Joanie clattered upstairs to get her shawl. 'I've changed my mind. I'm just going out! I'll catch Maddie up,' she called.

From the kitchen, Samuel John called back, 'Where's my twopence?'

She went into the kitchen and threw four halfpennies on to the table. 'There!'

At the far corner of the table, eleven-year-old Benjamin sat reading a book. He didn't even seem to have noticed that she was there and Samuel John turned away as soon as he got the money. She pouted as she walked into the hallway. No one really cared about her and whether she was happy. No one. And since Rebecca had got married, she could barely spare a few minutes for her younger sister, and even then, her talk was all of the house and how she was restoring the main rooms.

It was all right for some people! They didn't have to go to a boring old salon and sew until their fingers were raw. And after Rebecca left, you'd have thought Mary would have given Joanie a chance to meet the customers, which would be much more interesting than just sewing, but no! Instead, Annie had sold her interest in the salon to Janet Pover and Janet was just as bad a slave-driver as Annie had been. You could get round Mary sometimes, have a bit of fun with the other girls, but you couldn't get round Janet. The old witch didn't even like the girls to talk to one another as they sewed. It wasn't fair!

Joanie dawdled down the hill, then slipped down one of the back streets to avoid High Street, where she guessed Maddie and Harry would be walking up and down. 'I bet they don't stay long if I'm not there,' she giggled to herself. 'He won't waste his time on his sister.'

'They say it's the first sign of madness,' a voice said behind her.

She swung round to find Bart smiling down at her. She put one hand to her chest. 'Oh! You made me jump.'

'Who won't stay long?' he asked, falling into place beside her without so much as a by-your-leave.

'My friend Maddie. And her brother. They're out for a walk.'

'Harry Pickering.' Bart knew the man and didn't like him. As a clerk at the Gas Company, Harry enjoyed using his power to make customers wait – well, the unimportant ones, anyway. He clearly relished fussing over papers and small sums of money. He had made Bart wait in the office several times now, for no real reason at all, the stuck-up fool!

'Yes.' She sighed. 'Mr Harry Stupid Pickering.'

'I thought he was a friend of yours.'

'Not exactly. It's his sister who's my friend.'

'Oh? I'd heard that you were walking out with him.'

She gasped and stopped in her tracks. 'What! Who said that?' She didn't wait for him to explain, just groaned and added, 'Oh, I knew this would happen. I knew it.'

He stopped beside her, smiling. He'd heard it from several sources and Harry Pickering had hinted at it, too. But this wasn't the reaction of a courting woman. 'Knew what would happen?'

'I knew folk would think I was walking out with him if he always tagged along with us. Oh, what am I going to do?' Joanie didn't want to alienate Maddie. She didn't really have any other friends.

'Take a walk with another fellow?' he suggested, offering her his arm.

'Oh!' She looked up at him. Bart was exactly the sort of man she fancied, and always had been. He had such lovely hair, dark and wavy, and his eyes were brown and mysterious in a face tanned by the outdoor life of the market and his rounds for his father, who lent out small sums of money and made very sure that his clients paid him back on time. Bart had told her once that he wasn't fond of this side of his father's business, but it did bring in a steady flow of money. 'I thought we agreed there was no future in us seeing one another?' she said, staring down at the pavement.

He was staring at her. Anger and fresh air had coloured her cheeks a rosy pink and wisps of soft hair were already escaping from under her bonnet. 'Maybe I've changed my mind.'

'Oh.' She peeped sideways at him.

'Won't I do?' he teased when she didn't take his arm, clasping one hand over his heart and giving an exaggerated sigh. 'I'll be heartbroken if you refuse me.'

She chuckled. 'Silly!' But still she hesitated.

To hell with families! He didn't wait for her agreement, but reached out and took her arm, linking it with his and patting her hand with a proprietorial air. If his father saw them, too bad. Bart was nearly ready now to sever all connection with him and that damned chapel of his. Redemption House! Misery Alley, he called it to himself. All talk of sin and repentance, no pleasure in anything, not even the sun or the fresh air or the flowers. To hear his father talk it was a sin to bring home a bunch of flowers to brighten up the place.

'Is – is something wrong?' Joanie faltered, stopping. For a moment, he had looked so fierce.

He banished the thought of his father and smiled down at her. 'No. Sorry. I was just thinking of something else. There's nothing at all wrong with the world if I can take a walk in company with Miss Joanie Gibson.'

She blushed, but could not help smiling at him.

Soft and sweet, he thought. And yet my father would see her only as another sinner.

'Where would you like to walk, Miss Gibson?'

'To the park?'

'The Pickerings might see us,' he teased.

She raised her chin defiantly. 'I hope they do.' That'd show everyone she wasn't Harry's girl. And it'd show Maddie, too. Then another thought occurred to her. 'What if your father sees us, though? He wouldn't like you walking out with me.'

Bart echoed her own defiance. 'I hope he *does* see us. I've had more than enough of my father and his bullying ways.'

'He always looks very fierce.' She didn't want Bible Burns shouting at her, as he sometimes shouted at people in public.

Bart grinned. 'A lot of it is just noise. But I can be fierce, too, if need be. And I won't just make a lot of noise.' His voice softened. 'I won't let him hurt you, I promise.'

She looked up at him again through her long silky lashes, her eyes like pale blue crystal. 'Your father frightens me,' she admitted. 'And so do your brothers. They always glare at me when they pass me in the street. Why do they hate us Gibsons so?'

'To start with, because of our Nelly.' He frowned. 'But also, I think, because your grandfather is what my father pretends to be: a fervent Christian.'

'But your father founded Redemption House.'

'For his own glory, not that of the Lord.' It had taken Bart a long time to realise that, and once he had, it had helped him shake off the mental yoke his father had tried to lay upon all his sons. Pity Don and Bill hadn't done a bit more thinking. 'And lately, of course, there's the child. He hates to think of her being brought up a Gibson. He's severed all connection with Timothy Hill because of that.'

Joanie's face softened. 'Faith's such a lovely baby. You should see her. She's all soft and cuddly. I love babies.'

'I like soft cuddly things myself,' he whispered. 'But they're not always babies.'

Her steps faltered and she stared sideways at him.

'You're not frightened of me?' he asked gently. Suddenly it was imperative that this girl should not be afraid of him.

She shook her head. 'No. I've never been frightened of you, Bart.' Though he did fill her with strange feelings. But that wasn't fear. It was – she admitted it to herself, at least – attraction.

'Good.' He patted her hand and for the rest of their walk led the conversation into less controversial areas, teasing her, making her laugh and generally behaving as young men have always behaved with young women they find attractive.

Both of them found that they were enjoying themselves hugely. Then at one point they came face to face with Maddie and Harry Pickering and the laughter fled from Joanie's face. She gasped and held on to Bart's arm more tightly.

He would have just nodded and walked past, but Harry pulled his sister forward to confront Joanie.

'Your brother said you weren't feeling well,' Maddie said by way of a greeting.

With Bart's fingers warm on her own, Joanie felt more courageous than usual. 'I had a bit of a headache. It got better, so I came out for some fresh air.'

She stole another glance up at Bart, then looked sideways at Harry. The two men were eyeing one another like cockerels about to fight. Suddenly she felt afraid that they really would fight one another and tugged at Bart's arm to make him continue their walk.

He looked down at her and realised that she was anxious and distressed, for all her brave words. 'Well, we must carry on with our constitutional!' he said breezily.

In response to her brother's elbow in the ribs, Maddie said quickly, 'Let's join up.'

'No, thank you,' said Bart and pulled Joanie away. 'We're talking about something.'

When they were out of sight, they both stopped and looked at one another, then burst out laughing.

'Did you see his face?' Joanie crowed. 'Ooh, wasn't he surprised? That'll show him.'

He joined in her laughter, loving to see her face light up and her eyes sparkle. But afterwards, as their amusement died down, he said solemnly, 'I should watch out for Harry Pickering from now on, if I were you, Joanie. He can be a nasty devil sometimes. Or at least he was until he got that job and decided to become respectable. You should watch out for me, too,' he added, in fairness.

'Why? Aren't you respectable?' she asked without thinking, her eyes wide, but with something warm behind her anxious gaze.

'When I'm with you, Joanie Gibson, my thoughts are not at all respectable, but my behaviour is, and will always be with you, perfectly respectable. You can count on that. And don't let anyone ever tell you different.'

Her smile was shy, but glowing.

They walked around the park for about an hour. When the clock in Hallam Square chimed, she sighed. 'I'd better get back, I suppose.'

He hesitated. Was this the time to start his bid for independence? Then he looked into her trusting, hopeful eyes and knew that it was. 'Can I walk you home, Joanie? I'd really like to.'

'Oh.' She knew exactly what he meant by that. It was one thing to see a lad out in the park, even to let him give you his arm for a while, but quite another to let him take you home, where he might meet your family. Her breath caught in her throat for a minute, then she looked at him with a tremulous smile and said, so quietly that it was nearly a whisper. 'Yes. You can walk me home, Bart. I'd – I'd like it, too.'

'And can I see you again? Often.'

She nodded slowly, feeling for a moment as if she were floating on a cloud of happiness. 'Yes. I'd like that.'

'Next Sunday afternoon? Can I call for you? Take you walking?'

She nodded again, but a frown was creasing her forehead. 'I – I think my father would want to meet you first if you called at the house. He's a bit – a bit strict about who I go out with.' She waited for his answer, mouth half-open in breathless hope.

'I'd better go and see him at the junk yard during the week.' Bart decided. 'Have a talk with him. Make things a bit official, like. I don't think he'll stop you coming out with me, then.'

Her face was such a blaze of joy that it made him feel like the King of Bilsden.

The following day, John Gibson saw one of the Burns family approaching his yard and frowned. What did that fellow want? He went out to meet him. 'Can I help you?' His voice was guarded, suspicious.

'I'd like to speak to you, Mr Gibson,' Bart said. 'Privately, please.'

'Oh? What about?'

'Something that's not for other ears.'

John could not think what this might be, but his innate courtesy made him say, 'Well, I suppose you'd better come round the back, then.' He turned to Bill Midgely. 'Take charge, will you, Bill lad?'

When they were sitting in the little room where the staff took their midday meal and brewed up innumerable cups of tea, Bart hesitated for a moment, then took the bull by the horns. 'I met your Joanie on Sunday afternoon in the park. I've talked to her once or twice now. She's a nice lass, your Joanie is. I'd like your permission to call for her and take her for a walk next Sunday.'

For a moment, John could not frame a single word. This was the last thing he'd expected a Burns to ask him, the very last.

Bart watched him, so afraid suddenly that Joanie's father would say no straight out, that he rushed into speech: 'I know you have no cause to like my family, Mr Gibson, but maybe, if you give me a chance, you'll find out that I'm not much like the others. And – and I want this to be all open and above board. So that's why I've come to ask you straight out about Joanie.'

'You mean,' John hesitated to say it, but things had to be made clear, 'you mean you want to come courting our Joanie?'

'Well, I'd like the chance to get to know her. With your permission. And I think she'd like to get to know me.'

His face softened into a smile and it was that which made John relent, rather than the words Bart had spoken. But there would be other problems, so he asked bluntly, 'What does your father say about it?'

'I'm twenty-six, Mr Gibson, not sixteen. Old enough to make my own choices. I haven't asked him.'

'Does he know you're, um, interested in my Joanie?'

'No. Like I said, it's none of his business. And anyway, we both know what he'd say. He has no love for the Gibsons.' Bart hesitated, thinking things were not going as well as he'd have liked, then said, 'I'll not be working in the family business for much longer, Mr Gibson, though I hope you'll keep that to yourself. I'm not best suited with how my father runs things.' He faced something he'd refused to face before. 'And I'm not fond of debt collecting from poor folk as can hardly set bread on their tables. Not at all fond.'

There was silence, then John rubbed his forehead. 'Well, I don't know what to say and that's a fact.'

'Why don't you ask Joanie what she wants? And ask your wife what she thinks, too. I'm only talking about going for a walk, getting to know one another.' He hadn't intended to look for a wife for a long time yet. What was it about Joanie Gibson that tugged at his heartstrings so? Again his face softened into a half-smile at the thought of her, and again John noticed it.

'Well, I suppose that'd only be fair.' Though what Kathy would say, he didn't know.

'I'll pop in on Friday, then, for the verdict,' Bart said, standing up.

John watched him stride out of the yard, tall, muscular and radiating strength and energy. If he had been anyone but Lemuel Burns's son, John would have welcomed him as a suitor for Joanie. As it was, he didn't know what to think. 'Eh, it's a rum do. It is that! I think I'd better talk to our Annie as well. I'll go and see her after tea tonight. She'll know what's right.'

In a small terraced house in Waterby Street, Harry Pickering was in a towering rage. 'Why didn't you warn me she was seeing that Burns fellow?' he demanded, thumping his hand on the table and making Maddie leap in shock. 'Why didn't you say anything?'

'Because I didn't know, did I? She doesn't tell me everything.' Maddie hesitated. 'I told you she didn't allus want you tagging along. You've been pushing her too hard. It were all too quick.'

He looked at her scornfully. 'I've not been pushing her hard enough, I think. Not nearly hard enough.' He wasn't going to lose the last chance he had of marrying into the Gibson family. 'You go and get the tea ready. I need to do some thinking.'

He went to get out his pipe and settled in front of the fire, a frown on his face. Maddie tiptoed around him, as she always did when Harry was in this sort of mood. At times like this, she had to watch her step. He liked things to go as he'd planned them, Harry did. Always had. And he could get really nasty if they didn't. She'd had a few bruises to prove that in the past year or two.

16

Bilsden: Early May 1861

As Bart came home from a Sunday walk with Joanie a week or two later, he found a welcoming committee gathered in the parlour.

'Come in here and close that door!' his father ordered harshly. He was clutching his smaller Bible to his chest and anger was radiating from him. 'I want a word with you, son.'

Bart looked beyond his father to his two brothers, each of whom was standing with arms folded, glaring at him. He knew that stance. They had been called to attend their father and would jump to obey any order he gave them. Why had he been cursed with such stupid brothers? But worse than that, cursed with a father who was, he had often thought, quite mad.

'What about?' he asked to gain time, lounging in the doorway.

'Come inside this minute and shut that door!' Lemuel Burns's voice echoed down the hallway.

Upstairs, Prudence Burns clutched her hands to her chest in a vain attempt to still a heart that fluttered with terror. But she had to hear, just had to, so she crept closer to the banisters, trying desperately to make out what they were saying. Her husband's voice rang out loudly, but she could not distinguish the other voices clearly, especially the deep rumbling tone of her beloved youngest son. 'Don't anger him, Bartie,' she murmured. 'Oh, please don't anger him.'

Bart stayed by the door, staring at the three accusing faces. He could guess what had happened. Someone had seen him and Joanie and had told his father. He'd known it wouldn't be long now before they had a confrontation, but had decided to make the most of the time left to him to put a bit more money away. He would have expected his father to speak to him alone and it was Lemuel whom he watched now. He was such a wily old bastard you never knew which way he was going to twist next.

He suddenly noticed Bill's bunched fists and fighting stance. His brother glared at him. Only then did it occur to Bart that they might be going to try force. He'd expected biblical exhortations and an order never to darken his father's doorstep again, but not force. Ah, hell, if it hadn't been for his mother, he'd have gone years ago. He could guess that she was upstairs, listening. She did a lot of listening, his mother did, poor woman. He was surprised sometimes at the things she told him about what his father was doing, surprised and disgusted, as she was.

'Don't despise me for not standing up to him,' she'd murmured once. 'I tried when we were first married, but he beat me so badly—'

He'd assured her that of course he didn't dispise her, couldn't, no matter what.

'Ah, you're the light of my life,' she'd said then. 'The only decent one in the whole bunch.'

He forced himself to concentrate on the present, eyeing his brothers again. If they tried force, they'd have a hard job with him. But he'd have an even harder job beating two of them, though he was the strongest of the three now, taller than both his brothers and in some ways harder. They were sheep compared to him, sheep who allowed their father to lead them by the nose. Strong, but stupid. He shrugged. Even the worst of bruises soon healed and he doubted they'd go further than that, but prudently he remained just inside the door, ready to run for it.

'Come inside and sit down!' his father barked.

'No, I think I'll stand, thank you.'

Bill growled in his throat. Don shifted his feet. Lemuel Burns looked at his youngest son and scowled. 'Very well, then, stand. But make sure you listen and heed what I say. It's come to my attention that you've been consorting with a Gibson whore.'

With difficulty, Bart kept control of his temper. 'No.'

'"*Out of thine own mouth will I judge thee*,"' roared Mr Burns. '*St Luke*, Chapter 19, Verse 22. How can you lie to us like that? You've been seen with the woman. By several people.'

'No one's seen me with any whore,' Bart said, forcing a mild tone into his voice, for he knew his father hated it when he did not respond angrily to goading.

Lemuel Burns's voice rang out at full pitch. 'You've been seen with one of those Gibsons, the younger one, the one who flaunts herself all over the town of a Sunday with that giddy Pickering wench.' Maddie had openly mocked Lemuel once, since when he'd never lost an opportunity to blacken her name and that of anyone who consorted with her.

Bart found himself greatly tempted to smash his fist into his father's red face and bulging eyes. He resisted it and said, steadily and firmly, 'Joanie Gibson is a nice young lass, as innocent as anyone could wish. She is no whore.'

Breath whistled into his father's throat. 'So you admit it. You admit it! You'll repent of this publicly at chapel next week, Bartholomew Burns.'

'Repent of what? Walking out with a nice young lass? What's to repent of in that?'

'I'll have no carnal behaviour from my family!' roared the older man.

Bart was suddenly sick to death of his father's hypocrisy. Lemuel Burns might bray aloud his religion, might invoke the Bible with every alternate breath, but in fact, he was a cruel, vicious man. 'There has been no carnal behaviour between me and Joanie Gibson. I'm honestly courting a nice young lass. And,' he had to raise his voice to stop his father shouting him down, 'I won't take kindly to anyone blackening her name.'

'I'm not having it! No son of mine is going to wed a Gibson.'

'There's nowt you can do about it. I'm over twenty-one and my own man.'

'We *can* do summat about it. We can stop you going outside

this house until you repent of your sin,' Don said suddenly, his voice rumbling with anger. 'We can do that.'

'What? Keep me prisoner?' Bart laughed scornfully. 'Who'll collect the payments then?'

'We'll find a way,' Don said. 'There's allus a way if you seek it out and ask the Lord for guidance.'

'An' how long do you think you'll keep me here?' Bart demanded, but his mind was working furiously. It was just possible that they might be able to carry out their threat, if the three of them attacked him. Hell, he should have moved out as soon as he started courting Joanie and to hell with the extra money.

'We'll keep you here for as long as is necessary,' his father said, eyes wild and one hand thumping the Bible. 'Repentance! That's what we'll win from you. Repentance. "*For Joy shall be in heaven over one sinner that repenteth.*" *St Luke*, Chapter 15, Verse 7.'

'Allelujah!' cried Don.

'Ach, you're as mad as he is,' Bart said in disgust. 'And if it's quotations you want, how about this one? "*Therefore shall a man leave his father and his mother, and shall cleave unto his wife, and they shall be one flesh.*"'

'Take not the Lord's name in vain!' screeched his father, brandishing his Bible. '"*Honour thy father and thy mother—*"'

Bart had had enough of this and cut his father short. 'I honour my mother greatly for staying with a bully, but I have nothing save disgust for you, father or not. I'm taking my things and leaving this house today. And I'll not be back.'

Bill took one step forward. Bart tensed.

Lemuel gave a thin, triumphant smile. 'You're taking nothing. And you're not setting one foot outside that front door till you've repented your association with the harlot. However long that takes.'

Bart fumbled behind him for the door handle, trying not to show what he was doing. Had everyone run mad today in this joyless house?

Lemuel moved towards his erring younger son, Bible outstretched. 'You'll not even leave this room until you've sworn on this Bible that you'll not see that young Gibson whore again.'

Upstairs, Prudence Burns was rocking to and fro, praying soundlessly, over and over again: Lord, save my Bart! Lord, save my little Bart! Lord, save him, save him, save him!

Bart made a sound of disgust in his throat. There was no reasoning with them. They were mad enough to try to keep their word. He'd come back with a couple of friends later, when his father and brothers were at work, to get his things. He stretched out one hand, as if to touch the Bible, but instead gave his father a sudden hard push, sending him cannoning into Bill and blocking Don's way. Quickly, Bart wrenched open the door and ran outside. He was running down the street before his brothers had reached the front door.

Upstairs on the landing, Prudence Burns let her clenched hands fall limply to her sides and sagged against the wall. He'd got away from them. Her Bartie had escaped. 'Thank you, Lord,' she whispered. 'Thank you.' She felt faintness come over her and staggered into her bedroom to sit down. She had lost her only daughter and now she had lost her Bartie, the one son who mattered. The pain of that was over-whelming, but she tried to hold back the tears. If Lemuel saw she'd been weeping for her son, he'd beat her to assuage his own anger.

Instead, she concentrated on working out what she could do to help Bartie, to help herself. And when her husband came upstairs, face deep red and fury in his every word, she stared at him in amazement before bending her head meekly. For a moment he had looked so like her father that it had shocked her. But also it had given her a reason to hope. Her father, too, had been red-faced and prone to rages. Perhaps, she thought, the Lord had listened to her prayers. She had to believe that, believe it and work towards it.

'I'll write a new will,' he said. 'I'll cut him right out of it.'

'Yes, Lemuel.'

'Get out the writing things. We'll draft it now, then I'll think about it for a day or two. Not a penny shall that ingrate have. No, not a farthing.'

Head bent, she wrote to his dictation and when she had finished and he'd snatched the paper away from her, the idea struck her with the force of a blow, so that she gasped and sat rigid for a moment.

'What's wrong with you, woman?' he demanded.

'Nothing, Lemuel, just a touch of indigestion.'

A couple of streets away from the house he had called home for the past few years, Bart heard footsteps pounding along behind him and risked a glance back over his shoulder. Bill and Don were chasing him with that look of stupid determination on their faces that said they'd not give up. For a moment his mind refused to work, then he cursed under his breath and veered off into a side street, increasing his speed. He had not expected this much trouble in getting away. His father was even crazier than he had thought, and his brothers even more stupid. What the hell was he going to do? Two against one, and two brothers as big as his, was no fair fight.

Then, as he turned again, running towards High Street now, he saw the Police Station at the end of the little side street, and with a grin ran into it. 'Want to make a complaint,' he gasped, his breath rasping in his throat. He leaned against the counter, feeling exhausted, but there wasn't time to rest. He had to voice his complaint before his brothers arrived with whatever tale they decided to dream up.

'What's the matter?' The constable behind the counter stared at him in surprise. He knew Bart Burns by sight.

'Two men,' Bart said, 'pursuing me down the street.' He decided on the truth. 'My brothers. I'm trying to leave home. They won't let me get my personal possessions and they're threatening to lock me up in the house if I won't stay.'

The constable's mouth dropped open. At that moment, Bill and Don shoved open the door and strode across to the counter.

Bill lunged for Bart and grabbed his arm. 'You bloody fool! What do you think you're doing here?'

'Get him off me, Constable!' Bart made no attempt to fight back, just clutched the counter and tried to keep his brother from pulling him away from it.

'Now, you just stop that!' the constable blustered.

But Don ignored him and joined the fray, grabbing his erring brother's other arm – only it wasn't a fray, for Bart was still making no attempt to fight back, just pleading for the police to help him.

'Let go of him!' the constable ordered, more loudly this time.

'You stay out of this!' Don growled.

The constable began to get angry. He was not used to being spoken to like that. But he looked at the two huge men holding the complainant and decided he needed help. 'Sergeant!' he yelled. 'Come quickly! There's trouble!' He ran from behind the counter and took up a strategic position near the external door as Don and Bill got Bart's hands away from the counter and tried to drag him out of the station.

Authority entered the scene in the person of Sergeant Gerald O'Noonan, Gerry to his friends, among whom the complainant numbered himself.

Bart sighed with relief. The Lord had certainly been on his side today. 'Let go of me, you two!' he yelled suddenly, and slid to the ground to stop them dragging him out. 'Help!'

'What the hell's happening here?' demanded Gerald O'Noonan.

'This fellow rushed in and made a complaint,' the constable offered, pointing to Bart. 'He said his two brothers were pursuing him and that they wouldn't let him take his possessions from their house. Then the other two arrived and tried to drag him away. He hasn't done anything that I can see. It's them as is causing the trouble.'

Bill and Don continued to ignore authority, striving to pull Bart to his feet and drag him off home.

'Get your hands off him this minute!' roared Gerald, incensed to see an affray taking place inside his station.

'He's our brother, you fool!' Bill said, making no attempt to let go of Bart. 'This is a private matter.'

'Not if a citizen comes in and makes a complaint, it isn't.' Gerald slammed one meaty fist down on the counter and roared in his parade-ground voice, 'I said, *let him go!*'

For a moment all hung in the balance, then Don let go of Bart's arm and Bill followed suit. Bart pulled himself up, moved strategically closer to the men in uniform and began to dust down his clothes.

'Now,' the sergeant reached for his incident book, 'name?'

Don, who was nearest, responded automatically to the tone of authority. 'Don Burns.'

Gerald fixed him with a gaze which had once made raw recruits in the army shiver in their shoes. 'Not you, the complainant's name.' He knew perfectly well who the complainant was, since the two of them were friends, but this was now official business, so he acted accordingly.

'My name is Bartholomew Burns and I'm here to complain about—'

When the complaint had been taken down, the sergeant turned to Bart's two brothers. 'Now your side of it, if you please?'

Don thumped the counter. 'There's nothing to tell. It's a family matter and none of your business.'

Bill saw the sergeant's face grow a shade redder and nudged his brother. 'Bart is our younger brother. He was defying our father. Just let us take him home. We can settle it ourselves.'

'That's the problem,' Bart put in quickly. 'There are three of them at home and one of me. I'm trying to move out, and they're trying to stop me. I'm twenty-six, Sergeant O'Noonan. This is England, not some savage heathen country. At my age, I have a perfect right to live where I choose. And to take my possessions with me.'

Bloody right you do, thought Gerry. And so I've been telling you for months, me boyo. Aloud he simply said to the two older brothers, who were now standing shoulder to shoulder, 'The charge would be kidnapping, then.'

Bill and Don, who were definitely not the quickest-witted of fellows, just goggled at him.

'What do you mean, charge?' Don demanded at last.

'If you deprive Mr Bartholomew Burns of his liberty, whether he's a family member or not, the charge would be kidnapping. And,' he paused to let his words sink in, before adding, 'if you drag him off forcibly now, I shall add a charge of assault.'

The two of them stared at one another and took a step backwards.

'I could withdraw my complaint,' Bart said quietly, 'if they'd let me get my things?' He winked at Gerry.

The sergeant did not respond to the wink, nor did his face show a trace of feeling. 'Very generous of you, sir.'

'He's taking nothing from the house,' Bill said, and would have left the station, except for the fact that the constable, who was considerably braver with his sergeant there, was still guarding the door.

'We'll see about that,' Sergeant O'Noonan snapped, the light of battle in his eyes. 'As duly appointed representative of the law, I shall accompany you two and the complainant to the house in question. There I shall wait while he gathers together his things. Once I'm satisfied that justice has been done, I shall remove the charge from our incident book. And not until.'

There was a pregnant pause, then Bill looked at Don and nodded. 'Best leave it to Father to deal with when we get home,' he muttered.

Don's face brightened. 'Aye.'

The small procession clumped towards Sefton Street. Bart was trying hard not to smile as he walked. The sergeant, afraid that if he caught his friend Bart's eye, his composure would crack, was studying the world around him with his usual bland official gaze, one that hid both a shrewd mind and a kindly soul. Strictly speaking, he could be said to be exceeding his authority here, but no Bilsden magistrate would reprimand him for that. Not with property involved. He knew them all and knew, too, that they trusted their sergeant's judgement.

When the group of men got to Sefton Street, their booted feet making a loud clumping sound on the cobbles, Mr Burns, who had been watching through the window, flung the door open himself. 'What—' he began.

The sergeant had always found it helpful to take the initiative in this sort of situation. He pointed to Bart. 'Is this person your son?'

'That depends on whether he's come to his senses or not.'

'I asked you a question,' roared the sergeant. 'Kindly answer it. Is he or is he not your son?'

'Well – yes.'

'And has he, until this date, resided here?'

'Yes.' Mr Burns raised one finger to point at Bart and opened his mouth. 'But—'

'I believe your son – who is twenty-six and a free citizen of Her Majesty, Queen Victoria – wishes to pack his things and leave. Are you attempting to deny him that freedom?' The sergeant's voice was penetrating.

Mr Burns looked hastily around and saw to his dismay that curtains were twitching in nearby houses and some of his neighbours were standing openly at their doors, watching. 'You'd better come inside. We'll sort this out in private.'

'Thank you, sir.'

In the parlour, Bart looked at his father and all the fear, all the years of being browbeaten, suddenly combined inside him until he could barely speak for rage. 'I don't want to talk. I just want to get my things and leave,' he snarled. 'In fact, if I never talk to this lot again, it'll be too soon.'

'If you leave, you take nothing with you,' Mr Burns said instantly. 'Everything you have, you've earned by working for me. If you leave, I'll have it all back again.'

Gerald O'Noonan held up one hand. 'Just a minute, sir, if you please. If the gentleman has earned these things by working for you, you have no right to take them back. They now belong to him.'

Upstairs, Mrs Burns bit her finger hard to prevent herself

from weeping. It was the right thing for Bart to do, but oh, she would miss him! And Lemuel would be in a rage for days.

'I'd be pleased if you'd be present when I go up to get my things, Sergeant,' Bart asked formally. 'I don't want to be accused of stealing anything.' He glared at his father. 'Because I don't intend to take a farthing, not the smallest piece of rag, that isn't mine by rights.'

Mr Burns, who had been planning to accuse his son of theft at a later date, ground his teeth audibly. If his two fools of elder sons had thought to make a counter-complaint of theft at the police station, there'd be no problem preventing Bart from removing his things now. 'I intend to be present as well, and I shall examine every single item you take with you.'

The sergeant inclined his head graciously. 'That would seem fair, sir.' He pointed to the two elder brothers. 'I think Mr Burns and I can deal with this. You two stay down here.'

They looked to their father and he nodded, because there simply wasn't room for them all in the tiny attic bedroom Bart occupied.

As she heard them coming up the stairs, Mrs Burns picked up her mending, which she often did by the window there, to catch the best of the light. She recognised the shirt she was holding as one of Bart's and let out a soft whimper of pain. Rolling it up suddenly, she thrust it under the pile to the bottom of the basket, where she kept her books. Lemuel would never think of looking into her mending basket for anything, since mending was women's work. But she must have something of his to remember Bartie by. She must. She would keep the shirt.

In silence, he packed his things, occasionally pausing to refute a claim by his father that something wasn't his. He tied his clothes up in his nightshirts for lack of a bag or case. When he could find no other way of carrying everything, he turned to his father. 'Will you give me a loan of this sheet to carry my things? It'll save us both a deal of trouble at a future date.'

'He's taking nothing that's not his!' Mr Burns said immediately, ignoring his son and addressing the sergeant. 'Nothing.'

'I'll promise faithfully to have it laundered and return it within three days,' Bart said through gritted teeth, looking at the figure of the law.

'It might be wisest to let him borrow the sheet, sir,' the sergeant said, fixing Mr Burns with a stern expression.

'I'll return it to the police station,' Bart said, 'or bring it back here, as my father pleases.'

'I am no father of yours!' Mr Burns hissed. 'Bear witness, Sergeant, that I disown this fornicating rogue, and that once he leaves, I'll not have him back in my house.' To Bart, knowing his fondness for his mother, he added, 'Very well, take the sheet. But you can return it to the police station. You're not coming back here. And you'll not see your mother again. Ever. I'll make sure of that.'

And I'll make sure I do see her, Bart thought, but said nothing, just continued to empty the contents of his drawers into the sheet.

'And I'll make sure everyone in the town knows why I've disowned you,' Lemuel Burns added out of sheer spite. 'I'll tell them all about you and that Gibson whore.'

Bart began to lose control of his temper. He was not having anything said that would damage Joanie's reputation. 'If you accuse me – or anyone else – of things we haven't done,' he said, shoving his face close to his father's, 'then I'll take legal action against you. And that would cost you a pretty penny. There's been no fornication between me and the young person concerned. None at all! She's a decent lass and I'm not having her name bandied about in town by such as you. One word – just one – and I'll go to Pennybody's and take out a writ.' He wasn't quite sure how you did that, but he would bet his father didn't understand the law of slander, either.

Lemuel Burns gabbled furiously, unable to say a coherent word for the anger that was thumping through his veins, beating like a drum at his temples. 'The Devil has possessed you,' he screeched. 'Possessed you entirely. Get you gone from this household. Get you gone!' He held the Bible up between them as if to protect himself, then suddenly started intoning the seventh Psalm.

Gerald O'Noonan rolled his eyes. The old fellow was barmy. Utterly and completely barmy. He had long suspected it. As he had long mistrusted the screaming and chanting that came from Redemption House. Sometimes, it sounded more like an orgy than a service of worship. If he had his way, he'd close that place down, for it bred only misery and bigotry – and something else, something unhealthy.

As they walked downstairs, Gerry eyed his friend with covert interest, though his face was still set in its calm, official mask. So Bartie had fallen for someone, had he? And a Gibson at that. Well, there was only one Gibson lass unwed that Gerald knew about. The youngest. He did not allow himself to smile, but felt gladness wash through him. If the relationship with the Gibson girl had led to Bart's leaving this house of doom and misery, then as his friend Gerry could only be glad – though he wouldn't tell him so until he came off duty and stopped being Sergeant O'Noonan.

'Where shall you go?' he asked quietly as they walked away from the house.

'To Stonelea Street, just to give me time to look around?' Bart looked at him questioningly. That was where Gerry lived.

The sergeant shook his head. He didn't want Lemuel Burns having any excuse to tell the captain that the two of them were in cahoots. 'No, not yet.'

'Where, then? Damned if I expected to leave home today.'

'I believe there's a widow in Church Lane who takes in lodgers. Number seventeen. Try her first. You'll want somewhere decent if you're courting.'

'Thanks.' Bart frowned. He didn't want all his mates laughing at him. Best play that down. 'But I'm not sure yet that I'm courting. We're just – just getting to know one another.'

The sergeant allowed himself one smile. 'You'd better be courting after all that fuss.'

Bart found himself smiling back and admitting to himself

for the first time that he wanted to marry Joanie Gibson. He knew Gerry approved. And so would Gerry's wife. She'd been telling Bart for a while to find himself a girl and set up his own home. The wonder of that thought made him slow down, then he picked up his stride and beamed round him. What a lovely day it was!

17

Bilsden: May to June 1861

When John Gibson went up the hill to talk to Annie about Bart Burn's request to walk out with Joanie, he surprised her so much that for a moment or two, she could only stare at him.

'One of Bible Burns's sons?' she gasped, unable to believe her ears.

'Aye. An' I'll give him the credit that he came to ask me openly.'

'One of the men who beat up Mark?'

He nodded. 'That sticks in my gullet, too. But Joanie's fair taken with him.' After another pause, he added, 'An' I have to admit I weren't so happy before, wonderin' whether she might be thinking about that Harry Pickering, so in a sense this is better than that. I don't like that Pickering fellow, I really don't. And my Kathy agrees with me.'

'I don't know much about him.'

'No, well, it seems it's Bart Burns we need to know more about, not Pickering.'

'Have you spoken to Tom?'

'Not yet. I don't want him getting involved, to tell you the truth. After what they did to Mark, he hasn't a good word for any of the Burns family. He'd not be able to see straight about this.'

'Why didn't you forbid it straight off?'

'I say it every day: "*Forgive us our trespasses, as we forgive them that trespass against us,*"' he replied quietly. 'The only time I forgot that was with our Mark, an' my action drove him away, all the way to Australia. So I've promised mysen never to make that mistake again.'

She sat fiddling with the folds of her full black skirt, not knowing what to say. She didn't like the thought of Joanie's being courted by Bart Burns any more than her father did.

'Look, love, would you have a word with Joanie? Try to talk a bit of sense into her?'

'I suppose so. But we've never been close, Dad, so I'm not sure she'll listen to me. Ask her to come and take tea with me next Saturday. I'm sure Mary will let her go from the salon early.'

And on Saturday, when Joanie came, Annie was astonished again, for her half-sister was a young woman transformed. Her face was softly lit with happiness, all the old sulkiness gone – until Annie broached the subject of Bart Burns. Then Joanie's face shadowed over and she stared angrily at her half-sister.

'I wondered why you'd invited me to tea. You never invite me just for the pleasure of my company, like you do Rebecca! Well, Bart is none of your business, Annie Hallam. Who I walk out with is my business alone.'

'It's Dad's business, too, and he's asked me to talk to you.'

'What for? You can't stop me seeing him. Neither of you can. I'm nearly twenty-one, so soon I'll be able to do as I please. Leave home if I have to.'

Annie was shaken by the animosity in Joanie's voice and not for the first time felt guilty for how close she was to Rebecca and how distant from Joanie. She knew nothing of the girl's hopes, nothing much about her. 'I wasn't trying to stop you,' she said, keeping her tone deliberately mild. 'I just wanted to find out how you felt.'

'I feel happy. For the first time, I feel really happy,' Joanie threw the words at her, but her expression was softening even as she spoke. 'No one else understands me or cares about me. But he does.' In spite of her resolve to say nothing to her sister, she could not help adding, 'He's a lovely man, Annie. Kind. And so good-looking. He's not at all like his brothers. And he hates his father. It's just his mother he cares about.

That's why he's stayed at home for so long. He says she has a rotten life.'

'Oh.' Annie could remember the one time she had met Mrs Burns, who had come to tea with her daughter Nelly because the girl was pregnant by Mark. Mrs Burns had looked faded and beaten, lost to all hope and happiness.

'And when I'm out with Bart, I feel – I feel like I could fly.' Joanie's tone changed again, becoming very determined, more like Annie's, though neither of them recognised that. 'So I'm not letting anyone stop me seeing him! No matter what you say.'

Annie smiled at her and saw how puzzled Joanie was by this. 'Then if you love him, let him court you openly and we can all get to know him. I'd be the last person to stop any girl marrying the man she loves.' Her voice faltered for a moment as she added quietly, 'I was very happy with Frederick. I do understand what it's like.'

Joanie didn't know what to say for a minute. She watched Annie wipe away a tear. 'You must miss him.' The words were out before she had time to think.

'Every minute.' Annie shook her head, blinked away her tears and asked, 'Could you use a cup of tea? I know I could.'

Joanie nodded.

As they were waiting for Winnie to bring in the tea, Annie said quietly, 'I know we haven't always been close, but I do care about your happiness, Joanie. And if Bart Burns shows that he can make you happy, then I'll be glad for you and I'll do everything I can to help you.'

For the next couple of months, all went well with Joanie and Bart. He started up his own business at the market, selling bits and pieces, all sorts of things, something like a pawnbroker, except that folk sold him the things outright. Tom got one of his men to keep an eye on the little stall, and the man reported that Bart was offering fair enough prices.

'The stall isn't bringing in much yet, but it will,' Bart assured

Joanie. 'I'm not afraid of hard work.' The trouble was, he was beginning to suspect that his father and brothers were trying to damage his fledgling business, but he didn't tell her that. And if he got one shred of proof of it, he'd put a spoke in their wheels, family or not. But as usual his father was clever in his malice. Nothing happened that you could put a finger on, but it was enough to slow things down for Bart. The odd piece knocked off the stall by a lad running past. The odd person turning up at a busy time and complaining loudly that he had not paid a fair price. Things like that.

When the weather was fine at weekends, Bart and Joanie walked out together. When it was wet, they sat in the parlour of Netherhouse Cottage, talking quietly, with the door half-open. The family grew used to his presence and he was unfailingly polite to Kathy and John, but no one made any real attempt to get to know him.

Kathy began to say that he was not as bad as she had expected. John held his peace. He, too, had heard of the trouble at the market and wanted to see how Bart dealt with it. That seemed very important. He didn't want his daughter wedding someone who resorted to violence. Not like that fellow out near Luke's. He and his son had had several chats about Gorton. Luke wanted to intervene, but John had counselled him not to. 'You can't come between a husband and wife, lad,' he'd said, 'however much you'd like to, however badly he's behaving. The law is on his side.'

'Then the law is wrong.'

'Aye, well, this isn't a perfect world, is it?'

Urged on by her brother, Joanie's friend Maddie did all she could to mock Bart Burns and break up the relationship, but Joanie wouldn't hear a word against him. And anyway, she didn't have much time to go out with Maddie now. Her thoughts were all of Bart, and secretly she'd started filling a bottom drawer, sewing pillowcases and hemming sheets, stitching all her tender young dreams into them. For the first time she was glad of her skills as a needlewoman. Kathy knew what she was doing, of course, but Joanie had her own bedroom and Kathy said nothing to the rest of the family.

One night, Annie was driving home from Tom's. He insisted on accompanying her in her carriage, saying he'd welcome a brisk walk home afterwards. Really, he wanted to talk to her in private about Joanie.

'What do you think of that fellow Bart?' he asked.

'I don't know him. But he seems to be making Joanie happy, that's for sure.' None of them had ever seen the girl so lit up by happiness. She seemed to be blossoming daily, growing prettier. And when Annie had offered to buy her a new summer dress, instead of making some sarcastic remark, Joanie had accepted with a blush and confided that she could do with a new dress for best.

'Aye. An' he seems to be running that stall of his fairly, too,' Tom admitted. 'But I just can't like the thought of being connected to the Burns family.'

'Nor can I.'

'The old fellow is a usurer, you know,' Tom added. 'Bart used to collect the payments for him. He didn't push folk too hard, but now Don's taken over, there are tales of beatings and threats. I had a word with O'Noonan the other day. He's keeping an eye on things. Trouble is, according to Mr Burns, he's just helping his fellow beings in distress, and the money lending is not really a part of his business. Bloody hypocrite!'

Suddenly, Robert the coachman exclaimed loudly and reined in the horses, shouting, 'Mr Gibson! Mr Gibson! Come quickly!' Tom was out of the door before the carriage had even jerked to a halt and he, too, exclaimed and then shouted, 'Stop that!' Together with the gardener's lad, who always came with Robert when the ageing coachman took the carriage out at night, Tom ran towards the figure struggling against several attackers.

Annie poked her head out of the window, then grabbed the umbrella that was kept in the carriage and followed her brother, ready to protect herself if necessary. There wasn't much crime in Bilsden, but just occasionally thugs seemed to drift in from Manchester or other towns to try their luck.

The tangle was a group of men beating a figure who had just been felled from behind and was lying on the ground, groaning. As Tom ran towards them, a voice called, 'Come away!' and they backed off. One of them ran towards Annie and would have bowled her over if she had not stabbed out at him with her umbrella. He yelled and raised one fist, but Robert flicked his whip and caught the man a glancing blow.

The same voice yelled, 'Come away, I said!' and the men ran off into the darkness, for here near the top of Ridge Hill, the houses were far apart and there were no street lamps.

'Annie, he's hurt badly!' Tom shouted, and she hurried to where he stood over a groaning figure.

'We can't do anything here. Let's lift him into the carriage. Sim, you take his feet and I'll take his head. Annie, can you hold the carriage door open?'

Together, Tom and the gardener's lad carried the man towards the carriage. By the light of its lanterns, Annie could see that his face was badly beaten and covered with blood.

It was Tom who recognised him. 'Hell, talk of the devil! This is Bart Burns.'

'Oh, no!' Something clicked in Annie's memory, from a time she had seen another man who had been beaten mercilessly, her brother Mark. 'I thought I recognised the voice that called them off. It was one of the Burns brothers, I'm sure. Oh, Tom! His own brothers beating him up. How dreadful!' As she spoke, she was putting a cushion under Bart's head and wiping his poor bloodied face with her handkerchief. He was moaning faintly, nearly unconscious but not quite. 'Lie still. We have you safe,' she said and he quietened down. 'Tell Robert to drive slowly,' she whispered to Tom.

'When does he ever do anything else?'

At Ridge House, Tom and Sim carried the injured man inside and Annie sent a goggling Winnie scurrying to fill a hot-water pig. 'We'll put him in one of the spare bedrooms,' she decided.

While she was overseeing this, Tom took the carriage and went to fetch the doctor.

When Jeremy opened the door in his dressing gown, Tom grinned. 'We've got an injured man up at Ridge House. I think our Annie will only trust you to see to him.'

'Who is it? How was he injured?'

'It's Bart Burns, and I think it's his brothers and a few of their friends who have just beaten him senseless – though it'd be hard to prove, it being so dark. Dammit, why wasn't it a full moon tonight? We'd have been able to see what was happening then.' But Tom knew why it hadn't happened on a moonlit night. Cowards like to sneak up on folk in the darkness.

Another question, which had been hovering at the back of his mind, surfaced as he waited for the doctor. 'What the hell was the fellow doing near the top of Ridge Hill at this hour, anyway?'

Jeremy came running downstairs, dressed anyhow, his hair still ruffled. 'Let's go, then.'

'I've got Annie's carriage outside for you.' Tom led the way.

When they got to Ridge House, they found Bart conscious but in great pain. Jeremy examined him gently, with Tom standing by. 'Well, I think you'll live to see another day,' he said quietly, 'but I'd like you to rest for a while. You're concussed.'

Tom leaned forward. 'How did it happen? Who attacked you?'

Bart's lips closed firmly. 'I don't know. I didn't recognise them.'

Tom opened his mouth to tell him he was lying, but Jeremy laid one hand on his arm and shook his head warningly, so Tom left the invalid to sleep, with Jimson listening to Jeremy's instructions as to how to tend him.

Annie had kept the old valet on after Frederick died and Jimson now made himself useful as and when he could. He had aged a lot, but seemed happy to be given the task of watching the invalid.

'That old fellow needs pensioning off,' Tom said to Annie as he followed her downstairs.

'It'd kill him if I did that. He likes to make himself useful. And,' she smiled slightly, 'everyone on the staff conspires to need his help. I can't think what we'd do without him.'

'Ach, you're a soft touch,' he mocked.

'Why not? I can afford to be.' Then her smile faded. 'What are we going to do? Call the police out?'

Tom shook his head. 'We'll see what the patient says about it in the morning first. It's my belief he's going to pretend he doesn't know who attacked him.'

'And get his revenge privately?'

Tom's face was grim. 'I hope not. I don't want our Joanie mixed up with a family feud.'

Jeremy came down to join them, but refused to join Tom in a brandy. 'Keep Burns quiet for a day or two and he'll mend on his own. Is it all right if he stays here?'

She snorted in amusement. 'Did you need to ask me that?'

'Not really.' He took her hand. 'Annie, I'd just like to say again how very much I admire what you're doing to help the poorer folk.'

She shrugged off his compliments. 'I'm only doing as Frederick would have wanted.'

'I think you're doing a great deal more than that, my dear.'

When Bart woke up in the morning, he groaned and cursed as he tried to sit up. He seemed to ache all over and someone with a hammer was beating his head.

'You should lie still, sir, you really should,' a voice said to his right.

Bart looked round and saw an old fellow sitting next to the bed. He was very scrawny, with a faded yellowish look to him. 'Who are you?'

The man leaned forward to lay one hand on Bart's forehead. 'My name's Jimson, sir. I used to be Mr Frederick Hallam's valet, but now I like to consider myself a general factotum to Mrs Hallam.'

Bart closed his eyes. 'What the hell's a "general factotum"?' he demanded.

'Someone who helps as and when he can. I've been sitting with you during the night. We were afraid you might have been restless and hurt yourself. But you slept rather soundly, if I might say so.' Jimson beamed down at him in a fatherly manner.

'I need to piss,' Bart said, suddenly conscious of a great need that transcended everything else for the moment.

'Would you like me to help you to the bathroom? Or would you prefer me to fetch you a chamber pot?'

Bart grunted in his throat. He wasn't a baby to need a pot. 'Bathroom. And quickly.'

Jimson hurried to fetch a dressing gown and then helped Bart along the corridor to an elegantly appointed bathroom, like nothing he had ever seen before. It seemed a shame to pee on the flowered porcelain of the lavatory, but this was obviously the place.

When he had finished, Bart spent a minute fingering the appointments: shining brass taps, sink in flowered porcelain to match the lavatory, huge white bathtub with running water. Now that was luxury, he thought, staring at it. A bath you didn't need to carry water to, or empty, jugful by jugful, once you'd finished. Then he realised what Jimson had said. *Hallam.* Was he in Ridge House, then? How the hell had he got here? He leaned against the wall, groaning as his head thumped.

Jimson opened the door and peered inside. 'Are you all right, sir? I'm sorry to intrude, but I was afraid you might be feeling ill.'

Bart stared at his own bruised, puffy face in a mahogany-framed mirror on one wall. 'Am I at Ridge House?'

'You are, indeed, sir.'

'How the – how did I get here?'

'I believe you were set upon last night. Mrs Hallam and her brother, Mr Gibson, happened to be driving past during the attack and drove off the villains. You were lucky, sir. You could have been hurt very badly if they had not seen what was happening.' He didn't say 'killed' but they both knew that was what he meant.

'I'm trying to remember what happened,' Bart said slowly, as Jimson helped him back along to the bedroom.

'I think you should just lie down and rest, sir, give yourself a chance to recover. Dr Lewis said you should stay in bed today until he had seen you. But perhaps later you'd like a nice, hot bath?'

Bart gave a twisted smile. 'Called in the doctor, too, did they? Kind of them.'

'Mrs Hallam is always kind,' Jimson said simply.

Bart stared at him. Yes, the old fellow really meant it. Bart's father always said the Gibsons were a nasty bunch, who had made their money by taking advantage of folk, but Bart had seen nothing to prove that. Joanie's father and step-mother were still a bit suspicious of him, but they'd made him welcome enough. As had Luke. He was sorry now about thumping Mark. He'd been angry about his sister, but even then he'd thought that Don and Bill had gone a bit too far. And now, here he was, in the enemy's main citadel. Only perhaps she wasn't an enemy after all. Or, at least, not his enemy.

'Shall I send for some breakfast, sir?' Jimson asked, wringing out a cloth and putting it on Bart's forehead without being asked.

It felt so blessedly cool that he sighed with relief. 'That helps,' he admitted, and was surprised to see Jimson's face light up. General factotum! he thought. I bet she's just keeping him on out of sheer kindness. She won't need a valet with her husband dead. No wonder folk spoke so well of her in the town. Most folk, anyway. 'I could eat a horse,' he admitted, suddenly realising what Jimson had asked. He was finding it hard to concentrate.

'Then I'll make sure Cook sends up a nice tray of food for you. I won't be long.' Jimson bustled out.

Bart lay there, staring at the room. Luxury, sheer luxury. A big square of patterned carpet, velvet curtains, a sofa upholstered in the same velvet, gleaming mahogany furniture – it must be wonderful to live like this. But Annie Hallam hadn't got all this by cheating and over-charging, like his father did. She'd got it all quite honestly, if the tales were true. And when so many people spoke well of someone, you had to believe them.

Bart ate hugely, then lay back. Ridge House. He was safe here, right in the middle of the Gibson family empire. His family wouldn't be able to touch him.

'I think you should try to sleep now, sir,' Jimson said softly, straightening the covers and tiptoeing out.

But Bart couldn't sleep. He lay there in the big soft bed and one thought chased another round his brain. Suddenly, he wanted desperately to be like these people. He wished his name wasn't Burns. And how a girl like Joanie could love him, he didn't know, but he loved her, too, and wanted to marry her. Only he had to find some way of supporting her. And it had to be honest. That seemed very important, if he was to be respected by these Gibsons.

Just before noon, Dr Lewis called, examined Bart, congratulated him on the toughness of his skull and gave him permission to get up. 'But take things easy for a day or two, eh?'

Jimson came back to help, carrying Bart's clothes, all freshly laundered and mended.

Bart looked back as he left the bedroom. I'll have one like it one day, he thought. For Joanie. And I'll earn it honestly.

As he went down the stairs, a fat woman with frizzy hair came bustling out of a door at the back of the hall. 'Mrs Hallam wants to see you,' she announced. The tone of her voice and the look she gave Bart said she considered him a creature of no importance, so he stared right back at her and she took a step to one side.

'Well, I'd like to see Mrs Hallam, too,' he said, when he was sure the fat woman wasn't going to speak to him like that again. 'I'd no intention of leaving without thanking her.'

'Oh. Well. Yes.' Winnie felt flustered. Mr Burns was so large and powerful-looking. And he had terrible bruises on his face. He was walking a bit stiffly, too. 'If you'll come this way, sir.'

She would never know how much he treasured that 'sir', accorded to him, Bart Burns, by a servant of the rich.

She opened one of a pair of double doors and showed him inside. 'Mr Burns, ma'am.'

He turned to look at her, holding the door for him, as if he couldn't do it himself. 'Thank you.'

Winnie walked away, mouth pursed, thinking, Well, he might be a Burns, but at least he has a few manners.

Inside the library, Annie looked up. 'Do come and sit down, Mr Burns. You look terrible. Are you sure you're fit to be up?'

'Yes, I'm fine, thank you.'

She smiled and indicated a chair. 'You don't look fine.'

He took the chair, studying her. She was beautiful, with pale, delicate skin and that glory of auburn hair, with just a touch of silver at the temples. But he was glad his Joanie didn't take after her eldest sister. He didn't think he could live with such a beautiful woman. His father said this one had married Hallam for his money and had been happy to see him die, but the time or two Bart had seen her, she'd looked sad, as if she really mourned her husband.

'Well, I have felt better,' he admitted. 'And I've looked better, too.'

'Do you know who those men were?'

He shrugged.

'The voice that called them off sounded to me like one of your brothers. I met them when they beat up my brother. They seem to make rather a habit of using violence.'

He sighed and eased himself a little to accommodate a big bruise on his arse. Someone must have put the boot in. 'Aye. It was probably them.'

'What are you going to do to protect yourself in future?'

He shrugged again. 'Keep my eyes open. Avoid dark alleys.' But they'd not stop hounding him, he knew that. So he'd have to think of some way to keep them off. He had been considering moving to another town, perhaps Bolton or Bury. His mother had relatives in Bury. But Joanie said she didn't want to leave her family.

'Do you intend to – to try to get back at them, to attack them in your turn?' asked Annie.

He looked at her in surprise. What a funny question! Then he shook his head. 'No. I've done with that sort of behaviour. How my father's got away with it for so long, I'll never know.' He looked her straight in the eye. 'I want to make a decent life for myself and Joanie.'

'You've asked her to marry you?'

'Not yet. But I will. And she'll say yes, too.' He looked down at his hands, big lumpy hands with bruised knuckles. 'I do love your sister, Mrs Hallam. Very much.' Annie's smile made him blink.

'I can tell that. I've never seen her so happy in all her life.'

He relaxed a little. 'I used to watch her and wonder why she was so unhappy. She always looked lost. I think that's what drew me to her. I felt lost sometimes, too, at odds with my family.'

Annie took a sudden decision. 'I've been making enquiries about you, Mr Burns.'

He stiffened. 'Oh?'

'Yes, For Joanie's sake. I care very much about my family.'

He scowled. 'And what did your enquiries show?'

'That you're trying to earn an honest living in the markets. And that someone is trying to stop you.'

'Ah.'

'Your family again?'

He nodded.

'Tom and I were talking about it all after we brought you back last night. He says you're having trouble at the market stall.'

'Mmm.'

'So we wondered if you'd like to come and work for us in the junk yard instead?'

Bart gaped at her. 'Me? At the junk yard?' Then the scowl came back. 'I don't want your charity, thank you. I'm—'

She held up one hand. 'It's not charity. Let me explain. My father runs the yard. We had expected one of my brothers to take over there eventually, but all have found other ways of earning their living. We have good employees, but we're concerned, Tom and I, that Dad works too hard managing everything. He is getting on, after all. He's fine now, but he won't always be. And the yard earns good money for the family. It could continue to earn good money. So if you were to try it, and find that you liked the work, then it could solve a problem for us, as well as for you, if you gradually took over.'

He couldn't believe what he was hearing. 'You'd do that for me?'

'For Joanie. And, most important of all, for my father. But,' her eyes stabbed him like spears, 'we'll expect you to work hard and honestly. If not, we shan't keep you on, believe me. Not even for Joanie's sake.'

Bart blinked. She was behaving more like a man, and a strong man at that. Words came into his mind, words to describe her. Steely-eyed. Determined. No wonder she'd done so well for herself.

'Well?' she prompted.

Bart could not speak for the huge lump that had come into his throat, for he had just realised what she had offered him. A future. A wonderful future. He could only look at her and try to blink the sudden tears away from his eyes. 'And if my father gets up to any more dirty tricks?'

'Then we'll have to do something about him. But understand,' her gaze was level and confident, 'we run a totally honest business. No tricks, no violence.'

'It sounds like paradise to me,' he said gruffly and was glad when she got up to fetch something from the desk, for it gave him time to rub the tears from his eyes. Now he could do something that would make Joanie proud of him. And – he gave a little nod as he stared across the room at that slender upright back – this woman, too, the one who was giving him this chance. He'd make them all proud of him, glad to have him in the family.

A sudden grin creased his face. And how his father would hate it!

18

New York: June 1861

Two weeks later, as Tian dismounted from his horse, there was a hiss behind him. He turned, to see Igor Dalowski, dressed in shabby clothes, lounging near the gate.

'Come out to the stables at midnight,' Igor whispered, then said loudly enough to be heard by everyone in the camp, 'Would you be Mr Tian Gilchrist, by any chance?'

Tian nodded, hearing footsteps behind him. They were being unusually watchful of him at this camp. Captain Greeshall's warning, no doubt.

'I have a letter for you, sir,' Igor went on, still in the same loud voice. 'From Mr Brownsby of New York.'

A hand descended on Tian's shoulder. 'I'll take that.' His new commanding officer, Captain Formbin, moved him aside and reached for the letter.

Igor's expression was the epitome of stupidity. 'But the letter's for Mr Gilchrist. I was paid to bring it to him personally.'

'And he shall have it, as soon as I've read it. That's how we do things in the army, fellow. Return to your quarters, Gilchrist. And you, be on your way!'

Tian saluted and strode away. Was the letter just to fool people, or had Thaddeus really written down his escape plans? Surely not! All the time he was getting ready for the evening meal, Tian fretted and worried, expecting to receive a summons from the captain.

After the evening meal was over, Formbin signalled to him to stay behind and handed over the letter. 'Sorry. Don't like to read another fellow's mail. But Captain Greeshall told me about the circumstances of your enlistment and one has to be a bit careful. Tough break, eh?'

'Yes, sir.'

'You're doing well, though. Might be a new chance for you, eh, forget all that arty stuff?'

'Yes, sir. Thank you, sir.' Tian saluted and walked briskly away, seething inside at this casual dismissal of his talent, but hoping his feelings didn't show on his face.

When he was on his own, he read the letter and relief coursed through him. Thaddeus merely said that he had exhausted all avenues of appeal and that he deeply regretted his daughter's behaviour. He would, he assured Tian, be pleased to send him money to supplement his army pay for as long as the war lasted, and to receive him in his own home in New York any time Tian could get leave. The missive ended with pious sentiments about the need to defeat the rebels and a hope that he would do his part for the country which had welcomed him so warmly.

He laughed softly as he finished reading it. Thank you, Thaddeus, he thought. I know what you were trying to do. But this letter won't stop them keeping an eye on me. Their suspicions have been roused and a few words won't change their minds. So if I do decide to go on with the escape, it'll be hard to get away from them.

Now all he had to decide before he went to meet Igor was whether he really wanted to risk his life trying to escape. He had made one or two friends in the army. The life an officer led was not nearly so hard as that of an enlisted man. But – he sighed aloud at the thought – Annie was waiting to hear from him, Annie, who was free now, free to be wooed. Only, he had to get to her as soon as he could, and hope that some other fellow didn't come along and start wooing her in the meantime. A woman so beautiful would not be long without admirers once her period of mourning had passed.

He let out a long sigh. He was inclined to take the chance and try to escape. Could he trust Thaddeus to plan things well enough? Dare he trust him? Round and round went the thoughts in Tian's mind. It was one thing to get free of the Union Army by legal procedures, quite another to desert and risk being shot.

In the end, he laughed softly. What the hell? Faint heart never won fair lady.

'Shut up!' someone muttered.

Tian faked a small groan. 'Guts are bad tonight. Must have eaten something.'

'Then go and void yourself. Don't just lie there keeping others awake. You've been tossing and turning for hours.'

'Mmm. I think I'll have to.' Tian made his way quietly down the hallway to the small room with the large, noisome bucket that was the best the army could provide for the officers in this camp – although it was emptied twice a day, at least – and there he stood for a moment, working out his best route. He jammed a piece of wood under the door, pulled the lid down over the receptacle and climbed on top of it to stare out. Suddenly, he chuckled. His escape route had been staring him in the face, for this was the only place in the whole camp in which he was allowed to be alone.

Using his pocket knife, he pried open one corner of the shoddy frame, occasionally pausing to groan, as if his guts were in torment.

'You all right?' someone called through the door.

'I think it's easing now,' he called back. 'Are you wanting to go yourself? I think I could come out for a minute, as long as you're quick.'

'No. I'm fine. It's just that the captain told me to keep an eye on you.'

Rage coursed through Tian. Not even here would they let him be! He didn't let anger overpower his caution, though. 'You can come in and watch if you're that keen!' he called, managing by a huge effort to keep a cheerful tone in his voice.

'Nope. I'll just wait around for you out here.'

'Ah, hell! That's a bit embarrassing.'

'I'll go to the end of the corridor if you're so shy!' The man chuckled. 'After all, there's no other way out of here. And you'll grow out of your shyness when you've been in the army as long as I have. There ain't nothing you can do that I haven't done, too, believe me.'

Tian stood there, listening to the footsteps move along the corridor. 'Damn!' he said softly. Then he turned and tugged at the window frame. If it didn't come free, he was lost. If the watcher realised what he was doing, he was also lost. And he was already late for his midnight appointment.

But suddenly, the rest of the window frame came away in his hand. Ill-fitting and badly attached, it just fell out of its aperture and in his surprise, he nearly dropped it. Then he stood there on the lidded bucket, clutching it to his chest and grinning as the fresh air blew in to replace the unpleasant fumes. 'Well, that's a sign if ever there was one,' he whispered. 'Into Thy hands, O Lord!' He laid the frame down quietly, shuffled his feet and groaned again, then stepped back up on to the bucket lid as quietly as he could.

There was one terrible moment when he thought he was stuck in the small opening left by the window in the wall of rough planks, but then, with a last desperate wriggle, he tumbled to the ground. He lay there for a moment, sure that someone must have heard the noise he made, but no footsteps came running, no voices called out.

He let out a long shaky breath of relief and got to his feet. He'd banged his elbow and it hurt to move his arm. He was only partly dressed and his trousers were slipping down. But he'd taken the first step towards freedom and the thought was sweet. Fastening his braces, he crept around the edges of the drill area.

When he reached the stables, he went even more cautiously. There was only one person he wanted to see here. As he hesitated near the door, a dark figure stepped out of the shadows and Tian drew in his breath in a hiss of alarm. It was so dark in here that you could only make out shapes.

But it was Igor. He came forward with a shaded lantern

which he used to show his face and also to check that the newcomer was indeed the man he was waiting for.

Tian let out his breath again, relief shuddering through him, and sagged against the nearest stall for a moment.

'You're late!' Igor hissed.

'I had the devil of a job getting out. And they won't be long coming after me. They've been watching me night and day since I got here. So how the hell do you plan to get us out of here?'

'I've made a hole in the wall at the back of the stables. I never saw such shoddy work as these buildings. You'd think the war was only going to last a couple of months.'

'That's what they're all telling one another.'

'Well, I reckon it'll go on for a year or two, at least.' As he spoke, Igor was guiding Tian forward through the darkness until they came to the hole he'd made. 'You'll have to crawl through. I didn't dare make it any bigger. But it backs on to the street, so once we're out we can run for our lives.'

You never spoke a truer word, Tian thought. Igor gave no further explanations, just got on to his hands and knees, whispered, 'Follow me!' and crawled away into the darkness.

Tian was after him so quickly that he nearly bumped his face on Igor's heels. When they were through, Igor hissed, 'Shh!' and walked off along the street. Tian could do nothing but follow him. His spine was prickling with apprehension, he was sure they would be pursued, sure he would be caught and shot, but it was too late now to do anything but give it his best, so the fear had gone, leaving only an enormous sensitivity to every sight and sound around him.

In his mind, he repeated her name over and over again like a litany and it comforted him greatly. Annie, Annie, Annie, Annie.

At the end of the street, Igor disappeared down a dark, narrow alley and Tian followed, stumbling on the uneven surface. There was the sound of horses moving their feet restlessly. A figure stepped forward and Igor murmured something.

Coins chinked, footsteps walked away and then Igor hissed at Tian, 'Get up on the horse, you idiot! What are you waiting for?' He had already mounted.

The two men walked the horses quietly out of town, then Igor said curtly, 'Now, gallop for your fool life!'

Afterwards, Tian could never clearly remember that night. It seemed almost as if he and the horse flew through the darkness together, with Igor and the other horse making a vague shape in front of him that never really came into focus. They passed farms, peaceful in the fitful moonlight, fields with the dark shapes of sleeping cattle clumped in corners, woods where only providence preserved them from over-hanging branches, small towns where no light showed and an occasional dog barked. But none of it seemed real. All Tian cared about was that the horses should press forward, that the hooves should pound the road and that the sweating animals should eat up the miles that still lay between him and freedom.

Gradually, inevitably, the horses tired and their pace slackened.

They slowed down to a walk to rest the animals. 'I've got a change of horses waiting a couple of miles down the road from here,' Igor said in a low voice. 'I've made a trial run or two to see what was needed.'

'Good.'

Another dark figure was waiting at a crossroads with fresh horses. More coins changed hands, and the two men were off again.

'Sure, you certainly know how to ride, for a townie!' Tian called as they left another hamlet behind them.

'Let's see if I know how to plan an escape!' Igor threw back at him. 'I've a lot of money waiting for me if I succeed, not to mention the hand of Miss Lyn Brownsby.'

'Hah! You're welcome to that hellcat.'

Igor's teeth gleamed in the moonlight. 'Oh, I've fancied her for a year or two, fancied being a member of the family, too.

And I think she'll find me a little less easy to fool than her father.'

Dawn was just breaking as they rode into New York.

'I think we've the hardest part yet to come,' Igor admitted as Tian beamed at him in the pale light of early dawn. 'They're hell on deserters. They'll have telegraphed ahead. They'll be searching for you.'

'Well, I'm sure you've planned for that, too.'

'I have. I've found a place where you can lie low for years if necessary, but it's getting you on to a boat that's the risky part, and I'm not sure whether we shouldn't wait for a while.'

'No!' Tian realised his voice was too sharp and made an effort to speak more moderately. 'I want to leave as soon as possible.'

Igor grimaced. 'Yes. I thought you'd say that. You're eager to get back to her, aren't you?'

'Very.'

'You'll not be going back home with a good opinion of New York.'

'It was good in parts,' Tian said. But at the moment, he felt he never wanted to see the place again.

'Keep quiet now! We're here.'

Igor handed the horses to yet another man who stood waiting behind a fence and who led the two animals away without speaking a word, then Igor led his companion through a series of alleys and narrow streets until Tian had lost all sense of direction. Labourers were stirring, women tossing dirty water out of their front doors, snotty-nosed children playing in the dirt, but no one gave two dusty, sweat-stained men more than half a glance.

Finally, Igor led them through a narrow ginnel between two buildings and lifted a wooden cellar cover. 'In here.'

Tian ran lightly down some rough wooden steps which had bands of wood laid to each side to roll barrels down, and found himself in a cellar full of ale. He wrinkled his nose at the overpowering smell.

Igor grinned at him. 'Perfume not to your liking?'

'Not much. But I'm not complaining.'

'We've managed the first part all right, anyway.'

Tian held out his hand. 'Thank you. I'm greatly in your debt.'

Igor shrugged, but took his hand. 'It was to both our advantage. Now, come and let me show you your hiding place.' He led the way to the back of the cellar, where a narrow space had been made behind a row of barrels. There was a blanket, a bucket, what looked like a bottle of water and something wrapped in a cloth. 'Stay out of sight if you value your life, my friend. I'll be back this evening to take you to the ship.'

'I'm sailing tonight? I thought we'd be waiting a few days.' Tian did not wish to seem ungrateful, but it was going to be risky. Very risky.

'Well, we can delay things if you like. But there's a ship with a co-operative captain sailing tonight and heaven alone knows when the next one will be going to England.'

'Ah. I see.' He'd been shut away so long that he'd forgotten that the war would be affecting all the normal services.

'Well?' Igor cocked one eyebrow at him in the dimness of the cellar. 'It's your choice, my friend. If you want to wait . . .'

'Hell, no! We'll go with it.' Surely, surely nothing could go wrong at this late stage? Why would the army put a huge effort into catching one deserter when they had a war to fight?

Igor nodded. 'Must go now. I have to be at work, looking smart and well rested. What's the betting they come and check out all Brownsby's haunts?'

'Not worth betting. If they're hunting for me, those will be the first places to check in New York. He came to see me at the camp, after all.'

'Mmm. It had upset him, Lyn tricking you like that. He wasn't himself for days when he found out. He prides himself on his loyalty to his friends. And,' Igor hesitated, then admitted, 'Thaddeus hasn't been well lately.'

'He's all right?'

'Oh, I daresay he'll survive a few years longer, but he's aged a lot these past few weeks.'

Tian was puzzled. 'Worrying about me?'

Igor chuckled. 'No. Worrying about his investments. There is a war on, you know.'

Even before it grew dark the next night, Igor came for Tian. Again, he was dressed like a labourer and since he was a big man, looked the part. He brought some similar garments for Tian and waited impatiently for him to change, then said, 'We'll go out the same way as we came in.'

'Aren't you going to tell me what you're planning?'

Igor grinned. 'I'm planning for you to earn your way on to the ship. You'll be helping load the passengers' luggage. We'll get you on board at the last minute and I've bribed the First Mate to let you hide in his quarters until the boat leaves. Then you can go to your cabin and change back into your own clothes and become a first-class passenger. Your things have been on board for two days now. Oh, and by the way, your name is now Fergus Downing. You're a married man and your wife is waiting for you on the ship.'

'Wife!'

'Aye. A lady friend of mine happens to want to go back to England. And it suits me to have her leave, now that I'm about to marry. She'll be your cover.' Igor grinned. 'She'll have to share your cabin, but she's a cosy armful, so that should be no hardship.'

Tian was amazed at the scope of his friend's planning. But with so many people involved, so many stages to go through, many things could still go wrong. It had gone well so far. He prayed that their luck would hold.

At first, it seemed as if Igor's plans had worked perfectly. When they got to the docks, he handed Tian over to a taciturn giant with an Irish accent. 'You can trust Dan, here, with your life.'

Tian nodded.

Dan counted out the money Igor handed him and then nodded.

'There'll be as much again, mind, once I've received a letter from my friend to say he's arrived safely in England,' Igor said softly.

Dan nodded again. He looked at Tian and felt his muscles, nodding in satisfaction. 'He'll do.'

For nearly an hour, Tian humped boxes from here to there, and from there to somewhere else, under Dan's curt orders. If this had happened while he was still just a painter, he'd have had a struggle to keep up, because the boxes were heavy. But the stint in the army had built up his muscles and he found the work needed only a reasonable effort on his part.

When most of the piles of luggage had vanished, Dan's hand on Tian's shoulder pulled him away from the others. 'You can help me take the last lot of stuff on to the ship. This way.'

As he walked up the baggage gangway, loaded like a pack mule, Tian's heart felt light and easy. He stopped to stare back at New York, but a shove from behind made him stumble forward again.

'Watch what you're doing, you fool!' Dan grumbled. 'Do you want to drop that luggage in the harbour? I'll have your guts for garters if you stop again.'

At the top, Tian deposited his load in the same place as Dan did and joy surged through him. He'd done it! He'd escaped.

Then, just as he was turning to leave the deck, a man stepped out of the shadows with a gun in his hand.

'Too bad, Gilchrist. You almost made it!' Captain Greeshall gave his skeleton's grin. 'I knew you'd try to escape. Had a bet on it with Formbin. But I'm almost sorry to catch you. You don't deserve to face a firing squad.' He nodded to someone over to his right.

As the captain's attention wavered for just a few seconds, Tian acted. He didn't wait for anyone to come and take hold of him. Better death now than imprisonment and execution.

In one swift movement he turned round and flung himself over the side of the ship.

His body whistled down towards the murky waters and he held his nose, as he had done in his boyhood when he and his brothers went to swim in the river. He had been a good swimmer then. Pray heavens, he hadn't forgotten his skills.

What he hadn't counted on was the debris floating in the water. He could see the plank as he fell towards it, slowly it seemed, so slowly. But he could do nothing to avoid it. He felt pain as his head hit it, then nothing more as blackness swallowed him.

Captain Greeshall stood at the rail and cursed, then yelled orders to the men he had stationed below. They ran forward through the patches of yellow thrown by the dockside lights to peer into the water. Bubbles rose. More bubbles. But no body. And then the bubbles stopped.

'He could be fooling,' Captain Greeshall called out. 'Don't move from your posts and don't take your eyes off that water till I tell you!'

But no body surfaced and as the ship slowly pulled away from the docks, Captain Greeshall gave it an ironical salute. 'Well, Tian Gilchrist, you're either dead or you've escaped. And either way, you're no business of mine any more.' But just in case, he left men stationed at the docks for the next two days.

19

Bilsden: July 1861

Annie was worried. Not just about one thing, but several. It had been that sort of year, and the general situation wasn't improving as the months wore on. Today, however, she tried to push aside her worries and concentrate on her appearance, nodding approval of the lilac day dress as she looked at herself in the mirror. Five flounces edged in black lace ran round the bottom of the huge skirt from knee to hem, and the pagoda sleeves were edged with two similar flounces over *engageantes* of silk muslin.

Frederick would have laughed and said it was ridiculous to wear such a huge skirt, and it was – but still, it was very pretty, even though these enormous pyramid skirts were difficult to manage sometimes. It was a relief, she decided, nodding again at her reflection, to be out of mourning, for wearing black seemed to depress your spirits, somehow. She was still wearing only quiet colours, of course, but it was a year now since Frederick's death, so it would not be thought strange if she put off full mourning.

The things we do for appearance's sake, she marvelled. As if the colour you wear makes any difference to the grief you feel when you lose someone! Adjusting her lace cap, she thanked her maid and left Rose to tidy up the dressing room. She was a competent worker, but Annie hadn't got as close to her as she had to her former maid, Laura. Well, this year she'd had too many other things on her mind to get close to anyone.

It wasn't quite time for breakfast, so she walked over to the window for a moment and stood looking down at the lake and the masses of flowers in the beds around it. Such a beautiful display! Nat Jervis had excelled himself. She must remember to tell him so.

But the garden only distracted her for a moment and her thoughts turned inevitably back to her problems. She tapped impatiently on the windowsill and frowned. Jonas Pennybody had contacted her the previous day to ask whether she'd heard from Mr Gilchrist. She hadn't. Tian's one letter had come from America and had said that he'd be here by now. So why hadn't he turned up? Neither she nor Jonas had heard from him to explain the delay and that seemed so unlike the considerate, innately cour teous Tian Gilchrist that it was beginning to worry her. As if she hadn't enough to worry about without that!

She turned and began to pace up and down the bedroom. Perhaps he had changed his mind about painting her portrait. Perhaps he wasn't coming. No. She stopped and shook her head. Every time she tried to contemplate that possibility, something inside her said that he wouldn't change his mind, he would come and do the portrait, as he'd promised.

And she wanted him to come. It had become very important to her to fulfil Frederick's last wish. She had grown used to life without him now – well, more or less used to it. She missed his companionship most and always would, she supposed. But she would not feel easy until she had had the portrait painted, as he had wanted. She owed him that. He had done so much for her.

The gong sounded from the hall. Annie pulled her thoughts back to the day ahead and went down to breakfast. 'Good morning, everyone!' The sight of her family cheered her up and she smiled at her children and their governess. She had felt much closer to Tamsin and Edgar since Frederick died. People were right, your children were a comfort to you. Footsteps ran down the stairs and there was a break in the sound as the person jumped the last two steps.

'That's William.' Tamsin giggled. 'He always jumps down the last bit.'

William came in, beaming round at his family. He absolutely

radiated happiness nowadays, a man fulfilled, a man doing the work he wanted to. 'What a lovely day it is!' he said by way of a greeting.

There was a chorus of agreement, then silence for a while as they all addressed their food. All the family at Ridge House had hearty appetites. No fussy eaters here.

'Perhaps we'll hear from Tian today,' Edgar said, as he worked his way through a plateful of food.

That boy's growing again, Annie thought to herself. He'll be needing some new clothes soon. 'Mmm.' She deliberately made no further comment on his remark. But she might have known that he'd not be satisfied with that.

'Do you think we'll hear from Tian today, Mother?' he repeated.

'How should I know? Get on with your breakfast, do!'

'But he said he'd be here in June or July and it's nearly the end of July and he still hasn't come.'

Annie chewed her way through a forkful of ham that suddenly seemed dry and tasteless. The children didn't make things any easier, asking her nearly every day when Tian was coming, wondering if they'd hear from him that week, or whether he'd just turn up. She was amazed at how eager they were to see him after such a short acquaintance.

'I think he'll just appear one day,' Tamsin said, voicing her usual opinion as she waved a forkful of food around.

'You'll drop it!' Annie warned.

No one paid any attention.

'Well, I think he'll write first,' Edgar retorted.

'He might not be able to.'

'Of course he will. He's coming so far that he'll have to plan ahead, won't he, Mother?'

'He won't if he has an emergency, will he, Mother?'

The two children had stopped eating and were glaring at one another, though this was not the first time they'd had the same argument. 'Mother?' they prompted in unison.

'What do I know about his plans? All I do think is that the

pair of you had better spend your time on your lessons and stop bothering me about Tian Gilchrist!' Annie snapped. 'I can't think why you keep going on about him. He's only a painter, after all.'

Elizabeth and William exchanged surprised glances, while Edgar and Tamsin stared resentfully at their mother.

Annie scowled round impartially at them all.

Tamsin gave an exaggerated sigh and began to fiddle with the food on her plate. Edgar opened his mouth to say something, but closed it again when William kicked him under the table and shook his head in warning. Elizabeth remarked quietly on the promise of a fine day and asked the children if they'd like to go for a walk across the moors.

Gradually, Annie began to relax.

William, watching her more closely than she realised, was relieved to see it. He worried a lot about his mother. Always the pivot of the family, she carried so many responsibilities. And he had let her down by not going into the business. He could have taken some of the burdens off her shoulders, only he had had the call to the ministry and been unable to do anything but respond to it. But that didn't stop him feeling guilty sometimes.

After breakfast, Annie went down to the mill, glad to get away from her family. But there were worries awaiting her there, too.

'I hear the Confederate States have officially recognised that they're at war,' Matt said gloomily. 'Things don't look good.'

'What do you mean, "officially recognised"? They've been at war since April. In fact, they sound to have been the ones who started the stupid war in the first place!' She heard the sharpness in her voice and stopped abruptly at his look of surprise. What had got into her today?

'Well, now they've passed an act officially declaring war between them and the North.' Matt clicked his tongue in disapproval. 'We're facing a crisis, Mrs Hallam, a very serious crisis indeed.'

'We and all the other cotton masters,' she replied. 'Well, we've all been through hard times before and we'll no doubt go through them again.'

'But we've never had the cotton supplies cut off completely before. And if the war continues, they will be. I don't like to think of putting off our operatives. How will they manage? How will they live?'

'They'll manage, because we'll not put them off. If it comes to the worst, we'll help them somehow. We'll make special relief payments, set up work schemes.'

He shook his head. 'We can't support them all. There are just too many, I'm afraid.'

'We'll find a way. I'll not see any of our people want.' She was utterly determined about that – as Frederick would have been.

Matt leaned forward, his hands clasped on the desk between them, addressing her formally, as he always did nowadays. 'Mrs Hallam, we need to face facts. There's no way we can continue to support all our workforce if we can't obtain the raw cotton. We can't run down our financial reserves completely or we'll have nothing left to buy more cotton with when the war is over.'

She leaned forward, eye to eye with him, and quiet as it was, her voice was strong with emphasis, 'I am facing facts, Matt. I've been facing them for weeks now, trying to work out what we'll do if – no, when – the cotton supplies dry up.' She passed across some papers. 'This is my first estimate of how we'll stand at Hallam's, taking into account all my sources of income and my accrued monies.' She deliberately used the formal financial language she had learned from Jonas Pennybody, because it seemed to have more effect on Matt than saying the same thing simply.

He looked down at the papers and then up at her in amazement. She never ceased to surprise him.

'You're not the only one who's been worrying, you know.' She got up and paced across to the window and back again as he read through her notes. When he had finished, she looked at him earnestly. 'I won't let our people starve, Matt. If I have to sell everything I own, I'll not let them starve.'

He looked down again at the top piece of paper, which summarised matters. Its neat rows of figures would have done credit to any man. How many hours had she laboured over this, alone? He sighed. But even if the figures were accurate, it was still impractical to keep the operatives on without work for them. 'But you're putting everything you have into this,' he chided. 'We must keep up a better reserve than that. What if the war goes on for years? What shall we do then?'

'Whatever we have to. I must be able to live with my conscience.' She smiled at his disapproval. 'Don't worry, Matt. I'll keep enough back for myself and the children, and see that you have enough to manage on. I don't need to live in a rich style. I can make great economies on my present way of living if I have to. But Frederick would want me to care for our people. I know he would.'

'Mr James and Mrs Mildred won't like it.'

She shrugged. 'They don't have the power to stop me, though.'

His voice was more tentative as he added, 'I don't think I like it, either.' He looked at her anxiously as he said that.

She stared him, steely-eyed. 'Then I shall just go ahead alone.'

He was shocked rigid. 'Annie – Mrs Hallam – you have to be prudent!'

'Matt, I can only be as prudent as my conscience will allow.' She forced a smile. 'And we do have some other reserves that I haven't taken into account.'

He looked puzzled.

'The cotton goods, Matt. Don't you think that if there's a shortage of raw cotton, the made-up goods we already possess will increase in value?'

He nodded slowly. 'Well, yes – they might.'

'So we'll make sure that the warehouse is kept dry and watched carefully at night.'

'Ye-e-es.' But it was a reluctant agreement.

'And you did buy in some more raw cotton, as we discussed in April. So we'll be able to continue spinning for a while yet.'

He fidgeted. 'Well, I didn't buy as much as I'd have liked. It was too highly priced, you see.'

She froze. She should have asked this before. Why had she not checked the current stores as part of her calculations? 'How much did you get, then?'

He named an amount that made her cry out in protest. 'Oh, no! Matt, whatever were you thinking of? Surely you could have bought more than that?'

He wriggled his shoulders uncomfortably. 'I could have. But it was sheer robbery for them to charge that much and it made me angry. And besides, we can't spend all the money we have now. We simply can't.' He had to make her understand that. His own living depended on it as well as hers – his living and that of his family.

She didn't answer. If she had opened her mouth, she'd have shouted at him, called him a dithering coward – which he was, in some ways – and that would have destroyed the relationship between them for ever. She did not dare do that, because she simply couldn't manage without him. Whatever Tamsin said, a woman openly doing business as a millowner would not be welcomed. So Annie needed Matt to do certain tasks on her behalf. And anyway, she didn't want to spend her life dealing with the everyday details of the mill. He did that better than she would have.

'Oh, Matt,' she whispered at last when the silence had dragged on for too long, 'I was sure you'd have bought more than that.'

He looked across at her, anguish in his face. 'It's not my money. I just couldn't spend so much without consulting anyone, and you were so – so preoccupied just then.'

She swallowed hard. 'Well, then. I'll – I'll have to revise my plans, think what to do. And maybe you could ask around and find if there's any more cotton to be had. You can let me know what you find out, how much is being asked, and we'll decide together what to do.'

He sat there miserably, staring down at his hands, knowing he had failed her. He just could not feel comfortable handling such large sums of money. And sometimes, he didn't feel comfortable doing what she told him, either. She was, after all, only a woman. She had learned a lot from her husband, but women just didn't have the mental capacity to handle large businesses. Even exceptional women like Annie. He sighed. Nor did he. If only Mr Hallam had lived a year longer, he'd have been able to make plans for this emergency! How they all missed him!

'Perhaps,' Annie said thoughtfully, 'we can provide our people with some other sort of work.'

Matt looked up at her as if she had just said something totally ridiculous. A handsome man, she thought, not for the first time, but without the moral strength that Frederick had had. And without the fierce determination *she* sometimes felt. She would not let their people starve! She would not!

His tone was condescending. 'What other sort of work could cotton spinners do, Mrs Hallam?'

'I don't know yet. Do the sums for me, Matt, will you? Work out how long our present supplies of cotton will last. And if you hear of any other cotton being offered, come to me at once.'

She pushed herself upright from the handsome mahogany and leather chair that had once been Frederick's and walked slowly across the room. At the door, she turned. 'And, Matt – when you're in Manchester, if you hear of any other ideas for relief schemes, things other millowners plan to do, if you hear of anything at all that might suit us, find out all about it, please.'

They looked at each other across the room, then his eyes fell and he nodded acquiescence.

'We are going to keep our people in some sort of work for as long as this crisis lasts,' she said before she went through the door. 'Make up your mind to that.' She heard his heartfelt sigh as she walked along the corridor and echoed it, albeit more quietly, with one of her own.

When she got outside the office, Annie found the carriage waiting in the mill yard, but the horses still had their nose bags on.

Robert came hurrying across from the mill stables. 'You should have sent word that you were ready, ma'am.' He opened the carriage door. 'But I won't keep you waiting for long. Home now, is it?'

She stared at him, then shook her head. 'No. Not yet. I feel like some fresh air. Leave the carriage windows open, if you please. We'll go for a drive.'

'And where would you like to go, ma'am?'

Where? For a moment, she stood motionless, her thoughts still in a tangle, then she smiled. 'I know. We'll go and visit Luke. Can you get the carriage down Hey Lane, Robert?'

'Oh, yes, ma'am. Mr Luke's widened it at his end and there's plenty of clear space to turn round in front of his cottage now. And it won't be muddy on a day like this. I wouldn't risk it if there were any mud. I wouldn't like to get you stuck anywhere.'

He had always been over-protective with his employers and his horses, she thought, but since Frederick's death it had become more marked. Well, there were worse faults than that. 'All right, then. Let's go.'

Robert drove at his usual slow, careful pace, but today that suited Annie's mood very well. She was in no hurry to get to Luke's. What she wanted was some time alone, without anyone making demands on her. Luke was usually a very quiet, peaceful sort of companion and it did her heart good to see his pride in his market garden. She would enjoy spending a little time with him and he always seemed glad to see her.

But today, Luke was not alone and as he came out to greet his sister, she saw Mrs Gorton moving about inside the cottage. And for some reason Luke's face was reflecting distress and pain. He had such an open face that no guile or deceit was possible.

'I'm sorry!' Annie apologised. 'I forgot today was the day Mrs Gorton comes in to clean for you.' When he didn't answer, she asked gently, 'Is something wrong?'

He hesitated. 'It's – yes, there is a – a bit of a problem.' He looked at her, naked misery in his eyes. 'Could we go for a little walk, Annie? I'll show you my crops. They're doing well, at least.' He looked at her full skirt. 'But you'll get your pretty frills dirty.'

Her heart sank, for it was clear that he had something on his mind, but she replied steadily, ready to help him as she always was with her family, 'If you're in trouble and need to talk then I don't care if my frills get absolutely plastered with mud, Luke.'

For a moment, his expression lightened. 'No, you wouldn't care about that.' Another hesitation, then, as they turned and began to walk away from the cottage, he admitted, 'I shouldn't be burdening you, Annie love, and it's not me who's in trouble, but – but I do need to talk to someone about it, if you can spare me some time?'

'I can always spare time for you.'

He squeezed her hand, as it lay on his arm. 'Thanks, love. I've got a bench that looks out across the valley. We'll go and sit there, shall we?'

When they were seated, she waited for him to begin, thinking that the view and the cottage were both like Luke, pleasant and modest, rather than showy.

'It's Amy Gorton,' he said at last. 'I'm – I'm afraid for her life.'

This was the last thing Annie had expected. 'The woman who cleans for you?'

He nodded.

'But isn't that her husband's problem?'

He stared down at his hands, clasped so tightly that the knuckles shone white against the callused, earth-stained skin. 'He *is* the problem. He beats her. Badly.'

'Oh.'

'And it's getting worse. He's started hitting the children, too.' He looked at her, sheer misery in his kind blue eyes. 'Oh, Annie, they're only little. Tess is four and Adam's six. Gorton broke Tess's arm this week.'

'A child of four? Oh, no!'

'I can't bear it. I just can't bear it. Sometimes, when I see how bruised her face is, I want to go down there and beat him to a pulp. But I haven't the right. And he'd only take it out on her afterwards. It'd make things worse, not better.'

Annie's heart sank. The way he said 'her' gave away a great deal about his feelings. 'You're fond of Mrs Gorton?'

'Yes. I – I know I have no right to be. But I am. It just happened.' He reached out to clasp her hand. 'Not that I've done anything about it, Annie. I wouldn't. I have too much respect for her. She works so hard and endures it all so patiently.'

'I wish I could help you. Or her. But he's her husband. We can't interfere between man and wife.'

Luke sighed. 'Yes. I know that, really. But he's a drink-sodden brute who's getting worse, not better.'

They were both silent, then he gave a sad smile. 'But it's helped to talk about it to someone. I'm sorry to burden you with my troubles, though. We all do that, don't we?'

She patted his shoulder. 'Yes. But that's what families are for.'

'You've got enough troubles of your own. I shouldn't have said anything.'

'I'll soon have enough troubles for anyone,' she admitted. 'At the mill, I mean. The supply of cotton is running out because of the war, though we had better stocks than most. I have to think of some way to look after our people. I must find some other sort of work for them.'

He was astonished. 'Surely the war can't last for long? Not in these modern times?'

'Matt thinks it'll be over within a year. I'm not so sure. I've been studying the map of America. I'm very ignorant, but it's such a big country that surely it'll take much longer than a year for one side to overrun the other physically?' She sighed. 'It's at times like this that I miss Frederick's wisdom most.'

'But how can you afford to look after all your operatives if there's no work?'

'I'm quite a rich woman, Luke. Can you think of a better use for my money than to stop people starving?'

'Will it really come to that?'

'It might well.'

'They could apply for help to the Union.' But his voice was hesitant. The Bilsden and District Poor Law Union was not well thought of in the town, and folk said the Guardians were always at loggerheads with one another about how things should be run.

'And if they did apply, if they had to rely on the Union for long, they'd still starve, more slowly but just as surely. You know how relief is offered. In tokens. Redeemable only at certain shops.'

'Shops which are run by cheats,' he finished for her.

'Precisely. I couldn't sleep at night if I left our people to starve.'

He set his hands on her shoulders and moved her round to face him, looking at her with admiration clear on his face. 'You're a wonderful woman, Annie.'

She blushed bright pink. 'Don't be silly!'

'I'm not. And you are. Wonderful, I mean. I'm proud to be your brother. If I can help in any way,' he let go of her and gestured around him, 'even if it's only to give work to a couple of lads, then I will.'

She stared at him for so long that he stared back in puzzlement, then she gave him a huge hug. 'Oh, Luke, thank you!'

'Whatever for?'

'You've given me an idea of how to start.'

He gaped at her. 'What do you mean? Start what?'

'We'll start in small ways, by finding bits and pieces of work with folk like you. We'll pay you and other people to make extra work, meet half the wages, perhaps. That way we'll all benefit. For I won't have Hallam's people sitting around idle. That would only lead to mischief.'

She frowned into the distance. 'But if the worst happens and the war does continue for more than a year, then I'll have to find some bigger tasks for the majority of them to work on. There must be something we can set up.' She smiled wistfully. 'Frederick would have done it so much better than I could. He'd have said—' she stopped short and stared at her brother, eyes lighting up '—he'd have said to do something that would beautify our town.'

'Aye, he would, too. He set a great deal of store on improving Bilsden,' Luke agreed. 'The town owes him a lot. I never see the square but I think of him.'

For a few moments they sat there in silence, then she smiled. 'I don't know what I'll do yet, but it's a start to get some ideas of where to look. Talking to you has helped me.'

'I'm glad of that, at least.'

She was feeling more cheerful. 'I'll think of something – something Frederick would be proud of. Now, let's go back to the cottage. Do you think Mrs Gorton would make me a cup of tea?'

'Of course. But,' he paused, then pleaded, 'don't say anything about the bruise on her forehead.'

'No, of course I won't.'

But the size of Amy Gorton's bruise shocked Annie rigid. As did the tenderness in Luke's eyes when he looked at the woman and the pale child with her arm in a sling, who clung so closely to her mother's skirts and shrank back, terrified, when a stranger followed Luke into the cottage.

What next? Annie wondered as she drove home. It seemed sometimes as if the world was filled with troubles. Then she remembered how she had felt when she was seventeen, and pregnant after being raped. She had coped with that, more than coped, and would deal with all the things that faced her now, too! And she was beginning to get ideas. If the war went on for long, they would set up some project to beautify the town. Some major project. No one could object to that. And if the cotton spinners did things less efficiently than experienced labourers would have, what did that matter? As long as the spinners were gainfully employed. As long as they felt they were earning their way.

20

Bilsden: August to September 1861

In early August, a letter came for Annie. It was sent from Liverpool, but gave no clue as to the owner's address, as if the writer did not want any further connection with her. It was annoyingly brief and uninformative.

Dear Mrs Hallam,

Mr Gilchrist, who was part of the group I was to travel with from New York to Liverpool, failed to catch the ship.

Unfortunately, his luggage was already on board. As I haven't heard from Mr Gilchrist in the month since I arrived, I have taken the liberty of sending the luggage on to you and it will be with you in a few days. I believe, from what was said, that he was intending to stay with you and the luggage is labelled accordingly.

Yours sincerely
P. Downing

Annie showed the note to her family. William and the children were as puzzled as she was.

'What do you think can have happened to him?' Edgar asked, wide-eyed. 'I mean, he must have been intending to catch the boat if his luggage was already on board.'

'Perhaps his horse went lame,' Tamsin suggested, 'and he missed the boat.'

'He was staying in New York,' Edgar pointed out, with the sarcasm he was starting to use against his sister's sharpness. 'People in a big city go around in cabs, especially when they're about to leave, so he wouldn't have been riding a horse.'

'Well, something happened to the cab, then.' She glared

at him. Less and less was she able to control and influence him.

'If it had, he'd have caught the next boat, wouldn't he?'

'There might not have been another boat.'

Edgar gave a weary, exaggerated sigh. 'Don't you ever read the newspapers? Boats are still sailing.'

'You always think you're right—' Tamsin began.

Annie cut in. 'We can't know who's right, so it's no use quarrelling.' She was growing accustomed to stepping between them, and she and Elizabeth both thought it a good thing that Edgar was beginning to assert his independence. He had been too subservient to Tamsin as a small child. Now, at nine, he seemed to be changing in so many ways and was, the adults all agreed, very mature for his age; far more in control of himself and his temper than Tamsin, that was sure.

A week later, a carrier pulled slowly up Ridge Hill, with a load of bags, luggage and painting paraphernalia on his cart. The man hailed Nat Jervis, who was working near the gate. 'Where shall I deliver this to, Nat, front or back?'

Nat straightened up and came over to the cart. 'What is it?'

'Gentleman's luggage.'

Nat frowned. Mrs Hallam hadn't said they were expecting anyone, and he knew Robert hadn't been asked to meet any trains. 'Are you sure it's for us, Tad?'

The carter was affronted. 'A-course I'm sure, Nat Jervis. Think I don't know my own job? It says so here, doesn't it?' He pulled a piece of crumpled paper from his pocket and read laboriously from it. 'Mr T. Gilchrist, care of Hallam, Ridge House, Bilsden.'

He thrust it at Nat, who perused it and nodded slowly. 'It does say it's for us, but we haven't heard that anyone's coming. We do know a Mr Gilchrist, though. Painter fellow. He stayed here last year and did a picture of the family. Lovely picture it is, too. Who gave you the luggage, then? Didn't he come with it?'

Tad shook his head. 'No. No sign of the owner. Station master just told me to deliver it. Carriage paid at the other end, it was. It come in on the afternoon train from Manchester.'

'Well, you'd better take it to the front door and ask Winnie what to do. She'll know if anyone's expected.'

Tad pulled a face. 'She'll flap her mouth at me, that one will. Never satisfied, she isn't, whatever you do for her.'

Nat grinned but didn't comment, just waved farewell and went back to his work.

A few minutes later, Winnie puffed her way across the hall to the library and tapped on the door. 'Mrs Hallam, there's a carter at the door with some luggage. It belongs to Mr Gilchrist, but there's no sign of him, just his bags. You didn't say he was coming today.' The last was spoken in an accusatory tone. 'Shall I have it brought in? And shall I have Peggy make up a bed for him?'

Annie stood up. These must be the things sent on by the mysterious P. Downing. 'Yes, of course they must be brought in. Have them put in one of the spare bedrooms, will you?'

'Yes, ma'am. And shall I have them unpacked, ma'am? The things inside will be terrible creased if they've come all the way from America.'

'I don't know. Perhaps we'll wait a day or two, then if we hear something we can unpack.' But she was reluctant to do that. It would feel as if she were invading Tian's privacy. She went out to look at the luggage and the sight of his painting equipment added to her unease. Surely he wouldn't abandon it? Painting was the most important thing in his life.

That night over the evening meal there was further specula-tion from everyone except Annie about where Mr Gilchrist could be.

'Things'll be in turmoil with the war,' William said at last. 'But I'm sure he'll be here soon.'

Annie hoped so. She didn't want to add Tian to her list of problems. She tried not to listen to a voice inside her which insisted that he was already on the list. She told herself she had no responsibility for him, none at all, but still she couldn't help worrying.

In mid-September, William celebrated his twenty-third birthday with a family party at Ridge House. After the meal, when they were all gathered together in the drawing-room, he called for silence and went to stand in front of the hearth.

'I have something to announce.'

They all looked at him expectantly, smiling, some couples touching one another without realising it, the younger folk sitting in small groups. As he looked at them, William felt, not for the first time, that he had a very special family.

'I'm to be admitted as a Junior Minister next month,' he said quietly.

There was silence in the room, then John Gibson stood up, not caring who saw the tears of joy running down his face. He went to shake his grandson's hand, shake it and clasp it in both his and then shake it again. 'Eh, I'm that proud, lad, that proud. I don't know when something's pleased me as much as this, I really don't.'

'I thought the training was longer than a year? You said at least two years when we spoke of it before, possibly three.' Annie got up to give her son a kiss. 'You should have told us this was in the offing.' She didn't like being told news with the whole family when it was her son involved.

'I didn't say anything because it wasn't at all certain.' He smiled down at her. 'And because you have enough things to worry about, Mother.'

'I don't worry about you,' she said softly. 'Not nowadays.'

'Good. Because there's nothing for you to worry about,' he replied, putting his arm round her shoulders and giving her a quick hug.

John watched them, thinking how good it was that Annie had reconciled herself to William's call to serve the Lord. One day, perhaps she would be truly proud of the lad, not just accepting of what he was doing. John hoped so, anyway.

'How come you don't have to stay for the full training?' Tom asked, queuing up to pump his nephew's hand in turn.

'Mostly because of Grandfather and Saul Hinchclif fe.'

'Because of me?' John gaped at his grandson. 'How can it be because of me? What have I got to do with your training?'

'You're a lay preacher, and know more about theology than most of the other students do. And we've often discussed things, you and I. John Hannah, with whom I've been studying, is very satisfied with the basis of my beliefs. When I said I owed it to you, he said to tell you that you should have been a Minister yourself.'

John went pink and exchanged delighted glances with Kathy. 'Eh, to think of that!'

'And of course,' William continued, 'my time at the Mission was important, too, a sort of preliminary training. And my general education was good enough, even when I started. I have you to thank for that, Mother, and Saul Hinchcliffe, too. He's a wonderful teacher. But at the Institute, they put more emphasis on our calling and our understanding of the Lord's word than on our knowledge of Latin, so that was the most important thing for me to understand.'

William didn't say that many of his fellow students at Didsbury were ill-educated generally, even though they had felt a genuine call to enter the ministry, or that few of them had ever studied Latin, as he had. 'We had to wait for a decision to be taken about me. There's a rule, you see, that all students admitted to residence should remain their full term, save in extreme cases. It seems that I'm an extreme case.'

He looked around, his eyes so luminous with happiness that they seemed to shine with their own inner light. 'And the work I've been doing for Mother lately has been taken into account, too. My tutors really approve of what you're doing, Mother. So, although I shall be expected to preach in the smaller chapels near here, under Nathaniel Bell's guidance, I shan't be expected to go out on the Circuit until the need for my help in Bilsden is over.'

Elizabeth went to give William her own congratulations later, when the family had dispersed to stroll around the gardens. As they talked, she found herself walking alone with him and was enjoying his company so much that for once she did not hurry away.

As they turned along one of the sheltered paths through the shrubberies at the side of the house, they seemed so cut off from the others that they might have been totally alone in a green-shaded world. The day was warm and there was a ripe, drowsy feel to the air. Even the insects seemed to be buzzing around more lethargically than usual.

'You must be very happy,' she said quietly.

'I am. I worry sometimes at how happy I feel. It doesn't seem fair with so much trouble and want in the world.'

'It's very fair.' She hesitated, for she rarely allowed herself to speak about personal matters with him, then decided to continue. 'You carry joy with you wherever you go, William. It lifts people up, helps them. Don't ever feel guilty about that. Use it in your work. I don't think religion needs to be gloomy and full of misery and repentance. Do you?'

He didn't answer, just turned to stare at her, and for a moment they stopped talking, standing alone in this quiet sanctuary.

She stared up at him. He was the only man she knew who made her feel small. Her breath caught in her throat at how handsome he was. And yet he was five years younger than she was, and her employer's son to boot. She had no right to feel like this about him. No right at all.

Something of her feelings must have shown on her face, for surprise crept into his, surprise and something else. 'Oh, Elizabeth,' he said softly.

She could not think what to say or do, could not even move as he reached out and put his arms around her. 'Elizabeth,' he said again, wonder in his voice.

'No!' She tried to push him away, but instead found herself grasping his upper arms, staring at him, wanting his love, wanting it so much that she ached with the need. As his head bent towards her, she gasped and made a feeble protest: 'Oh, we – we shouldn't.'

But he paid no attention to that. He just pulled her closer and began to kiss her. And though his kiss was as gentle as everything else about him, it seemed to burn on her lips, to burn and to fuse the two of them together. 'Dearest Elizabeth,' he murmured as he drew away, saying the words softly, his voice filled with tenderness, saying them as if the very sound of her name gave him pleasure.

Conscience made her push at his chest. 'No! Oh, no, William!'

This time her agonised tone got through to him and he let go of her, his face filled with sorrow. 'I'm sorry. I didn't mean to – if you don't share my feelings—'

And, heaven help her, she couldn't bear him to think that. 'No!' She reached out to take hold of his hand. 'No, it's not that, William. Never think that I don't – that I wouldn't like to—' She faltered to a halt.

'Then what's wrong? Why do you not want me to kiss you?' He asked the question as simply as a child would.

Her face was scarlet as she admitted, 'I did want you to kiss me, but – but I shouldn't have.'

'I don't understand.'

'You're my employer's son. And – and you're five years younger than I am. I have no right even to think of – of growing fond of you.' She gasped. What had she said?

William was looking at her with that steady, trusting expression he had, the look that had already disarmed many people whom the harshness of life had made bitter and twisted. Before it, Elizabeth felt like candle wax melting in front of a flame. 'Oh, please, don't look at me like that, William! And – and don't – we mustn't ever—'

He stretched out one hand and gently laid his fingertips across her lips. 'We need to talk about it. I think I have a right to help make any decisions about us, too.'

'No!'

'Yes.'

'But—'

Voices were calling his name from the front of the house. William took hold of her hand and pulled her through the shrubbery, heedless of any damage to her full skirts or to the plants which Nat tended so carefully. He had spent some of his childhood tracking through this part of the gardens, imagining great adventures, dreaming his boyhood dreams, so now he led her unerringly along a little-used path, round the side of the kitchen garden and along the outer wall until he came to a high gate with a rounded top set in the thickness of the tall walls. 'Aha!' He smiled as he lifted the well-worn latch. The gate opened without a sound, for this was the way the outdoor staff entered the grounds in the mornings and left in the evenings.

She looked back over her shoulder. 'William, we really shouldn't—'

'Yes, we should. We need to talk. And we're liable to be interrupted any moment if we stay near the house. Come on. Let's stretch our legs for a few minutes on the moors.' Still holding her hand, he led her across the rough ground, following another little path between the thick tufts of wiry grass and other vegetation. Only when a hollow hid them from the house did he stop and gesture to some tumbled rocks. 'Shall we sit?'

She chose a rock with room for only one person and perched there nervously, her arms around her knees. If she had been a lady of fashion, with hooped skirts she couldn't have done that, but she was not, or ever likely to be. It was her favourite position when she wanted to think about something.

He smiled at her. 'I've been waiting to speak to you,' he said, in that quiet reasonable tone that he used to everyone, rich and poor, 'until I was further on in my training. I've had such a lot of reading and studying and thinking about my beliefs to do, that I couldn't concentrate on anything else. Though I knew you were there, knew I would one day want to talk to you like this.' He stretched out and took her hand. 'And I think I've been taking it for granted that you would wish to hear what I have to say.'

She was blushing furiously again.

'And, Elizabeth,' another long straight look emphasised the seriousness of his words, 'I'm not like my uncles, not interested in – in loose women and – and such things.' Now it was his turn to blush. 'I think I'm rather a simple person, really.'

'But you could find someone of your own class, someone your mother would be proud to have as a daughter-in-law. Why should you be interested in me? I'm poor. And,' she stared down at her skirt, bitterness clenching into a tight hard knot in her belly, 'I'm not even pure. My Cousin Lewis saw to that . . .'

Sobs shook her. She had never forgotten that dreadful night when he had come to her bedroom and forced himself upon her. She hadn't told her aunt, just fled from her cousin and found this job through an agency in Manchester. And even then, her cousin had followed her, had tried to take her back, so that he could have the convenience of her body. It was William who had driven Lewis Melby away, with Frederick Hallam's blessing. So he knew all about her shame.

Before she knew what was happening, he was kneeling beside her, cradling her in his strong arms, just holding her close. 'As if that matters!'

'But it does! It does!'

He was kissing her forehead, her cheeks, murmuring endearments. 'No, it doesn't, love. I met your cousin, remember. I know what he's like. It wasn't your fault and it's long past now. And, anyway, it doesn't matter at all to me.'

She sobbed against him for a while, giving in to the pain she had locked away inside herself for nearly three years, the pain she had never been able to confide in anyone about.

'Now,' he said, as her sobs died down. 'Can we talk about us?'

'Oh, William, we shouldn't!'

'I won't change my mind. I've grown to love you, Elizabeth.'

Still she forced herself to shake her head. 'We mustn't.'

'What am I going to do with you?' he teased. 'Spurning me like this! I shall go into a decline.'

She was betrayed into a gurgle of laughter, but it ended on a half-sob. 'William, please think about it. Think very seriously. I know that I'm not the sort of woman your mother would want you to . . .' She flushed scarlet, unable to finish the sentence.

He finished for her '. . . want me to marry.'

She nodded.

For a moment, his face was sad. 'But then, I'm not the sort of son she wanted, either. Don't think that I don't know how disappointed she is in me. The last thing she wanted was for her son to become a Methodist Minister. She wanted one who would go into the family businesses and made even more money – as if we need any more! But I'm not that sort of son. Maybe Edgar will be.'

'I doubt it. I think he's actually more like you than his mother or father.' She wouldn't mention Edgar's obsession with drawing and painting. After all, he was young yet. He would probably change his mind several times about what he wanted to do with his life. But she knew that he still wheezed every time he went into the mill, so how could he ever work there? 'It's Tamsin who's like your mother, really,' she said on an afterthought.

'That little minx!' said William fondly.

They looked at one another, then Elizabeth forced herself to say, for William's sake: 'Please. Think about it all very carefully. Take several months and – and look around at other young women.' It nearly tore her in two to say that, to turn down what was probably the only chance she would ever have to marry the man she loved, had loved for a long time now. But she did it. Because she cared about him, really cared.

He frowned. 'I'd rather—'

'Please!'

He was enough like his mother to get the terms of their bargain straight. 'And in six months, if I still feel the same?'

'Then we'll talk about it again.' But he wouldn't feel the same. She knew that. She was not beautiful or graceful or any of the things men usually admired in a woman. She was only his calflove. Abruptly she stood up and began to walk back towards the house. Thoughtfully, he followed.

'My face must be all red,' she said as he opened the gate.

He studied it, wishing he dared kiss her again, but he didn't want to upset her. 'It is a bit, I'm afraid.'

'You go ahead of me, then, William, and I'll try to slip up to my room. I'll say I have a headache or something.'

She managed to escape notice, but lay awake for hours that night, alternately smiling tenderly at the thought that a man like William Ashworth could love her, or telling herself sternly that she had no right, no right at all, to love him, or to expect anything to come of that love.

Then the very next day, something happened which drove all thoughts of love and marriage out of William's head, and Elizabeth's too. For the most unlikely member of the Gibson family got into really serious trouble.

21

Hey End Farm: September 1861

On the Friday, when Amy did not come at her usual time to clean his house, Luke began to worry. She was always so punctual. And he enjoyed seeing little Tess, who had not yet started school like her brother Adam. He had got into the habit of waiting for Amy and her daughter inside the house and sharing a cup of tea with them when they arrived at eight o'clock. On this particular day, growing more anxious by the minute, he alternated between standing at the kitchen window looking down the lane, and pacing up and down outside near his glasshouse, from where he would also be able to see her coming. His dog gave up the struggle to understand what he was doing and went to sleep in the outhouse.

But hours passed and still she did not arrive. Nor did he see any sign of the children, who often played out with their bat and ball near the farmhouse in the morning before Adam went to school. What he did see, an hour or so before noon, was Ted Gorton, standing at the gate, staring down the lane towards Luke's cottage. Ted was usually out and about in the fields and rarely spent any daylight hours in or near the farm-house, except for meals. But today he was just standing around, and by his stance and his restless pacing, he was not in a good mood.

Coming to the conclusion that he'd better not do anything which might betray his worries about Amy, Luke went back inside the cottage, but continued to watch the farm through the kitchen window. After a few minutes, Ted went back indoors, too. The fact that he swayed as he walked towards the house suggested that he might already have been drinking. That did not bode well for poor Amy.

Quietly, Luke tidied up the kitchen, then spent the rest of the day observing his neighbours, anxiety for Amy fretting him so much that he could not settle to work and could barely force down any food.

Several times Ted Gorton came back out to stare down the lane. Each time he seemed to sway more markedly, and Luke, who had excellent eyesight, once saw him shake a clenched fist in the direction of the cottage, as if angry with its occupant. There was no sign of the children or Amy, though Luke watched with particular care at the time Adam usually came home from school.

Around dusk, he saw Ted stroll out of the house and turn down the road which led towards the hamlet of Hey End, not walking straight but rather rolling from side to side.

Only when he had disappeared from sight did Luke leave his cottage. Something made him take a circuitous route to the end of the lane. Better safe than sorry, he told himself. Don't want Gorton coming back, seeing me and blaming Amy for that. So he slipped behind the glasshouse and then ducked down behind the taller plants until he came to the drystone wall which ran along between the edge of Gorton's fields and the lane. He crawled over it at a spot where it had collapsed and should have been remade, if Ted had been a better farmer. Instead, it had a few rough planks stuck in the gaps to keep the sheep from escaping.

At the farm, Luke peered over the wall and ducked back down immediately, for Gorton had crept back and was crouched in hiding there, watching Luke's cottage. Luckily, he had his back to his own side wall and did not see his neighbour. Moving quietly, Luke returned home, walking between the glasshouse and the cottage quite openly, as if he'd been working out there.

The next day followed much the same pattern. No sign of Amy or the children, just Gorton. The man did only a minimal amount of farm work and spent most of the day moving in and out of the house, mostly standing staring in Luke's direction when he was outside. It was as if he was daring Luke to come down the lane. Luckily Luke had no deliveries to make that day. And even if he had, he doubted he would have made them. Somehow, he felt that he had to stay near Amy, felt that his very presence at the cottage protected her from – dread shuddered through him – the worst.

As the day wore on, Gorton's gait became more unsteady and at dusk he crept off down the lane, as if trying to go to the local pub without his neighbour noticing. But Luke did notice. He had noticed everything which happened that day.

He stood in the kitchen, debating with himself, then decided to slip along to the farm, as he had done the previous evening, and wait to see if Gorton returned secretly again. No, better still he would go into Hey End and check whether Gorton really had gone to the pub.

When there was no sign of his neighbour at the farm, Luke walked into the hamlet, again trying to keep out of sight. He peered through one of the small side windows of the pub and saw Gorton sitting in a corner, with some of his boozing cronies, laughing and swilling down ale. Not until a new round was brought to the table did Luke move, then, still keeping himself as much out of sight as possible, he ran all the way back to Hey Lane.

At the farmhouse, he hammered on the door.

No one came.

He peered into the windows, determined to find out what had happened, and kept on knocking. 'I won't go away till you speak to me, Amy!' he called. But his heart was thumping with the fear that she might be lying inside, injured, unable to respond.

A blur of pale face appeared at an upstairs window and then it opened a little. Amy's voice, sounding weak and breathless, floated down to him. 'Go away, Luke! You'll only make things worse.'

At least she was alive, then! 'Come down and talk to me. Let me see that you're all right. Then I'll go away.'

When there was no answer, he called desperately, 'Ted's still drinking in the pub. If you hurry, he won't catch us. But I'm not going away till I've seen you. And every minute that passes makes it more dangerous for me to stay here.'

'Oh, Luke, just leave me alone!'

'I mean it.'

Footsteps came down the stairs, slow footsteps, not like Amy's usual light tread. Luke felt as though his hearing had become extra-sensitive, as though his whole being strained to be inside the house with her. The footsteps didn't come to the front door. Instead, they went towards the parlour. So he followed them, standing outside the window as a shape moved towards it and opened a small hinged pane.

'Ted has the door keys,' she whispered. 'Oh, Luke, please go away. He'll kill me if he sees you here.'

As she stood there, he could see that she was swaying. He moved towards the small opening and gasped at what he saw, tears coming into his eyes. 'What has he done to you now?'

'Beaten me.'

'But—' There were no words to describe the horror of her once lovely face, for it was now puffy and battered, her lip split, one eye completely closed and her hair, her beautiful hair, cut off, leaving jagged ends around the fragile skull. After the first shock, he forced himself not to show his concern and asked calmly. 'What about the children? Are they all right?'

Tears came into her eyes. 'He's taken them down to his mother's.'

'But are they all right?' he repeated.

Silence told him that they were not.

His voice was low and harsh as he tried to keep his anger in check. 'What did he do to them this time?'

'He's broken Tess's leg as well as her arm, now.' Amy could hardly speak for sobbing. 'He threw her downstairs when she and Adam tried to help me. Then he beat poor Adam, too.'

'He's a monster!' Luke couldn't think of anything to say,

anything to do to help her. 'Will – will his mother support him in this madness?'

'What can she do? He gives her the money to live. Without him, she'd be a pauper. She'd have to go into the Union poor-house. But I think she'll try to protect the children. She does love them.'

Luke was nearly shaking with the hot rage that was coursing through him. Never, in all his life, had he felt anger like this. Never even thought to feel it. For the first time, he understood why some men killed.

Already she was reaching out to close the window. 'Please leave now, Luke. He'll kill me if he finds you here. Get someone else to clean for you from now on. Don't even speak to me when you pass me in the lane.'

'But why? Why is he doing this?'

'He's grown insanely jealous of you.'

'Of me? I don't understand. Why should he be jealous of me?'

She hesitated, then said quietly, 'Because I'm fond of you. Because you're the man he never has been, never could be. And because the children speak so well of you.' Then she closed the window and walked away.

Luke could not return home, could not face an empty house, so he went back into Hey End. Afterwards, he could not be sure whether he'd gone there to call Gorton to account, or whether he'd just felt a desperate need to be with people, normal people who didn't beat their wives, didn't break their children's limbs. He also felt a desperate need for something to numb the pain he was feeling. He rarely drank more than a glass of beer, but now he felt he needed several glasses to wash the pain and horror from his throat. If anything would do that.

When he got to the pub, he hesitated, then stood outside the window again and peered in. If Gorton was still there, he'd walk down the hill to the next pub, the one at the crossroads, so that he could drink in peace. But Gorton wasn't there. Thank heavens! Luke pushed the door open, wincing at the brightness inside, and walked across to the bar. He ordered a pint of beer and stood there, still feeling numb.

'Feeling thirsty tonight, Mr Gibson?' the barmaid joked. 'You never normally have more than a half.'

Luke looked at her rosy unmarked face and felt bile rise into his throat at the contrast with Amy. He forced himself to reply quietly. Jenny was only doing her job, taking an interest in her customers. She was a pleasant enough lass. It wasn't her fault that Amy was hurt. 'Yes. I'm feeling right thirsty tonight,' he managed, but he couldn't force a smile.

He paid for the beer and found himself a small table to one side, where he could be on his own. He wanted people around him, normal, cheerful people, but didn't want to have to make the effort to talk to them. He picked up the beer, sipped, then put it down again. It was tasteless. It nearly choked him. He rested his forehead on one hand, not knowing what to do to help Amy. And those poor little children.

Suddenly the room seemed to explode around Luke. His arm was knocked away so violently that he had to grab the table to stop himself falling. The glass went flying, scattering beer over all those nearby, who exclaimed and jumped up. Luke knew, even before he looked up, who had attacked him. And as he raised his eyes, Ted Gorton swung his fist again. Drunk as he was, he managed to connect with the side of Luke's head, so that he was knocked backwards off his stool.

From a million miles away, he heard the publican's voice calling, 'Hey! No fighting!' Around him, everyone had stopped talking. People were moving out of the way. Quietly. Warily. Eyes on the attacker. The sudden silence seemed to press down upon the whole room.

Gorton laughed hoarsely and came at Luke again, sure of his prey. He was a fighter of some renown locally, a man who enjoyed his own brute strength.

And that was his mistake. For, like most lads in the Rows, Luke had had to learn to defend himself, however little he enjoyed fighting, and he had not forgotten the basics. He scrambled to his feet and ducked backwards, yelling, 'Stop it, you fool!'

'Stand up an' fight like a man!' Gorton roared.

The publican tried to grab him from behind, but one of Gorton's drinking mates dragged the publican away. 'Let him be. He has a right to thump this bastard's head in.'

Luke dodged round a table and picked up a chair to fend off Gorton. 'This is stupid!' he shouted. 'What quarrel could you possibly have with me?' He knew by now what Gorton thought, but he also knew that half the population of the hamlet was listening, so he intended to do his best to protect Amy's name.

'*What quarrel?*' Gorton paused to yell. 'The best damned quarrel a man could have. You're a fornicator, like all the Gibsons. An' you've been at my wife. So I'm goin' t'beat you senseless an' teach you to leave other men's wives alone from now on.'

Luke put the chair down and spread his arms wide. 'I've not touched your wife,' he pleaded. 'There's no need for this.'

'Hah! I'm not a fool. I've seen you an' her together, seen the way she looks at you.'

Luke took another quick step backwards as Gorton advanced towards him, fists raised menacingly. The men were of roughly the same height, but Gorton was more heavily built, a big man going to seed. Luke still had a young man's body, trim and yet muscular from all the physical work he did.

'Stand still and fight, y'bastard! Let's see if Gibson blood is as red as other folk's.'

'There's no cause to fight,' Luke protested again. 'I've never laid a hand on your wife. Never. I swear it!'

'Liar!' roared Gorton and lunged forward.

Even then, Luke would have avoided his drunken attack, but one of Gorton's friends joined in, pushing Luke from behind, forcing him right into Gorton's path. And the other men from that group of drinking friends formed a rough circle around the two of them, so Luke could not escape.

'Stand up and fight like a man!' one man shouted, his face red and angry.

'Give him stick, Gorton!' another growled. 'Teach him a lesson.'

'Punch his lights out!'

'Show the bastard!'

Behind them the landlord was pleading with them not to fight indoors and other men were calling, 'Shame! Stop it!' But no one did anything, no one tried to break up that circle of men who stood with arms outstretched to keep the other drinkers away.

At this moment, Luke knew that he would have to fight – and win. For Amy's sake, as well as his own. He seemed to go cold inside, cold and detached, and remembered all the self-defence tactics Tom had once taught him, Tom and his brother Mark. In front of him, Gorton was rocking to and fro, grinning, stupid with drink – and stupid with confidence, too.

He realised he would have to keep out of the way of those fists and use Gorton's drunken overconfidence against him. He dodged hastily as Gorton threw a round-arm punch at his head, and his lips tightened in satisfaction as it missed him.

'You won't beat me up as easily you beat your poor wife!' he taunted. 'Remember that I didn't want this fight. And there's no reason for it. I've not touched her!' But his final appeal fell on ears just as deaf as before.

Drunk as he was, Gorton was a shrewd, experienced fighter. He growled with anger at missing and rushed forward. The two men closed and broke apart, fists rising and falling, grunts signalling a hit. Then, as Luke dodged backwards, knowing how dangerous it was for him to let Gorton get too close, he bumped into the human circle around them.

As he moved sideways, quickly wiping the sweat from his eyes, Gorton shouted, 'She's a whore, she is, an' when I've done with you, I'll go back an' teach her another lesson. No one'll ever want her again by the time I'm done with her.'

The thought of Amy being beaten yet again terrified Luke.

Gorton might well kill her if he carried out his threat. Strength seemed to well up in Luke and determination to protect the woman he loved. He watched as Gorton swung another wide blow at him and swayed backwards just enough to avoid it. Then, at the precise moment when his opponent was off balance, he acted, swinging his fist with all the force he had in him.

As it connected with Gorton's jaw, the red angry face suddenly went slack with shock and Gorton crashed backwards. He did not rise again.

Luke stood there, panting, as Gorton's friends pushed past him to tend their mate. Someone touched his shoulder and he jerked round to find a man he knew by sight pushing a handkerchief at him. It was an elderly farmer he'd spoken to once or twice and Len Daley was looking at him approvingly. 'You did well, lad. He's a mean fighter, Gorton is.'

'I shouldn't have fought at all. There was no reason to fight! I've never been near his wife.'

'I believe you. She's related to my wife an' she was allus a nice lass, Amy were. She'd no sooner go whoring than she'd walk into town naked.'

Then a voice from the hearth roared, 'He's killed him!' and every eye in the place turned to the figure sprawled in front of the fire.

Luke gasped and shuddered, clutching at Len Daley. 'He can't be dead!'

Gorton's friends turned to glare at him and one took a step forward.

'Don't let that murderer get away!' another yelled.

A third man ran to the door and stood there, guarding it, arms outstretched, as if he thought Luke would try to escape.

The publican hurried forward and bent over Gorton. When he stood up, his face was ashen. 'He *is* dead.'

For a moment, it seemed as if Gorton's mates would rush at Luke, but Len called out, 'Now then, let's not do owt else stupid!' He jerked his head to his own friends, a group of older men who were more or less sober. They got up and walked over to join him, forming a barrier between Luke and Gorton's mob.

'Someone go an' fetch the constable!' the publican called.

'I'll go!' One of Gorton's mates stood up.

'You go with him, Fred,' Len said quietly to the man next to him. 'See the tale's told properly, eh?'

Fred nodded and went out into the darkness.

Luke could not move, could only stand there numb with shock. He'd killed a man. Killed him! He hadn't meant to, but that's what he'd done. He looked down at his right fist and shook his head disbelievingly. He shouldn't have come here tonight, shouldn't have let Gorton goad him into a fight. No, that was silly – he hadn't been able to avoid the fight. 'Oh, hell,' he said, clutching Len's arm. 'I'm going to be sick.' And he was, vomiting in the nearest corner, after which he collapsed on to a bench, white-faced.

When the constable came, there was a babble of voices as each man tried to tell the story. The constable yelled, 'Quiet!' and the noise subsided. Then he asked, 'Where's the fellow as killed Gorton?'

Luke could not frame a word, so Len spoke for him. 'He's here. And it were an accident.'

'That's not how this chap told it.'

'This chap's drunk and he's best mate to the dead man,' Len retorted.

'An' so I telled the constable,' Fred said loudly, 'but he wouldn't listen.'

The constable still seemed reluctant to believe him and the chorus of voices rose once again as each man put in his half-penn'orth, one side calling out 'Murder!' and the other protesting that it had been an accident.

'Has someone sent for a doctor?' the constable demanded.

Heads shook.

'What's the point?' a deep voice asked. 'Ted's bloody well dead.'

'Someone fetch one. Dead or not, we need a doctor to see him.'

There was an awkward silence and the constable used it to take charge. 'No one is to leave till we've got to the bottom of this. And you,' he glared at Luke, 'stay where you are.'

Luke just stared blankly at him. He didn't think he could walk more than a few paces, he felt so dazed and wobbly. This was a nightmare, surely. He'd wake up in a minute and be grateful for that.

But the long, slow minutes ticked past and he didn't wake up. The horror just went on and on.

'He hasn't tried to leave,' Len said angrily, when Luke didn't protest on his own behalf. 'And he didn't want to fight, neither. That fool brought on his own death, with his drinking and his lies. He *forced* the fight on this young chap.'

Half the men in the room nodded and made noises of agreement, the group around the body tried to yell them down, and it was a moment or two before the constable could get order again.

'Someone go an' fetch Sergeant O'Noonan!' he ordered, feeling it was beyond him to sort this out.

Another man ran out of the door.

Ten minutes later, Dr Spelling arrived and pronounced life extinct.

'This one killed him,' one of Gorton's friends cried. 'He's a bloody murderer.'

'I can see no sign of murder,' Dr Spelling said, in his usual quiet tone, 'only the signs of a fight. I doubt it's anyone's fault.' He then examined Luke, who was sitting hunched in a corner, feeling faint and distant. 'You'll live, but he copped you a few good blows. You'll be black and blue tomorrow.'

Luke just stared at him.

'This man is in shock,' Dr Spelling pronounced. 'He should be put to bed, given a cup of hot, sweet tea, and kept warm.'

'He's not leaving here till the sergeant comes to lock him away!' said Clifford Sykes, one of Gorton's closest friends.

'It were an accident,' Len insisted yet again.

'Well, it'll be your word against ours about that, won't it?' Sykes said, spitting in Luke's direction. 'An we'll just have to see who they believe.' He raised his voice, 'Constable, I saw this brute kill my best mate an' I'm going to make sure justice is done.'

Len glared at him. 'Well, me an' my mates will be able to tell folk what really happened. Do you think they'll take your word against mine, Clifford Sykes? You're a drunken ne'er-do-well, an' you allus have been.'

Still Luke did not speak. He heard the voices, but they seemed a long way away and nothing to do with him. He just sat there, staring at the body near the hearth in horror. Someone had covered it with a blanket, but it was there – the bump of the covered head, the boots poking out – a reminder of what he had done, accidentally or not. Killed a man! The words kept echoing in his head.

Dr Spelling looked at him and frowned. 'Aren't you Luke Gibson?' he asked suddenly.

At this, Luke's eyes flickered towards him and he nodded.

'Good heavens, man, how came you to this?'

'He were attacked. That's how it happened,' Len declared. 'That fool lying dead there deserved all he got.'

Sergeant O'Noonan bustled in then and took charge. He had Luke taken into the small room at the side where some of the old women from the hamlet usually did their drinking. He ordered the body left where it was until the magistrate could come and see it, then turned and found himself faced by two opposing camps. So vehement was each in its insistence that Luke Gibson had – or had not – attacked Ted Gorton, that in the end the sergeant decided to take Luke down to the police station, just in case.

'You go an' tell Gorton's wife what's happened,' he said to the constable.

Luke stopped by the door. 'Dr Spelling, will you go with him? I saw Mrs Gorton today at a distance. She'd been badly beaten. I think she needs your help.' He debated whether to say anything about her being locked in, then decided not to. It might make it sound as if he were in the habit of visiting her when her husband was out. He would do anything to spare her trouble. Anything.

Dr Spelling nodded and Luke sighed with relief.

'Someone should go and tell his mother, too,' another man said.

But someone had done that already, and before the doctor could leave Maidie Gorton was pushing her way into the pub, rushing forward to the body on the floor and raising the blanket to stare at him. 'How did it happen?' she asked in a flat, dead voice.

'That 'un killed him,' one man said.

But Len Daley was already moving forward. 'It were an accident, Maidie. Just an accident. Your Ted forced a fight on this chap and he hit his head when he fell. He was rotten drunk again. Come away with me and I'll tell you what happened. Come round to our house.'

She stood up, slowly and painfully, like a very old woman. 'I can't. I've got my grandchilder at home.' She went across to the doctor, who still had not left. 'Could you come back with me and see to the little lass, sir? Our Ted threw her down the stairs yesterday an' I think he's broke her leg. He wouldn't let me call anyone in. He'd already broke her arm a week or two ago. But he can't stop you from seeing her now.'

There was a gasp from those listening.

She ignored the mutters that followed and wiped her sleeve across her eyes. 'He were a lovely lad,' she said in a broken voice, 'a right lovely lad. I don't know what happened to turn him into a drunken sot.' Then she looked across to Luke. 'I doubt you did it a-purpose, Mester Gibson. And it's probably saved Amy's life. He were crazed an' getting worse by the day.'

Len put his arm round her and guided her towards the door. 'I'll come with you, Maidie love. Doctor, better go to her house first to see to the child. I'll show you the way to the farm afterwards.'

Sergeant O'Noonan touched Luke's arm. 'Better come down to the station, lad. We'll need to look into things. An' you'll need to make a statement. Besides, you'll be safer there.'

Luke nodded and stood up. As he and the sergeant walked down the hill, followed by Gorton's friends, less vociferous now but determined to see him locked away. Luke began to shake and clutched at the sergeant's arm for a moment. 'I didn't mean it. I didn't mean to kill him. I didn't even want to fight him. Oh, God, I've killed a man!'

As the sergeant told his good friend Bart Burns, who had been passing by and turned to follow him and Luke to the station: 'Never saw a man so upset as Luke Gibson. Never. I reckon he's telling the truth about the fight. But there'll have to be an enquiry now. Those drunken sots who were friends of Gorton are hell-bent on accusing him of murder.' He hesitated. 'Look, would you go and tell his family for me? I can't leave the station at the moment.'

Bart nodded. 'All right.' Not a job he'd enjoy. It'd shock John Gibson rigid to hear that Luke had killed a man. And since he had gone to work at the junk yard, Bart had grown to respect and like John. But someone had to tell the family, and better him than a stranger.

Hell, he said to himself as he strode off down the street, Luke Gibson was the last person you'd expect to be involved in a fight, let alone kill someone. The poor bastard had looked shocked and sick. He needed his family.

And Bart had no doubt that the Gibsons would rally round to help.

22

Bilsden: September to October 1861

Bart was first to Netherhouse Cottage, where he knocked up John Gibson and told him, as gently as possible, that his son Luke was down at the police station.

John, dressing gown hastily dragged on over his nightshirt, scrawny shanks showing beneath it in worn felt slippers, stood in the doorway, gaping at him. 'Our Luke?' His voice quavered like that of a very old man, not his normal steady tones at all.

Bart nodded, feeling sorry for the old fellow, who was teaching Bart all he knew about dealing in junk and gently guiding him in ways of absolute honesty and trust in his work-mates – ways that seemed wonderful to Bart after his father's carping and often dishonest methods.

'Our Luke? Are you sure?' John blinked like a man who had not managed to gather his wits together.

'Aye, I'm sure.' Bart hesitated, but the old man had to know. 'He's killed a man.' He saw an expression of horror and disbelief on John's face and added hurriedly, 'In a fight. It were an accident. He didn't do it a-purpose.'

'Our Luke in a fight? I – I can't believe even that.'

'It's true. Folk say he didn't start the fight, though.'

'Who were it? The man as died, I mean?' John was clutching the door frame and looked as if he would have fallen without its support.

'Ted Gorton.'

'The fellow as farms up near Luke?'

'Mmm.'

There was a patter of footsteps and Joanie came rushing down the stairs. 'Bart! I thought I heard your voice. What's wrong?'

Behind her, Kathy said, 'Come inside, lad. No need to stand on the doorstep shivering.' She looked at her husband. Bad news, she thought, but said nothing, just ordered gently, 'And you, John, let's get you near that kitchen fire.'

Upstairs, another bedroom door banged and the two boys came pounding down the stairs to join them, followed by Lally, looking even thinner and more like a starving sparrow than ever in a tightly belted dressing gown with her hair tied up in rags. Without needing to be told, she began to poke up the kitchen fire. A cup of tea always helped when there was trouble, and from Mr Gibson's face, this was trouble, right enough. She kept an ear turned to the conversation and what Bart had to tell them made her stop what she was doing and stare over her shoulder in horror at Joanie's young man.

John's hands were shaking and his face so white and fragile-looking, it might have been made of paper. Bart wished he had been able to soften this blow. 'He didn't do it on purpose,' he said again and again. 'You know your Luke. He didn't want to fight in the first place.'

'Then why have they taken him to the police station, if it were an accident?' John demanded.

'The sergeant told me it's for his own protection. Gorton's boozing mates are standing outside the station shouting for his blood.' Bart didn't say exactly what they were shouting and was relieved when John didn't ask. It'd only make matters worse. 'The sergeant daren't let Luke go. He's afraid they'll attack him.'

'Nay!' John whispered. 'Nay, did you ever hear the like?' He clasped Kathy's hand tightly and turned an anguished face on her. 'What should we do, love? I can't seem to think straight.'

There was silence, then Bart realised that everyone was looking at him, relying on him. And he realised, too, that he felt part of this family now, that he wanted to help them. 'I think we should tell your Tom and Annie. I'll go and do that, if you like, Mr Gibson, while you're getting dressed. Then I'll bring them back down here to see you. We can talk it over together, work out what's best.'

John nodded, relieved. 'Yes. Yes, you're right, lad. You go an' fetch our Annie. She'll know what to do. An' our Tom, too.'

'We'll be ready to go too, Luke, by the time you get back.' Kathy exchanged worried glances with Lally. She had never seen her John like this. Joanie was just standing there, watching Bart, eyes shining with pride. He was a good man, her Bart was.

It did not take long to explain matters to Tom, who nodded and said, 'Right. I'll get dressed and meet you back at Dad's. You go and fetch our Annie.' As Bart turned to walk away, he added, 'Thanks, lad.'

Bart turned to nod. 'I'm happy to do owt I can t'help, Tom. We all know your Luke would never attack anyone.'

Worried as he was, Tom spared a moment to watch him go. 'He'll do,' he said aloud. He had doubted Joanie's choice of a man, but Bart Burns was all right. Nothing like the rest of his rotten, cheating family.

So the tale was told, a third time to Annie, who had rushed down to open the door herself when she heard someone knocking and shouting her name. William stood at his mother's side, his arm round her shoulders. 'I'll come, too,' he said simply.

Bart waited while they got dressed, conscious of Winnie, in a faded blue dressing gown, pattering to and fro, lighting lamps and muttering about getting the fire going. All the time, she kept shooting sideways glances at Bart, as if she didn't trust him. She's acting like she's the mistress, instead of Annie Hallam, he thought to himself, somewhat annoyed, for Winnie always seemed to radiate disapproval when he was near.

A few minutes later, he was astonished to see Annie hurry downstairs, dressed in a simple skirt and top, under a dark mantle, with just a scarf on her head. No hoops or fancy clothes, simply a woman off to help her family. It was the first time he'd seen her like this, the first time she'd seemed a flesh-and-blood figure to him, instead of a being far above him. She'd be lovely if she smiled more, he realised in surprise, but she had always seemed so stern and managing to him.

At Netherhouse Cottage, they found John dressed and looking a bit better, but still in shock. He turned at once to his grown-up children for support and guidance. They both hugged him, Bart noticed, and John hugged them back, holding on for a little longer than usual, as if he drew strength from touching them.

Bart felt jealousy sear through him for a moment. His father had never hugged any of them, and in fact, the only time Lemuel Burns had touched them in any way as children was to cane or smack them. His mother had hugged him, though, his poor mother, whom he saw sometimes staring out of the upstairs window and who had once or twice raised a hand in greeting as he walked slowly past, or blown him a kiss. He wished he could get her out of that house, bring her somewhere like this. She must be leading a miserable life lately. 'Are you coming with me to the police station, then?' Tom asked Annie.

'Of course I am. You stay here, Dad, and keep Kathy company. We don't want Luke coming home and finding no one to greet him.' Her eyes slid sideways to Bart, as if questioning him.

He nodded and banished all thoughts of his mother. 'I'll come, too, if that's all right with you, Mrs Hallam? I may be able to help in some way, even if it's only to run messages.'

'Thank you. And isn't it about time you called me Annie?'

'Annie, then.' Well, well, he thought to himself, imagine him on first-name terms with the owner of Hallam's Mill.

Joanie, who had been hovering nearby, beamed at him. John nodded approval and sank into his favourite chair. Behind him, Kathy also nodded and gave Bart a little smile.

The three of them walked briskly into town, glad of the moonlight that showed their path clearly. Annie and Tom questioned Bart again in hushed voices as they went, but he could only repeat what he had told them before. 'I wasn't there when it happened. Sergeant O'Noonan knew I was – well – connected to your family now, so when he saw me in the street, he asked me to tell you. And I was glad to help. Though I'm not really that much use.'

'You've been a great help. It's not everyone who'd walk all over the town at night like that.' Annie sighed. 'Poor Dad's not taking it well. It upsets me to see him like that, looking so frail.'

'I'm not taking it well, either,' Tom said, his face tight with anger. 'If I find anyone calling out for our Luke to be hung,' for Bart had told these two exactly what the mob was shouting, 'I'll make him regret it, I will that.'

'And I'll help you do it,' Bart said quietly. Luke Gibson had accepted him from the first. He had never had to prove himself to Luke, and he thought a lot of Joanie's brother.

There was still a small group of men waiting outside the police station, though most of the crowd had dispersed. At the sight of Tom and Annie, they began to stir and shout.

'Watch out! Here's some more bloody Gibsons!'

'Hang that murdering bastard!' Clifford Sykes made a crude gesture of pulling a rope tight round his neck.

Tom instantly veered sideways, walked right up to the group and stood eyeball to eyeball with Sykes, who seemed to be the leader. 'What was that you were saying about my brother?' he demanded, prodding Sykes in the chest.

The other man shuffled his feet and took a pace or two backwards, but Tom followed him step for step, and when Sykes looked to his mates for help, he found that they'd moved even further back than he had, leaving him on his own in a prom-inent position. He swallowed, feeling suddenly nervous, but tried to stand his ground. Tom Gibson had a reputation in the town – honest but a hard man to cross, and had been good with his fists when younger.

'I saw your Luke kill Ted Gorton an' you'll not get me to say different, 'cos it's the truth,' he muttered.

'I don't want you to tell anything but the truth.' Tom's voice was silky, but with acid beneath its soft tones. 'The exact truth, though. Not something you made up to get at us Gibsons.'

Clifford said nothing, but someone to the side of him muttered, 'Bloody murderer!' so Bart took it upon himself to walk towards that fellow, who moved quickly backwards like the coward he was.

'What are you doin' siding with them Gibsons, Bart Burns?' a voice asked from the very back of the group.

'I'm looking for the truth, same as Tom is,' he replied. 'An' why shouldn't I be with them?'

'Your daddy won't like to hear about this,' another voice said, in a whining falsetto. 'He'll tell the Lord on you.'

Bart glared round, but in the deep shadows it was difficult to tell who was speaking. He suspected who the first speaker was, though. 'My father can do what he chooses. He's nothing to me,' he called. 'An' if you've gone in working with him, you'll regret it, Sim Jones. Folk allus do.'

There was silence from the back and after a minute or so Bart nodded. It had been Sim Jones.

Then, from the shadows, a taller man stepped forward. 'Keep your mouth shut about our father, Bart, or I'll shut it for you!'

'You can try, Don. You can certainly try,' he tossed back. Was Don going out drinking with fools such as these now? He glanced round, feeling disgusted to see his own brother, estranged or not, among scum like these. What a contrast to the Gibson family! He wished he were not a Burns, wished it quite desperately sometimes.

Tom took a step away from the group of men, but his eyes were hard as he said, 'I think it's time you lot went home.'

'We'll go when we choose,' Don Burns threw back at him, 'and no bloody Gibson will tell us what to do.'

'But I will!' a voice from the police station doorway shouted, a very loud voice. Sergeant O'Noonan had finished taking the statement the law required from a man so shocked by what had happened that, in the sergeant's expert opinion, he could not possibly be telling lies. 'I've had enough of your noise,' he roared. 'My constable told folk a while back to get off home. Some of 'em had enough sense to go. This is the last warning to the rest of you. If I don't see the back of you, and quickly, I'll arrest you all for disturbing the peace! So get moving.'

A couple of men broke away and hurried off down the street, others took a few steps away then slowed down, loitering, as if they still expected something to happen.

'Right!' the sergeant called and started to cross the road. The ones who had been hovering began to walk away more quickly and more men joined them as he drew closer, leaving only Clifford Sykes and Don Burns standing there. 'Can I help you, Mr Sykes?' the sergeant asked, with heavy sarcasm.

'I'm not going till I know what you're going to do with that murderer,' Clifford's jaw jutted pugnaciously and his fists were clenched.

'That's it!' Tom snapped. 'If I hear you call my brother that name once more, Sykes, I'll have the law on you for slander.'

The phrase 'law on you' seemed to penetrate even Sykes's drink-sodden brain. 'Eh? Whass that?'

'Slander is a misdemeanour,' the sergeant told him cheerfully. 'They sue you for making untruthful statements that damage someone's reputation and then, if they win their case, they take everything you own in compensation. They'd have that little corner shop of yours, Sykes, I promise you, if they proved you'd been slandering anyone, though it's not worth as much as when you inherited it. You spend too much time boozing and not enough looking after your business. But they'd have it off you, anyway.'

'Not if I'm there to bear witness that you've been threatening him,' Don growled.

The sergeant's expression was mild, greatly at variance with the alertness of his eyes. 'Me? I never threatened anyone. Sykes asked what slander was and I told him. That's all that happened here.'

Sykes muttered something, then turned and walked off down the street, joining two men who had been waiting for him at the corner. There he paused to yell, 'Luke Gibson had better watch out if you let him go! We'll not put up with him killing our friend.'

The sergeant ignored them. 'Nothing better to do, sir?' he inquired of Don, who had not moved.

'Just stretching my legs. No law against taking a walk, is there?'

'No, sir, so long as that's all you're doing.'

Don stood watching as Bart disappeared into the police station with Tom and Annie. His dad was right to be angry. Bart had betrayed the family, absolutely betrayed them. And they'd make him pay for that one day, him and his little whore.

When Bart left the station again, to go up the hill and summon Annie's carriage, which was thought to be the safest way to get Luke home, Don followed him, not hiding his presence. But he did not quite dare go past the gates of Ridge House, where one of the gardeners lived and kept watch on who went in and out.

'You're a bloody turncoat, you are,' he muttered, as he watched Bart disappear from view. 'And we'll get even with you for that one day. Eye for an eye, tooth for a tooth. You'll regret your defiance of Father, you and the Gibsons both. "*Honour thy father*",' he muttered as he walked away. 'That's what the Bible says, an' if you don't do it of your own accord, we'll teach you to do it. That lass is going to be sorry she took up with you, too. She is that. Real sorry!'

Since Ted Gorton's friends continued to make a fuss about his death, the magistrate authorised Dr Lewis, as town's medical officer, to perform an autopsy on the dead man to find out the exact cause of death. Jeremy, assisted by Dr Spelling, duly did this in the basement of the town's small hospital, but refused to tell anyone what he had found, reserving his findings for the public hearing. The magistrate had deemed this necessary, in view of the dissension the affair had caused in certain quarters.

Hamish Pennybody came along to the magistrates' court to represent Luke's interests, but he could not understand what all the fuss was about. 'Regrettable, of course, but these things happen. It was clearly an accident. No doubt about it.'

Luke had been released on Tom's surety: 'Just a formality, that,' Sergeant O'Noonan had apologised. Luke had been staying with Tom since then, but had insisted on going up to work his land at Hey End in the daytime. Tom had tried to dissuade him and when he failed, set a couple of fellows he knew to keep an eye on things up there, as unobtrusively as they could. He didn't want anyone attacking their Luke, especially as one or other of Bart's brothers often seemed to be hanging around lately, either up at Hey Lane or near the yard.

The whole family was worried about Luke, who had lost weight and was looking gaunt and unhappy. He had talked with Nathaniel Bell, Minister at the chapel, about what had happened, but although Bell had assured him that he could not be held to blame, it had not taken away the dreadful feeling of guilt. '*Thou shalt not kill*', the Bible said. And he had killed.

Luke was even more worried about Amy than about himself. He had not seen her since that dreadful day, for she had gone down to live with her husband's mother, leaving the farm empty and neighbours to tend the stock. He wished he could just catch a glimpse of her or the children, but she had not poked her nose out of the door all week. Perhaps she was worried about her hair? As if that mattered! Eh, the poor lass had suffered, and he wished he could make things right for her again, wished it most desperately. Instead, he seemed to have made them worse.

On the day of the hearing the courtroom was full, with people standing up along the back and more waiting outside, unable to get in. When Luke entered from the rear, some of those inside jeered at him, but Sergeant O'Noonan crossed over to them immediately, smiling round like a tiger choosing his prey. 'Next one to make an unseemly noise gets thrown out,' he said, with his usual cheerfulness. It was commonly held that he'd smile even if he had to hang you. 'This is as court of law, not an alehouse, and I'll thank you,' he raised his voice, 'all of you, to behave with due respect.'

When the magistrate entered and took his place, he made a brief speech summing up why this hearing was being held, then asked the officer in attendance to call Dr Lewis.

Jeremy walked in, tall and elegant in dark grey, a figure well known in the town, and a man whose word would not be doubted.

'Please tell the court what you found in your autopsy.'

'The dead man had a tumour on the brain. He must have been close to death for a while. The fighting only accelerated the process. It's probable that his behaviour had changed during the past few months. He could have become violent or morose. His wife and mother will be able to tell you about that.'

There was a mutter as people exclaimed to one another.

The magistrate banged his hammer for silence. 'Thank you, Dr Lewis. You may step down. Call the proprietor of the Hare and Hounds!'

Jake Remsworth was nervous. He answered the questions put to him so quietly that the magistrate ordered him twice to speak up.

'Did you see the fight start?'

Jake shook his head. 'Not really, Your Honour.'

Luke looked up at that, puzzled. Jake had tried to stop the fight. He must have seen it start.

Other witnesses were called and their testimonies were quite contradictory. Ted Gorton's friends looked triumphantly across at Luke as they stepped down from the witness box. He tried not to show the fear that was beginning to curl quietly in his stomach, fear that they'd threatened the witnesses and were about to pervert the course of justice. Surely that couldn't happen, could it? Not in England in this day and age.

Fred Daley was the next witness and made quite an impact, giving his evidence in a quiet firm voice and telling the truth, though his story conflicted greatly with that of some of the others.

'I am beginning to think that some of the witnesses are committing perjury,' the magistrate said as Fred stepped down. He had a loud, booming voice which echoed round the court-room. 'I wish to make it quite clear that if anyone is found guilty of perjury in my courtroom, then I shall commit that person to prison. I will not have Her Majesty's justice mocked, even in a simple inquiry like this one.'

After that, the remaining pair of Ted's cronies claimed not to have seen anything, causing Clifford Sykes to glare at them across the court.

'Call Mrs Gorton!'

Amy came in, a bonnet hiding her shorn head, though fronds of hair stuck out untidily around her forehead. Her face was colourless, and she looked frail and haunted. Yet under oath she spoke firmly. Yes, the doctor was right. Her husband had indeed been acting strangely for several months before his death. When pressed to say how, she started weeping and confessed that he had beaten her and the children. 'Badly, sir,' she ended with a sob.

'I'm afraid you must tell me more clearly what you mean by "beating", Mrs Gorton,' the magistrate said, his voice sympathetic.

'He h-hit me, slapped my face, threw me to the ground and – and he kicked me while I lay there.' She was sobbing now, trying to stop but not succeeding.

Luke's knuckles were white on the edge of the pew-like bench in front of him.

'Any other strange behaviour?' the magistrate prompted.

'He c-cut off my hair, sir.'

'For what reason?'

'Because he said he didn't want me,' her voice faltered for a moment and she drew in a breath that was more of a groan as she struggled to answer the question, 'f-flaunting myself at other men.'

'Was it likely that you'd do that?'

'No, sir. Never.'

'Anything else?'

'He kept accusing me of things I hadn't done, sir.'

'Again, I regret that I shall have to ask you to be more specific. What sort of things, Mrs Gorton?'

Her voice was so low that the magistrate interrupted to ask her to speak up. She took another deep breath and said, 'He accused me of – of having a – having relations with our neighbour, Luke Gibson.'

'I ask only to set the record clear, because I have no doubt about the answer you will give me, but did you have such relations, Mrs Gorton? Was there anything between you and Mr Gibson?'

'No, sir. I cleaned his house for him, and he was very kind to me and the children, but I never, ever would have behaved in such a way. Never!'

'How was Mr Gibson kind to you?'

She flushed bright red. 'He used to give us food, sir. He knew that Ted kept us short.'

There was a gasp in the courtroom and then a murmur ran round it. This was the last thing anyone would have expected her to say, for Gorton had been a free spender in the pub, often buying drinks for his cronies. No one liked to think of little children going hungry, especially those men who had been recipients of the dead man's generosity.

Ted Gorton's mother was called next and was also able to testify to her son's changed behaviour. She was still angry enough to add of her own accord that he had broken little Tess's arm a week or two before and then later, just before his death, her leg as well, when he had thrown her down the stairs. 'Oh, sir, he refused even to let a doctor be called to the child. He weren't like my son any more,' she ended. 'I hardly recognised him sometimes. An' I were ashamed to have borne him when I saw that poor child, I were that.'

'And has the doctor seen the little girl now?'

'Yes, sir. He came to see her the very same evening as Ted died. Dr Spelling, it were.'

'And what did he say about her injuries?'

'He says our Tess will limp for the rest of her days because of what her father did to her, and the way we had to wait to get her leg set.'

Before anyone could stop her, Mrs Gorton added a comment of her own accord. 'Nor I don't believe that that young fellow,' pointing to Luke, 'would ever have started a fight, an' you should be ashamed of yourself, Clifford Sykes, for hounding him like you have. Luke Gibson is as nice a fellow as you could meet, an' allus a friendly word, or carry your basket back up the hill from market for you.'

She turned back to the magistrate. 'I'm glad the doctor cut my son open, sir, and found what were wrong. I didn't like the thought of it at the time, but now it's shown me it weren't all my Ted's fault, at least. It were his illness, like. An' that's a comfort to a mother, it is indeed.'

The court was filled with a heavy silence, and even Clifford Sykes, who had been glaring at Luke until now, was unable to deny Maidie Gorton's evidence and was scowling instead at his own hands, clasped together in his lap like a bunch of gnarled roots.

The magistrate nodded benignly. In a case like this, where people in the community were taking sides and some were clearly making threats, it was best to let folk have their say. The mother had made an excellent witness. 'Call the doctor,' he said, and proceeded to question Dr Spelling about little Tess's broken limbs, then about Amy Gorton's injuries.

The people in the courtroom were silent, listening now to the evidence in an embarrassment that made them avoid one another's eyes. It was one thing to know a man was giving his wife a thump or two from time to time; quite another to hear serious beatings discussed openly, to see a decent young woman with a face still badly bruised and hear of a child maimed for life. It was not how they liked to think of themselves in Hey End.

In his summing up, the magistrate gave everyone a lecture on perjury. 'I shall not prosecute anyone today, though it's quite clear that some of you have been lying to the court. But we have uncovered the truth, which is why we came here, so I shall let it go at that. I give down a verdict of Accidental Death. And, Mr Gibson,' looking across at Luke, 'you should not blame yourself in any way. You tried not to fight. You were forced to defend yourself. The whole unfortunate business was, quite simply, an accident so far as you were concerned.'

Luke nodded, but his heart was still heavy. He knew it would always be on his conscience that he had killed a man. Always. His face was bleak as he walked out of the court. He searched the crowd outside for Amy, but she had hurried out with her mother-in-law the minute the session ended, and he could see no sign of her.

That night, he sat in his cottage and for the first time did not feel a sense of pride in what he had wrought with his own hands. Instead he felt lonely. He could not settle to his new seed catalogue and stood for a long time in the doorway, looking in the direction of the farm. But there was no light in the windows. She was gone.

Would she ever come back?

23

Bilsden: October 1861

In October, a man got off an early afternoon train in Bilsden. He was either very tired or had been ill and was not fully recovered. His forehead bore a nasty jagged scar and another crossed his chin, where a half-grown beard straggled untidily. He was rubbing his temples like one whose head is aching and it was a moment or two after the train had left before he noticed the porter standing beside him, staring.

'You all right, sir?'

'Yes. Yes, I'm much better. I'll just—' His words trailed away and he picked up one small bag, leaving his other luggage lying there. But when he walked out of the station, he seemed to lose the impetus to move on and paused once again, staring round Hallam Square as if he had never seen the place before.

'Are you sure you're all right, sir?'

The man turned round to find that the porter, a large fatherly man, had followed him outside. He managed a half-smile. 'I'm very tired, that's all. I've been ill and the travelling's taken it out of me, but I'm getting better now.' And he was, he told himself firmly as the fear that had haunted him for a few months crept into the corners of his mind again. He was much better. Every day he was remembering more and more.

'Has this place changed?' he asked suddenly, gesturing to the square. 'I feel I ought to recognise it, but I don't.'

The porter nodded. 'Yes, sir, it's changed quite a bit. There used to be just the street and then the station at the end, but Mr Hallam – very civic-minded gentleman, greatly missed – had it rebuilt.' He turned to nod at the wide space surrounded by elegant buildings. 'We're proud of our square, sir, very proud. Named it after him, Hallam Square.'

'He's dead?'

'Yes, sir. He died last year.'

The man was frowning. 'Would his first name have been Frederick?'

'Why, yes, sir. Did you know him?'

'I think I did.' The man sighed. 'I had a bad knock on the head. I don't even remember how it happened.' Though they'd told him about it afterwards, told him that he was lucky to have got away from the military, even if he had been badly injured in the process. And had it not been for an Irish dockworker, who loathed the military, pulling him out of the water and concealing him inside a crate, he wouldn't have escaped.

'I've forgotten a lot,' he said, more to himself than to the porter, 'but it's coming back to me, bit by bit. Frederick Hallam.' He nodded. 'Yes, I do remember him. Tall fellow?'

The porter nodded.

'With silver hair? Rather distinguished?'

'Yes, indeed.' It was the porter's turn to frown. It was beginning to seem to him that he ought to recognise this gentleman, because for all the untidiness of his appearance, he *was* quite clearly a gentleman, and Sam Jeary prided himself on never forgetting a face. 'So you've been to Bilsden before, have you, sir?'

'So they tell me. And I think they're right.' He hesitated, then asked the question which was so important to him, trying but failing to sound casual. 'I keep remembering another name, a woman's name. It might be someone I knew here, for I always think of it in connection with Bilsden. She was called Annie.'

Sam stared at him. 'Well, I don't know her personally, of course, but Mr Hallam's widow is called Annie, so if you knew him, you'd definitely have met her. Devoted couple, they were. Everyone was very sad for her when he died.'

The man was only half listening. 'And does she have auburn hair – curly?'

'Yes, sir. She does. Very elegant lady, Mrs Hallam.'

'And she has a son called – called – Edgar?'

Sam beamed at the poor gentleman. How sad to lose your memory like this! But he obviously knew the Hallam family. 'Yes, sir. A fine lad he is, too. His father would be proud of him.'

The man's voice was harsh, as if he couldn't control it properly. 'How do I find Annie – Mrs Hallam? I've come all the way from America to see her.' He saw the porter staring and added hurriedly, 'I'm hoping she can help me regain my memory. I remember her so clearly, you see, that she must know me, must be able to help.'

Sam was impressed by the tale. America was a long way away, and they were having a nasty war over there at the moment. Perhaps that was how the gentleman had got injured so badly. There was nowhere like England, if you asked Sam. And no part of England as good as Lancashire. Salt of the earth, the folk of Bilsden were. Couldn't find finer people anywhere, nor ones who worked harder. He was proud to have been born here. 'Well, now, fancy that,' he said indulgently, trying to humour the poor gentleman, who didn't really seem to know what he was doing.

'How do I find Annie – Mrs Hallam?'

'Well, the best thing would be for you to get a cab and tell the driver to take you to Ridge House. That's where she lives. If she's not at home, I'm sure they'll let you wait for her, you not being well and having come so far.' The poor fellow was pale, and thin. Looked like a strong wind might blow him away. 'Shall I call you a cab, sir? And fetch the rest of your luggage?'

The man was staring at Sam as if he hadn't understood what he was saying. He half closed his eyes and whispered, 'Ridge House. Yes. I remember that name, too.' He sighed and seemed to make a huge effort to pull himself together. 'Yes, porter, please call me a cab. I must go there at once, must see her.' He saw the porter frown and realised this might give rise to talk. 'And her children. There's a girl, too, isn't there? Red hair, like her mother. But I can't remember her name.'

'That'll be Miss Tamsin. Image of her mother, she is.'

The porter watched the cab drive away and wondered if he'd done the right thing. The poor gentleman didn't look dangerous, but he certainly wasn't well, not well at all. Still, Sam consoled himself, there were plenty of people up at Ridge House to protect Mrs Hallam. Servants and family. Quite a devoted family, they were, too. Just like the dear Queen. A fine example to everyone.

Annie was talking to Nat Jervis near the rose beds when one of the station cabs turned into the drive and rumbled up to the front door. There seemed to be only one occupant. She frowned. She wasn't expecting anyone. 'Excuse me, Nat. I'll just see who that is.'

She walked across the grass towards the front of the house, but the cab door opened before it even drew to a halt and a man half fell out of it. He stumbled, righted himself and stopped to gaze around him. At first she thought her eyes were playing tricks on her. It looked like – but it couldn't be! Tian Gilchrist was much younger than this gentleman, who was staring across at her as if he'd never seen her before. Perhaps it was a relative of Tian, his older brother or—

Suddenly, the man shouted, and it was definitely Tian's voice. 'Annie! It is Annie, isn't it?' Then he ran towards her and before she knew what was happening, he had swept her into his arms and was kissing her passionately.

For a moment, she responded instinctively, as her body had always responded to his, even though she had done nothing about it before. Now, before she knew what was happening, she had melted against him, kissing him back. When she realised what she was doing, she panicked and began to push him away.

From across the garden, Nat called out, 'Hey!' and footsteps thumped across the lawn towards them.

But by the time Nat arrived, the man had let go of Annie

and was just holding her at arm's length, staring at her. 'I've dreamed of you,' he said, in a hushed, reverent tone. 'At night in crowded barracks . . . in Brownsby's house when I couldn't even remember who I was. I always remembered your face, Annie. Always.'

She forgot her fear. 'Tian? Is it really you?' A surge of joy at seeing him took her by surprise. 'Oh, Tian, welcome back!'

He smiled down at her, his face radiant. 'I really am back.' Then he gave a loud sigh and collapsed at her feet.

Nat moved forward as he bent over the crumpled figure. 'Is he all right, ma'am?'

'He's just fainted, I think. He must have been ill. I didn't recognise him at first.'

'Nor did I, ma'am.' He cleared his throat and decided not to refer to the embrace.

Annie blushed and also decided to ignore the kiss, as well as the feelings which were still throbbing through her body, feelings long unsatisfied. She pushed the thought of that aside and ran her fingertip over the scar on Tian's face. 'He must have been in a bad accident. He said – he said at one time he didn't even remember who he was.'

'Mother!'

Winnie was waddling down the steps, eager to see what was happening, but Edgar pushed past the maid and rushed across to Tian. The cab driver and the gardener's lad had also joined them and were staring down at the unconscious man as if he had two heads.

Annie stood up. 'What am I thinking of, standing around here like this? Mr Gilchrist has been hurt. Can you carry him inside, please, Nat? And perhaps you'd help him, driver?' She caught hold of her son's arm. 'No, let them get Mr Gilchrist to bed, Edgar.'

She turned to the gardener's lad, who had grown so much lately that he was more a man than a lad. 'Sim, will you go and fetch Dr Lewis as quickly as you can? Hurry, now!'

Sim was off at once, pounding down the gravel driveway.

You didn't argue with the mistress when she gave you orders in that tone. As he ran, he marvelled. He remembered Mr Gilchrist, the artist gentleman. Well, they all did. Lovely man, he was. What could have happened to him?

Annie turned to the maid, her voice crisp and businesslike again. 'Winnie, please show Nat and the driver the way to the corner bedroom at the back!'

Winnie nodded and set off, overtaking the men and giving a running series of orders to mind their step, not bump into the paintwork and watch out for Mr Gilchrist's head when they turned the corner of the stairs.

As Annie and Edgar followed the small procession into the house, they looked up to see Tamsin and Elizabeth peering over the banisters. When she realised who was being carried up the stairs, Tamsin's mouth formed a big 'O' of astonishment. 'What's happened to Tian?' she asked in a loud whisper.

'He's had a bad accident,' Annie explained yet again. She followed Nat upstairs into the spare bedroom and watched him and his assistant lay Tian carefully on the bed. 'Thank you, Nat. I'll see to him now. Winnie, will you pay the cab driver, please?'

'Yes, ma'am.' Winnie left reluctantly. 'Did he say anything about what had happened to him?' she hissed at the driver as they walked down the stairs together.

'Hardly spoke at all. I had to ask him twice where he wanted to go. He was just staring round like he'd lost his wits. Who is he?'

'A friend of the family,' Winnie said loftily. She might probe for information, but she wasn't giving anything away to outsiders. I'll go straight back up, she decided. The mistress might need me. 'You fetch the luggage in and I'll go and get you your money,' she ordered.

When she had paid the driver from the purse kept in the servants' quarters, she almost pushed him out of the house, seized the small portmanteau as an excuse and ran up the stairs as fast as her plump legs could manage.

Meanwhile Annie stood staring down at the man lying on

the bed. Tian looked so pale. Without realising what she was doing, she sat down on the edge of the bed and smoothed the chestnut hair from his brow. He murmured something indistinguishable and reached out blindly to grasp her hand.

A noise behind made her look up to see the doorway filled with curious faces. 'Good heavens! He doesn't need an audience. Elizabeth, can you persuade the children to leave Mr Gilchrist alone until the doctor's been?'

'Yes, of course. Come on, you two.'

But Tamsin had to ask first, 'Is he going to die, Mother?'

Annie looked up, understanding why Tamsin had asked this. Since their father's death, both children were afraid of losing anyone they loved. Even the death of one of the elderly stable cats the previous month had had both of them in floods of tears. 'No, of course he isn't going to die. But he's been ill. We'll have to nurse him better. You can help me, but not now. I've sent for Dr Lewis. He'll tell us what to do.'

They walked away with Elizabeth, slowly and reluctantly, with many backward glances.

'Dr Lewis will make him better,' Edgar declared, once they reached the schoolroom door. 'He's the best doctor in town.'

'He didn't make Father better,' Tamsin muttered, then shut her mouth in response to a glare from her governess.

Before Annie could examine Tian again, another noise made her look up. Winnie reappeared, holding the portmanteau in front of her like a shield. Annie sighed. Sometimes you could have too many servants. 'Thank you for carrying that up, Winnie, but would you please wait downstairs now? I need you to bring Dr Lewis up here as soon as he arrives.'

The maid bobbed her head. 'Yes, ma'am.' She bustled down, clicking her tongue in exasperation at the sight of the shabby suitcase and trunk which the driver had left right in the middle of the hall, just where they would trip people up. 'Some folk haven't the sense of a rabbit!' she muttered, and tried to pick them up, exclaiming aloud: 'What on earth has he got in these? They weigh a ton.'

She saw Nat bending over a flower bed near the front door, examining a rose bush, and beckoned to him. 'Could you just come and help me upstairs with these, Mr Jervis, please? I don't like my hall looking untidy and we don't want Dr Lewis to trip up over these cases, do we?'

Nat grinned and came back in. It wasn't strictly his job, but never mind. 'All right, Winnie. Where do you want them?'

'In the room next-door to Mr Gilchrist's for the moment. We don't want to disturb him.'

'All right, love. I'll take them up.'

'And mind you don't bump my paintwork!'

'No, love.'

'And don't call me "love"! How many times do I have to tell you that?'

He grinned as he went out to get help. She had a sharp tongue on her, old Winnie did, but her heart was in the right place and she was a good worker.

Annie didn't even hear her maid close the bedroom door the second time. All her attention was focused on the man lying so still. She was surprised at the joy welling up inside her: joy that he was safe, that he had come back, that he was here. She stroked his hair away from his forehead again, but it tumbled back. At one side it was shorter than the other, where a small scar broke the hairline. What could have done all this? And how thin he was!

Without realising it, she continued to stroke his forehead gently, remembering what he had looked like the last time she had seen him – so young and strong, vibrant with life. And now, he might have been his own father, or at least an older brother. 'You poor thing,' she whispered. 'Who did this to you?'

He opened his eyes even as she spoke. 'Annie. Are you real? I've dreamed about you so often and woken in tears because I couldn't find you. Is it really you?'

'Yes.' Her voice was low and without realising it, she cradled his cheek in her hand. She couldn't believe what she was hearing. Dreamed of her? Wept because she wasn't there? Did he still care about her, then?

He fumbled for her hand, carrying it to his lips. A shiver ran down her neck and warmth welled up inside her.

'I forgot everything else, but I never forgot that I loved you,' he said, smiling. 'Never. And I always remembered your name, even when I couldn't remember my own.'

She realised suddenly how strange it would seem if people heard him talking like this, so she tried to turn the conversation in to more sensible paths. 'Tian, you mustn't say things like that!'

'Why not?'

'Because – because—' She had been going to say because she was a married woman, but she wasn't, not any more, though she still had trouble remembering that sometimes. But that didn't mean that she was going to let him – to—

He kissed her hand again, reverently, like a knight who had found the Holy Grail, and her protests trailed away. Then his eyes closed and he sighed himself into sleep, still holding her hand tightly.

Jeremy found them like that when he came into the room.

Annie was unaware that she had tears in her eyes as she nodded to her old friend in greeting. 'It's Tian Gilchrist, the artist. He's been injured – a blow to the head – though I think it happened some time ago. He says he even forgot who he was at one time.' She blinked away the tears. 'Oh, Jeremy, he just collapsed at my feet. Is he going to be all right? He must be all right!' She couldn't lose him as well.

Jeremy came to put his arm round her. 'It must have been a shock for you to see him like this.' And she had had enough shocks lately, with poor Luke. 'Let me examine him and then we'll talk. And, Annie, if you don't need him elsewhere, could you send Jimson to me? He's marvellous with sick people. By the looks of it, you'll need someone to tend Mr Gilchrist for a while.'

She didn't want to leave, but knew it wouldn't be right for her to stay, so she went out reluctantly to ring for Jimson. But she didn't join her children afterwards. Instead, she went and sat in the library, blushing again as she remembered the sweetness of Tian's kiss and smiling to herself from time to time. She could not deny how happy she was to see him.

Half an hour later, Jeremy came downstairs to join her. 'Tian's roused himself once or twice, but he's sleeping again. It seems a normal sleep and some colour has returned to his cheeks.'

'Good. Good.'

'Jimson's keeping watch and has promised to call out if the patient stirs.'

'He loves to be needed.'

The doctor accepted a cup of tea and a piece of cake. 'I can find nothing physically wrong with your Mr Gilchrist, apart from the scars, and as you say, they happened a while ago. There's no congestion in his chest, but he looks utterly exhausted. I'd hazard a guess that what he really needs is to rest a lot and be cosseted back to health.'

'He said he even forgot who he was at one time,' she said softly. Tian had also said that he had never forgotten her, but she did not tell Jeremy that. She held the thought inside her, marvelling at Tian's devotion. It made her feel good – and very alive.

'Not surprising after a blow like that. Shall I have him admitted to the hospital, or do you wish to keep him here?'

The very thought of turning Tian away to the care of strangers made her angry, even though the town's small hospital was well run under Jeremy's supervision. 'We'll keep him here, of course. Did you really think we'd turn a sick man away? A friend of the family, too.'

Jeremy didn't even try to hide a smile. 'No.'

'But you'll have to tell us exactly what to do for him.'

'I doubt there's anything specific you can do. Just look after him, keep him tranquil, feed him well and let him recover in his own time. He shouldn't have been travelling in that condition.'

But she could guess why Tian had been travelling. He had been coming to find her. The thought made her shiver. She knew he had fallen in love with her nearly two years ago when he'd painted the family portrait. He had made no secret of that when he left. In fact, it was why he had left so precipitately. And his love seemed to have endured. The thought warmed her, warmed something that had been feeling cold for a long time. Oh, Tian! I'm not ready for it, she thought suddenly. But she did not allow herself to think beyond that, to admit what it was that she was not ready for. 'Well, then, we'll nurse him back to health again,' she said aloud, trying to sound her usual decisive self.

Jeremy hid a smile. He had known Annie since she was ten years old and could see, even if she didn't realise what was happening, that today's events had started to soften the brittle shell behind which she had been hiding since Frederick's death. And about time, too. A person could not mourn for ever, or live like someone made of stone. He did not comment on the soft glow that filled her face, just said quietly, 'I'll leave you to it, then, Annie. Send for me if you need me, but otherwise I'll pop in to see Gilchrist again in the morning.'

It was evening before Tian awoke and he could not, for a moment, think where he was. But he was used to that so did not allow himself to panic, just lay still and allowed the room to come into better focus around him. A very comfortable room, with velvet curtains and well-polished furniture.

'Would you like a drink of milk, sir? It's fresh from the farm.'

He looked round to see an elderly man hovering by the bed. 'Should I know you? If so, I'm afraid I can't remember who you are.' It was always best to admit that, because if you tried to hide it, you'd be sure to betray yourself and usually quite quickly, then the person would take offence.

'My name is Jimson, sir. I work for Mrs Hallam. I used to be Mr Hallam's valet.' He gave a rusty chuckle. 'Now she calls me her general factotum. She's asked me to look after you.'

'Annie.' The word was a whisper, but a smile lit Tian's face to brilliant life. 'I did find her, then? It wasn't a dream.'

Jimson had been warned that Mr Gilchrist had been injured – well, you could see that for yourself – and he'd been warned, too, that the poor gentleman might not remember things very clearly. So he spoke slowly as he explained, 'You're at Ridge House, sir, Mrs Hallam's home. You came to Bilsden by train, took a cab up here and then you fainted clear away.' Winnie had described the scene to the other servants quite graphically.

'Ah. Ah, yes. I was very tired. The journey – sure, it seemed to go on for a black eternity. We had such bad weather crossing the Atlantic that I spent most of the time in my bunk.'

'That must have been very unpleasant, sir.'

'It was.' Tian looked round. He wanted to see Annie again. He had to assure himself that she was real. 'Is – er – is Mrs Hallam free? I'd like to – to thank her.'

'She's having dinner with the children and Mr William at the moment, sir. She said she would come up and see how you were afterwards. I'll send word down that you're awake, shall I? And then perhaps you'd like me to wash you? And shave you?' Jimson did not like beards. They always looked untidy to him. Ungentle-manly. A neat pair of side whiskers or a well-trimmed moustache was one thing, but he did not approve of beards and never would, whatever the current fashion.

Tian ran his fingers across his hairy chin and gave the ghost of a laugh. 'Yes, that would be wonderful.' It had been too much of an effort to shave on the boat and once he touched English soil, all he wanted was to get to Bilsden, to see her.

So when Annie and the children came up to see their guest, it was to find Tian looking more like his old self, although very much thinner. She had warned Tamsin and Edgar not to pester him with questions and not to make a lot of noise, so at first they just stood and stared at the figure in the bed.

Tian looked across at them, frowning. 'You must be Edgar and – and—' he remembered the name the porter had told him '—and Tamsin? I do apologise for not recognising you, but the blow to my head seems to have damaged my memory.'

Edgar stepped forward. 'Are you feeling better now, though?'

'Certainly more comfortable, thanks to Jimson.' But there was a dull ache in Tian's forehead, as there often was since the accident, and he rubbed it without realising that he was betraying its presence.

'Do you remember how you painted a portrait of us all just before Father died?' Edgar asked.

Tian stared at him blankly, then understanding crept slowly into his face. It was like this sometimes when people prompted his memory. 'Ah! Yes, I think I do remember, now that you've mentioned it. You were all in the garden.' He looked around. 'But there was someone else as well. You two. Your mother. Your father. And – another man?'

'William,' Tamsin volunteered, even her ebullience dampened by the sight of this pale shadow of Tian Gilchrist. 'Our elder brother.'

Tian was staring at her. 'You look very like your mother.'

Tamsin pulled a face. 'Everyone says that. I'd rather look like myself, actually.'

He chuckled, but then let his head fall back on the pillow and sighed, as if even that short conversation had tired him.

'Run along now, you two,' Annie said. 'I'll join you in a few minutes.'

Overawed by this encounter and by the changes in Tian, they nodded and tiptoed out. But by the time they rejoined Elizabeth and William downstairs, their natural liveliness had returned and they kept interrupting one another as they tried to explain how the patient was looking and exactly what he had said to them.

In the bedroom, Tian opened his eyes again, looked up and pleaded softly. 'Will you stay for a few moments, Annie?' He could not bear to call her Mrs Hallam, for she seemed almost a part of him. 'I seem to have spent a lot of time alone in bed in the last few months. I'd welcome a little company.'

Annie hesitated, then sat down. 'Very well. If you're not too tired to talk.'

'No. Not too tired.' Never too tired to talk to her. 'Thank you for taking me in, wild and untidy as I must have looked.' He rubbed his chin and smiled at her. 'And thank you for lending me your general factotum. I don't know which of us was happier to see that beard go.'

She smiled back. 'Jimson doesn't approve of them.'

'No. He made that quite plain.'

Tian's eyes were devouring her again, as if were feeding from the very sight of her. She didn't know what to say or do. Not even Frederick had looked at her with such naked hunger, such a depth of longing.

Before she had realised it, Tian had captured her hand again. When she would have pulled it away, he whispered, 'Please, Annie. I need to hold you, to believe that you're real, that you're not just another dream.'

And it seemed churlish to deny a sick man that comfort.

'Would you like to stay here at Ridge House for a while?' she asked. 'The doctor says you need cherishing and, heaven knows, there are enough people here to look after you.'

'It's you I want to cherish me, Annie. You that I need.'

She did not know what to answer. And that was strange, because she could usually fend off unwanted compliments and had no trouble turning conversations into safer channels when they threatened to embarrass her. But with him she felt, had always felt, a little off balance.

After a moment, Tian forced himself to let go of her hand. He had no right to hold it, however much he loved her. 'I'm being too forward, I think, Annie. Annie . . .' He repeated her name as if just to say it was a pleasure, then he shook his head and tried to concentrate. 'But to answer your kind offer, yes, I'd love to stay here, I would so. I'm sure I'll get better more quickly in your house. Are you certain it's all right?'

'Of course.'

'And I might remember something more if I stay here. Ever since I arrived at the station, I seem to sense memories creeping up behind me, just out of reach.'

'It must be very frustrating for you.'

'It is. Very.'

After that they said very little and, gradually, his eyes closed and his breathing deepened. But she sat on, staring at him, wondering at how comfortable she felt with him, as if she had known him all her life. As if – again she cut off that dangerous thought and tried to focus on something else. But it would not be driven away completely and she dreamed of him that night, dreamed of how he had been before, so young and strong, charming everyone. Even Frederick had liked him. And he had liked Frederick.

And – she admitted it at last – Tian Gilchrist was still in love with her!

Even in her sleep, she tensed and tried to drive the idea away. But it would not be driven and was still there when she awoke. She lay watching the early dawn brighten into full light. Frederick had known very well that Tian loved her, and yet he had still invited him back to do the portrait of her.

Was Frederick trying to match-make? She tried to banish the thought, but like Tian's memories it crept up and hovered behind her, refusing point-blank to go away.

Which was exactly what Frederick would have wanted.

24

Bilsden: Early November 1861

'I won't do it!' Maddie cried. 'Harry, don't ask me! Please!' She cringed back as he stepped towards her and grabbed her arm.

'You'll do it. There's no one else as can, so you must.' He shook her to emphasise his words, shook her very hard.

Maddie burst into tears. 'But Joanie's my friend! Oh, Harry, she doesn't love you. She loves Bart and—'

Her words were cut off abruptly as he slapped her across the face – a vicious blow that knocked her halfway across the kitchen and tumbled her into a heap near the table. He followed her across the room and dragged her to her feet, holding her by the hair with her head bent backwards and thrusting his face close to hers. 'If you don't agree to do it,' he said, his voice softer now but no less vicious, 'then I'll have to persuade you. And you won't like that.'

'I'll do it,' she whispered instantly. Tears rolled down her face but she did not dare sob aloud, not while he was still speaking to her. When Harry got this mood upon him, there was nothing you could do but obey. She'd found that out to her cost a long time ago, when they were both children. Perhaps . . .

But as usual he outguessed her. 'And if you mess it up, I'll hold you accountable. Remember that, too.'

She shivered. 'Yes, Harry. I – I won't mess it up.'

He stared at her, his face set and determined, then gave a little nod and let her go. He did not even seem to notice when she crept out of the room and went to hold a cold damp cloth to her sore face. He was lost in thought, going over his plans again and again. Nothing must go wrong. Nothing. He'd never have another chance like this one.

The following Sunday, Maddie called for Joanie, as they had arranged during the week, and they set off up to the moors.

'Thanks for coming out today,' Maddie said. 'Having you to talk to means a lot to me.' Tears gathered in her eyes.

'What's wrong?'

She looked down at her gloved hands. 'I'll tell you later. We'll find somewhere to sit down where no one can hear us, then we'll talk.' And they had walked on in silence for a while, Maddie star ted to worry that Joanie would become suspicious so she said brightly. 'Tell me about you and Bart. How are things going?'

Joanie smiled and for the next ten minutes talked in a soft voice, her eyes shining with love, about the man she was walking out with, the man she'd agreed to marry as soon as he had a bit more money put by. She'd have married him without the money, but he was determined to do the thing properly. 'And since Luke's troubles, Bart's family have left him alone, so everything's wonderful, Maddie. Just wonderful,' she repeated.

Maddie tried to suppress a sob, but couldn't.

Joanie put her arm round her friend's shoulders. 'What's the matter, love? You can tell me. Are you in some sort of trouble?'

If they hadn't arrived at the prearranged spot just then, Maddie would have given in to an almost over whelming impulse to tell Joanie to run away home as quickly as she could, and to hell with how her brother punished her, but as they breasted a small rise and walked down into the tiny sheltered dell, a figure rose to greet them and the impulse died instantly.

'Hello, Joanie.'

She stopped dead. 'Harry.' Then she looked sideways at Maddie in reproach. Her friend knew perfectly well that Joanie didn't want to see him. But Maddie was avoiding her eyes. At that moment, Joanie started to feel frightened. She didn't question that fear, just turned instinctively to run.

But Harry was after her, and before she had gone more than a few paces, he had caught her and thrown her to the ground.

She screamed then, but he sat with his knees astride her, holding her arms above her head and just laughed. 'There's no one to hear you, Joanie Gibson. No one at all.'

'Maddie, help me!' Joanie pleaded. 'Maddie!'

But she was backing away. 'I'm sorry, Joanie. S-sorry.'

'Go and do the rest,' Harry ordered, and even before his sister had left, he started to pull Joanie's skirt up.

She screamed and fought, displaying more strength than he would have thought possible, but he was a well-built man and she was a small woman. Everything happened so quickly, so horribly quickly. He lifted her skirt, pulled her pantaloons carefully off, so that nothing was torn, and started thrusting inside her almost before she knew it.

Pain lanced through her and she screamed again. It hurt so much, so very much. And although she begged him to stop, he just ignored her and continued to thrust until suddenly he stiffened, groaned and sagged over her.

When he climbed off, he was breathing more rapidly, but he was smiling, too. 'You're mine now, Joanie Gibson, mine! And no other man will want you when he knows I've had you. Not even your precious Bart.'

As he reached for her skirt, she opened her mouth to scream again, but he just put one large firm hand across it, squeezed hard and said, 'A bit late to scream now, eh?' Then he began to pull up her pantaloons and straighten her clothes.

She lay there like a twisted doll, horror still shuddering through her, so terrified that she couldn't resist. 'Why?' she whispered as he pulled her into a sitting position within the shelter of his arm and held her there. 'Why?'

'Because I'm the one as is going to marry you, not that Burns fellow. And I've just made sure of that.'

'I won't marry you! I won't!'

He smiled and bent his head closer, adding, 'But there might be a baby on the way now, so you can't possibly marry another fellow. Even if he still wants you. Which he won't, believe me.'

Shock held her so rigid that she didn't hear voices or see her father and Kathy until they were almost upon her.

'It's all right, Joanie love,' Harry said, with a fond look. 'I'll explain to them.' He pulled her up, but beneath the folds of her skirt held her wrist so tightly that she couldn't have moved anyway, even if shock hadn't held her rigid. 'I'm sorry, sir,' he said, looking at John. 'It's all my fault. I got carried away. Joanie fell and hurt her ankle, so Maddie went for help. But when Joanie said she wasn't really hurt and just wanted to talk to me, well, I was so happy. And when she hinted she had made a mistake about Bart and that it was me she loved, I was so set up, I – I just couldn't help myself. I'm sorry.' He bent his head, as if in shame.

Joanie pulled her hand from his and jerked away from him. 'It's not true! I don't love him! He made me do it!'

Harry turned a reproachful gaze upon her and shook his head. 'Nay, Joanie, love!'

And Maddie, after a quick glare from her brother, gulped and added her mite. 'Oh, Joanie, you were egging him on all the way up here. You know you were.'

At that, Joanie gave way completely to the hysterics that had been threatening. Kathy ran across and put her arms round the sobbing girl. 'Eh, love, don't take on so. Whatever happened is done now. Let's just get you back home and then we can think how to mend it.'

Unfortunately, Kathy's words echoed Harry's. It was done now. Bart wouldn't want her now. How could he? She wasn't a virgin any longer. She was ruined. *Ruined* . And what if there was a baby? Harry was right about that. Bart might perhaps forgive her this, believe her, even, but he would never accept another man's baby.

'I could carry her,' Harry offered.

Joanie shrank closer to Kathy, trembling. 'I can walk.' But Kathy and John had to guide her, for she seemed bewildered.

When they got back to Netherhouse Cottage, Kathy took Joanie upstairs and John took Harry and Maddie into the front parlour. Again he questioned them, but again they kept to their story. Harry in particular was very convincing in his contrition.

'I do want to marry Joanie,' he insisted several times. 'I always did. And I thought she loved me till that Bart came along and dazzled her. I beg you'll forgive me, sir. I never meant things to go so far. Oh, I do hope I've not got her with child!' He buried his face in his hands and managed a sob or two, but out of the corner of his eye he watched John's reaction to this last statement with great satisfaction. That'd done the trick, as he'd hoped it might.

It was unlike John to act precipitately and make decisions for Joanie without even asking her, but ever since Mark had got Nelly Burns into trouble, he had a horror of any of his children fathering another illegitimate child. He didn't even send up the hill to ask Tom or Annie to join them, just talked the whole thing over soberly with Harry, who at least was prepared to do his duty by the girl and who seemed truly repentant.

'I do love her,' he kept insisting. 'I do.'

John remembered with a twist of pain how he had not forgiven Mark and then Mark had run away. He must forgive Harry now, hard as that might be.

In the end, it was decided between them that John would speak to Bart the next day and tell him that Joanie had made a mistake and no longer wished to marry him. Then Harry would wed her as soon as it could be arranged, for as he carefully pointed out again, there might be a baby on the way.

'I can tell Bart for you, if you like,' Harry volunteered. 'We don't want Joanie doing it. He might get angry and hurt her.'

'No, no, I'll tell him,' John insisted. He owed it to Bart to break the news gently. The poor lad would be upset, he would that. He was very fond of Joanie. And he was a good lad, too, a real hard worker. John would have much preferred him to Harry as a son-in-law.

Kathy was more doubtful about the hasty decision when she and John discussed it later that night in the privacy of their room. 'I'm not sure our Joanie did lead him on,' she whispered, cuddling up to her husband. 'She says she didn't, anyway. She says he forced her.'

'Nay, love. The other lass said she led him on. She said it quite clearly. Maddie wouldn't lie about something like that. She's been our Joanie's best friend for years.'

'But Joanie insisted she didn't.'

'Young lasses don't know half the time what they're doing,' John said. 'They don't realise how they're stirring the lads up.'

'But still—'

'And anyway, love, what if there's a baby?'

Kathy sighed and let the matter drop. She'd talk to him again in the morning.

But the next day, Joanie woke up weeping and sobbing. When Kathy went in to see her, she begged her step-mother not to leave her alone, so there was no chance for a quiet word with John before he went to the yard.

Kathy laid one hand on her step-daughter's forehead and found it hot. Indeed, Joanie seemed so feverish that Kathy debated sending for the doctor, but then, what could a doctor do in a case like this?

'Bart won't want me now, will he?' Joanie sobbed, clinging tightly to Kathy's hand. 'He won't want me.'

'Harry told your father he'd marry you. He said he allus did want to wed you, love.'

Joanie shuddered. 'Well, I don't want to marry *him*. Never did. Never! And I won't marry him!'

'But what if there's a baby?' Kathy knew that the Gibsons were good breeders. Well, all of them except Annie. They seemed to beget children as easily as other people caught colds.

Joanie buried her face in the pillow and sobbed as if the end of the world was nigh. As for her it was.

Kathy could think of nothing to do but sit there, stroking her hair and letting her cry it out. The lass was probably right.

Even if there wasn't a baby, Bart Burns wouldn't want her once he knew what had happened. But Kathy still didn't like that Harry Pickering. And she believed Joanie, believed he had forced her. If there was no baby, she didn't see why the poor lass should have to marry a man like him, and so she'd tell John.

At the yard, John asked Bill Midgely to watch the front and took Bart into the tea room. There, he told him the bad news in a few simple words.

Bart cursed fluently and thumped the table so hard that a cup jumped off and smashed to pieces on the stone-flagged floor. 'I don't believe it! I don't. My Joanie wouldn't have egged another fellow on.'

John shook his head. 'Her friend says she did.'

'Maddie's that slimy sod's sister. Of *course* she'd support his story. They probably planned it between them.'

For the first time, real doubt crept into John's mind. Then he remembered Harry's contrition, his insistence that he loved Joanie, and banished the doubt. No, it would take a truly wicked fellow to rape Joanie and make up a false tale like that. John wouldn't, just couldn't, believe it of anyone who seemed so straightforward.

Bart thrust himself to his feet.

John jumped up. 'Where are you going?'

'I'm going to kill him!'

John got between him and the door. 'You're not going anywhere.'

'Mr Gibson, don't try to—'

'Lad, you'll have to knock me out of your way to get through that door,' John said, with all the authority he could muster.

'But—'

'Sit down!'

Bart hesitated, saw the sympathy on John's face and sagged down on to a chair, burying his face in his hands. And suddenly he was unable to stop the tears. The mere thought of Harry Pickering taking his Joanie, leaving his seed inside her, doing who knew what to her, made him feel . . . 'I'm going to be sick,' he said suddenly.

John grabbed the tin bowl they used to wash up the dishes and thrust it at him.

Bart threw up his breakfast, retching until there was nothing left in his stomach. When he had finished, John took the bowl outside and emptied it, then came back to stand beside him, patting him awkwardly on the shoulder. 'There, there, lad.'

The sympathy was too much to bear. Bart began sobbing – hoarse raw sounds that went to John's heart. They stopped after a while and Bart looked up at him fiercely. 'She wouldn't have let him. He must have forced her.' Then he took the handkerchief John was offering and scrubbed at his eyes and his damp face. 'I'll never believe she egged him on. Never.'

'She won't have meant to. She'll just have been – playing. Like young lasses do.'

Bart shook his head. 'Not my Joanie.'

John sighed. 'I'm not letting you leave here until I have your promise that you won't seek him out and attack him.'

It was a long time before Bart looked up and said, in a voice that was more like a growl, 'What good would it do now?'

'No good. No good at all. And look at what happened to our Luke. You don't want to make trouble now. It's too late.'

'You should report him to the police for rape.'

John shuffled uncomfortably. 'Eh, lad, we all get carried away at times.'

'Did you ever force yourself on a lass?'

'No!'

'And neither did I.'

'But Maddie says—'

Bart glared at John. 'His *sister* says.'

John was quiet for a few moments, then shook his head helplessly. 'But if we take him to the police, it'll be all over town within the hour and Joanie's good name will be destroyed for ever.'

Bart swore and thumped the table.

'And there might be a child,' John added. 'Us Gibsons get childer so easily.' Too easily, as he had learned to his own cost with his second wife. Poor Emily hadn't been able to cope with the almost continual pregnancies. He still felt guilty about that sometimes.

Bart turned and thumped his fist against the wall, not seeming to notice the blood running down his knuckles after wards.

Silence lay heavily between them.

'You won't go after him?' John asked at last. 'Promise me.'

'I'll not go after him.'

'Promise.'

Their eyes met, then Bart's fell. Already John Gibson seemed more like a father to him than his own ever had. 'I promise I won't go after him,' he said at last. Though if he met Harry Pickering in the street, he might not be able to hold back.

'Do you – do you want to see our Joanie? Kathy thought you might like to talk to her. To say goodbye.'

Bart gazed sightlessly at the floor. Did he want to see Joanie? What could he say to her? 'I believe you, love, but you're spoiled meat now? You've been marked by another man, and you might even be carrying his child.' Bile rose in his throat at the mere thought. 'I think it'd do more harm than good,' he said through the last remnants of his self-control. 'Look, I need to get away. I'll be back tomorrow.' He stopped dead and looked at John. 'If you still want me to work here, that is?'

'Of course I do, lad. I don't know what I'd do without you, now.'

Bart nodded, turned and walked out of the yard, taking his grief up to the privacy of the moors, ignoring the cold wind and the drifting rain that followed it across the tops.

He kept his promise not to go after Harry Pickering, but if he had come face to face with the man during the weeks that followed, he would not have been able to stop himself thumping him.

But Harry Pickering, afraid of retribution, took care to go to work early, using the back roads, and to leave the office late, moving from alley to back street like a thief in the night, and always entering his home from the rear yard.

When Annie was told what had happened, she felt anguish twist inside her and her heart went out to her young sister. She knew exactly how Joanie was feeling, for she'd been in a very similar situation herself when she was seventeen. Only she had not had much help from her family, for her step-mother, Joanie's mother, had never liked her and had only wanted to get rid of her and her problem. How ironic that Emily's daughter was now in the same position. And how sad. Men! Annie thought bitterly. They're only after one thing.

She tried several times to talk to Joanie, but she had never been close to her youngest sister and could get no real response from her. Neither could Rebecca. Joanie wasn't talking to anyone. She sat in her bedroom at Netherhouse Cottage, refusing to go to work, refusing to discuss her situation. Day by day she grew thinner, looking like a pale ghost of herself, and only bothering to eat when Kathy or her father coaxed her.

I won't be pregnant, she had thought at first. Not after just one time. When her monthly courses did not come, Kathy said that meant nothing. A big upset could stop things for a bit. They'd have to wait for a clearer indication of pregnancy.

But then, as the days passed, Joanie had to face the fact that she probably was carrying that man's child. She felt sick at the mere idea and could keep no food down for days. But it wasn't morning sickness; it was horror that was doing it to her, try as she might to think of the innocent child – and even Kathy urged her to do that. But with a child, however innocent, came the need to marry *him*, to live the rest of her life with *him*. And she couldn't do it. It was the only thing that was at all clear in her mind during those weeks: she couldn't, wouldn't, face a lifetime of Harry Pickering, with his evil ways and his hard hands that hurt and hurt and hurt.

When she was told that Harry was asking to see her, she

became hysterical. But she became equally hysterical at the suggestion she see Bart, who was also asking to speak to her. Time passed in a slow blur, and she found it hard even to tell night from day sometimes. Why did people keep pestering her? She didn't want to see anyone.

For the next few weeks, Harry tried hard to persuade the Gibsons to let him marry Joanie straight away, but Annie and Tom backed Kathy up on that one and the idea of a wedding was set aside until the need for it was proven beyond any doubt.

For all Harry's feigned repentance the family was no more than curt with him. And when he brought some flowers for Kathy, she threw them away the minute he'd left, breaking their stems and throwing them on the compost heap herself.

'They'll remind me of him. I can't bear the sight of them,' she told Lally as she came back in, rubbing her hands on her pinafore.

'I can't take to him, either, though he's allus very polite to me.'

Others were of the same opinion. 'I don't like Pickering,' Annie said to Tom as they discussed it privately. 'I really don't.'

'If it were up to me, I'd beat his head in,' her brother said. 'And if I were Bart, I'd have done it already.'

'Dad made him promise not to.'

'Dad would. All he cares about is the child.'

She nodded.

They were both quiet for a few minutes, then Tom changed the subject. 'How's your guest coming on, then?'

'Tian's doing a lot of sleeping, but Jeremy says that's to the good. And he is beginning to remember things.' She didn't look Tom in the eyes as she spoke. She found herself colouring up when she spoke of Tian, and in one sense was glad her family had other problems to occupy their minds just now, though she wished poor Joanie wasn't suffering so.

Like her sister Annie before her, Joanie at last had to admit that she was pregnant by a man she loathed, a man who had forced himself upon her. Unlike her sister, she found the man eager to wed her. If she had discussed it with Annie, she would have found out that her sister was quite willing to go against their father and help Joanie do what she wanted, but she wouldn't discuss it with anyone except Kathy.

When her father came up to her bedroom one evening and started talking gently of the need for her to marry, suggesting a day – when even Kathy said there was no alternative – Joanie panicked.

The next evening, when Kathy sent Samuel John up to call his half-sister down to tea, he came clattering back down the stairs, shouting that her bedroom was empty. It was Kathy who panicked then, sending the boys running out to search the streets.

John was sent for, but there was still no sign of Joanie, so they sent Ben running up the hill to fetch Tom and Annie. Between them, the family organised a street by street search.

'Should we call in the police?' Kathy wondered.

'Not yet,' Tom said curtly. 'Let's see if we can find her ourselves first. It'll cause less talk that way.'

'You don't think she's—' John broke off, his eyes begging Kathy to deny that Joanie would even think of doing away with herself.

But much as she loved him, his wife couldn't give him that comfort. 'I don't know, love. She were that unhappy.' She hesitated, then said, 'Even if she does have a baby, I don't think we should force her to marry that fellow, John. For it would be forcing. She'd never do it of her own accord. I just can't like him. For all his talk of loving Joanie, I can't believe him, either. He's cold and – and he frightens me. He does.'

'Eh, love, we've talked it through time and again. To have a child out of marriage will ruin our Joanie's whole life. She'll lose her good name. Folk won't want to associate with her. What sort of life will she lead then? I can't want that for her. Nor I don't want the child scorned for its lack of a father.'

'Or is it yourself you're worried about?' she asked, drawing away from him for the first time ever.

He stared at her aghast.

'You're a lay preacher,' she said, her voice hard and tight. 'It wouldn't look good if your daughter had a bastard child.'

He was white with shock and horror. 'You can't believe that of me, love. You can't!'

'I can't believe any of this has happened,' Kathy said tiredly. 'But I don't think Joanie should be forced to wed him, all the same. He's a wicked man. Everyone except you thinks he forced her, whatever his sister says.' She gave her husband a long, level look. 'I know you, John. You allus think of the childer. And you allus think the best of folks. But I b'lieve you should consider our Joanie's feelings first this time. And what's more, if we find her, I'll not let you force her to wed him.'

'If!'

'Yes. If.'

He bent his head, tears glimmering in his eyes. 'Very well. If we find her – no, *when* we find her – I'll do anything you think right, love.' For he didn't want to lose another child, as he had lost Mark.

Down at the junk yard, Bart was about to lock up when he heard a sound in the back of the wood store. There had been several thefts in the town lately so he crept round the side, determined to catch the thief. And if the bastard struggled, so much the better. He'd enjoy a good fight. He never should have let John Gibson make him promise not to thump hell out of Harry Pickering.

Treading softly, he made his way to the wood store. A dark shape was huddled in one corner, just huddled there, with breath clouding the icy evening air. Whoever it was was making no attempt to steal anything and did not even seem to have noticed him approaching. It must be someone on the tramp, then, seeking shelter for the night, poor sod.

'Now look here, you—' he began, then gasped as the figure

stirred and a white, terrified face gazed up at him in the moonlight, a face he'd have recognised anywhere. 'Joanie!'

She burst into tears, sobbing wildly and curling up into a tight ball of anguish.

For a moment Bart just stood there, staring down at her, sick to his stomach to think of her doing it with that bloodly Pickering. Then her sobs got to him. They seemed to echo the pain that had sat like broken glass in his belly since that dreadful day John Gibson had told him what had happened. He knelt down beside her, stretching out one hand. 'Joanie, love,' he said before he could stop himself. 'Oh, love, don't.'

'He forced me!' she wailed. She had come here especially to tell Bart that. She couldn't bear him to think she'd egged Harry Pickering on, just couldn't bear it. Even if Bart never spoke to her again, he must know the truth from her own lips. But her courage had failed her at the sight of him, looking so grim and angry, and she had crept round the back to hide and try to think what to do. 'Oh, Bart, he forced me. He did. I'd never, ever have—'

He pulled her roughly into his arms, shushing her as if she were a child. Then he realised how thin she was and held her at arm's length, studying her beloved features. 'You're that thin,' he whispered. 'Oh, my bonny lass, you're nobbut skin and bone!'

He picked her up in his arms and carried her round to the tea room, setting her gently down on a chair and fumbling for the lamp he had extinguished only a few minutes before. When it was lit, he turned to her and gasped to see how ravaged her face was. 'What have they done to you?'

She swallowed and tried to find words to tell him. 'Nothing. I was just – just sick to my soul. I c-can't marry him.'

'Your father says you're—'

She looked up at him then, her face bitter. 'Aye. I'm likely with child. An' that's all they think of. The child. They don't think of me. But I decided – last night it was – I suddenly seemed to see it all so clearly. I decided to go away. I'll ask

Annie to give me some money to tide me over till the child is born. I think she'll do that.' Joanie looked down at her stomach in sorrow. 'And I'll set myself up to take in sewing.' A bitter smile twisted her face for a minute. 'I'm a good sewer an' I can cut out, too. I'm not interested in making fancy clothes for rich women who look at you like a worm, but I can make nice dresses for ordinary women, and—'

He couldn't bear it a minute longer. She looked so frail, as if a breath would blow her away, and yet she was planning to defy her family, defy everything the world would expect of her. 'Shh!' He touched one fingertip lightly to her lips. 'Let me say something.'

She closed her mouth and looked at him warily, waiting, expecting to be hurt again.

'I can't deny I were mad when your father told me – mad and sick to my soul.'

She just stared at him.

'But I've had time to think about things now. That's why I tried to see you. An', lass, you'd no need to tell me you didn't egg him on, no need to tell me he forced you. I knew that.'

Her face brightened for a moment and she said huskily, 'Thanks, Bart. I'll treasure that thought.'

'Shh. I'm not done yet.' He took a deep breath. 'I can't deny that the thought of his child sticks in my gullet.'

She put her hand protectively across her belly. 'It's my child, too.'

He stopped speaking and looked at her, surprised. 'Yes, it is, isn't it?' Then he took a deep breath and said, 'Well, I still think – if you agree – that we should get wed.'

She stared at him for a moment. 'Oh, you are a good man, Bartholomew Burns!' Then she shook her head, sorrow twisting her face. 'But it wouldn't work. You'd resent me, or hate the child. And I won't have its life made unhappy.'

Admiration ran through him, warming him. Frail as she was, she could still think of the child, protect it before it was even born. At that moment she reminded him so much of his own mother, who had often tried to protect him when he was a little lad, that he growled and pulled her up off the chair into his arms. 'I'll not be the one to make a child's life unhappy,' he said, and kissed her cheek gently. 'I promise you that, love.'

He didn't dare kiss her with the usual passion, because she felt so frail in his arms and he was afraid of being too rough with her. Instead, he turned and blew out the lamp, swung her up and began to carry her out of the yard. 'Come on! Let's go and tell your father right now.'

'Put me down. Bart, I can walk. Bart! What'll people think?'

He grinned in the darkness. 'I don't want to put you down, love.' He felt her hand come up to touch his cheek, his lips. 'Ever.'

'Oh, Bart,' she sighed, resting her head against him. 'I've been so unhappy.'

'Me, too, love.' But he wasn't unhappy now. And he didn't intend to wait to get wed, no, not a day more than he had to. He wanted her safe, where he could protect her, love her. And most of all, he wanted to beat that bloody Harry Pickering to a pulp, and would do if the fellow so much as laid a fingertip on Joanie again. If he even looked in her direction again.

Bart kissed the top of Joanie's head as he walked and the tears that fell down her face were tears of joy.

1862

25

November 1861 to January 1862

Annie walked down the stairs, wishing she felt more like going to a wedding. Poor Joanie! This would be such a shabby, hurried affair compared to Rebecca's. They had obtained a special licence, only the bride's family would be present, and soon the town would guess why.

Tian was waiting at the bottom of the stairs. 'I wonder, would you give the bride this from me?' He held something out.

'What is it?'

'A small painting. Some flowers.'

Annie's face lit up. 'You've started to paint again?' They were all worried that he had made no attempt to use his talent, though Edgar had lent him some materials and tried to get him interested.

He shook his head. 'No. This is something I did in New York. I found it in the luggage that had been sent on.' A bitter smile flitted across his face. 'I can't even remember doing it, but it's pretty. I think your sister will like it.'

Annie took it from him, trying not to let her pity show. 'Thank you, Tian. It's a kind thought.'

He caught her hand in his and held it tightly for a moment. 'Annie—'

She pulled quickly away from its warmth, feeling flustered, as she always did when he touched her. 'I really must go. I don't want to be late.'

'Annie—'

Tamsin and Edgar came clattering down the stairs, followed by Elizabeth, and there was no further opportunity to talk. Tian took a step backwards, lips thinned with determination. He could wait.

'I wish you were coming, too,' Tamsin said, stopping next to him.

His words came out too harshly. 'I'm not family.'

Her lower lip jutted out in the way it always did when she did not agree. 'Well, you feel like family to me.'

He forced himself to smile. Not the child's fault that the mother flinched away from commitment. But as he watched Annie go, he promised himself most solemnly that he would catch her alone soon, would insist on the private talk he needed so much. For the attraction was still flaring between them. The slightest touch, just being in the same room, set the currents flowing. But Annie would not admit that, or at least would not do anything about it, which amounted to the same thing. Well, he intended to make her talk about it, and before too much time had passed.

As he heard the front door close behind them, however, his shoulders sagged for a moment and he shook his head. Perhaps it would be wrong to force things. Perhaps he should be patient, should wait if she still needed time. But could he bear to wait much longer? His need for her was gnawing away at him. If she didn't start to show signs that one day she might return his love, he didn't know what he would do with himself. His thoughts always stopped there, as if he was on the edge of a high cliff and did not dare look over the edge.

But today he nodded to himself as a thought occurred to him – surely she wouldn't become so flustered when he was near if she felt nothing? And when he had arrived . . . his memories of the first day or two were not very clear, but had she not sat by his bed, let him hold her hand, caressed his face? Those were not the actions of a woman who was totally indifferent to a man. So what had made her draw away again?

Tom could have told him, or any of Annie's brothers and sisters. For many years, she had had to be the strong one in the family, and somehow, now, even when they were independent of her, she found it hard to let go of that sense of responsibility.

But Tian didn't ask Tom. He just tried to understand her himself. Tried very hard, for it was the most important thing in the world to him.

The little Methodist chapel, which was usually crammed full of people, seemed empty with just the Gibson family filling the first few pews. At the front, two vases overflowed with late flowers and greenery, provided by Nat Jervis and Luke. The bride, looking pale, clung first to her father's arm, then to that of her new husband. But when the time came, she gave her responses in a steady confident voice and as she looked up at Bart, her eyes were aglow with love.

The groom hovered over her in a very protective way and his feelings for her showed just as clearly in his face. Kathy nodded in satisfaction as the Minister declared them man and wife. Joanie would be safe with this man. And Bart would be happy with her. He was a steady, responsible fellow, already taking a lot of work off John's shoulders at the yard. And to Kathy, there was something more. Poor Bart seemed hungry for love, not just the love of a wife, but the love of a family. The way he watched them sometimes made her feel so sorry for him. He seemed to have led such a bleak life.

The newly-weds were to live at Netherhouse Cottage for the time being and Kathy intended to mother Bart – not to try to replace his own mother, whom he loved greatly, but to make him feel part, really and truly part, of the Gibson family. As she did herself now, though she had once been an outsider, the ill-treated child of drunken parents.

Wiping a tear away, for she always cried at weddings, Kathy shivered as she remembered how Tom had insisted on the need for them all to be careful for a while. Surely that dreadful Harry Pickering wouldn't pursue their Joanie any more? Wouldn't try to hurt her again? And Bart's family had left him alone for the past few weeks. Why should anyone start making trouble for him now?

Please, Lord, she prayed, look after those two. They've had enough trouble lately. And give Bart the grace to love the child.

Then little Faith, now a year old and sitting on Kathy's knee dressed in her best, pulled at her grandmother's bonnet ribbons and her thoughts turned away from her step-daughter to her fosterling. She and John loved Faith just as dearly as if the child were their own. And she was a taking little thing, for all her Burns blood.

Eh, it was sad that Mark could not see her grow up. Where was he now? The letters were so few and the time between them so long. And he didn't really say much. Oh, he wrote several pages, talked about Australia, talked about the people he had met, but he didn't say how he felt, didn't make Kathy and John feel that he was truly happy there. And although they'd written to tell him about Faith, they hadn't heard back from him. Surely there had been time for a letter to come by now?

There was none of the usual teasing and jokes as the group left the chapel, but when a few passers-by who had gathered outside, as people always do for weddings, shouted their good wishes, Joanie looked up and gave them a blushing smile.

Everyone went back to Netherhouse Cottage to find a surprise waiting for them, because Tom had engaged Mr Triffcott to take a photograph of the couple, and then another of the whole family. The town's chief photographer, showing the signs of his increasing affluence in his thickened waistline, had, with Lally's help, moved the furniture around and set up his apparatus in the parlour, since it was too dull and damp outside to take a photograph. Soon Joanie and Bart were posing near the fireplace between some of Luke's potted plants. At first they were stiff and awkward, then Tom made them laugh so much that they moved and spoiled one shot completely.

After that, everyone began to feel that the wedding really was something to celebrate and Kathy had the inspiration of having another photo taken of little Faith on her grandfather's knee to send to Mark. Surely that would bring him back? Only then John insisted she be in it, too, and it was hard to keep the child still for a whole minute. But if it came out all right, they would send it to Australia. A father should be able to recognise his own child.

After that, there was a hubbub of conversation as the men set the parlour furniture to rights and the women helped serve the meal, then everyone went into the dining-room to eat. Lally took Faith from Kathy, for the child was starting to grizzle, and gave her into the keeping of a cousin who sometimes came in to help and who was to feed the tiny child and put her down for a nap.

Joanie, sitting at the head of the table with Bart, was quiet and still looked much thinner than usual, but she kept smiling at her new husband in a way that excluded the rest of the family and made Rebecca and Simon share a satisfied glance.

With Lally muttering about things spoiling, they all squeezed round the dining table as quickly as they could, with the children squashed on garden benches round an old table that was sometimes brought in for large gatherings.

Annie had sent down some bottles of champagne from the stock in Frederick's well-supplied cellar, and Tom took it upon himself to act as waiter, pouring some into everyone's glasses, even adding a drop to the lemonade the children were drinking and calling Lally in from the kitchen to join them in a toast. When all the glasses were charged, he cleared his throat and looked at John meaningfully.

Primed by Tom and Annie, John stood up. 'It seems funny to be making a speech to you lot,' he began, and looked down at his glass. Some of the folk at chapel would not approve of any sort of alcohol, but he didn't think one glass now and then mattered. It was drinking too much that harmed folk, not the drink itself. He took a deep breath. He had not dared to say anything at Rebecca's wedding, not with all the grand people assembled there, but now he wanted to speak. 'Still an' all, it seems right to say something today,' he went on, looking at Bart and Joanie. 'I'm glad you two have got wed. I think you truly love one another, and that's what counts, as me and my Kathy well know.' He threw a fond look at his own wife as he spoke.

Samuel John rolled his eyes at Benjamin. Their parents were always being soppy like that.

Tamsin dug her elbow into Samuel John's ribs and mimed a shushing noise. He scowled back at her.

'So,' John went on, 'I'd like us all to drink to our Joanie and her new husband, Bart. May the Lord watch over them and may they be very happy together.' He raised his glass in salute as the rest of them echoed his last words.

Tom waited until everyone had taken a sip, then stood up. 'I'd like to say something, too.' His children groaned and he grinned at them. 'I want to take this opportunity to welcome you officially to the family, Bart. From now on, you have every right to quarrel with us, laugh with us and work with us. But most of all, you have the right to love our Joanie as a husband should. Welcome to the family, lad!'

Again, everyone echoed the last words, though David and Lucy were still pulling faces and whispering to one another.

Young Albert watched everything very solemnly, as he often did. He still seemed happier with the role of observer, still seemed in part an outsider, but Kathy was keeping an eye on him in her quiet way, making sure he was not left out when it mattered.

Bart nodded to Tom in thanks, his heart too full to say anything. Under the table he was holding Joanie's hand, and if she was clinging to him like a shipwrecked person holding on to a piece of driftwood, well, he understood that. He'd look after her from now onwards and if it was humanly possible, he'd make her happy. He squeezed her hand and she looked up, nervousness still mingling with the love in her eyes.

'I love you, Mrs Burns,' he whispered.

She gulped and tears filled her soft blue eyes. 'And I love you, Bartholomew Burns.'

'I like it when you use my full name.' It made him feel like a different person to the old Bartie Burns, son of a Bible-thumping hypocrite. At that moment, his mother's face rose before him. The day would have been perfect if she had been able to come to the wedding, but he'd known better than even to invite her. His father would only have made trouble for her if he had and there would have been no hope of her coming, anyway.

Joanie nodded. 'I like it, too. I think I shall call you Bartholomew from now on.' And taking advantage of a lull in the general conversation, she called out, 'Listen, everyone! I have something to say, too. My husband wishes to be known as Bartholomew from now on. So please remember that.'

For the first time, Kathy thought in relief, the lass looked like the old Joanie. 'Thank goodness!' she murmured.

'Bartholomew.' Several voices tried it out, heads nodded, glasses were raised and Tom winked at him.

'It sounds more dignified,' Rosie approved, 'more suitable for a married man.'

'And to me, it's a symbol of starting a new life,' Bartholomew added. 'A break with the old one.'

They all understood that and made noises of agreement. It was sad that a man should be cut off from his family, but with a family like his, what else could a decent man do but go his own way? And anyway, he was now an honorary Gibson. So he would never be alone in the world again.

Since it had turned fine, if still cold, the newly-weds were then escorted down to the station on foot. Their luggage was already waiting for them there and they were to catch a train to Manchester and then go on to Blackpool, where they would, of course, stay with Joanie's half-sister, Lizzie, who ran a boarding house in the north part of the town.

Bartholomew, who had never ever seen the sea, was feeling excited about this trip. His own family did not go in for things like holidays and he had never seen the ocean before.

As the family walked back up the hill, after waving the train off, Annie found herself next to Luke. He had been very quiet all through the wedding.

'Have you heard from her?' she asked, guessing what was on his mind.

'No. I wrote asking if I should see to her garden – she used to love her flowers and herbs – but there hasn't been a word in reply. I haven't even seen her in the street. I hear she's been back to the farm, but I haven't seen her there.' Amy was avoiding him. He understood why, because she would want all the talk to die down, but it still hurt. And he missed her and the children quite dreadfully.

'Who's looking after the place, then?'

'We all are, those of us who live nearby.' He had been grati-fied to be included in the neighbours' planning for this. It seemed a sign that they had forgiven him for killing Ted Gorton, though some folk in Hey End still turned away as he passed. In one sense, he would never forgive himself. It was such a dreadful thing to take a man's life, even by accident, even a man who was so ill that he was behaving wickedly.

'Things will work themselves out,' she offered in comfort.

'Will they?' It didn't feel as if they would. His little cottage seemed emptier every day and even his land had lost some of its attraction.

Back at Netherhouse Cottage, they all sat down to another cup of tea, and the young folk, at least, made heavy inroads into some plates of scones and cake.

When everyone was settled, Simon stood up and clapped his hands for attention. 'My wife and I have a small announce-ment to make. Given the circumstances, we didn't want to say anything while Joanie was here, but I can now inform you that we are about to become parents.'

Rebecca blushed and laughed as the family took it in turns to congratulate her. Given her Gibson heritage, she had expected to fall pregnant quickly, but it had taken over a year, so she was particularly happy about it now.

Annie tried to keep a smile on her face, but at times like this, when she saw a couple so much in love, she felt very alone. Tian's face with its reproachful gaze appeared in her mind.

She knew she was avoiding him, knew she was being cowardly, but she was so confused by her feelings. The strength of her first reaction to him still frightened her, as well as the fact that he had only to come into a room for her to sense to his presence – sense and begin to tingle all over.

I'm not ready for anything, she kept telling herself, not ready. But the words rang hollow in her mind, for her body said that she was ready and kept her awake sometimes at night to prove it.

November passed quickly after that. The speculation about Joanie Gibson getting married so hurriedly and quietly was soon forgotten as the country was rocked by the scandal of the Trent incident. The Americans from the North had dared to fire on the British flag, board the Royal Mail steamer *Trent* and remove four American passengers. The whole country was outraged, even those whose sympathies lay more with the Union.

Tian was naturally asked for his opinion about the incident. 'Tempers run very high in America over this war,' he explained again and again, for he was the only person in Bilsden who had been there and seen what was going on with his own eyes. 'The Northerners are not always thinking straight about what they're doing. You don't in wartime.'

'Well, they can just keep such crooked thinking for their own affairs,' Tom retorted. He had never expected to feel so strongly about something like that, but he did. He was an Englishman, wasn't he?

'I'd guess that worse things will happen before this war is over,' Tian replied gloomily. 'Far worse.' For he had remembered quite a lot about his days in the army now, especially his fellow soldiers' blind determination to win against those goddamned Rebels, win at all costs. As far as they were concerned, any man who was not with them was against them and therefore fair game for retaliation.

The perpetrator of the incident which the British considered an outrage, one Captain Wilkes, was treated as a hero when he returned to port in America with his prisoners and after that, relations between Britain and the Northern United States began to look even more fragile as 8,000 British troops were sent to Canada.

It was Prince Albert, ill as he was, who intervened so that the note sent to the United States government was modified and less inflammatory language used. Eventually, on the 26 December, the four prisoners were released.

Sadly, however, the Prince Consort died of a putrid sore throat before this happened and Her Majesty retired abruptly from public life, her grief, people said, extreme and debilitating. They were not to know that she would not return for almost fifteen years.

The Gibsons were sorry, of course they were. It was sad for anyone to lose a husband so young and the Queen had loved Prince Albert greatly. The whole nation knew that. But they had their own worries.

Dutifully, Tom ordered his staff to put a mourning wreath on the door of the Emporium for the Prince Consort, and Annie authorised Matt to close the mill early, so that the operatives could gather to pray for their poor grieving monarch.

With her own loss so recent, Annie felt particularly sorry for the Queen. And Tian, seeing how Prince Albert's death had affected her, let Christmas pass without attempting to speak to her about his feelings.

His memories were still very fragmented and that impaired his usual confidence. He woke sometimes in the dark hours of the early morning, sweating and gasping from a recurrent nightmare in which they had caught him, taken him back to the training camp, stood him against a wall and shot him out of hand. He always jerked awake just as the guns were about to be fired, and then he would toss and turn for the rest of the night, waiting for the chill and tardy winter dawn to lighten the oppressive blackness and bring the house back to life again.

Every day another memory would come back, often catching him unawares, making him freeze wherever he was. Then he would have to fumble his way to the nearest chair and sink down on to it till the shaky spell passed. The inhabitants of Ridge House had learned to leave him alone at such times, to ignore the blind look of pain and puzzlement on his face.

When he discussed it with Jeremy Lewis, the doctor was sympathetic but confessed himself unable to help.

'The human brain is a strange organ. We doctors know very little of how it functions. I've learned to leave it alone. Unless you have to, Gilchrist, I'd advise against taking laudanum or anything else to help you sleep. Just let nature take its course.'

Early in the new year, however, seeing how Christmas with her family had lightened her spirits again, he did manage to get Annie on her own. From his bedroom window, he saw her walking through the shrubbery, frowning to herself, and on a sudden impulse he slipped downstairs quietly.

Not too quietly for Winnie, however, who planted herself firmly in his path. 'Can I help you, sir?'

'No, thank you. I'm just going out for a walk.'

'It's cold, sir. Won't you need your coat?'

But he had already set her gently aside and left.

'He's as bad as Mr William,' she muttered, watching him go. 'He'll catch his death in this weather.' Then she grew thoughtful. The mistress had gone out without a coat, too, just a shawl around her shoulders. And though the sun was shining, it was full winter now and Winnie wouldn't fancy being out there without a coat in that icy wind. She began dusting the furniture in the hall, but absent-mindedly, without her usual vigour.

Suddenly she stopped dead. Now she came to think of it, the pair of them had been acting strangely for a while. Why, she'd seen the mistress slip into the old morning-room one day, as if to avoid meeting Mr Gilchrist in the hall. And she'd seen him hanging around when he thought no one was watching, trying to catch the mistress. It couldn't be— They weren't— A smile creased Winnie's face. Well, well. And the master only dead a year and a half.

At the thought of Mr Hallam, she sighed as she always did. The best master anyone could ever have. The very best. But he was dead now and life had to go on. Besides, the mistress was only forty-one – Winnie had no need to stop and work that out, for Mrs Hallam was exactly ten years younger than herself, almost to the month. Yes, the mistress was still young enough and pretty enough, too, to marry again, for all the threads of silver that misted the auburn at her temples. And Winnie had heard the master once saying that if anything happened to him, he hoped the mistress would marry again. Not that Winnie had been eavesdropping – she hoped she had more pride than to do a thing like that – but you couldn't help overhearing things as you worked.

She began to hum as she dusted her way round the hall, a totally tuneless drone that always made Rosie wince. She liked Mr Gilchrist. He, too, would make a good master. Oh, she did hope something would come of it! She enjoyed family weddings. When Miss Rebecca had married Lord Darrington, some of the servants had been allowed to go down to the church and Mrs Hallam had sent them real champagne to drink the bride's health with. That was what happened when you served a decent family. They looked after you. Just as you looked after them.

Outside, Tian caught up with Annie at the far side of the shrubbery, in a sheltered part of the gardens not overlooked from above.

She turned at the sound of footsteps and became very still and watchful when she saw who it was.

He stopped a pace away from her. 'Annie,' he said softly, just her name but with such a wealth of feeling in his voice.

She couldn't speak, was suddenly short of breath, her wits fractured into a thousand stray thoughts by the impact of his nearness.

'We need to talk, Annie.'

'I – I'd rather not.' She took a step backwards, but could not move further because of the leafless tangle of branches from a small forsythia shrub that lightened up this corner of the gardens into a yellow glory in early spring.

'It's not like you to run away from something.' He reached out and took hold of her hand. 'Annie, you know we need to talk about what lies between us.'

She stiffened at that. 'Nothing lies between us! Excuse me, I have to—' She tried to pull her hand away from him and push past him at the same time. She succeeded in neither.

He held her arm so firmly she couldn't move away, then pulled her slowly into his arms. 'Annie, my lovely Annie,' he whispered. 'I've been wanting to kiss you again for weeks. I couldn't believe it when I saw you in the garden that first day, looking so beautiful, with your hair flaming in the sun. For a moment, I couldn't catch my breath. And I feel the same way every time I set eyes on you.'

Mesmerised by the soft lilt of his voice and by the touch of his hand, she made no further attempt to pull away, just blinked up at Tian as his head bent towards hers. And when he put his arms round her to pull her closer, when his lips touched hers, she lay quiescent in his embrace. For a moment, she even responded to his kiss and put a hand around his neck.

Then she panicked and began to flutter against him like a caged bird.

So he let her move back. But still he kept hold of one hand. 'Ah, Annie, I love you so much!' he whispered, as if he did not dare say the words too loudly. 'Surely you feel something for me?'

'Tian, I'm not – I can't—' Her voice fluted to a stop and then she jerked out, 'I'm not ready for – for another man. Not yet.'

His eyes were searching her face, seeing the confusion in it. But a surge of triumph coursed through him. She was not rejecting him and she had for a moment responded to his kiss. It took all his strength to do so, but he made himself let go of her hand and move backwards. 'Could we just talk about things, then?'

She swallowed hard. If she were wise, she'd leave him, run back to the house. 'I'm not ready,' she said again, unable to think of anything else to explain her confusion.

'But you're not rejecting me?'

'I – I don't know what I'm doing.'

'Annie love, my beautiful, beautiful Annie, won't you give me a chance? Won't you let me court you properly?' He saw her eyes widen as she looked at him, as if she was surprised by her own feelings and reactions.

'I don't know. I – We'll see.'

Then she did walk away. And he didn't follow her. She hadn't rejected him. Suddenly he remembered the letter he had found in his luggage, the letter from Frederick Hallam. Strangely, he felt as if Frederick was there beside him for a moment, urging him to be patient, not to give up.

I'll show it to her, Tian decided. And I think, I really do think, that Frederick would be on my side. He'd not have wanted her to spend the rest of her life alone. No one who truly loved her would want that. And she deserves some happiness, for she's looked after the happiness of everyone else in her family. Very patiently, he had pieced together the story of her life from things the Gibsons had let drop, and it had filled him with admiration. She's a wonderful woman, he thought now. And she's still overburdened. I could help her, love her, share those burdens. Why won't she let me?

He began to pace up and down. That damned war in America was biting hard in this part of the world now. Cotton was short, and the spinners and weavers of Lancashire were feeling the pinch. And if the war went on for years, as Tian believed it would, then things could only grow worse.

When he went back to the house, he got out his painting things and began to set them in order. Pictures were flickering before his eyes, so many pictures, so many experiences from his trip to America. Suddenly he was itching to set them down.

A couple of hours later, the dinner gong rang and the family gathered in the dining-room. All except one person.

Edgar looked at his mother. 'Shall I go and call Tian?'

For a moment, Annie felt herself flushing and couldn't think what to say, then she nodded. 'Yes. But go quietly. He may have fallen asleep. He's not fully recovered yet.'

They heard Edgar running up the stairs, then heard him stop and begin to tiptoe, almost as noisily as he had run, along the corridor. There was the sound of a knock, followed by a door opening, then suddenly Edgar gave a shout of joy and his words were heard quite clearly by everyone below.

'Tian, you've started painting again!'

26

February to March 1862

Joanie's wedding was a bright spot in a gloomy winter for the Gibsons and their fellow Lancastrians. Not that the Gibsons went short. No, certainly not. But business at the yard inevitably slowed down, and wherever you walked in Bilsden you could see the operatives' distress.

Without work, men hung around street corners or gathered in groups wherever they could find shelter from the weather. Custom at pubs dwindled, for the men could not afford their usual tipples. Those still in work of some kind, rarely full-time, would make a half pint of beer last a whole evening. The drinking rooms which had been bright and cheerful now seemed to echo with the phantom cries of past enjoyment, and those who could still afford to go there spoke more loudly, as if trying to fill the emptiness.

Some men went off on the tramp, seeking work elsewhere, but it was hard on shoe leather and although the first few found jobs here and there, soon there was no more work to be had within two days' walking distance. Of those who went into Yorkshire, a few found work in the woollen industry, but again there weren't unlimited jobs to be found, and even if you got something, it was hard to pay for food and lodgings as well as sent home enough money for your family to live on.

For the women of Bilsden, it was perhaps hardest of all. They found it impossible to make the vouchers given out by the Poor Law Guardians purchase enough food to fill their children's bellies every day, for the grocery shops involved did not give generous value on the vouchers. And then the women had to try to comfort their hungry children. Since it was winter, there was the additional problem of heating and little or no wood left to be garnered from the countryside around the town. So the best people could do was gather in groups and huddle together in one room to conserve warmth, while they tried to ignore their stomach's rumbling and wished for better times.

To some women, their inability to purchase cleaning materials was an added misery, for they felt it a disgrace to have no soap, no blacklead, no hot water even. They had always taken a pride in their houses, kept everything sparkling clean and held their heads up in front of their neighbours. Now, they did what they could with cold water and hard scrubbing, but it never seemed enough, and clothes and skin all seemed to take on a greyish tinge.

It was Eva Bagley who thought of meeting this need. She was originally from a humble clerk's home herself, and had been one of the earliest of the town's ladies to accept Annie as Frederick Hallam's wife, at a time when Beatrice was trying to stir up trouble for her step-mother. Like most of the citizens of Bilsden, rich and poor, Eva's husband was feeling the pinch in his haulage business.

She, who had been happier helping him struggle to build up his business in the early days of their marriage than she had as the pampered wife of an affluent man, began to look full of purpose and determination again. She cut down her housekeeping cheerfully before Michael even had to ask her, and when her children complained of the lack of choice, she gave them a taste of what it was like to go hungry by sending them to bed without an evening meal or supper. After that, they did not complain again.

When Eva mentioned her idea of providing cleaning materials, it caught the imagination of a few ladies who objected to supplying food for those already 'on the Union' and therefore supposedly provided for. But they could see that the public money might not stretch to soap and soda and that the men on the Board of Guardians might not see these things as necessities. They were happy to fill the need from their own pockets.

Eva at first was dubious about how best to distribute the ladies' largesse. Then fate took a hand. When her shopping bag's handle broke one day, scattering her purchases across the street, a woman came forward to help her pick them up, a woman of the lower classes, with such a motherly look to her that afterwards, when they got talking, Eva plucked up the courage to confide her problem and ask for advice.

The woman, one Mary Jane Pitten, brightened and exclaimed, 'Eh, that'd be champion, that would!' She began at once to offer suggestions, ticking them off on her fingers, and they were so sensible that Eva invited her home for a cup of tea to discuss the matter in more detail.

'Nay, I'm not dressed to visit a house like yourn,' Mary Jane demurred, looking down at her plain woollen dress and faded shawl. She had already pawned her good Sunday shawl and did not expect to see it again.

Eva was not going to accept a refusal. 'Please come! We can sit in the little back room and no one will disturb us. It's warmer there anyway, since I don't light the parlour fire until the evening to save fuel.' She saw the surprise on Mary's face and gave her a wry smile. 'The lack of cotton is hitting us all, you know.'

'Eh, I never thought the rich folk 'ud feel the pinch, too,' Mary exclaimed.

'We don't go hungry like the poorer people do, but we've had to cut down.' Eva sighed. 'And anyway, I couldn't keep a lavish table when I see folk around me lacking bread. I just couldn't do it.'

Mary Jane gave in to temptation, sent her neighbour, who had been hovering nearby, home with a message that she'd be back later, and allowed herself to be taken to the Bagleys' comfortable residence.

She stopped again at the gate, staring at the commodious house with its neat, winter-bare gardens. 'Eh, I don't—'

'This way.' Eva took her arm and led the way inside, sending the maid, who was goggling at her strange companion, off to fetch tea. When it was brought, Eva ministered to her visitor herself.

'A cup of tea?' She had already seen the longing on the other woman's face, of course she had, but she behaved as if this were a normal visit. To do otherwise would embarrass her guest.

Mary Jane fought temptation and lost, giving in to the luxury of it all. 'That'd be very nice. Thanks.'

'And perhaps you'd like to try a slice of my fruit cake? I make it myself on Cook's day off. I miss doing the cooking since my husband came up in the world.'

The visitor sipped the tea delicately, sighing at the taste of it. 'I don't know when I've had a better cup.'

'You must let me give you a packet to take home with you.'

Mary Jane stiffened. 'I don't need charity. We're managing.'

'I wasn't offering you charity, but a present from – I hope – a friend. And anyway, you're going to be so much help to me that you can't possibly think of it as charity.' She held out her hand for the empty cup. After a few sips, Mary Jane had been unable to resist gulping the rest of the tea down while it was still so lovely and warm. 'Another?' But she didn't wait for an answer, just poured, then refilled the pot from the hot water jug. 'It'll only go to waste if we leave it, you know.'

She took a piece of cake herself to encourage Mary Jane to eat, then got down to business. 'Now, how best do you think we should . . .'

And somehow, the 'we' struck the right note and before long it was 'Eva' and 'Mary Jane' and an unlikely friendship had formed. For as long as the cotton famine lasted, Eva's own pet charity flourished and the poorer women of Bilsden could, if they wished, obtain cleaning materials. But it was Mary Jane who took charge of the distribution and who was able to prevent abuse of this largesse.

So when Eva insisted on making a small weekly payment for Mary Jane's services and started giving her parcels of food and leftovers, Mary Jane felt she could take them with a clear conscience. She had earned them. And if her husband dared to grumble again about her usurping his job as wage earner and leaving him to see to the children, she would go for him with her rolling pin, she would that.

Tian endured those troubled months as best he could. He did not try to leave Ridge House because Annie was there. And anyway, he still needed help at times, still needed to feel safe as he continued to regain his memories.

He wrote cheerfully to his family in Ireland, explaining that he had had an accident and lost his memory for a time. But he declined their pressing invitations to go home, minimising his problems and fabricating excuses for not visiting them. If he could, he would take Annie with him when he did go to Ireland, take her to meet his family. Until then, he would stay with her in Bilsden as long as she would let him.

Although he had started painting again, what he produced was different from his earlier portraits, less lyrical, more filled with drama, pain and sadness. It wasn't an expression of beauty, but a necessary purging of his troubled mind. After a while, he set to work on the big picture he had planned of ordinary working people setting off on a ship which would take them overseas, and that at least satisfied him. He tried to show the emigrants' sorrow, their anguish at leaving their loved ones – not from an excess of sentimentality, but because it was the simple truth and because their pain deserved a voice.

Edgar was in and out of the studio, quiet and watchful, his eyes full of the same longing to paint that Tian had once felt. But he could not encourage the boy too much, because one day Edgar would inherit his father's mill and other interests. You could not easily ignore such responsibilities and he knew that Annie, having been disappointed in her elder son, expected much of her younger boy, refusing even to contemplate the thought that he might not grow out of his wheezing weakness, which was, she insisted, improving somewhat.

Not until the big painting was finished did Tian show it to her. And then she just stood there, so greatly moved that tears trickled down her face. 'I hadn't realised how they felt,' she said simply.

'Few people do.'

'The Poor Law Guardians are talking about sending people from Bilsden to Australia.'

'Sending them? You mean – against their will?'

She nodded.

The idea horrified him. 'That would be wicked, absolutely wicked. Even when folk want to go it's painful for they know they'll probably never see their loved ones again. But to force them to emigrate—' He shook his head. 'No. That's downright immoral. Can't you stop them?'

She turned back to the painting, her eyes still full of tears. 'No. Frederick might have been able to, but all I can do is argue with the Guardians. We're in disagreement about quite a few things. That's why I set up my own relief scheme for our workers. I couldn't bear them to be treated like – like inconvenient cattle.'

'William seems to be doing well for you with it.'

'Yes. He's very capable.' It was still a surprise to her how capable her son was. 'But applications for relief are more than double what they were last year. And the town still expects me to pay poor rates, as well as look after our own people.'

'That's unfair.'

She nodded. 'I think so. I'm going to speak to the Town Council tomorrow. Again.' She gave a short dry laugh. 'I'm going to try to bluff them this time, make them believe that if they don't grant me exemption from paying the normal poor rates, then I'll toss all our people back on to them.'

'They'll not believe you. You're Frederick Hallam's widow. They'll know that you'll look after your own.'

'We'll see.' She rather thought that people *would* listen, because she was taking Matt Peters with her, and he had produced page after page of neat figures proving how much cheaper it would be for the Bilsden Town Council to remit Mrs Hallam's poor rates and leave her to care for her own people.

What's more, Matt did not approve of what she was doing, and that would show.

She hesitated, then asked a question that had been on the tip of her tongue for a while. 'Do you think – perhaps you could start painting my portrait now?'

He shook his head. 'Not yet, Annie darlin'. Not till I feel,' he shrugged his shoulders, finding it hard to explain it to her, 'not till I feel happier inside. I know exactly the sort of portrait Frederick wanted, I do most truly understand that. He wanted to show you in your prime, beautiful and glowing. I can't produce something like that yet. But if you want me to leave Ridge House, I can easily find lodgings in the town. I'm not short of money.'

Indeed, he was surprised at how much money he did have nowadays. His English agent, Miles Correnaud, had written to his home in Ireland to say that he had sold most of the paintings Tian had left behind in England, and Tian's father had passed the letter on. Thaddeus Brownsby had written from New York to report progress and had certainly kept his promise to make the money Tian had earned in America multiply.

'I suppose I really ought to move out,' he repeated. It was not the first time he'd made that offer.

'There's no need whatsoever for you to leave,' Annie snapped, not asking herself why she felt so angry at the thought. 'Are we not making you comfortable here?'

He smiled, a warm smile that lit up his face and made her blink at how handsome he was looking again, in spite of the scar. 'Well, if you're sure?'

He put his hand on her shoulder. He was always touching her, and it always made her feel restless. 'Of course I'm sure. But if you like, if it'll make you feel better, you could teach the children something about sketching. You know how much Edgar enjoys his drawing.' And had been begging her to ask Tian to teach them properly.

'I'd be happy to do that.' He lifted his hand to twirl one of her curls around his finger. 'Ah, Annie!'

Before she realised what she was doing, she had swayed towards him and he was taking her in his arms. When his lips touched hers, she did not draw back.

He kissed her gently, then he moved backwards. 'No protests this time, Annie darlin'?'

She just stared at him, as if she had no will of her own, so he pulled her towards him again and kissed her more ardently. Afterwards she leaned against him, shaking visibly, and he felt a surge of triumph. She must be growing to love him.

'Oh, Tian!' she murmured.

'What?' He held her at arm's length and smiled down at her.

She shook her head helplessly. 'I don't know what.'

'Then just accept what's happening between us. Give it a chance to grow. There's no rush. Sure, and isn't it the most natural thing on this earth for a man to kiss the woman he loves.' He put one fingertip lightly across her lips to prevent her speaking. He didn't want this moment spoiled.

Annie was very quiet that evening, but once or twice her eyes met Tian's across the room and she gave him a quick half-smile. And as he went upstairs to bed, he felt hope glowing warmly inside him. His patience was going to be rewarded. How could it not be when he loved her so much?

She went to bed to agonise over the incident.

27

April 1862

The next morning, before Annie could confront the Town Council, James Hallam arrived at Ridge House in the station cab, having set off from Leeds at a dark and chill hour of the early morning. He had received the latest accounting from Matt Peters the previous day and was sizzling with fury at how Annie was conducting his father's business, at how she was wasting the family's money on workers who were not earning it, who should be the responsibility of the town's Relief Committee. For once in his well-ordered life, he had behaved impetuously and simply set off to confront her.

'Ah, there you are!' James started trumpeting his disapproval as soon as the front door was closed behind him, while Winnie was standing waiting to take his coat. Annie, who had heard her maid's exclamation of 'Mr James!' came out of the library to greet him. She was so startled when he shouted at her that for a moment, she could only stand there in shock.

And so loudly did he continue to harangue her that within a couple of minutes, the whole household was listening to the altercation.

'This time you have gone too far, Step-mother. *Too far!* I have come to try to talk sense into you, for all our sakes,' he began, tossing his hat and gloves to Winnie, then unbuttoning his coat while the anger that had built up to explosion point during the train journey from Leeds, poured forth. 'Heaven knows, it's more than time someone did.'

Winnie stood there at the side of the hall, open-mouthed.

Annie recovered enough to glare at her step-son. 'Kindly

come into the library and stop shouting at me like an ill-mannered schoolboy, James.'

'Someone needs to shout at you,' he retorted, struggling with a final button, then in his haste getting his hand stuck in a hole in the seam of his sleeve lining, caused by his increasing plumpness which was starting to strain the seams of all his garments. 'If you go on as you are doing, you'll waste every penny of the money my father left you, as well as my own and my sister's inheritance.' He muttered under his breath, 'Damn the coat! What's wrong with it?'

'Allow me, sir,' Winnie said, stepping for ward, hands outstretched to ease it off him.

'I can manage.' He waved her away irritably and finally dragged off the sleeve, ripping the lining as he did so. He then cast the coat carelessly in the parlourmaid's general direction, not bothering when it fell to the floor, for what else was that fool of a woman paid for but to pick it up? Squaring his shoulders, he adjusted his cravat, then strode forward towards the library, ready to do battle.

Annie followed him inside, angry enough to shut the door behind her with a thump.

'Well!' Winnie stood for a moment with her hands on her hips. She knew what she thought of so-called gentlemen who treated servants as rudely as that, she did indeed. And she remembered Mr James as a boy, and a nasty, spotty lad he had been, too. His spots might have gone now, but his manners hadn't improved. Winnie was just glad she worked for a lady like Mrs Hallam, not him and that wife of his, who ill-treated little children. (The servants all knew what they thought of that incident!)

A pair of large feet pounded down the stairs. 'Did I hear shouting? Who was that, Winnie?'

'It was your step-brother, Mr William,' she said making no effort to pick up James Hallam's coat yet. She hoped it would get wrinkled, and she wouldn't be pressing it for him, as she might for someone with better manners, no she wouldn't. 'And if he's still talking to your mother as rudely as he spoke to me, she'll no doubt welcome an interruption from you.' See how you like that, James Hallam! she thought, smiling to herself.

Before William could move, a second set of footsteps thumped down the stairs from the dormer room where Tian had his studio. 'What on earth is going on? I heard shouting and—'

He broke off as voices were raised in the library.

'It's James Hallam,' said William by way of an introduction. 'Father's son by his first marriage. Not happy how his father left things. Fond of interfering. Or trying to interfere. And his wife,' his expression grew dark at the memory, 'is particularly fond of caning children and locking them in dark cupboards.'

'Well, whoever he is, he's not going to speak to Annie like that.'

Tian took a step towards the library door.

William put one hand on the artist's shoulder. 'Allow me. After all, I am her son. I have a more obvious right.'

'But I—' Tian broke off. From William's expression, he had no need to put his feelings for Annie into words.

'I think it would make matters worse if you interfered this time. He's the sort who jumps to conclusions, usually malicious ones.' He smiled. 'And your feelings for my mother are rather obvious.'

'Oh. You – you don't mind?'

'Of course not.'

'Thank you.' Tian shook his hand and said gruffly, 'Very well. I'll stay outside. Call me if you need any help throwing him out.'

William grinned. 'Oh, I think I can manage.' He opened the library door and strolled inside. 'Good morning, Mother.'

James, who had just opened his mouth to deliver another tirade, closed it, took a few deep breaths and said icily, 'Your mother and I were having a private conversation, young man.'

William smiled. 'How can it be private when you're shouting at the top of your voice?'

'I can defend myself, William,' Annie said, eyes flashing. 'And anyway, I don't intend to waste much more time with James when he's in this stupid mood.'

Her step-son swung round. 'You'll hear me out this time.'

William sucked in air very audibly.

Annie ignored her would-be champion and stepped right up to James, poking her finger into the softness of his belly, so that he took a half-step back, cast suddenly on the defensive, for he detested people touching him. 'I'll do as I choose in my own house, James Hallam, and don't you forget it. You'd have been out on your ear before now for the way you've been addressing me, if you weren't Frederick's son. Now be quiet and listen.' Again her finger jabbed him in the middle.

James took another hurried step backwards.

Their unwelcome visitor seemed, William thought, trying not to chuckle, as stunned by the fact that she was touching him as by the fact that she was defying him. When her pointing finger jabbed out again, James skipped backwards so hastily that he stumbled over a chair leg. William hid a grin. Trust his mother to look after herself.

'I don't care about profits at a time like this,' Annie told her stepson, each word carefully articulated, 'nor would your father and nor should anyone who calls himself a Christian. There is almost no work for the spinners. *No – work – at – all!* And this is not their fault. Do you really expect me to allow our people to starve?'

'There is poor relief. No one need starve in a modern country like ours.'

'Yes, poor relief.' There was a wealth of scorn in her voice. Martin Leaseby was doing all he could to minimise the relief, but she would not stand by and let people suffer, and so she'd told him, stopped him in the street and not minced her words. 'That does slow down the starvation process a little, I will admit.' She opened her mouth to continue, then her eyes narrowed suddenly and she paused, staring at James as if she had never seen him before. A smile began to curve her lips, and when she spoke, her tone had changed. 'But I do agree with you that our relief expenses must be kept down as much as possible, James. I do not at all wish to *waste* our money.'

'Oh?' He was very suspicious of this sudden volte-face.

'So perhaps you should come with me this afternoon to speak to the Town Council. I've requested them to waive my poor rates, on condition that I take full responsibility for our own people.'

'Take full responsibility! Are you mad? That's why the Poor Law exists, to protect those in genuine need. It would be enough for someone like you to pay the poor rates. More than enough.'

'Not for me it wouldn't. Don't forget that I come from the Rows myself.'

A sneer twisted his face briefly. 'I never forget that.'

'Good.' She forced her anger down. She needed his co-operation, however reluctant. 'Then perhaps you will come with me this afternoon and help me persuade the Town Council to remit the poor rate for Hallam's.' As he opened his mouth to refuse, she added in a firm voice, 'It's the only way you can help me to reduce my expenditure, James, believe me. I am utterly determined about this.'

He stared at her. She was much shorter than he was, much shorter than his own wife, but she radiated purpose and, yes, he had to admit it, power, too. He had never met a woman like her and she always made him feel ill at ease, for he could not, in her presence, consider her an inferior being, however much he managed to persuade himself when he was away from her that she was only a female, therefore fallible and in need of masculine guidance.

Behind him, William muffled another chuckle.

'I shall not be satisfied with that,' James said. 'If you go on as you are doing, there will be no profits at all for the family.'

Her smile was quite serene as she uttered her next heresy. 'No. I don't expect there will be any profits from the mill until the war is over. I hope you're making a good living from your legal practice, James.'

He could only stand there at this, opening and shutting his mouth like a stranded fish.

'But by keeping our people on, we shall preserve a skilled workforce, for we still have the best spinners in town. And when this war does end, when the cotton starts coming into Liverpool again, we shall not need to train new workpeople like those fools who are sending their operatives away.' She smiled. 'Indeed, we shall have the most loyal workforce in the town. Your own father taught me the value of that.'

'My father grew soft in his old age,' James said bitterly, wondering why he had ever thought he could talk sense into her. 'And I see that he infected you with his foolish ideas.'

'He did indeed,' she agreed, a soft smile transforming her face as she thought of Frederick. Then the smile vanished and changed to an implacable stare. 'Well, will you help me try to reduce my expenses in the only way I think proper?'

'I will. But it'll be a first step only. I shall not stand aside if you continue to give away our family's money.' But it was an empty threat and they both knew it. Anger had sent him here today, but in anger you believe you can do things which you know to be impossible in the cold light of calm reason. How could he have forgotten her presence, the way she always made him feel like a schoolboy, for all that she was only two years older than him? She was not like Judith, whom he had trained to bend to his wishes. This woman would never bend to any man's wishes.

'The money will not be given away, James. I intend to make the operatives earn it. That's why our mill went on to half-time before it needed to, so that they could still feel they were earning something. And I'm now looking for some other project to occupy them, something which will beautify the town, for your father would have thoroughly approved of that.'

James shook his head slowly from side to side, feeling a sour taste in his mouth. This was what came from giving power to a woman. Softness. A lack of sound business sense. He played his last card. 'If I do this, will you at least sell the cotton goods

331

you've been storing up? That will help maintain this coming year's profits.' He did not want to lower his comfortable standard of living, did not see why he should have to.

She shook her head. 'No.' Then she held up one hand. 'Just think for a moment. How much more valuable do you think those goods will become as the war continues?'

But it took her and Tian until after lunch to make James appreciate that, to make him realise that the war would probably go on for a year or two more. And Tian spoke with such authority about the situation in America that James became convinced and over the next few months, even found himself quoting the facts supplied to him by Tian to colleagues and acquaintances. As the years of war went by, he gained much respect for his shrewdness and foresight.

'And now,' Annie said, 'let's finish our lunch. I'm sure you're hungry, James. You must have had to leave Leeds very early this morning.'

'I am hungry, yes,' he admitted, despairing of talking any sense into her.

As James and Annie drove into town that afternoon in the Hallam carriage, he looked at her suspiciously. 'How long is that artist fellow going to be staying with you? It gives a very strange appearance for him to stay at Ridge House, sponging off you.'

'He's not sponging. He's our friend and guest. And he'll stay with us until he's fully recovered. Even then, he'll not leave until he's fulfilled your father's last request to me.'

'Oh? What's that?'

She felt she owed him some sort of explanation, if only to prevent gossip and speculation. 'Your father left me a letter, to be delivered some months after his death, expressing a final wish that I commission Mr Gilchrist to paint my portrait. He left a letter for Mr Gilchrist, too, asking him to undertake that commission. I shall not go against Frederick's wishes.' After which she refused to discuss Tian further, though she knew that people were beginning to talk. Well, let them!

The Town Council had met in all its pomp that day, prepared to deal firmly with Mrs Hallam, for what, after all, did a woman know of business? Even a woman like her. Like James, they were to find out their mistake very quickly. Certainly Mrs Hallam was quieter than usual and deferred to her step-son and manager, but there was steel behind her softness and both her companions turned to her frequently for endorsement of what they were saying, not the other way round.

First, Matt presented the figures he had gathered, whose totals shocked some Councillors rigid.

'But it won't come to that, surely, Mrs Hallam, Mr Peters?' the Mayor asked. 'I mean, most people think the war will be over by autumn at the latest.'

'Then most people are wrong,' she said. 'But please don't take my word for it. Ask Mr Gilchrist next time you see him. He's seen what's happening in America.' She then sat silently while James Hallam took over and argued her case with a lawyer's practised skill.

'So you see,' he summed up, when he had numbed the Councillors into resentful silence with a spate of long words and Latin terminology more suited to a court of law, 'that the longer the war continues, the more money you'll be saving the town.' He scowled at Annie. 'And I shall not allow my step-mother to continue to look after her own people unless you do agree to remit her poor rates, for I, too, own part of the business and it's my money which is being used, as well as hers. Do you think we Hallams have unlimited funds?' Awful scorn underlined his final words. 'Money to throw away?'

Annie lowered her eyes, so that they wouldn't see how angry she felt when she heard James talk like that, as if he could tell her what to do. She listened as the arguments raged backwards and forwards, then, when they could come to no conclusion, she cleared her throat and all eyes turned to her again. 'Why do we not come to some compromise? If the war ends, and I've paid out less than the poor rates I would have paid, then I'll gladly pay the difference to you.'

The Mayor exchanged glances with his cronies, sensed their approval and nodded. It was not likely that she'd expend less than the poor rates, but best to cover all options. 'That would, I think, be fair, Mrs Hallam, very fair indeed.'

'It'd be fairer still to agree also to remit my step-mother's poor rates for years after the war ends, because she's likely to pay out a great deal more by doing things in this quixotic way,' James snapped. He paused, a carefully calculated pause, then looked at Annie and shook his head. 'I'm not sure I can agree with what you're doing, Step-mother. Perhaps we should reconsider our position?'

The Council hastily took a vote, then, just as it was about to agree formally to remit Hallam's poor rates while the war lasted – providing they took complete responsibility for their own workpeople and their families – Michael Bagley, who was one of the Poor Law Guardians as well as a Councillor, spoke up.

'I don't think the Council actually has the power to remit the poor rates.' He looked apologetically at Annie. 'It's not that I don't approve of what you're doing, believe me, Mrs Hallam, but it's a question of what is legally permissible.'

Annie closed her eyes and prayed for patience. The ins and outs of the way the law was applied sometimes irritated her beyond bearing. Stupid laws made by stupid men, she often thought, men who in this case had little practical understanding of the suffering they were making half-hearted attempts to alleviate, men who seemed to enjoy making regulations more than they enjoyed doing something worthwhile.

There was silence in the Council Chamber, then the Mayor asked hesitantly, 'Does anyone know exactly how matters stand legally?'

There was silence, then Michael Bagley volunteered, 'We can hold a meeting of the Guardians in a day or two, an emergency meeting, and work out what may be permissible.'

'I shall come back and attend that meeting,' James declared, then looked in Mr Bagley's direction. 'If it's allowed, that is?

I'm sure we can work something out, if it's only for Hallam's to pay the money to the Poor Law Union and then have it paid back for services rendered in the relief of certain specified persons.' His gaze was that of a superior person assisting his inferiors. 'There is usually a legal way, if the goodwill is there. What we need to establish today is whether the goodwill is there?' He raised one eyebrow at the Council, who hastened to agree with him and to vote at once to support Mrs Hallam in principle, on behalf of the ratepayers of Bilsden.

Two days later, James again caught an early train from Leeds and attended the meeting of the Bilsden and District Poor Law Union Guardians. He found them much more amenable to the suggestion that Mrs Hallam be paid from the poor rates the amount she had paid in, as long as the emergency lasted and as long as she continued to provide totally for all Hallams' employees and their families.

'We shall, however, require Mrs Hallam to sign an agreement to the effect that if the war ends quickly, she will make good any monies not spent, or rather the Bilsden and District Poor Law Union will require it,' Michael Bagley concluded later, having been chosen to represent the Board of Guardians and make their decision known to Mrs Hallam.

Annie smiled brilliantly at them both, relieved at the news they had brought, relieved to have it sorted out so she could get on with things. She knew that James still thought she was behaving irresponsibly, but at least this small financial saving would keep him out of her hair for a while. She was sure she could spend the money to better effect than a bunch of old men like the Guardians could. 'Send the agreement to James first, if you please, Mr Bagley. I'm sure he'll verify that it's legally binding – on both sides.'

'I'll do that, Mrs Hallam, and let me just say how much I admire—'

When the visitor had taken a fussy leave of her, with much effusing about her 'true Christian charity', she turned to her stepson and smiled. 'Thank you, James.'

'Don't thank me for helping you to ruin yourself! And don't ever think that I wish to give away the family money.' James, who felt he had wasted more than enough time on Annie's vagaries, took out his watch, snapped the case open and nodded. 'I believe a train is due shortly. I'll take my leave of you, Stepmother.' Without waiting for her response, he went out into the hallway, demanded his outdoor garments from Winnie and set off for the station on foot.

Annie grinned at Matt, whom she had invited to attend the meeting. 'I think we did rather well, don't you?'

He shook his head. 'I fear I incline more towards Mr James Hallam's views about this.'

'So long as you obey my orders, you can incline where you want,' she replied cheerfully.

The next day was cloudy but fine. Tian sought Annie out. 'I'd like to walk up to Clough Knowle. I think it'd help pull some more of my confused memories together.'

She shuddered. 'I haven't been back there since that day.'

'Then perhaps you should come and face your devils, too?'

She was tempted, glanced out of the window and gave in to temptation. 'Very well. I think the rain will hold off.' She was not sure it would be a good thing to go alone with him, but she would enjoy a long walk. She felt as if she'd been cooped up indoors for a million years and wanted to get the sour taste of James's penny-pinching disregard for people's distress out of her mouth.

They didn't speak much as they strode out towards Clough Knowle. Both were energetic walkers and they had soon warmed themselves up, in spite of the chill wind that was soughing across the tops and whining through the rare, wind-twisted trees that fought to survive in the clefts and hollows.

When they drew near the spot where her step-daughter had tried to push her to her death, Annie slowed then stopped. 'She was utterly mad, but I wish Beatrice hadn't died like that, for Frederick's sake. It hurt him greatly.'

Tian nodded, beginning to remember the day he had coaxed Annie up from the ledge which had prevented her from falling to her death when Beatrice pushed her over the edge. He gestured to some rocks. 'Would you like to sit down for a minute?'

She nodded and sat there on the chill stone, staring into the distance. When she looked sideways, Tian had that rigid look about him which meant that he was remembering something, so she turned her attention back to the sweeping expanse of moorland, which from up here seemed to stretch away into the distance as far as the eyes could see. When she was on the tops, she sometimes felt as if she were alone in the world, alone and yet connected to the earth around her in an elemental way. She wasn't a fanciful person normally, but up here you could not help fancies creeping into your mind.

'What must it be like to fly, as those birds are doing?' she pondered aloud when she saw the grimness fade from Tian's face.

'It must be wonderful.' His voice sounded more Irish than usual, soft and lilting, such a contrast to the flat harshness of Bilsden voices. 'I've often dreamed of flying and on the ship going out to America, if you stood near the prow and let the wind possess you, you could almost imagine you were doing it. On the way back to England, it was too stormy to stand anywhere on deck, or even to stay upright in your cabin sometimes.' And he had not been the only passenger to wonder whether they would make it safely to Liverpool.

He put one arm around her, almost absent-mindedly. 'Isn't it grand?' he asked. 'I never thought to admire any other landscape so much, for I love my home, but this one takes hold of your heart somehow.' He pointed towards the valley below them. 'Though if this were Ireland, there would be a lake down there, glinting at you, full of fish just waiting to be caught.'

'A lake.' She closed her eyes. 'Yes, I can just see it.' Then she opened her eyes and blinked at him, clutching his arm in her excitement. 'Tian! That's it! A lake!'

'What do you mean: "That's it"?' He looked down at her vivid face and joy filled him again. More and more she was relaxing with him, confiding in him. They were building a relationship like a wall, brick by brick. And he hoped it would be strong enough to last for ever.

Words tumbled over one another as she tried to explain. 'Tian, that's what we can do with our people. We can pay them to dig out a lake. Frederick told me once that people built an artificial lake over Rochdale way, you know, at the end of the last century, to provide a water supply for the Rochdale Canal. If they could do all that in those days, then so can we. And our lake will provide water for the town, too. Jeremy Lewis is always saying how much we need another clean water supply.'

'It's a lovely idea, but your people are spinners, not navvies. They'll not have the muscles to dig out a lake.'

She laughed aloud. 'What does that matter? It just means we must employ more of them to do it. What shall we call it? Bilsden Lake?' She shook her head. 'We'll have to think of a better name than that.' She was silent for a moment, then she turned again to look at him, triumph glowing in her eyes. 'If the spinners create it, we should surely call it—'

'Spinners Lake,' he finished for her, throwing back his head and laughing aloud. 'Annie, you're a genius! I've talked to the men in the streets as they hang around on the corners, not knowing what to do with themselves. They're pining for something to do, something to give them back their self-respect. Creating a lake would make them feel they were earning their way again.'

'Spinners Lake,' she said in a reverent, hushed tone. 'Oh, how Frederick would have loved that idea!'

Tian had been going to kiss her. It had been agony to resist it for so long, with her shoulders warm beneath his arm, her softness tantalising him. But at the mention of her dead husband's name, he drew back, both physically and mentally, bitterness trickling through him like acid. It had happened several times now. Just as he thought they were making progress, she had thrown the ghost of her husband between them.

When would she start living for herself? When would she stop saying Frederick's name in that besotted way? The man was dead! Tian had liked him, too, but he was dead now. And Annie was very much alive.

Would she ever truly accept that? For if not, they had no future together. Tian knew that he could not accept a half-hearted love, not when he cared for her so much. He got up and started back down the hill. 'Come on. It's getting cold.'

She followed him, puzzled. What had she done to upset him? For he was upset, no doubt about that. But the idea of creating a lake was filling her mind and she did not take the time to find out why Tian's mood had changed.

28

Spring 1862

People say that good things happen in threes. Certainly, it seemed that way to the Gibsons that spring, in spite of the lack of cotton, the shortage of work in the town and the continuing bad news from America.

Luke was the first to bring the family good news. In April, he came to a decision. He had been very patient, but now he just had to talk to Amy. He had seen her occasionally in the distance and when their eyes had met, she had recoiled, shaking her head as if to tell him to stay away. And he had respected that, because of her widowhood. She always wore black, with a dark bonnet hiding her shorn hair, though he could see that the fringe on her forehead was growing longer. But it hurt him to see how she always hurried about her shopping, almost furtively, as if she did not want to speak to anyone, as if she felt some sense of shame.

He knew she had been out to the farm several times, for some of the neighbours had seen her, but she had chosen to go on days when he wasn't there. To do that, she must have been watching from her mother-in-law's window for him to go into Bilsden. One of the neighbours was now farming most of the land for her and tending the stock, on a shared profit basis, but others, including Luke, were helping out where they could. What Amy was living off, he didn't know. Perhaps Ted Gorton had not spent all his money? Perhaps old Mrs Gorton had had something saved?

In the end, he had to resort to subterfuge to catch Amy. He went off down the hill towards Bilsden in the carrier's cart early one morning, a market day, as he often did. But once out of sight of Hey End, he pretended to have forgotten something and got down from the cart, walking back across the fields in a route which he had chosen with care so that Amy would not be able to see him. He was well enough known in the district now to trespass on other men's lands, and – he hoped – he had been forgiven by his neighbours for inadvertently killing Ted Gorton.

Even Clifford Sykes now nodded to Luke when their paths crossed, though he had not gone beyond a nod. But the other men greeted him cheerfully, passing the time of day with him as if nothing had ever been wrong, and he judged it best to allow what they had done and said in the past, in the heat of the moment, to be forgotten, for he wanted to stay at Hey End, stay on the land he loved.

He crept back behind the dry-stone walls, as he had done once before, and then waited patiently near Gorton's Farm. And sure enough, Amy turned off the road and came walking briskly along the lane, stopping for a moment at the farm gate to stare along to Luke's house then turning towards her home. She stood on tip-toe to fumble above the lintel for the front-door key, which was always kept there, but muttered in exasperation when she could not find it.

Luke moved forward quietly until he was standing behind her, then he cleared his throat. 'Is this what you're looking for?' He held out the key which he'd taken that morning.

Instinctively she gasped and shrank back, but he said nothing more, did not move, just gazed at her steadily.

'Ooh, you did make me jump, Luke Gibson!' She stretched out her hand to take the key, trying not to touch him as she did so.

His fingers tightened around hers for a moment, then he let go, not wanting to force her into anything. She had been forced enough for one lifetime. 'I need to talk to you, Amy. And you've been avoiding me.'

She left the key in his hand and started fiddling with her shawl. 'I – I don't know what you mean.'

'You haven't spoken to me since that day. Not once. Do you hate me so much for – for what happened?' He had meant to speak gently and tactfully, had had a speech carefully prepared, but it all went out of his head at the sight of her dark eyes staring up at him so anxiously from a face which was not, at least, bruised now.

She sagged against the doorpost. 'Of course I don't hate you, Luke. How could I? You've been nothing but kind to us, me and the children. And what happened was an accident. Everyone admits that now, even Ted's mother.'

'So you don't hate me?'

Her voice was gentle and her eyes softened as a blush coloured her face. 'Of course I don't.'

He took heart from that and the words he had been longing to say for so long poured from him. 'Oh, Amy, I've missed you so! And the children. I can't help loving you, can't think of anything else lately but you. I can't even care about my work just now, for you're there in my mind every minute. And if you don't let me court you, be with you sometimes, I don't know what I shall do, how I shall face living. Amy, I—'

She laid one fingertip on his lips. 'Shh, Luke.'

Anguish ran through him. She was going to turn him down, tell him she wanted nothing to do with him. The pain of that thought was so intense that he missed what she was saying and when she looked at him expectantly, her face as bright as that of a little bird pecking in his field, he could only ask, 'What? What did you say?' and wait in dull misery for the blow to fall.

'I said, give me that key and come inside, you great daft lump.'

For a moment he couldn't move. 'You're not – not sending me away?'

She laid one hand on his arm. 'No, Luke. I'm not sending you away.' Looking at him, she realised that for once she had the upper hand and the last of her fear of remarriage fell away. This man could never resort to violence. She had always felt that, and now, looking at his plain honest face, the diffident expression, the anxiety in his guileless blue eyes, she knew it with utter certainty. So when he did not seem able to move, she took the key from him, turned it in the lock and led the way confidently inside, feeling the first shoots of a nameless joy twining delicately through her whole body.

When they were inside her parlour, which felt chilly and looked so strange and lifeless, she would have gone across to light the fire, as had been her original intention. But he took her hand, swung her round and asked humbly, 'I must hear you say it. Is there really hope for me?'

She nodded, her cheeks rosy again. 'If that's what you want, Luke. I wasn't sure how you felt. I thought I should keep my distance for a while, till the gossip died down a little. But now – now I should love you to court me. I can't think of anything which would make me happier.'

His face lit up with such a blaze of joy that her mouth fell open in delight and she could not help beaming back at him.

'I wasn't sure, you see,' he told her, still humbly. 'I couldn't believe that someone like you, so smart and pretty, would – would fancy someone like me. I'm not clever like our Annie, or good-looking like our Mark. And I doubt I'll ever be rich, for I can't seem to care for money, as long as I have enough for my needs.'

'I love your looks, Luke,' she told him, touched to the core by his lack of confidence in himself. 'The kindness of your soul shines from your face, and that's what pleases me most in a man, not handsome features. Nor I never expected to be rich. The wife of a small farmer seldom is. I don't mind hard work. I just,' for a moment her voice broke, 'want a man who will love me and my children, who'll treat us kindly. I understand that Ted was ill, towards the end, but he'd always hit me, you see, always. Though never like he did in the end.'

'No!' His voice was soft with shock and pain for her. She was so little to have faced years of violence like that.

'And I won't put up with it ever again,' she added, determined

343

that he should understand this. 'Not even once. I'd walk straight out and never come back if you laid a finger on me.'

A tremor of anger shook him for a moment. To think of it! To think of anyone doing that to someone smaller and weaker, someone they had promised solemnly in church to love and cherish. 'I couldn't hit you, Amy. Or your children. I'd love them like they were my own. I do already.' And then he reached for her, gathered her in his arms and kissed her until the room spun around them both.

'How soon can we be married?' he asked as they drew apart. 'I can't bear to wait a moment longer than I have to.'

'As soon as my mother-in-law thinks right.' She saw his surprise at this condition and tried to explain. 'Maidie's been so good to me and the children. And I know she doesn't hold what happened against you, but if she thinks we should wait a bit, then we will.' She hesitated. 'And – and we'll have to look after her. She has no money, you see, and she's not a strong woman.'

He shrugged, still smiling. 'Of course we'll look after her.' Then his face brightened. 'When we marry, she could come to live in my cottage if she likes, then she'd be much closer. Would she like that, do you think?'

'Oh, Luke,' her voice broke on the words. 'You're such a lovely man.'

He put his arm round her waist and hugged her to him. 'I'll come down with you and see her today. We'll ask her if she minds. And then we'll tell the children.' He had never resembled his father so much before. 'I like children,' he admitted. 'I do hope we can have some of our own.' Then he blushed even more brightly than Amy had.

The second good thing to happen to the Gibsons was a blessing in disguise. The same week that Luke proposed to Amy, and Gorton's mother gave her blessing to the union, Joanie slipped and fell on the icy cobblestones of Church Road, a bad fall that knocked the wind out of her. Almost immediately she started to feel uncomfortable, so she abandoned her shopping trip and made her way slowly home, stopping a couple of times on the way as pain stabbed through her belly.

Kathy took one look at her face and asked, 'What's wrong?'

'I fell over. And I feel . . .' Joanie clutched her stomach. 'I've got a pain here, a bad one.'

Within a couple of hours, she had lost the baby she was carrying, and try as she might, she could not regret it. She lay there in bed, weeping for what she saw as a fault in herself.

'Don't let her start another child for a few months,' Dr Spelling advised the worried husband after he had examined her.

'But she'll be all right?'

'She'll be fine, Mr Burns. Just let her rest for two or three days and treat her gently for the next few weeks.'

'And,' Bartholomew hesitated, 'she will be able to have other children, won't she?'

Dr Spelling smiled. They always asked that – well, they did until they had a house full of children and too many mouths to feed, then they asked how they could avoid having any more. 'There's no reason to think she'll have any trouble bearing children. This is a simple miscarriage, for which the cause is obvious – a bad fall.'

When Bartholomew went out through the kitchen to their bedroom in what had once been a dairy, he could not help feeling happy. He would have accepted Harry Pickering's child, because it would have been Joanie's child, too, but he suspected that he would always have felt resentful, though he would have tried not to let it show. Now, what Harry Pickering had done did not matter at all. Joanie was Bartholomew's wife, his alone, and the only children she would be bearing would be his, too.

'I'll sit with her for a while,' he told Kathy as he passed through the kitchen.

Joanie, who was lying back against the pillows, stretched out a hand to him, tears trickling down her cheeks. 'Oh, Bartholomew. I'm sorry to cause such an upset.'

He leaned across to kiss her cheek. 'The important thing is that you're all right.'

More tears filled her eyes and spilled over. 'I'm glad it happened,' she admitted. 'I know it's wrong, and I didn't do it on purpose, but I'm glad I've lost the baby. Is that wicked of me?'

He gathered her in his arms. 'Shh, now. So am I glad. If you're wicked, then I am, too.'

Had it not been for his father and brothers, he would have been totally happy now, in his new life, but he saw them sometimes in the street and the glances they threw in his direction were full of hatred still. And he knew, for he understood the way they thought, that they were still trying to find a way to get back at him.

Even Tom thought it was better for the couple to continue living at Netherhouse Cottage, though they would both rather have had their own home. 'Give it a year,' he told Joanie when he had a quiet talk with her. 'If those Burns fellows haven't forgotten their stupid grievances by then, you'll have to move away from Bilsden.'

'Are they so bad?'

He nodded. 'Aye.' And seemed to be getting worse lately, as if old Bible Burns had lost control over them.

The third good thing to happen to the family concerned William. In May, he decided that he had waited long enough. He knew his own mind and as far as he was concerned, Elizabeth MacNaughton was the only woman he wanted. He caught her on a balmy Saturday afternoon, when the children had gone down the hill to visit their grandmother, and such was the purpose on his face that when she saw him come into the schoolroom, she could not move, could not do anything but watch him, her heart in her mouth.

'I'd like to have a serious talk with you,' he announced. 'Here or on the moors. I don't mind if you want to get out of the house to do it. But it's more than time we talked again.'

She gulped and put one hand to her throat. 'I don't think we should – should—' Her voice faded before the determination in his face.

'I've done as you asked and waited. And my feelings have only grown stronger.'

He had done more than wait, she thought, he had watched her, stared at her, stayed near whenever he could, smiled at her in such a fond way that several times she had nearly told him how she felt about him. It was a wonder no one else had noticed William's attentiveness, but the family had had a few other things to worry about. Only Elizabeth's own strong sense of duty held her back, and the fear that Annie would be furious at the thought of her son marrying a governess. The last thing she wanted was to upset Annie, who had been such a good friend to her.

'I haven't changed my mind, Elizabeth. And I shan't.' He caught hold of her hand. 'Will you marry me?' Her face turned so white that he frowned and his voice became more gentle. 'You're not afraid of me, surely?'

She shook her head. 'But I still feel – I feel we shouldn't – your mother – I'm so—'

He could bear it no longer and pulled her into his arms, kissing her like a man who'd been starving for love. Neither of them heard Annie come in.

'Will you marry me, Elizabeth?' he asked again. 'You must. I don't want anyone else.'

Annie gasped and would have left, but they heard and turned towards her, shock on both their faces, guilt too. She took a hasty step backwards. 'I'm sorry. I didn't mean to eavesdrop.'

'Oh, Annie, I'm so sorry. I told him we shouldn't – I—'

Elizabeth looked so terrified that William instinctively put his arm round her shoulders and turned to face his mother, as if she were an enemy about to attack them.

Annie could not think what to say. What next? she thought. Whatever next?

It was left to William to take charge, which he did in no

uncertain way. 'I love Elizabeth, Mother, and I want to marry her. But she felt that you might be upset, so she asked me to wait six months. I did. And I haven't changed my mind at all.'

Annie was indeed rather upset, but she did not show it. Love grew where it would and you couldn't change that. She would far rather William married someone younger, someone with a loving family behind them, and yes, a bit of money of her own, for he would clearly never make much, or even care about that. But it was his choice, not hers. She smiled at them both. 'I'm surprised, perhaps, but not upset. Elizabeth, my dear, did you really think I'd disown William and throw you out?'

The governess sagged in relief. 'I – I didn't think I was s-suitable – g-given the circumstances.'

'What circumstances?'

Elizabeth flushed scarlet. 'My past.'

It took Annie a moment to realise what the younger woman meant – the fact that her cousin had once raped her – and then she made a scornful noise in her throat. 'As if that matters!'

William hugged Elizabeth and then smiled at his mother. 'Well, since we've now got that sorted out, perhaps you'll leave me to propose to the woman I love, Mother?'

Annie smiled again and backed out, but the smile faded as soon as the door was closed behind her. The strongest emotion she was feeling at that moment was envy. She missed having a man put his arms round her, missed it dreadfully. And it was Tian's face that rose in front of her as she faced that thought, not Frederick's, something which didn't make her feel as guilty as it once would have.

Inside the schoolroom, William repeated gently. 'You will marry me, won't you, Elizabeth?'

And for the first time she allowed herself to give him the answer she longed to. 'Oh, William, of course I will.'

He pulled her towards him. 'And soon?'

Colour flooded her face, making it seem soft and pretty for once, not taut and angular. 'As soon as your mother can find someone to replace me.'

'We'll get her to write to the agency this afternoon.'

But she still had to ask, 'Oh, William, are you sure?'

'Very sure.'

It was left to John Gibson to sum up the family's feelings about these changes. 'Eh, for all the troubles around us, I don't know when I've felt so pleased. Amy love, welcome to the family. And, Elizabeth, I can't think of a better wife for our William.'

From across the room, Tian watched the two newly declared couples even more enviously than Annie had. What would he not have given to have her look at him openly like that? He was making progress with her, but so slowly that it was agony at times. He would have to do something about that.

Start the portrait! a voice said in his head. *Start the portrait. It's time.* And the voice sounded like – it couldn't possibly be, but it did *sound* like – Frederick.

From the sofa nearby, Joanie was looking at her brother and her nephew, rejoicing for them, with Bartholomew's arm around her shoulders and a lightness in her mind and body that she hadn't felt for months.

'You're a lucky family, you Gibsons,' he whispered in her ear.

She shivered. 'Don't tempt providence.' It seemed for a moment as if shadows flickered around them, then she blinked and the room was again filled with light and happiness. What a silly thing to think! She didn't know what had got into her.

29

Early Summer 1862

As the war continued in America, hunger seemed to grow into a tangible presence in Bilsden, not just hunger for food, but hunger for something to do, hunger for a purpose to life again. And yet, those of the spinners who had bothered to think the matter through usually maintained staunchly that the North was right to fight for the freedom of the poor black folk. Slavery was wrong, and hadn't Britain showed the way to less enlightened nations many years before by freeing all its slaves?

Reading groups from the Working Men's Institute studied the progress of the war in the newspapers which were passed on to them by richer folk, for now they could not even afford to share the cost of one of their own. There at the 'Stute discussions were hot against the South, who not only kept slaves but put other people's livelihoods in jeopardy by their stubborn resistance to modern ideas. Still, they told one another proudly, Lancashire folk were managing somehow and would continue to manage.

When Tian, prompted by Luke, offered to go and talk to people at the 'Stute about America, his offer was accepted with alacrity, and his one lecture rapidly became three. He was then asked to talk to other groups in the town, and accepted those invitations, too.

There were several sorts of relief schemes operating now in the area covered by the Bilsden and District Poor Law Union, not only the official one provided for by law and the one Hallam's provided for its own people and their families, but others run by special interest groups. Each church had its own ways of helping those who worshipped there, several of the richer people in town had pet schemes operating and smaller efforts like that of Eva Bagley covered other areas of need.

Annie and Matt had managed to keep their own operatives on more or less half-time until now by buying more cotton at exorbitant prices. Matt grumbled at the percentage of badly cleaned and packed cotton in the bales nowadays, something he would never have accepted from suppliers before the war. But now, if you complained, they just shrugged and said to send it back and they'd sell it elsewhere for more than you had paid. What was the world coming to?

Annie had not let her idea for a lake lie idle, however, and had started gathering information about how to do it within days of that walk up to Clough Knowle. She also talked more generally to individual members of the Town Council about starting up some work scheme to beautify the town, using the labour of those who had no work. The reactions had been guardedly positive – so long as the Council was not called upon to provide the money. All except Martin Leaseby and one of his cronies, of course. Leaseby would oppose anything she said, on principle.

Bilsden had been one of the first towns in Lancashire to set up a relief committee, in an ill-defined way at first, with conflicting ideas about what the responsibilities of that committee were. Now it was reorganised to deal with the increasing needs of the unemployed operatives and their families. Annie would have loved to be on it, but only men were invited to become members, which infuriated her since she was running the largest single scheme in town. 'And look what the Committee had been doing', she raged to Elizabeth one day. 'Some of them probably couldn't even tie their own shoelaces, let alone understand the daily needs of the poor'.

Elizabeth was mildly surprised at her anger. 'That's how it's always been. Men run things publicly, women work in the background.'

'And when you and William marry, will you sit in the kitchen while he goes out and helps the poor?'

'Well, no.'

'So why should I not be involved?'

Elizabeth could only shake her head and decline to be drawn.

Of course, the Town Council was very proud of its progressive attitude, of the fact that it had been one of the first to start doing something, but Wigan had also set up a committee in January, with Rochdale and Preston following suit in February, so Bilsden would have to look to its laurels from now on if it was still to play a leading role in relieving the distress. Manchester and Liverpool were not, for once, showing the way, since their inhabitants were not so dependent upon what Frederick had often jokingly referred to as 'the Great God, Cotton'.

However, in April, two meetings to consider the prevailing distress were held in Manchester Town Hall. William attended them both, coming home disgusted because no action was taken, except for vague discussions about setting up schemes to grant loans to unemployed operatives. Liverpool was not destined to act until even later in the year.

'They're fools,' said Annie, when he told her what had happened. 'How will the operatives pay back loans? Even in good times, they don't have a lot of money to spare, not till their children have grown old enough to earn, anyway.'

Later, they heard that money was to be made available for projects to relieve distress. 'We must see if we can get some,' Annie decided. 'I'd have done something about the lake before now if I could afford to do it on my own, and I'd have done it more efficiently, too.'

But when they made enquiries, they found out that they had to work through a Local Committee of Charity, and that the Central Executive Committee was much more inclined to deal with Town Councils than with individuals. Annie became even more grumpy then, snapping at everyone, including Tian.

In the meantime, as cotton supplies dried up, Matt organised other work, systematically cleaning out and whitewashing the interior of the mill, going through it room by room, using the out-of-work spinners as labour. Some men were still needed for maintenance work on the machinery, of course, though it was a part-time occupation. And after much discussion between Matt and the chief engineer, a Scot whose obsession with 'his' machinery was legendary in the town, some of the older pieces of equipment were replaced.

Annie grew even more tense as May passed, snapping at everyone indiscriminately. For the first time, she and Tian quarrelled, though they took their disagreements out on to the moors, where they could shout to their hearts' content. And they did shout at one another, until suddenly he dissolved into laughter.

'What's the matter with you?' she demanded, astonished. 'Why are you laughing?'

'I know you need to quarrel with someone, but sure, I can't keep it up any longer.' He pulled her to him. 'Oh, Annie, you bad-tempered witch, give me a kiss.' And he took it before she could protest.

'Do you feel better now?' he asked as they walked back.

Reluctantly she grinned. 'Yes. I do, actually.'

'Can I ask what's making you so out and out grumpy?'

She hesitated. 'If I tell you, will you keep it to yourself?'

'Of course.'

'I'm trying to buy the land for Spinners Lake.'

'On your own? Can you afford it?'

'I can if the vendors will be reasonable, but they've got unrealistic ideas about its value.'

'You never cease to amaze me.' But he felt somewhat annoyed that she hadn't seen fit to confide in him.

'Well, we have to get on with things. But afterwards, even if I do get the land for a reasonable price, I won't be able to afford to employ enough workers to dig it out in less than fifty years. Oh, Tian, it's all so frustrating! And have you seen people's faces? They look so – so dispirited.'

He put his arm round her. 'Could you not work out a less ambitious scheme?'

353

'No, I couldn't! We're going to build a lake. I'm determined on that.'

'Sure, you're a terrifying woman.'

While she was waiting to hear whether her latest offer for the land had been accepted, Annie summoned a council of war at Ridge House, a council which included Jeremy Lewis, who was delighted at the idea of a better water supply, and who was to provide the scientific information about the town's need for this to those sceptics who said things were all right as they were.

'It's time to work out how to build a lake,' Annie declared to her supporters. 'I'll find the money somehow. But how do we set about the actual work?' Business she understood, but engineering schemes were beyond her.

Matt shook his head. He still hoped she wouldn't be able to do it. It made him wake in a cold sweat sometimes to think of how much money she was pouring into the scheme, even before she had any other support.

Tian shook his head as well. He knew nothing of the making of lakes.

William cleared his throat and the others turned to him.

'Do you have any ideas?' Annie prompted.

'Well, I do know of an engineer, Mother. And even if he can't help us with this project, he may know of someone else who can.'

'Who is he?'

'The brother of a fellow who studied with me at Mr Hinchclif fe's. My friend's name is Peter Thorby and he comes from the Colne Valley. I'll write to him at once.'

Three days later, he had his reply by the second post, opening it just before lunch and sharing the news with his family and his fiancée as they ate together. 'This is from my friend Peter. His brother can't help us himself, as he has no experience of making lakes, but he's given me the name of another man who may be able to do something. Someone called Hervey Bamforth. I'll write to him this afternoon. He lives in the Colne Valley, too.'

'Isn't it exciting?' Edgar beamed round at them. 'Fancy making a lake. I can't wait to see it begin.'

'Well, I don't think it's exciting at all,' Tamsin grumbled. At twelve, she had grown moody, her temper fluctuating so much lately that Annie sometimes lost patience with her, though Kathy said it was just her age and would pass.

'Then you don't need to listen when we talk about it!' Annie snapped.

Tamsin gave one of her exaggerated sighs.

Tian intervened between mother and daughter, as he was doing increasingly. 'When you see the lake start, *alannah*, you'll find it interesting. We can go out there one day soon and sketch how we think it'll look, then we'll see who's closest when it's finished.'

But Tamsin was not to be won over. 'I can't draw like you two can, so it's silly to include me.' She hunched a shoulder and scowled down at her plate.

After lunch, Tian waited behind to speak to Annie. 'I think it's time for me to start on your portrait now,' he said without preamble.

'Oh?' She had enough on her plate without sitting around being painted.

He raised one eyebrow. 'Frederick's last wish,' he reminded her.

'Yes. But I wonder sometimes whether—' Her voice faded away and she stared down at her skirt, stroking the material and smoothing it carefully. 'You're right,' she said at last. 'And I've sworn to do it, so I must make the time. When do you want me to sit for you?'

'This afternoon?'

Alarm flared in her eyes, then she shook her head. 'No. I'm far too busy. Next week, perhaps.'

His voice was firm. 'Tomorrow, then.'

'Tian, I – oh, all right, then. Tomorrow morning.'

'I want to do the preliminary sketches out on the moors, not here.'

'You can't mean that!'

'But I do. I want to paint you with your hair blowing free and that look of determination on your face, against a background of rolling hills. And, Annie, I also want to know why you've been avoiding me lately?'

Another silence stretched between them and she was tempted to deny it, but her innate honesty won. He was right. She had been avoiding him. That was because she was shocked at how much she missed him when he was away – for he had taken two short trips to nearby towns to paint the distress the lack of cotton was causing, staying away for several days. But there was no way she could get out of this. 'Well, all right. Tomorrow, then. If it's fine.'

'It'll be fine. I've already checked that with Nat. Straight after breakfast.'

'Perhaps the afternoon would be better,' she said perversely.

'In the morning, Annie.' He did not intend to give her a chance to back out.

When they met after breakfast the next day, Tian was carrying not only his sketching gear, but a picnic basket.

Annie hesitated at the door. 'I really don't think I have time to stay out all day.'

He pushed her gently outside. 'Then you must neglect your other duties for once and steal the time.'

She stared at him, opened her mouth to speak, then shut it again.

As they walked across the moors, it soon became obvious where he was heading. When they stopped for a breather she confirmed it. 'Clough Knowle again?'

'Yes. You at the summit, with the moors spread out around you, and below, the valley that will become our lake. In fact, I intend to paint a lake there.' He saw that she was frowning, not convinced that this was the right thing to do. 'I can't do an indoor portrait, Annie, not if I'm to capture your spirit.'

'Frederick would have—'

Tian's voice was as harsh as a crow shrieking from a treetop. 'For heaven's sake, don't mention his name today, Annie, don't set him between us any more! He wouldn't want it and it's killing me!'

She swallowed hard and continued walking. Had she been doing that? Setting Frederick between them? Yes, she had. A pang shot through her. It was so hard to let go. She looked sideways. And so hard to open a new door. She felt angry with herself. It was not like her to dither and prevaricate. The word hovering in the back of her mind was 'cowardly'. She squared her shoulders without realising it. She did not want to consider herself a coward.

When they got to the summit, Tian set up his painting gear on the little plateau where they had once picnicked with Rebecca and Simon, where Annie had once nearly lost her life. But somehow, the place had lost its dark connotations, thanks to Tian, and had become once again a place she loved, a place she had often visited before the tragedy.

'I want you to stand here, near this outcrop of rock, facing into the wind.' He took her and positioned her.

His closeness made her feel breathless, but he didn't take advantage of it, as he had at other times. She was sorry, yes, sorry about that, she admitted to herself. She would have liked him to hold her, just hold her close, as Luke held Amy, or Bartholomew held Joanie. As Frederick used to hold her. She pushed the thought of Frederick away. In silence, she watched Tian sit down with his sketching block and take out a piece of charcoal.

'Look out across the valley, Annie. Look out and challenge the world.'

She obeyed him, but felt vulnerable under his gaze. Then gradually time slowed down and she did begin to feel as if she were facing up to the world and whatever it could toss at her. He was right about that. It was how she had survived. The wind whispered soothingly in her ears, the sun shone down from a nearly cloudless sky and the moors, ah, they embraced her, cushioned her spirit, set her free from her obligations and duties – they made her only Annie, not anyone's mother or sister or daughter. And most certainly not a millowner with lives hanging on her every decision.

She was quite surprised to hear Tian announce, 'We'll take a break now. I don't want you getting stiff.' He patted the rock beside him. 'Come and sit down here for a while, woman. If you ask me nicely, I'll pour you a drink of lemonade.'

Still feeling light, free from responsibility, suspended in a magical place where anything was possible, she took the tin mug he held out to her and drank it thirstily. 'It's delicious.' Then she made the mistake of looking at him.

He drained his own mug, his eyes holding hers steadily. Without speaking, he reached out, took her mug and set it down beside the rock with his own. 'It's time to talk again, Annie.'

'Do we have to?' She didn't want to spoil the mood of this lovely day.

He nodded. 'Oh, yes. We most definitely have to.' But he made no attempt to take her in his arms, just looked at her seriously. 'I'm better now. Oh, maybe I've still a few more memories to get back, but I've recovered enough to feel that I know myself again. And so I must start this conversation by thanking you for looking after me, for bringing me back to health.'

He took her hand and raised it to his lips for a very gentle kiss, then kept it in his.

She could only let him hold it. Nervousness was shivering in her belly. She was not sure she could – not sure of anything.

'The one thing I didn't forget in all that time was how much I loved you, Annie. I think you are the only woman in the world that I can love like that. It took me so long to find you. It's consuming me, my love is, burning within me like a great fire. If you don't love me back, if we don't do something about our love, I fear it will devour me entirely and leave only an empty husk. I can't wait for ever. Not even for you.'

She swallowed, eyes falling for a moment, veiled in the long dark lashes that lay quivering against the delicate ivory of her complexion, then she looked up again, staring at him. But she didn't say anything, for he deserved this opportunity to speak freely. But did she deserve such love? Could she live with it? Was there enough fire still left within her to meet his?

His voice was as soft as silk in her ears. 'I've loved you almost from the first moment I saw you in that art gallery in London, you know. I didn't believe in love at first sight before that, but you changed my mind. I've never been able to decide whether it was the sunlight on your wonderful hair, or the bright intelligence in your eyes, that first caught my interest.'

'You stared at me so,' she said in a low voice. 'I didn't know where to look.'

'I couldn't take my eyes off you,' he agreed.

'And then you saved my life.'

'I certainly saved you from injury.' He sat still, gazing into her eyes, and she let out a shuddering sigh without realising it.

'You saved my life up here, too,' she went on, still caught in the strangeness of the day, snared by his will and by the power of his love.

'Only partly. It was the thought of Frederick which saved you.'

Her eyes were suddenly veiled, as if the name of her dead husband had come between them.

'Look at me, Annie!' he commanded. 'Look at me and realise that I'm alive and Frederick is dead.'

She was not aware that she had made a soft sound of pain, but she did look up at him again and caught her breath at the sight of him. So handsome. So very much alive.

He reached into his pocket and pulled out a tattered, water-stained piece of paper with a torn corner. 'This is the letter Frederick sent me. I had it with me when I was injured. I want you to read it now.'

She made no attempt to take it from him. 'I don't want to.'

'You must. You must see what he said, what he wanted for you.' And, he thought, you must face the fact that he's gone.

Reluctantly she took it from him. What she read made her grasp in shock and stare at him.

'Read it aloud,' he ordered, his voice harsh with the effort it was taking to restrain himself. 'Read that paragraph about us aloud.'

Her voice faltering, she did as he asked:

And, Mr Gilchrist, if the attraction between the two of you flares again, then know you will have my blessing upon it. I don't want my lovely girl to spend the rest of her life alone.

She gulped, let the paper drop and, as he bent to pick it up before the wind could snatch it from him, she put her face into her hands to hide the tears that would not be held back.

Tian stuffed the letter into his pocket and pulled her into his arms, letting her cry against him.

When the tears had stopped, he fumbled in his pocket again and shook out a handkerchief. 'It's not exactly clean, but I don't think the paint smudges will come off on your face.' He began to wipe it for her, but before he had finished, he looked into her eyes, gave an inarticulate exclamation and began kissing her instead. 'Ah, my love, my Annie, can you not feel something for me? Because if you can't, I'll have to leave. I can't bear it any longer. I've tried so hard to be patient, but I've a need for you that's as deep as the ocean, and as little likely to be satisfied as the ocean is to dry up.'

'I don't – don't want you to leave,' she whispered. The thought of not seeing him again made her feel dreadful, bereft. 'I – I value your – your friendship.'

'Hah!' He shoved her away from him abruptly, making her cry out in shock. 'Is that all it is? Friendship? Because if so, I'll be gone tomorrow. No, tonight!'

Silence crept between them and sat there for a moment, then Annie broke through it. 'No! It's not all I feel.' She looked at him pleadingly, but he sat there and gave her no help. 'I –

you know there has always been an – an attraction between us. Even when F—even before.'

He shook his head. 'That's not enough, either. I want your love, Annie, love or nothing. Attraction isn't enough. And I scorn mere friendship from the woman I love.'

She blinked at him. 'I don't – don't know what to say. I'm not used to – to—' Her voice faltered to a stop. 'Tian, can't you be patient for a little while longer?'

He shook his head. 'No. Not a day, not an hour longer, not if you won't give me anything of yourself. Sure, you're as tightly guarded as a citadel of the old times. You have walls around you, Annie, high walls. And I can't see over them. You need to open your gates. Only you can do that. Open up and let me in, my love. You need me and my love as much as I need you.'

She was terrified of the very thought. 'There's safety in walls,' she whispered, her throat dry with fear. 'If you give your love to someone, you risk so much. Too much, perhaps. I'm not sure that I can face that risk again.'

He looked at her steadily. 'Two face the risk when there's love between them. It's the price you pay.'

She tried to explain. 'When Frederick died, I had to be strong. And you're right. I did build up barriers around myself. Oh, Tian, it's not easy to tear them down again!'

'You can make a start,' he pointed out. 'Brick by brick. I don't expect the barriers to fall all at once.'

'Can I?' she asked bleakly, the landscape around her a blur through tear-filled eyes. 'All my life, I've kept making starts. Again and again. And things have kept happening to destroy my hopes. I don't know whether I have the courage to do it all again. I just don't know—'

'Then I'll leave you to think about it. I'll go back to Ireland and if you ever manage to break out of your prison, you can come and tell me.'

'No!' The word was out before she could stop it and she clutched at his sleeve. 'I don't want you to go, Tian. You've become a friend, a very close friend.'

'You can make other friends. And you have your family. They're a very wonderful family. If friendship is all you have to offer me, then tell me so and I'll leave. You can't keep me hanging on a string like this. It's cruel, Annie.'

Without realising what she was doing, she stood up and began pacing to and fro. Then she stopped and answered him elliptically. 'I thought I knew what I wanted. Now I'm not sure.'

But he was as hard as the rock beneath them. He had to be. It was his whole future he was fighting for. 'Then I'll leave you to think it through.' He stood up and began packing away the mugs. 'We'll go back to the house now. I'll catch the evening train to Liverpool, take a boat to Ireland from there.'

'No!' The plea was torn from her again. 'Tian, no! Don't go!' She took a step towards him, but he gave her no help. He waited, implacable, determined. So she took another step, and another, till she was standing close to him. Then his self-control broke and he pulled her into his arms and began to kiss her. This time, he did not hold back. He kissed every inch of her face, starting gently and ending with her lips. The kiss deepened and she began to respond, moaning in her throat and pressing against him, kissing him back.

Without either of them realising how it came about, they were somehow lying on the ground, and he was touching her, caressing her, feeling the softness of her breasts, and even through the clothing that covered them, able to feel her response to his touch. In the end, he put her violently away from him, drawing a cry of distress from her.

'If we don't stop now, I'll not be able to control myself, Annie. Do you want that? Are you ready for that?'

Her lips were swollen and her eyes languorous with passion. It was a moment before she could respond, then she flushed and swallowed hard. 'Not – not yet. Not like this, anyway.'

'I love you, Annie. Love you so deeply that there's nothing else matters to me in the world.' He paused and added, 'So you tell me where we go from here. For if it was up to me, we'd be down at the church tomorrow begging the parson to marry us.'

She gasped and one hand flew up to her throat. 'It's very quick.'

He sighed. 'I might have known you'd say that. Very well. I'll wait a little longer to get married. But only a little. And I'm not doing anything if you don't make a formal commitment to me, show me that you're not ashamed to love me. Show your family, too.' He let the silence echo around them for a moment, then asked quietly, 'Shall I be seeing your father? Shall we be telling your family? And then will you at least name a bloody day, woman?'

'Eventually.'

His eyebrows rose and he took a step backwards. 'Eventually? What sort of word is that?'

Anger rose in her. 'It's the best I can do. Yes, we'll tell my family. And yes, we'll get married. Eventually. You have to give me a little more time, Tian. I – I have to get used to it.'

His voice was sad. 'Is it so hard to marry me?'

She shook her head. 'No. Oh, Tian, no. It's not that. It's – what people will say, how they'll stare at me, at us, that I have to get used to. The public side of things is what worries me.'

He understood and relief surged through him. 'Because for the past few years you've been the strong one, who kept herself aloof. I'm not sure you didn't keep something of yourself aloof even from Frederick.' And although his voice was teasing, his words were deadly serious. 'Well, woman of stone, it's about time you softened, let the world see that you're only forty and still young enough to marry again.'

'Marry again!' She sighed at the prospect.

'You were thinking of living in sin with me, maybe?' he teased.

She glared at him. 'Of course not!' Though she knew there were rumours in the town about why the artist had stayed on at Ridge House, rumours she had scorned to notice.

'Then it'll have to be marriage,' he teased. 'You'll have to make an honest man of me.'

But she could not treat it lightheartedly. 'What will the family say?' she worried.

'There's only one way to find out. Come on, let's do the dreadful deed now, today.' She hadn't said she loved him, not as he loved her, but he was afraid to ask more of her today. He had breached the gates, but the rest of the citadel still stood strongly around her. One step at a time, he told himself. Pull the walls down one brick at a time. Aloud he said, 'So I'll go and see your father today. And we'll tell your children tonight.'

She stared at him and it seemed a long, long time to him before she sighed and said, 'Yes.'

He walked back with one arm around her waist and his other aching from the weight of the uneaten picnic and the sketching materials. But it was the first time she had allowed him so close and he wasn't going to pause, even to change arms, in case that made her change her mind.

He thought he understood how she felt, how hard it was for her. He hoped he could continue to be patient with her. And he was, he admitted to himself, afraid to push any harder. He had crept up on her over the past few months, and today, he had taken her by surprise and forced her to make a decision. Now he had to make her so dependent upon him and his love that she would never want to leave him. And he would. He would do just that.

30

May to July 1862

It was a busy time for the Gibsons, and a happy one, too. At the end of May, Rebecca gave birth to a son, a healthy baby with his father's long limbs.

John Gibson trudged up to the Hall after work the next day and was admitted to her ladyship's bedroom, to the dismay of the nurse Simon had hired, who didn't even believe in fathers spending much time with their new-born offspring, let alone grandfathers. John held the infant in his arms and beamed at his daughter and her husband. 'Eh, he's a bonny baby, isn't he? And so like you, lad.'

'Who else should he be like, pray?' Simon's arm tightened around his wife.

'He could have looked like us Gibsons,' said John, taking the remark literally. 'But the Gibson men aren't allus blessed with much by way of looks.'

'Our Mark's good-looking,' Rebecca protested.

'Eh, if I didn't forget!' John fumbled in his pocket. 'We got another letter. He sounds pleased about our Faith, says he's got her photo standing on his mantelpiece.'

As he walked back down the hill to Netherhouse Cottage, he beamed around him. The Lord had been good to him and his childer, He had that.

Once the worry of childbirth, always a dangerous time for a woman, was over, the next few weeks were very busy, with three weddings to be arranged. Tom had expressed loud and instant approval of Annie's engagement to Tian, but the rest of them were still not quite used to the idea of their Annie remarrying: nor, come to that, was she, which sometimes led to awkwardnesses. Only a man as charming as Tian Gilchrist could have smoothed things over quite so well at family gatherings – and smoothed his fiancée's ruffled feathers, too, when people spoke less than tactfully about her approaching marriage.

'Are you sure about this?' John Gibson took her aside to ask after Tian had spoken to him. 'You don't look like a woman longing to be wed, love. In fact, I think you spoke to him a bit sharply just now.'

'I feel embarrassed by it all, if you must know,' Annie said, speaking equally sharply to her father. 'I wish Tian and I could just go somewhere and get married in private, without all this fuss, I really do.'

'Eh, our Annie's a funny one, sometimes,' he confided to Kathy later as he sat in the kitchen and watched her prepare a meal. 'Does she really want to wed him, do you think?'

Kathy fingered her rolling pin. 'I don't know. Sometimes she looks at him as if she's never seen him before, sometimes she looks irritated when he asks her to do something she doesn't want to, and other times she looks at him as loving as you please. I don't understand her, John. I don't think I ever have, really. Though I admire her, admire what she's made of her life. And I'm grateful to her, too.'

'I used to think Frederick was the only one who understood her.'

'That's something else that worries me.'

'What do you mean, lass?'

'I think it'll be hard for Tian to follow a man like Frederick. And – and I think they should set up a home of their own, not live in Ridge House. I told her so, too, but she just said she was too busy to change houses now and that Tian didn't care where he lived. I wish she wasn't allus so busy. That mill seems to eat her life up. Can't you speak to her about it?'

He stood up and went to put his arms round her from behind, cuddling her to him, as he often did. 'She's never listened to me before, so I'm not going to try to interfere. She snapped my head off just now for asking if she was really sure she wanted to wed him.'

William and Elizabeth were to marry in August, but it would be a much bigger affair than Luke's wedding, in spite of William's pleas to his mother to keep it simple.

'We have too many social obligations,' she had insisted. 'And since Elizabeth has been our governess until now, it will look better if we do the thing in style. We don't want to give the appearance of being ashamed of her, do we?'

That silenced him, but he still looked unhappy.

Annie sighed, guessing what he was thinking. 'I won't be extravagant, William, I promise you. Not in times like these.'

'You're sure it's the right thing to do, Mother?'

'Very sure.'

'For Elizabeth's sake, then.'

'And have you thought about living here?'

'Yes. We'd love to for a while, until the war is over and I get my own church.' He put his arm round her for a quick hug. 'Cheer up! For a woman who's about to get married herself, you look like you're going to a funeral sometimes.'

It always amazed her that she could have produced this large son. She gave him a mock tap on the hand. 'Don't be so cheeky.'

He didn't smile, just looked down at her, very solemnly. 'I thought I ought to make it clear that I approve. I really like Tian. I think he's good for you – and for the children. He's the only one who can slow you down. Even Father couldn't do that, could he?'

That made her think.

On a fine morning in July, Luke and Amy were the first of the three engaged couples to get married, at a simple service in the Todmorden Road Methodist Chapel. Only the immediate families attended, but that now included Maidie Gorton, who had helped so much by publicly welcoming Luke as her daughter-in-law's intended.

Maidie was overwhelmed by the number of Gibsons present, not to mention their exuberance and confidence, but held herself proudly erect in a new violet and cream outfit made for her by Joanie, who had recently decided to set up as a dressmaker to more modest clients than she had served at Annie's salon.

'What about when we have children?' Bartholomew had teased as he watched her sew.

She had just smiled. She smiled a lot nowadays. 'When we have children, I'll get some daily help and continue to work from home. I'm not ambitious like Annie, but I do like sewing, so long as I can do things my own way. Annie doesn't like bright colours, but I do, and so do a lot of women.'

'I like them, too, when you wear them,' he breathed into her hair, and the sewing fell to the floor.

Annie had insisted on providing a reception for Luke and Amy at Ridge House. Amy had begged Luke to find a tactful way to refuse and just to offer everyone cakes and a simple drink of ale or tea at the farm, as was the custom in Hey End, but he had shaken his head. 'No, love. We'll do that later, for the neighbours, but I think we should accept Annie's offer. It'll look better, for one thing, and for another, she likes to do things for people.'

'I feel out of place there,' she muttered.

'Look, Amy, she's my sister, so you'll have to get used to going to Ridge House, because I'm not going to stop seeing her.'

'It's so big, and the servants frighten me,' she confessed, twisting the edge of her pinafore and avoiding his eyes. She had barely spoken a word on her one and only visit there.

He put his arm round her and gave her a hug, then put a finger under her chin and forced her to look up at him. 'The servants frightened me, too, Amy, the first time I went there. But I found out that they're just people like anyone else, and most of them have worked there for so long that they're almost part of the family now.' He chuckled. 'Winnie, who usually opens the door, will nag you and remind you to wipe your feet, but if she thinks you look cold or tired, she'll fuss over you like a grandmother.'

Amy remained patently unconvinced.

'The third reason I want to accept,' Luke went on gently, 'is to show the world how proud I am that you're marrying me.'

She blushed a rosy pink. 'Oh, Luke.'

'So we'll say thank you very much to Annie and we'll accept her kind offer, eh?'

'I suppose so.'

'And we'll make sure that Maidie comes, too.' For Ted's mother was as frightened of the big house and Luke's rich relatives as Amy.

The children, Tess and Adam, rode up to Ridge House after the wedding in a hired carriage, with their grandmother and Joanie and Bart. They clutched one another's hands and stared out of the window. It seemed strange to ride like this and they exchanged delighted glances and waved when they saw someone they knew. But the house was even bigger than the chapel they had just left, and they clung to their grandmother's hands in terror as they went inside.

Luke and Amy, who had been sent off from the chapel alone in the first carriage, were now standing in the hall to greet the guests. Annie stood nearby, smiling so warmly at Amy and Luke that there could be no doubt she was pleased with the marriage. Amy began to lose her fear of her new sister-in-law from that moment onwards. Tian stood beside Annie, very much the loving fiancé, as always in public, though they had had sharp words only that morning about how hard she was working.

After the reception, Luke took Amy away for the first holiday she had ever had in her whole life, though they were going only as far as Blackpool and Lizzie's.

'Why would you not come to the wedding?' he asked Lizzie soon after he arrived. 'Dad was upset. You haven't been back to Bilsden for years.'

She shrugged. 'I have my guests to look after. You're not the only ones here at the moment, you know. In fact, you were lucky I could fit you in at such short notice. If I hadn't had a cancellation, I wouldn't have been able to, family or not. And anyway, I like it here and I don't like Bilsden.' She saw he was unconvinced and added, in her usual scornful take-it-or-leave-it tone, 'I never fitted in with the rest of the family, you know, though we've made peace between us now. The only reason I've ever gone back there was for Dad's sake.'

Beside her William's half-brother on his father's side was scowling at the newcomers. Jim Coxton didn't like it when any of the Gibsons came to stay. They always seemed to upset the woman he called his 'Auntie Lizzie'. The two of them got on all right here in Blackpool, made a decent living. Just him and her. They didn't need anyone else.

Once, when he was a lad, he'd thought he needed his half-brother, and William, the older of the two, had seemed to need him, too, but the family had kept the two of them apar t until William had grown up. And by then, his half-brother had become too different, too posh for Jim's taste. Now he had Lizzie, and they were as close as a real aunt and nephew, which was how they both liked it.

'I'll take you up to your room,' he growled, breaking up the conversation and seizing Luke and Amy's suitcases.

Lizzie looked at the hall clock. 'Heavens, is that the time? I'd better get on with the teas. Six o'clock sharp, you two. No honeymooning till afterwards.'

Amy's face was scarlet as she followed Jim upstairs.

It was an eventful summer in other ways. Two weeks after Luke's wedding, Lemuel Burns dropped dead in the middle of the weekly tirade he called a sermon: a tirade which focused mainly on hell fire, damnation and sin, and which usually had the congregation of Redemption House swaying and moaning by the end. On this particular day, he broke off in the middle of a phrase, his face turning dark red. He gasped for air and found none, then slowly he keeled over, knocking the lectern and Bible aside with a greater and lesser thud than the dull thump of his body striking the ground. He lay twitching for a moment, then froze into an eternal stillness.

The congregation gasped, and for a moment no one moved. When Lemuel's two sons ran forward to kneel by him, his wife did not move for a moment, just bent her head to hide the relief she was sure would show on her face. Thank you, Lord! she prayed. Thank you for delivering me from bondage. Then she raised her head again and walked forward to join her sons, face expressionless.

'Carry him home,' she ordered Bill and Don, making no attempt to touch her husband. 'And then send for the undertaker.'

At the house, Prudence Burns took charge as she had never been able to do in her husband's lifetime. 'Put him in the spare bedroom.'

'Surely his own bed?' Bill murmured.

'And where would I sleep then?' she demanded. 'No. We have a spare bedroom, we shall use that. Straighten him out decently and cover him with the bedspread. Come downstairs when you've done all that. We have things to discuss while we wait for the undertakers.'

'Aren't you going to see to his body yourself?' Don asked, bewildered.

'No. The undertaker's men will do all that. I've never been able to stomach dealing with dead bodies. It fair makes me shudder.' She swung into the parlour before they could argue.

While they were upstairs, she fumbled on the mantelpiece for the key, then unlocked the bottom drawer in the bureau that Lemuel had used for his business papers. She paused for a second to listen for anyone coming down, then took a folded piece of paper from the bottom drawer.

Then, still with an ear for sounds from upstairs, she fumbled in her mending basket for another piece of paper, one sealed in exactly the same way with red wax. This had lain hidden beneath an old, frayed napkin for some time. She had prepared it when her Bartie left home. Now, she pushed it beneath some other papers and relocked the drawer, then replaced the key on the mantelpiece.

As there was still no sign of her sons coming down, she hurried into the kitchen and flung the piece of paper she'd taken out of the drawer into the hottest par t of the stove to burn, poking the curling black remnants to break them up. Then she swung the big kettle over the flames as an excuse for being there.

When her sons came downstairs again, she was sitting with her hands folded, staring into the fire. 'Don't you think we'd better get his will out? It's in the bottom drawer.'

'He kept it here? Didn't he let a lawyer draw it up and keep it safe in his office?' Don demanded.

'No. He didn't trust lawyers.' Which was true as they well knew. She hardly breathed as Don opened the drawer and fingered through the pieces of paper there. 'I think this must be it,' he said, in his slow way.

She could have screamed at him to hurry up, but somehow she kept quiet. She was taking a great risk and had to tread carefully, for she had written this will herself. When she'd written down Lemuel's real will, at his dictation, she had been so angry at the unfairness of its provisions that she'd decided to do something about it, if she could. Watching him get redder and more apoplectic by the year, just as her father had done, she had hoped desperately that he was of the same physical make.

Now, her prayers had been answered. Like her father, he'd died suddenly, while still a man in his middle years. Like her father, he'd left a widow glad to see him go.

'He never said aught to me of a will,' Don grumbled, holding the piece of folded paper with its red wax seal and staring at it as if it were written in Chinese.

'Why would he? He thought he'd live to make old bones. But he had me write it out for him – and then he changed it a while back. Open it up and you'll find out what he wanted done.'

Don fingered the paper once more, then shook his head and passed it on to his brother Bill. 'You read it.' No need to explain why. Don was no good with long words and they all knew it.

Bill took the will as if it were red hot, then shook his head in turn and handed it to his mother. 'Best you read it to us. He was your husband, after all. And you'll understand it better than we could. I could understand his writing at the shop, but not this fancy writing of yours.'

Having a much clearer hand, she had written all formal letters for Lemuel for years and all he had done had been to sign them. She breathed slowly and deeply to dissipate her relief. 'I don't like to,' she protested half-heartedly.

Bill's voice was impatient. He spoke to her just as his father had, scornfully, as if she were nothing. 'Go on, Mother. Let's get it over with.'

So she broke the seal with her pencil-sharpening knife, opened out the paper and smoothed it, pretending to run her eyes down it. Her hands were shaking, but she didn't think they would see any significance in that. 'It's been a while since he had me write this,' she said apologetically. 'I'd forgotten how he put things.'

They were jigging about with impatience now and spoke almost in unison. 'Go on, Mother!'

She looked down at the paper again, keeping them waiting deliberately, enjoying even this tiny moment of power, then, just as Don opened his mouth to growl at her again, she began to read it out, very slowly: '"I leave everything of which I stand possessed to my wife, though it is my earnest hope that she will pass it on intact when she dies to any of my sons who are still working in the business when I die."'

'He can't have said that!' Don roared, snatching the paper from her, tracing each word with a thick fingertip and mouthing them before he pronounced each syllable aloud. He also examined the signature, looking up when he had finished, bewilderment in his face. 'He said he would leave everything to me and Bill, half-share each. He said it often. Promised, he did.'

Bill took the paper in turn. 'It's his signature, all right. I'd recognise it anywhere.'

She had wondered what Lemuel had told them about his intentions. Fury burned through her at the thought of how he had planned for them to have it all and for her to have nothing, to be dependent upon them for the rest of her life. 'If that isn't just like him!' she exclaimed. 'He always had a tricky way of getting to his goal.'

'But he said—'

'He often did say one thing and do another,' she reminded him. 'You know that.'

'Nor he didn't believe in women managing money,' Bill added.

'Well, he'd know that I'd ask your advice, now wouldn't he?' she asked in a reasonable tone. 'It won't make much difference, really.' Another lie. It'd make a great difference to her, but she couldn't tell them that yet, not until she'd carried out the rest of her plans.

Bill passed it back to her. 'Read the rest out. We might as well know it all.'

She read it, then looked up at them. 'What do you think we should do with the will?'

'Take it to a lawyer and see if we can't change it,' Bill snarled, snatching it again. 'I've heard somewhere that you can overset wills.'

'But you have to prove that the one who made it was not in his right mind,' she protested.

'We'll find some way to prove that, don't worry.' He turned and beckoned to his brother.

'Where are you going?' she asked as they opened the door, terrified that they'd do something to spoil her careful plans.

'Down to the shop, to see if there's not another will hidden there. I reckon he made this one when he was upset about something and then forgot about it. He must have made another.'

She sagged back in relief. They'd find nothing. She'd had to clean the shop out thoroughly every Saturday for as long as she could remember. She'd have known if there had been any other will. She'd always kept a careful eye open and she knew where Lemuel hid his most important papers. No, her husband had relied on her in this one matter of formal documents and it would be his undoing – and her vindication. Like his sons, he detested writing, preferring to leave that to her and keeping for himself the accounts. He loved the rows of figures, loved paying money into his bank and hated to pay out any of the money which had come in.

But as she stood by the parlour window and watched them walk off down the street, fear still shivered through her. What if they destroyed the will? For a moment, she froze at the mere thought, then determination surged up within her. She'd prepared for that, hadn't she? She would not be denied! No, she would not! She had thought this through very thoroughly over the years and made other preparations, too, just in case. Now, she had only to stick to her plan and keep calm. There must be no mistakes made by careless actions.

An hour later the undertaker arrived, prepared to deal with a weeping woman. He found a calm one instead.

'Before you start, we need to discuss a few things,' she said. 'Please come into the parlour.'

'Mr Burns has already been to see us,' he said gently. 'I'm sure he wanted to spare you the anguish at such a time.'

She was surprised. 'When did he come to see you?'

'Oh, he came in quite often, every month or two at least. He always wanted to see the latest caskets, discuss the arrangements. I have it all written down, everything he had selected.'

Trust Lemuel! He wanted to control things, even from the grave. 'Well, that's a pity, because I have my own ideas about funerals, and I'm the one with the money to pay for it.' She heard how sharp her voice was and tried to speak more calmly. 'I want the cheapest casket you've got and the cheapest funeral, Mr Purbreck. Not a pauper's funeral, but a cheap one.'

He goggled at her. 'For a gentleman of Mr Burns's stature? Surely, he has earned something a little more – well, impressive?'

She smiled then, a clear joyous smile. 'It doesn't matter what he's earned, or what his standing was. He's dead now and has left everything to me. I don't want to spend my money on vain show. Let my husband be remembered for his deeds.'

'But—'

'If you aren't interested in handling things, I'm sure Dolan's will be.'

The rivalry between the two funeral companies was bitter. 'There's no need for that,' Mr Purbreck said. 'We'll do as you ask, of course we will.' Shock did strange things to people. Perhaps she was worrying about how she would manage. But with two grown-up sons and several businesses in the family, she shouldn't have anything to worry about, surely?

'I wonder,' she said as they were leaving, 'if you could send your boy to deliver this letter to my other son? As soon as possible. The family has not always been united, but he would want to know about his father.' When Purbreck scowled, she dropped the letter and a florin into his hand with a murmured, 'For your trouble,' and his reluctance vanished.

'Of course, madam.' The coin disappeared and he made his stately way to the front of the closed funeral van. 'Drive back!' he ordered his colleague.

'You never can tell how grief will take them, can you?' the other man whispered as he shook the reins and drove off at the usual sedate pace.

'That you can't. Here, we have to drive past this address. Just stop for a minute and I'll see if anyone's home. Perhaps the other son will be able to talk a bit of sense into her. A cheap funeral for a man like that! Did you ever hear the like?'

Prudence closed the front door behind them, leaned against it and looked up. 'Forgive me, Lord,' she said aloud, 'but I have been sorely tried.' She would, she decided, as she went upstairs to look for a black dress, tell the boys she'd ordered the funeral and leave them to find out the details on the day. By that time, she hoped to be out of their reach.

When her sons came home, they found her quietly preparing the evening meal in the kitchen, her eyes lowered as usual, so they talked in front of her with the same abandon their father always had, as if she were too stupid to understand anything, as if it did not even matter whether she could understand. But she did hear. And understand. She always had.

The following day, both her sons disappeared again straight after breakfast without a word of explanation. She watched them go and nodded. She had hoped for that.

For once, Prudence Burns didn't get on with her housework. Instead, she put on her best bonnet and mantle, and made her way along High Street to Pennybody and Pennybody, where she asked to see Mr Hamish Pennybody as a matter of urgency. 'I think my son may have made an appointment for me.'

'Yes, your son came in yesterday,' the clerk said, his voice gentle, as always with the bereaved. 'In fact, he's waiting for you now with Mr Pennybody.'

Inside the lawyer's office, she found her beloved Bartie, who stood up and came to hold her tightly in his arms. Neither of them could speak, so he just hugged her again and she patted his cheek, finding it as wet as her own.

Bartholomew had already explained to Mr Pennybody how matters stood in the family, so Hamish watched the reunion benevolently.

As they moved apart, Prudence made a special request of Bartie, who was confident enough now of his new family's ways to assure her that it was perfectly possible, that he was sure the Gibsons would be happy to oblige. 'Good,' she said, as softly as ever, then she turned to the lawyer and explained about the will, how her other sons had taken it away. She thought it prudent to weep softly into a handkerchief and worry that they might destroy it because it didn't say what they wanted.

'I have to do as my husband wanted,' she repeated again and again. 'It was all written down.'

'It's also what the law now requires,' he assured her. 'And if they destroy the will, they'll be breaking the law. We must get hold of it.'

'There are two other copies. Would they do?'

'*Two* other copies?' Hamish could not hide his surprise.

'My husband was a—' she hesitated as if reluctant to say the word, '—a rather suspicious man. He trusted no one.'

'Where are the other copies?'

'One is hidden in the bedroom, behind one of the pictures. I don't know where the other is. He wouldn't tell me.'

'You can rely on us,' he assured her. 'Now, this is what I think we should do—'

When Don and Bill came home at noon, scowling, they found no signs of dinner cooking and their mother, dressed in her best, sitting in the parlour with a police constable and the senior clerk from Pennybody and Pennybody to keep her company.

'What's wrong?' Bill gasped.

'Do you still have your father's will, sir?' the clerk asked. Bill stared at him, eyes narrowed. He and Don had made their plans. 'What will? Father didn't leave a will.'

'Your mother says there was a will found yesterday.'

Bill shot her a quick glance and took a step towards her, fists clenched. 'The grief has turned her brain. You go up to bed and have a lie down, Mother. We'll deal with this.'

Prudence remained where she was. 'There's nothing wrong with my brain. And we did find a will. Yesterday. In the bureau.'

Don sighed and made a gentle clicking noise with his tongue. 'Poor Mother!' he said to the two visitors. 'She's worried about how she'll live if we get all the money. She made the story up.' He moved forward, arm outstretched, as if to propel her bodily from the room.

The clerk from Pennybody's stepped between them, not without trepidation, for Don was a burly man. 'Your mother told us there was another copy of the same will in the bedroom, which we duly retrieved.'

Don froze, his mouth falling open.

'And,' added the constable, enjoying himself, for he knew the Burns brothers and had no time for them, 'we found another copy of it in the attic – which your mother did not know about.'

'What's this all got to do with you? If there's a will, we should be the ones to deal with it.' Bill held out his hand. 'Give it to me.'

'In a moment. I have to inform you that your mother has appointed Mr Hamish Pennybody to deal with matters pertaining. I'm his senior clerk and he has asked me to look into things for him today.' He held out one of the copies of the will. 'However, I should be glad if you'd look at this and identify it.'

Don's expression as he snatched the piece of paper would have frightened anyone and the clerk was suddenly glad Mrs Burns had suggested getting a constable along as witness and for protection.

'What have you done, you old fool?' Bill demanded of his mother, trying to push the clerk aside to get to her.

'Hey, stop that, you!' snapped the constable.

But what really stopped Bill was the expression on his mother's face. He had never seen her look so decisive, or heard her speak so firmly.

Prudence stared across at her son, and laughed, a short, dry sound. 'What have I done? I've made sure your father's last wishes will be carried out. As any dutiful wife would have done.' She laughed again. 'Now, give the will back to the clerk, son.'

'What do you think, Bill?' Don asked, still holding the piece of paper.

He glanced at the constable, a large man, who was fingering his truncheon. The two of them could still have dealt with him and the clerk, and destroyed the will, but that would have brought the law down upon them. 'Better do as she says.' His glare promised his mother retribution later.

379

Don handed the paper back to the clerk.

'You do recognise this signature as your father's handwriting?' the man asked as he took it and showed it to the constable in turn.

'Aye.'

'You're absolutely sure about that?'

Don nodded wearily. There was no denying it. His father's spiky writing was easy to recognise. Anyone at chapel could identify it. Trust the old fool to keep more than one copy. They should have thought of that and searched the house. 'Aye. I said so, didn't I?'

The clerk turned to Bill and again held out the piece of paper. 'And you, sir? Do you recognise it as your father's handwriting?'

'A-course I do. But it's not what he said he wanted. He must have run mad to write a will like that. There'll be another one somewhere.' And Bill intended to find it, hire another lawyer and prove that the money was his.

The clerk fixed him with a very firm stare. 'Unless you can substantiate that statement, I'd advise you to watch your tongue, sir.'

The constable turned to Mrs Burns. 'If you're ready now, ma'am, I'll call in the men and then escort you across town.'

Bill stared at the constable. 'What do you mean "call in the men"?'

'And where do you think you're going, Mother?' Don demanded, barring the doorway. 'You've not got our dinner ready yet.' And besides, he wanted to have words with her. She was going to regret what she'd done, regret it bitterly before he was through. But even if she had got the money officially, they'd make sure she never laid hands on it. Women were weak vessels, as their father had never tired of pointing out, as their whore of a sister had proved with that bloody Mark Gibson.

Prudence waited until she had the complete attention of her two elder sons. It would, she hoped, be the last time she needed to speak to them. 'The constable is going to call in the removal

380

men,' she replied, perfectly composed. 'I'm leaving this house for good. I've been nothing but unhappy here and I hope never to return.' This, too, she had dreamed about, planned for. And Bartie had not let her down.

'I'm not having that!' Bill roared, making a lunge for her. 'Your place is here, in your husband's house.'

The constable jumped in front of Mrs Burns and for a moment the two men stood face to face, on the verge of a struggle. 'It's not up to you to tell your mother what to do,' he said to Bill, disgusted by the way they spoke to poor Mrs Burns.

Don had more sense of what was possible. 'Back off, lad,' he said, then he turned to his mother as he added, 'for now.'

There was the sound of footsteps in the hall and two men walked in. 'What's to go, then?'

Mrs Burns stepped forward. 'This and this and . . .' How often she had planned to herself what to do! Worked out lists in her head of what she'd want and what she'd leave behind. It had been a cherished dream that consoled her greatly through the years. Now, she spoke rapidly, crisply, and her two sons alternated between glowering at her and gaping in amazement.

Just as she was leaving, Don came to the door of the parlour. 'You'll regret this, Mother.'

'No, I shan't.'

His voice was very quiet. 'I'll make sure you do.'

'Quiet, you!' roared the constable, for Mrs Burns had gone white. 'If you make any more threats, I'll arrest you myself.'

Don smiled, a particularly nasty smile. 'No threat. Just saying she'll miss us, regret leaving.'

Prudence turned her back and hurried along the street. When the cart pulled away, she walked beside it without a backward glance. But a shiver ran down her spine as Don's words came back to her. She'd have to be very careful for a while, very careful indeed. But her Bartie had arranged things. And Don and Bill's anger wouldn't stay at white heat for more than a few weeks. Anger never did. In the end, they'd accept things.

After all, they'd still have most of the businesses. She didn't want anything to do with money lending and pawnbroking and such trades. She just wanted enough money to live on comfortably for the rest of her life. She'd send them a message in a day or two, outlining her decision, telling them what she was giving them.

'You feeling all right, ma'am?' the constable asked gently.

'I haven't felt as well in thirty years,' she replied, holding her face up to the sun. 'Isn't it a beautiful day?'

31

August 1862

For her wedding and a few days thereafter, Annie had promised Tian to set aside her worries, but as she said to him, when he discovered her frowning into space one afternoon and tried to cheer her up, it was hard not to worry.

He put his arms round her and tried to listen patiently, but he had held back his desire for her for so long that it was growing more and more difficult. Did she think of nothing but Hallam's operatives and their families?

'Money's running short all over Lancashire,' she said. 'That Mr Tiplady was right when he sent a letter to *The Times* in April appealing for help from the rest of England. And so was the other man who wrote – though how silly to call himself the "Lancashire Lad"! What dignity or standing does that give him? But the government will have to do something. We absolutely must have national assistance for our distressed operatives. We in Lancashire can't do everything ourselves.'

'Well, the Lord Mayor's Fund is doing quite well now in bringing in relief money.'

'It didn't grant any of it to us for the lake, though, did it?' She sighed. 'But it did help others, and for that, at least, I'm glad.' She turned to smile at him, a very strained smile. 'I'm glad I've got you. You're a great comfort to me, Tian.'

'Now, isn't that an admission from an armoured lady?' he teased.

There was a knock at the front door and they stood together, listening to Winnie's flat tread go across the hall to answer it.

'That woman is a joy to me,' Tian murmured. 'One day, I want to paint her portrait.'

'*Winnie's?*'

'Yes. In her working outfit, with that ridiculous cap that makes her head look like it's been flattened.'

Annie pulled a face. 'I tried to design her a more attractive cap, but she insists on wearing that sort. Says it feels more seemly.'

The heavy footsteps returned and Winnie knocked on the library door. 'His lordship to see you, ma'am,' she announced in the obsequious tone of voice she always used with Simon Darrington. Tian gave a muffled snort of laughter and turned to face the window in an attempt to hide it. He did not want to offend someone who couldn't answer him back.

'Show him in, Winnie.' Annie's voice betrayed only a slight tremor of amusement. 'Simon, it's good to see you. How's Rebecca?'

'She's well. I've left her and young Johnny sitting in the garden.' He nodded to the other occupant of the room. 'Tian.'

'Come and sit down,' Annie urged. 'Or we could follow Rebecca's example and sit outside.'

'No, let's stay here.' Simon sat down and smiled. 'Annie, I may have good news for you.'

'Oh?' It would be something about the child, perhaps. She waited to hear it, smiling. He was such a devoted father.

'I think I may be able to get you some funding for your lake.'

She jerked forward, mouth half-open and eyes alight. 'Really? Oh, Simon, how wonderful!'

Watching, Tian wished he had been able to make her glow like that. As if it wasn't hard enough to follow a man like Frederick Hallam, he also had to compete for her attention with a major cotton crisis! If she wasn't thinking about the lake, she was persuading the better class of people in and around Bilsden to take on extra help and use some of her operatives for other sorts of work. Luke, for instance, now had two thin boys working for him, learning about market gardening. Her voice recalled Tian to the present.

'Where will the money be coming from?'

Simon smiled. 'The Cotton Districts Relief Fund. I know Lord Derby quite well, so I called on him and told him about your idea for a lake. As you know, most of the money they collect is to be distributed through the Manchester Central Relief Committee, but—'

She pulled a face. 'In which case, it'll come to the Bilsden Relief Committee, not me.'

'No, I think they're making one or two exceptions for par ticularly worthy causes. Will you let someone come and see you to find out more about your project? Derby said he'd send a friend of his, who's interested in helping with a few schemes.'

'I'd see the devil himself if it'd get me some money for the lake.'

He smiled. 'Then I'll bring Adrian here tomorrow when he arrives. I'm afraid I took your acquiescence for granted, Annie.'

'Good. You're the best of brothers-in-law.'

But the visit of Lord Derby's representative proved to be rather disappointing. Adrian Seton was another man who seemed to find it difficult to deal with a woman. He spoke patronisingly to Annie, congratulating her on what she had done as if speaking to a child, and addressing most of his remarks to Tian or William. By the time he left, she was boiling with suppressed rage, and the family had a hard time with her that night, for the slightest thing made her snap at them.

However, after an agonising few days of waiting, they received word that some money was to be granted for the construction of Spinners Lake, though it would be conditional upon a suit-able committee of local dignitaries being formed to oversee the lake's construction, and a reliable accountant being appointed to take charge of the monies. Mr Seton was a cautious admin-istrator of funds, it seemed.

'That means forming a committee of men,' sighed Annie.

'I'm afraid so, my love,' Tian agreed. 'But if we choose them carefully, they shouldn't slow us down too much. And I daresay we could find you a place on the committee, too, even if you couldn't head it. Now, can we get on to planning our own wedding?'

'What? Oh, yes. Yes, I suppose we'd better.'

He didn't comment on her lack of enthusiasm. He would win her over after they were married, teach her to love him as much as he loved her, and teach her to enjoy life more, as well. Had she ever had the opportunity to do that? He wondered sometimes.

The wedding was to take place in St Mark's Parish Church. Tian went to see the parson and was forced to confess to having been born a Roman Catholic, which the parson seemed to regard as a heinous crime.

'I have no real interest in sectarian approaches to religion, so surely it doesn't matter if I get married in the Established Church?' Tian protested. 'We're all Christians, after all.'

The look he received said it did matter, so he tried harder to explain. 'When I get out on the moors, I can see that God himself is above all that sort of thing, so I just follow suit and worship him wherever I happen to be.'

'I think it better if we hold a few discussions about what it means to marry a member of the Established Church and bring up a child in its ways. Not that – hmm – Mrs Hallam is very likely to have children – hmm – not at her age.'

Tian bit his tongue and endured a couple of visits to the parsonage, visits that bored him to tears. Eventually, however, he did pass some sort of invisible test and they were able to settle on a day.

Only then did Tian write to his family, a long letter, telling them about Annie and inviting them to attend the wedding. 'My mother will be upset that I'm not marrying a Catholic,' he admitted to Annie. 'She's very devout. Don't let her upset you.'

Tian's father wrote back, accepting the invitation but warning that Tian's mother was very hurt that her son had not come home before this, and that she was deeply concerned for his immortal soul if he were to marry outside the Catholic faith.

*She would have taken it better had you brought your
betrothed over to meet us first. Surely there's no need for such
haste, Tian? Can we not postpone the wedding until you've
talked things over with the priest here? Maybe the good father
could also talk to your Annie. Have you even asked her to
consider converting to the truth faith?*

Tian didn't show the letter to her, just pulled a face. 'Religion!
Why do people let it raise barriers between them, when they're
all supposed to be worshipping the same God?'

'I presume your mother's upset?'

'Yes. I'm afraid so.'

'But they will be coming to the wedding?'

'I think so. They want us to postpone it, though, go and see
them first.'

'Then perhaps—'

'No!' He looked at her very steadily. 'I'm giving you no
chances to build up your walls again, Annie.'

He didn't show her his reply, but the result was another,
much shorter letter from his father agreeing to come over to
the wedding. 'I'm to find them rooms at the Prince of Wales,'
Tian finished.

Annie stared at him. 'But they can stay here! We have plenty
of room. Surely you told them that?'

'I did, but they don't want to put you out. Sure, there are
even more Gilchrists than there are Gibsons.'

'Well, just let your parents stay here, then.'

'No. They all want to be together.' He was beginning to
realise just how unhappy he had made his mother, but it made
no difference to his determination. Nothing was going to delay
his marriage. Nothing! And he knew his father would do his
best to smoothe things over.

Annie didn't like the idea of his family staying in a hotel.
Indeed, she was growing somewhat nervous about meeting
Tian's family if they did not approve of the marriage.

The only member of the family to write a warm, loving letter was his sister Sarry. 'She's sure you're a wonderful woman and she's dying to meet you,' he told Annie, looking happier. 'She says she'll bring the other picture of you with her.'

'She sounds lovely. I'm looking forward to meeting her. I feel I know her already from the picture of yours I bought for Frederick.'

'Yes. Though she's almost grown up now.' His eyes went to the wall, where his painting of his sister Sarry as a child hung. It had been Annie's gift to Frederick, and that was not a good thing to remind her of, and yet it had been the reason they first met. How tangled everything was!

Personally, he thought Kathy was right and it would be better for him and Annie to find themselves another home, but his beloved was adamant about that, as about so many things. She had neither the time nor the money to find another house, let alone move. And she was right about one thing. They couldn't really afford it just now. He still had money in America, where Thaddeus continued to help increase it for him – he suspected partly out of guilt for his daughter's actions – but Tian couldn't touch that money yet. Indeed, he'd just sent word to Thaddeus, who had ways of getting messages to Liverpool, to go ahead and invest three-quarters of it in a rather risky venture.

Annie was very abstracted that night and glad to let the question of Tian's family drop, glad to sit quietly with her hand in his and watch the sunset over the moors through the big library windows.

Then she looked at the living man beside her. 'I do love you, you know,' she said quietly. 'I might seem abstracted sometimes, but I do love you.'

He pulled her closer and dropped a kiss on her cheek. 'I know you do, Annie, I know. If I didn't believe that, how would I ever put up with you?'

She smiled, but had an idea that he wasn't really joking.

In the end, the meeting between Annie and Tian's family did not take place until the day before the wedding, when they all came to take tea at Ridge House. They had left the children at home in Ireland and it was just a sober group of adults who appeared, Tian's parents, three of his brothers and two of his sisters, together with their spouses, and Sarry, the youngest, who would be the only one left unmarried after the wedding.

The meeting was not a great success, though everyone was extremely polite. Tian, watching the Gilchrists behave like wooden puppets, not the lively family he loved, felt almost in despair. Would nothing go right with this marriage of his?

'She's older than you,' his mother said disapprovingly when he walked back to the hotel with her on his arm. 'You didn't tell us that.'

'Because it doesn't matter.'

She reached up to touch his face with her gloved fingertips. 'And you didn't tell me about the scars, either.'

'Sure, I'd completely forgotten them. It happened a long time ago.'

'Only last year. And why you couldn't come home and see your family, let us nurse you better, instead of going to strangers, I'll never understand.'

'Now, me love,' Tian's father said. 'Let that rest.'

Tian ran his hand through his hair and prayed for patience. 'I didn't think you'd be so upset. And if you must know, I completely lost my memory for a time. The only thing I remembered was Annie, so I came to her.'

'Completely lost it!' His mother stopped walking to stare at him, aghast. 'You never said that before.'

'It was a bad time, Mother. I try to forget it.'

When they reached the hotel, she kept hold of his arm. 'You will come in and talk to us, son?' It was more an order than a request.

His heart sank. It sank still further when she led the way upstairs and settled down with just himself and his father in a small private parlour.

'Is your Annie still able to have children?' his mother asked bluntly.

Tian shrugged. 'The doctor says she shouldn't have any more. She doesn't give birth easily. And at her age—'

'How old is she?'

'Forty-two.'

His mother burst into tears. 'Even older than I'd guessed. I never thought I'd get no grandchildren from you. Oh, Tian, the church tells us that having children is one of the main reasons for marriage and—'

'I don't care about that, Mother. It's not children I want, just Annie.' He had never hungered for children. Sometimes, he thought his painting replaced that need. 'And I'll have Annie's children,' he added. 'I get on very well with them. You met them. They're a delightful pair – well, they are most of the time, anyway.'

But his charm had no effect. His mother was sobbing in his father's arms now.

Tian clenched his hands into fists and tried to speak quietly. 'I don't know why you're taking on so. You've got plenty of other grandchildren, haven't you? For goodness' sake, Mother.'

But she was not to be comforted and he left her still in tears.

That night, Annie lay awake for hours, as she had done many times in the past month or two. She thought about the coming day, about the wedding, and wondered if she was doing the right thing. She wept a little for Frederick, then worried that she wouldn't make Tian as happy as he deserved. His family certainly didn't think so. His mother in particular had been very short with her.

In the end, sheer exhaustion overcame her and when she woke up, there was too much to do to worry any more. She had made her decision and it was too late to change it. Besides, she did love Tian. She really did.

None of the guests filing into the flower-filled church the next morning knew that it had been broken into during the night and the elegant flower arrangements torn apart and strewn over the floor. If the verger hadn't been passing and seen a supposedly locked door standing ajar, no one would have known until it was too late to do much about them. As it was, the verger had gone to close the door, seen the damage to the lock, peered inside the church and run in panic for the parson.

Only the wedding preparations had been affected. Nothing else in the church was damaged or stolen. After some thought, the parson sent for Mr Thomas Gibson, and Tom sent word to Luke, asking if he had any other flowers to decorate the church with. So the damage was more or less repaired without Annie's needing to know about it.

'Who could have done this?' Tom raged to Sergeant O'Noonan, as they waited for Luke and Nat Jervis to bring the new flowers. He was furious to think that his sister couldn't even get married without something going wrong.

'Someone who hates your sister did it.' A thoughtful look came over the sergeant's face. 'Or maybe it's aimed at all the Gibsons. Does your family have any enemies you think might have done it? Other than the folk we already know about who're jealous of them, that is. Or does your sister have her own enemies?' He knew the answer in part. He and his men had had a few dealings with the Gibsons in the past year, one way or another. Not just because of Luke and Bartie, but more recently through wilful damage to the yard and a brick thrown through one of the expensive plate glass windows at the Emporium, though presumably the night watchman who patrolled inside had kept the intruders out.

There had even been an anonymous letter to the Minister of the Methodist Chapel, saying that John Gibson was a fornicating liar, who cheated folk at the junk yard and should not be allowed to preach. The Minister had shown it to John and assured him that he knew it to be all lies, but it had still hurt John.

Prudence Burns was also a target for mischief. She was now living with Joanie and Bart, who had recently moved out of Nether-house Cottage to share a house with her, and there had been several incidents of damage to the house – washing pulled off the line and trampled in the mud, offensive matter left on the doorstep, stones thrown at the windows in the middle of the night.

Everyone could guess that this had been done by Don and Bill Burns, but no one could prove it. The two brothers could always produce a witness who had been with them at the time of any incident. Even Prudence was now dubious that her sons would ever come to terms with her inheriting, though they had not refused the businesses she had transferred to them. A new woman, Prudence, and would have been extremely happy but for these troubles, for she got on well with Joanie.

'It depends what you call enemies,' Tom said thoughtfully. 'There are plenty of people jealous of our success, but real enemies, well, I don't think so.'

'There was the trouble with Mrs Barrence a few years ago.'

'And Beatrice is dead now. Anyway, she was mad.'

'So we're back to the Burns family? Or even maybe to friends of Ted Gorton? Do you think some of them could have done this?'

'I can't think why they should start again now. Since the inquest, Luke says things have been all right up at Hey End. And surely their quarrel wouldn't be with Annie?'

'You can never tell when people are filled with hatred,' the sergeant said thoughtfully. 'They strike out at anyone close to the person they hate. Myself, I'd plump for the Burns brothers, but they've been bloody clever about it, more clever than I'd have expected.' He grew more angry with each new incident, feeling he was letting people down, not doing his job.

'Well, I'm sure you'll do your best to find out who it is, Sergeant,' Tom decided to increase the number of night watchmen to three for a while.

'I'll try, sir. I will, indeed.'

'In the meantime, don't tell my sister about this. Luke and Nat Jervis say they can replace the flowers.'

'We ought to mention it to Mr Gilchrist, perhaps?'

Tom shook his head. 'Not on his wedding day! Let the poor fellow enjoy his honeymoon.'

Later that day, St Mark's Parish Church filled up so that every pew was crowded with guests. Annie knew it would have given offence if she hadn't invited all the major citizens of Bilsden, especially now, when she needed the full support of those on the Lake Committee or the Town Council. So she'd sighed and invited anyone who had even half a claim to attend.

Sitting at the back were some of the servants, ready to slip out the minute the ceremony ended and be driven back to the house in the waiting station cab. Winnie was among them, wearing a ghastly hat as unflattering as her indoor cap, but beaming with pleasure. Some of the operatives had been chosen, too, to represent Hallam's people. The two latter groups had had places specially reserved for them, at Annie's own request. The operatives were scrubbed and polished, and had borrowed as much finery as they could, to honour their employer, but they still looked shabby and hollow-cheeked against the well-fed and smartly dressed servants.

James, at the front of the church, leaned towards his wife. 'Fancy inviting operatives to a wedding!'

Judith grimaced. 'That woman has no idea of how to behave. I'm amazed you wanted to come today.'

He shrugged. 'It would have caused talk if we'd refused. I prefer to keep our disagreements within the family. Besides, I must be on good enough terms to come and check what she's doing.' He still hoped to contain the worst of her extravagance towards the operatives.

Beside him, Mildred was whispering to her husband. 'His family are very Irish, aren't they?'

'Very.'

'Poor Father must be turning in his grave.'

'Indeed.' Peter twirled the end of his moustache and hoped it wouldn't be a long wedding. He didn't know why Mildred had insisted on attending. If it had been up to him, they'd not have come. Peter had never forgiven that woman for inheriting the majority of Frederick's estate and he never would. He had had to curtail his expenses quite drastically as a result.

'But Father would have wanted me to attend,' she'd said tearfully. She kept remembering that the last time she had been in this church had been for her father's funeral.

Peter stifled a yawn.

When Annie walked down the aisle on John Gibson's arm, she looked so beautiful and so young for her age that many of the congregation stared in surprise and not a few of the women felt a pang of envy. She was wearing a gown of ivory satin. It wasn't an expensive gown, though no one could tell that, for she did not intend to waste money just now. She had designed and finished the gown herself, trimming it with lace taken from an old evening gown.

Tian, waiting for her at the front of the church, watched the shafts of sunlight play upon her hair as she walked through them down the aisle. After a brief glance at her gown, he had eyes only for her face, the face of his full-length portrait today, a woman defying the world. That was the best painting he'd ever done, but he would never sell it. It meant too much to him. William had asked for the one he had painted earlier, which his sister had brought over from Ireland, and Tian was inclined to give it to him.

He glanced sideways and saw by the stiffness of her carriage just how embarrassed Annie was by today's fuss, and knew, too, that his family's coldness had further upset her. Such a burden of responsibilities lay on those slender shoulders, but he hoped to lighten that, somehow. He had to find ways. He worried about her, and knew John Gibson worried, too. She could not go on like this for much longer. She was as taut as a bowstring.

Then he dismissed such thoughts as she came to a halt beside him. He took her hand and looked at her with his love shining so brightly in his eyes that she softened into an equally loving smile as she began her responses.

She did love him, she thought, love his relaxed charm and innate kindness as well as admiring his artistic talent. It was hard sometimes to show her feelings, with all the troubles she had to deal with at the moment, but she loved him greatly. Differently from the way she had loved Frederick, for they were very different people.

Both of them were so lost in their thoughts that they made their responses automatically and were surprised to hear the words, 'I now pronounce you man and wife.'

Tian didn't wait to be given permission to kiss the bride, just gathered Annie to him and kissed her firmly on the lips. 'We'll be very happy. I'll make sure of that,' he breathed into her ear.

She stared at him as if she'd never seen him before. Today was bringing back so many memories of her wedding to Frederick that her joy was spliced by occasional moments of sharp pain. 'You're a lovely man, Tian,' she said at last. 'I'll try to make you happy.' Then she realised that everyone was waiting for them to sign the register and moved across to the side of the church, with her hand laid lightly on Tian's arm.

Even in this, he thought, looking down at her arm, she doesn't lean and cling as other women do.

The reception caused its own share of comment. The invitations had said bluntly that, given the distress in the area, the meal would not be a lavish one. But its simplicity amazed everyone.

'How mean!' whispered Mildred.

'Blazoning her charity at a time like this,' replied Judith, who had not visited Ridge House since her quarrel with Annie and was very much on her dignity today. Edgar and Tamsin had avoided her, refusing point-blank to come and say hello. Even William, the most forgiving of men normally, had given her only the coolest of nods.

But Tamsin and Edgar were delighted about the marriage, for even in this, their father had prepared the way, hinting that if anything ever happened to him, he hoped their mother would one day remarry. And they both adored Tian, vying when they got back to Ridge House, to stay near him, calling him 'Step-father', at every opportunity.

'Are you not afraid I'll grow very strict now I really am your wicked step-father?' he teased, ruffling Edgar's hair and giving Tamsin a quick hug.

Hanging upon each of his arms, they laughed at the mere idea. 'You're not that sort of person,' Edgar said. 'Not at all. You're always very gentle.'

'Am I now?' Tian was intrigued by this insight.

'Yes.' Edgar looked at him, for a moment like one grown man to another. 'I think you'll make my mother very happy, if anyone can. And perhaps you can stop her working so hard.' He hesitated, then said in a gruff voice, 'And I think my father would approve.'

'I'll certainly try to make your mother happy.' But it would be very difficult, for she was still pushing herself too hard and nothing Tian said, nothing seemed to slow her down.

In another part of town, all the operatives had gathered for their own feast, and there were no complaints about the refreshments there. Indeed, it was a bright spot in these hard times.

'Mrs Hallam – no, Mrs Gilchrist now – deserves to be happy,' they told one another. 'She's a good employer.' For they were under no misapprehension that Annie left everything to Matt.

'And isn't Mr Gilchrist a nice chap? Treats you as civil as Mr Hallam used to.'

'Eh, what do you think *he* would say if he saw her getting wed?'

'I think he'd approve. He weren't mean, not about anything, an' he can't be here with her now himself, can he, after all?'

On the way to the railway station, Annie and Tian stopped at the church hall to see the operatives and to listen to a stilted speech of congratulations.

'Look after our Annie, Mr Gilchrist,' an anonymous voice

shouted from the back and a rumble of laughter ran round the room.

'I'll do my very best,' Tian smiled. It was good to hear how well thought of she was. And it was good to have her to himself, for once. He meant to make the most of that.

When they were sitting in the second train, on the way from Manchester to Scarborough, Annie leaned against Tian and let out a long, low sigh. 'I'm glad all that fuss is over.'

'Me, too. Let's just sit quiet for a while now, eh?' He knew she was exhausted and was not surprised when she fell asleep leaning against him. She had grown thinner over the past few months, her eyes seeming larger in her face, and often, when she didn't know anyone was observing her, lines of worry would etch themselves on her forehead and she would chew at her thumbnail. Today, for a while, she had lost that harried look, seemed younger again, but he knew it wouldn't last.

The hotel at Scarborough was large, their suite luxurious in the extreme.

'Should we be spending so much money?' Annie worried.

'*We* are not spending anything. I'm paying for the honeymoon, love.'

She looked at him. 'Then should you be spending this much?' He had refused to discuss his finances with her, saying only that he had enough for his own needs and a few more investments brewing. Oh, and he'd like, after they got back, to pay the indoor servants' wages as his contribution to the household expenses.

'Yes, I should be spending it,' he said firmly. 'I only intend to get married once and I want to make it special.'

And it was special. The wedding night itself, about which both Tian and Annie had secretly worried, was wonderful. They had always had this instant physical response to one another, even before Frederick's death, and for once did not need to rein it back or try to ignore it. Nor were there any distractions. There was no guilt, no holding back, just joy in one another.

The next three days went by so swiftly and happily that neither could believe it when their last night came.

'I don't want to go back,' Tian admitted, lying in bed with Annie nestled in his arms, her glorious hair spread over his shoulder, and moonlight filtering through the curtains. 'Couldn't we stay on for another night or two?'

'I wish we could. But I have a meeting—'

'You always have meetings.'

'This one's important.'

'Aren't we important, too?'

'Yes. Very important. And I love you very much, Tian Gilchrist, but I also have to look after our people. When the war is over, when the mills are on full time again, then I promise I'll hand over some of my responsibilities to others. But until then—'

'Until then, you'll nearly kill yourself trying to look after them all.' But he said nothing else. He knew she wouldn't change until the crisis was over. But he intended to find ways of helping her, reducing her burden. He would. He must.

1863

32

September 1862 to February 1863

After the North's victory at Antietam, President Lincoln proclaimed that on or after the first of January, 1863, all slaves in the rebellious states would be free. The news was well received in England. John Gibson, who had taken an intense interest in the fate of the poor, enslaved, black people in America, had tears running down his cheeks as he read about it in the newspaper.

'It makes it all worthwhile, somehow,' he told Kathy. 'Lancashire folk have suffered, and they're still suffering, but they're free men and women, and so should everyone be, else what progress have we made in this rushing modern world of ours?'

All over town, people were spreading the news and nodding to one another. It helped, somehow, in the suffering of the cotton towns to know that the cause was just.

When Tian heard people talking, he grimaced sometimes and once confided in Annie, 'I'm not sure the reasons for this war are as simple as that, but I don't like to say anything to spoil people's illusions about why they're suffering.'

'Well, it is being fought for the freedom of the slaves, isn't it?'

'Only partly. It's also being fought to preserve the Union.' And, he suspected, for various business reasons.

He changed the subject to something more pleasant. Miles Correnaud had just written to say that Tian's latest batch of paintings was selling well in London. He also had some hopes that the huge painting of the emigrants on the docks would be accepted for hanging in the Royal Academy's annual exhibition, a great honour. Tian shrugged at that. He had never sought honours, and was proud of the painting whether it was hung or not. He had achieved what he wanted, and that was enough for him.

'But you deserve the recognition,' Annie protested.

'I get recognition every time someone buys one of my paintings.'

'They are good. They always were, but since you got back from America they have,' she paused to search for the word, 'they have a depth of emotion that sometimes brings tears to my eyes.'

He took her hand and kissed it. 'I'll treasure that remark.' Then they separated, each heading for a different busy day, during which they sometimes met over shared tasks, and sometimes didn't. They both knew that people thought them strange, but neither of them cared about that.

Since he had got back from his honeymoon, Tian was spending long hours painting. Not just because he needed some money coming in, but because it was something he had to do, a fire burning in his belly. The portrait of Annie had been hung, at his insistence, in the dining-room, though she said she felt embarrassed to see her own face staring back at her from the wall. But everyone else loved it and John would often go and stand in front of it to marvel at how Tian had caught her indomitable spirit.

However, as the year passed, Tian began to fret over his secret investments. News came so very infrequently. He had told Annie only that he had some money invested in New York with his friend Thaddeus Brownsby. What he had not told her was that the majority of his money was now invested in a ship to run the blockades and bring cotton from the embattled Confederate States. He was surprised that a man as patriotic as Thaddeus should involve himself in a nefarious enterprise like this, for some said it was undermining what the North was trying to achieve. But Tian knew that Thaddeus would not be able to resist such a profitable gamble.

And it was a gamble, for some ships did not make it through the blockades with their loads of cotton. But when they did, the profits were huge. Tian had decided that if the gamble paid off, he would then withdraw his capital and invest it in a safer project in England. He wanted something to set against Annie's money, something to make him independent, but he had never cared about being rich.

That winter, work started on Spinners Lake. There was still not enough money available to complete the project, but since the Lake Committee had received a grant from Lord Derby, some of the local businessmen had joined Annie in putting money into the project and the general mood was that they would find the rest of the funding somehow. For the idea had caught people's imagination and was the talk of Bilsden. Even the Town Council had voted a penny rate towards the lake, for it was a form of charity towards the spinners which would reap dividends for the whole town. And the spinners themselves were longing to work on something so tangible, something they could be proud of.

One golden weekend in October, Annie and Tian went across to Hollingworth Lake, near Rochdale, to see what was going on there, what they could expect their lake to become.

'I wish we were going,' Tamsin said several times before they left.

'Another time,' Tian insisted. He lowered his voice. 'I need to get your mother away from all her responsibilities. I told you that, Tamsin.'

'Well, it's boring here. I hate Bilsden.' She was at the age when everything was black or white and was prone to making such sweeping generalisations according to her mood.

But this time she was not able to get round her step-father.

Tian and Annie stayed at the Queen's Hotel on the south side of the lake. They found the place a thriving holiday and excursion centre, with several pubs and hotels. Trips came, the landlord told them proudly, from as far afield as Manchester and Leeds. 'Though attendance has dropped off a little since the trouble with America,' he admitted. Then he brightened. 'But it's given us a chance to do up our accommodation and we'll be ready for the increase when we get the cotton again.'

'No wonder they call it the Weighver's Seaport,' Annie said, using the local dialect phrase, as she and Tian strolled round the lake. 'It's amazing that all this has developed inland.'

'It's a grand little place.' Tian was enjoying the crowds, the festive air and the innate good humour of those holidaying there.

Some of the hotels had wooden stages outdoors for dancing, lit after dusk by huge gas lamps. Others had gardens by the lake. And there was a steamer to ride across the lake on. As the Gilchrists had gone dressed simply, Tian persuaded Annie to join in the dancing, persuaded her to pretend that she was merely an artist's wife, persuaded her simply to sit and relax.

While he was busy sketching the holiday makers at the lake, for he could not resist the lively scenes, Annie sat and listened to the people talking: people of all classes, from labourers to clerks to a few more affluent families.

One day, the tiny resort was even more crowded because a charitable gentleman in Rochdale had hired wagons and had brought some of the operatives on an excursion, providing a simple dinner for them in the middle of the day and giving them a brief respite from their worries about where the next meal was coming from. They were easy to recognise, for they were the ones with mended clothes and worn boots, the ones with desperation barely hidden below the surface.

'Why don't we bring our own people here next spring?' Tian suggested that night. 'Give them a break from worry. If we hired a whole train and some charabancs, it wouldn't cost too much.'

She looked at him with tears in her eyes. 'That's the first time you've said it.'

'Said what?'

'Said "our people" as if you're really a part of Bilsden now.'

'I feel it.' He pulled her close. 'But I still like to persuade my overworked wife to take a little time off now and then.'

'You could persuade anyone that black was white,' she retorted.

He wished he could. Another incident had had to be hidden from her. Someone had broken into the kitchen gardens at Ridge House and trampled down some of the plants. Luckily, Nat had heard the stable dog barking and had come rushing out. Even more luckily, he had had the wit to tell only Tian in the morning. Since then, Tian had hired out-of-work spinners to keep watch on the grounds at night, paying for their services from his own pocket.

And Tom, who had suffered similar predations at the back of the Emporium, had done the same. He now had two outdoor watchmen as well as the usual indoor man.

'If I ever catch the sods who are doing this,' he confided to Tian, 'I'll make sure they regret it for the rest of their lives.'

But when the Gilchrists got back from their weekend away, the work seemed to pile up and Annie soon began to look drawn and weary again. This caused regular arguments between her and Tian, some quite fiery. It was a new thing for Annie to have a husband who shouted at her, threw things across the bedroom or stormed out of the house, and it was a side of Tian she had not been fully exposed to before their marriage.

'It's you who should have the red hair,' she shouted at him one day.

That stopped him short. 'Why the hell do you say that?'

'Because you just – just erupt into rage.'

His mood changed at once and he walked over to her, taking her in his arms, though she struggled against him. When he kissed her, Annie melted against him. His loving was also fiery, very different from Frederick's skilled touch. And, though she felt guilty to think it, it was wonderful to have a younger lover.

'I don't like the way you can do this to me,' she grumbled, trying and failing to scowl at him.

'I do. I like it very much.'

Over the next few months, they both had a struggle to adjust to one another. It was inevitably a stormy marriage, and all the more difficult because it was being played out in front of so many other people: family, servants, business colleagues.

'Frederick would never have shouted at me in front of the children like that,' she told Tian stiffly one night. 'It's – it's ungentlemanly.'

'I'm not Frederick. And who the hell cares about being a gentleman?'

'Why can't you just understand that I have to look after our people?'

'And I have to look after you. Besides, you don't have to kill yourself in the process. Not even your precious Frederick would have wanted that.'

'Don't you dare speak of him like that!'

'I'll speak of him how I like. I sometimes think we've got a marriage for three, that he's still lying there next to us in bed.'

Her face turned white. 'That's a horrible thing to say.'

'Well, you make me feel horrible sometimes.' He stamped off along the corridor to his studio and she tried to settle to work in the library. Within an hour, they had sought one another out and made up.

The children learned to tiptoe around on such occasions, and took their worries to Elizabeth and William, who reassured them that most married people quarrelled now and then.

'You two don't,' Edgar pointed out. 'And Mother didn't quarrel with Father.'

'William is exceptionally hard to quarrel with,' Elizabeth replied. 'I know. I've tried.'

'And so was your father,' William added.

There were times when Annie and Tian's love burned brightly, when everything seemed to be going well. And there were other times when things grew cooler, especially if Annie got abstracted and left Tian out of what she was doing, some-thing which never failed to infuriate him, or if he became too touchy because a painting was not going the way he had wanted.

Tian's relationship with the children was the easiest part of his new life, for both of them adored him. He got on well with William and Elizabeth, too, but so did everyone. William had always had a sunny, lovable nature and Elizabeth's happiness since her marriage was equally infectious.

It was William who suggested to his mother that Tian be invited to join the Lake Committee. 'He needs to be more a part of things, Mother. You cut him out too much.'

She sighed. 'I do try to think of him, William, but sometimes there are so many things to sort out that I can't see straight. He does have his painting. And he is involved in some things.'

'Not in the main decision making. You keep that to yourself still.' He hesitated, then added, 'You don't seem to want to let go of the reins.'

Her voice was sharp. 'Why should I let go of them?'

To argue about that would not forward his cause, so William did not pursue the point. 'Will you at least think about putting him on the Lake Committee?'

She frowned. 'I'm not sure I should do that. People might talk. Say he's only there because of me.'

'I'm sure you should do it anyway. With old Benson dying suddenly, there's a vacancy. Besides, there's a genuine need for someone to oversee the artistic side of things. We don't just want a lake, we want a pretty lake, surely?'

'I sometimes wish,' she said, her voice tight and controlled, but her hands clenched into two fists, 'that Tian and I had not met again until after this war.'

'And I'm glad you did meet now, Mother, for he's the only one who can make you slow down at all. None of us wants you to kill yourself.'

She thumped her fist on the table. 'This is not a time to slow down, William, not with so much trouble in the town.'

He just looked at her fist and she realised how angry she

was getting. She breathed in deeply and slowly. 'I'm sorry. All right. I'll suggest that Tian be invited on to the committee.'

Afterwards, she was thoughtful as she remembered this conversation, for it seemed to mark another turning point in her relationship with William. He had grown in so many ways lately. Perhaps it was his work with the operatives, his marital responsibilities or his management of many of his mother's charitable efforts – whatever it was, he had become a man whom people consulted. They sought him out, confided in him, asked his advice, wanted him with them when they were dying or after their loved ones had died. And when he preached in the smaller chapels near Bilsden, they were always full.

'He makes you feel there's hope in the world, Mr Ashworth does,' one old lady told Jeremy when he visited her in hospital. 'I shall die happy if he's by my side.'

The last of Annie's resentment at her son's becoming a Minister faded that winter. He was born to do something like that, and Elizabeth, dear Elizabeth, pregnant now with her first child, seemed born to be his wife.

And far from resenting Annie's suggestion, the other committee members approved it. Tian Gilchrist was invited to become a member of the Lake Committee, with a special brief to oversee the artistic side of things. Even hard-headed businessmen, who thought little of a man who painted pictures for a living – such a poor way to make money – could see that their lake ought to be as pretty as possible.

'We mun all pull together now,' said one older man, who owned a small mill just outside Bilsden which spun coarse yarn.

'Aye,' said another, 'and yon sod Leaseby should think shame to himself for the way he diddles folk. I had a word with Bagley last week. We s'll have to think of a way to stop it, a way to make that damned Relief Committee help folk in a fairer way.'

'Aye. Mrs Gilchrist is right about that.'

So the succession of small incidents, damage here, trouble there, was a puzzlement to the males of the Gibson family, who had managed to keep most of them from their womenfolk.

However hard they tried, they could not manage to tie them to the Burns brothers. And yet, who else could it be?

The committee made a good start on getting the lake project going that winter. First Mr Hervey Bamforth came over from near Burnley to be interviewed. He proved a capable man, if rather blunt in his ways and speech, and was offered the position of engineer in charge on the spot.

He accepted the commission equally promptly and was back in Bilsden within two days with his things, ready to start. The speed of this, after all the delays, took even Annie by surprise.

Within a month, the plans were all made and approved by everyone who saw them, thanks to Tian's sketches, which showed what the lake would look like. They pleased the Town Council, the Lake Committee, and even Mr Adrian Seton on behalf of Lord Derby, who sent word that he would contribute more money in the new year if the start seemed promising.

An office for Mr Bamforth had been set up in the old farmhouse where Beatrice Barrence had once stayed when she was trying to harm Annie, and where her body had been carried after her plunge to death. Annie never liked visiting the place, which seemed filled with malicious echoes, fanciful as that sounded. She was glad that the building would be drowned when the lake started to fill up.

In the meantime, Mr Bamforth requested tables and benches to work on and filled them all with sketches and figures about water flow and calculations and plans for doing the work in several distinct stages.

By early in 1863, he was ready to start.

'In the winter?' the committee members asked. 'Surely we should wait till the spring?'

'Those without work need to earn money now,' Tian and William insisted, supporting their engineer. So the committee spread word around that people were needed to labour on the lake.

Men who had once worked in the mills came in droves to

offer their services. Hervey Bamforth frowned at them and said he would let them know.

'They haven't the muscle,' he told Annie, when he met her in town. 'You'd be better hiring proper navvies, men who have worked on the railways. You're wasting your money on weaklings like these.'

Annie felt quite comfortable arguing with Mr Bamforth, who had never treated her like an ignorant female and could be brought to listen to her views if she stood up to him. 'The whole point of the lake is to give these people work. We have to pay them relief, so we might as well pay them to work. It doesn't matter if they're less efficient.'

He sat frowning down at the plans. 'Then at the very least, we must hire some foremen who have worked on the railways. And you must either provide wagons to take your operatives to and from the town, or build us a shanty town near the lake. They'll be too exhausted to walk far at the end of the day for the first few weeks, believe me.' Another scowl and a furious tapping of fingertips on the pocket knife which seemed to go everywhere with him and be more often in his hand than his pocket. 'You'll have to provide some good red meat for them, too.'

Annie looked at him in surprise. 'What do you mean?'

'Muscles such as we need to dig out a lake won't be built up without good food in the men's bellies. You'll need to feed them up.'

She nodded. It made sense. 'Very well. I'll see what we can do.'

'There are a lot of engineers who wouldn't work on a job like this, with such unskilled workers,' he added.

Annie's heart leaped into her mouth. Was he going to resign?

He grinned at her. 'But I always did like a challenge.' His smile faded. 'And besides, I admire what you're doing. You're a good woman, Mrs Gilchrist, and you've a good husband there, too. I reckon this'll be one of the prettiest lakes I've ever built if he has his way. I hope to work with him again.' For

Mr Bamforth specialised in creating lakes and was delighted with Tian's artistic input.

It was Tom who solved the problem of feeding the workers on the lake. Business had inevitably dropped off at the Prince of Wales Hotel during the cotton shortage. 'You buy the meat and potatoes,' he told Annie. 'I'll get 'em cooked for you. My contribution.' He grinned. 'And that'll ensure I keep my cook here. He's getting a bit fed up with so little to do.'

'You won't have enough room. There are going to be a couple of hundred people working on the lake.'

'I've an outhouse we can convert just to prepare the food to feed your flock. It won't cost much. And we can hire a few more people to help. You leave that side of things to me.'

'So long as you hire our female operatives for that.'

He rolled his eyes at her. 'Heaven preserve me from a managing woman.'

'But will you?'

'Of course.' He watched her go, frowning. He could understand why Tian got angry with her sometimes. She was obsessive about her people.

If it hadn't been for the odd incident, always directed against the Gibsons, the only cloud on the horizon for Tian would have been Annie's working too hard. But the incidents continued. More broken windows. One of Tom's heavy wagons damaged, so that the brakes didn't work and there was nearly a nasty accident.

'I thought it had all stopped!' he grumbled to Rosie. 'What the hell are we going to do? People are going to get hurt at this rate.'

'Do you still think it's Don and Bill Burns?'

'Who else can it be? I've built up my business honestly and haven't made any real enemies that I know of.' He stopped pacing to stare bleakly into the fire. 'And anyway, it's not just me. They tried to break in at Bart's house last week. I wish he and Joanie would move back into Netherhouse Cottage.'

'I thought his mother was looking worried when I saw her in town.' Rosie stretched out her toes towards the fire, sighed and changed the subject. 'I think I'll cut down on my concert programme next year. I'm getting too old for all this travelling.'

'You don't have to do any travelling if you don't want to.'

'Don't start on that again,' she said, yawning. 'I like singing to people. In fact,' she looked sideways at him, 'I've been thinking of putting on a couple of benefit concerts. Very select audience. Make people enjoy supporting the spinners. I'll give my services free and I'll pay for the hire of the hall in Manchester, though I'll expect the Bilsden Town Council to give me the Town Hall here free of charge. Money to go towards the lake. What do you think?'

He stopped his pacing to sit beside her on the sofa. 'I think you're a wonderful woman, Rosie Gibson. And I'm glad I married you.'

She cuddled up to him. The servants often found them like that and had grown used to it, for their mistress had little sense of dignity, except where her work was concerned.

But Tom continued to feel uneasy, as did other members of the Gibson, Gilchrist and Darrington families. If it was one of the Burnses, how the hell were they doing it?

And what if they tried something really dangerous next, something that got innocent people killed?

33

March to April 1863

In March, the Prince of Wales got married and Bilsden Town Council loyally decorated High Street and Hallam Square with civic bunting, kept for these occasions and beginning to look a bit faded and frayed. A couple of members of the Council proposed that a big public meal be held in the park for the out-of-work operatives, to celebrate, but that was outvoted very quickly. Instead, an engraved silver plate was sent to His Royal Highness and his bride, together with a fulsome message of congratulations.

'They say Nero played his fiddle while he watched Rome burn,' Tian joked when he heard.

'Well, if Bilsden were burning, I'd throw that silly Council on top of the fire!' Annie snapped. 'As if the Prince needs more silver plates!'

'Aren't you even interested in what the bride wore to the wedding?' he asked.

She just looked at him. 'I might have been once, but not now. What are you going on about it for?'

He sighed. 'It's called humour. Something you might have understood once, but have surely forgotten about now.'

And they were off into another quarrel, and strangely, when she stormed away from him, Annie felt better for it.

He didn't feel better, though he had provoked the argument on purpose. 'She can't go on like this,' he muttered. 'But how the hell do we stop her?'

One evening, as Joanie was hurrying home from a visit to Kathy, a figure stepped out in front of her and grabbed her arm to stop her.

Joanie clutched at her chest. 'Ooh, Maddie! You did make me jump.' Her first reaction was to walk on, for she had not forgotten how her former friend had tricked her. But she didn't. Instead, she stood staring at her in shock, for the other woman was gaunt and haggard, looking years older than her actual age. 'Are you all right?'

Maddie shrugged and looked around furtively, as if worried that they might be seen. 'I'm as well as I can be. Look, just step into this doorway for a moment.' When her companion hesitated, she said, 'I'm not trying to trick you this time, Joanie, I promise you.' She had such desperation in her voice that Joanie followed. 'I need to talk to you, warn you, to make up for − for what I did before. But I don't want anyone telling Harry I've been talking to you.'

'Warn me about what? If it's my husband's brothers, you needn't bother. I know they hate us.'

Maddie gave a sniff, as if scornful of Joanie's ignorance. 'It's not just them, that's the whole point. It's our Harry, too.'

Joanie tried to move away, but the other woman was now blocking the doorway. Joanie looked around, suddenly afraid, but there were plenty of people close enough to call to for help, even if they couldn't see her at the moment. 'I don't want to talk about your brother.' She hated even to think of him, to remember what he had done to her, how he had almost ruined her life.

Maddie kept hold of her. 'Don't go. Please.' She began to speak in a low, urgent voice. 'Harry hates you now, Joanie. Hates all you Gibsons.'

Joanie just stared at her.

'And he hates your Bart most of all,' Maddie continued. 'He's allus been a nasty sod if you go against him, Harry has. He'll get his own back on you if it takes him years. He's like that. I should know. The number of times he's thumped me—' She broke off. 'Well, I haven't time to go into that. How he treats me is my problem, isn't it?'

Joanie couldn't understand where all this was leading. 'Even if your Harry does still hate me, what does that matter?'

Maddie shook her. 'I told you. Listen, will you? He intends to get his own back.'

Joanie began to wonder if Maddie was quite right in the head. 'But it's me as was hurt. What has *he* to get his own back for?'

'Harry can never see anyone else's side. Never. An' he's got together with Don and Bill Burns now. I don't know what the three of them are planning, but it's something nasty if I know our Harry. So you watch out for yourself, Joanie. And watch out for your husband and his mother, too. I've heard them mention her as well.'

'What are they—'

But a noisy group of people they both knew were coming down the street, and Maddie gasped and slipped away, leaving Joanie leaning against the hard panels of the door, staring, feeling a chill shiver through her. Then, as the people passed without seeing her, she realised how dark it had grown. Bartholomew didn't like her to be out after dark, so she hurried off home.

But when she got there, further bad news was waiting for her. Prudence Burns put her arm round her daughter-in-law and said gently, 'Your father's been hurt, love. Bartie sent word. He said he'd go over to Netherhouse Cottage with you when he got back from the yard.'

'Dad? He's hurt? What's happened?'

'The lad Bartie sent over told me your dad's been attacked – beaten – Joanie, come back!'

But she had gone flying out of the house, shawl slipping from one shoulder, shopping lying scattered where she had dropped it. The only thought in her head was to see that her father was all right.

Netherhouse Cottage was ablaze with light. Joanie ran inside without knocking and found Tom in the kitchen, sharing a cup of tea with their half-brother, Samuel John, both of them hunched over the warmth of the drinks, looking stern and serious.

'Dad?' she gasped, stopping in the doorway to clutch at her side and pant for breath.

Tom got up and came to put his arm round her. 'He's all right, love. Just badly bruised and a couple of broken ribs, we think. The doctor's with him now.'

Footsteps came down the stairs and they turned towards the hall.

Dr Spelling stopped at the sight of them. 'He's all right. A couple of weeks' rest and you won't believe it ever happened.' He paused. 'Do you know who did it?'

Tom shook his head. 'I can't imagine anyone wanting to hurt Dad.'

'I suppose it must have been someone after his money, then. There are enough people in want in this town.'

'His money wasn't taken,' Tom said flatly. 'So it can't have been that.'

'Perhaps they were disturbed before they had a chance to—'

Again, Tom shook his head. 'No. They finished what they'd set out to do, then left him lying there. He'd be lying there still, but someone from chapel was passing by, found him and helped him home.'

'You'd better tell Sergeant O'Noonan about it, then.' Dr Spelling turned towards the front door. 'I must go. I'm due at the hospital for a difficult birthing.' It was one of the main uses of the town's small hospital, for sick folk much preferred to be looked after in their own homes, if at all possible.

Joanie took a step towards the stairs. 'I want to see Dad.'

Tom shook his head. 'Better wait till Kathy comes down. He might not feel up to seeing anyone. He was only half-conscious when they brought him home.' Then he thumped one clenched fist against the other and added in a tight, clipped voice, 'Someone's going to pay for this. I'm not having Dad attacked. He's done nothing to deserve that. Nothing.'

There was the sound of a carriage outside and the front door flew open again. This time it was Annie who rushed inside, closely followed by Tian and Ben, who had gone running up the hill to fetch her.

She looked at the solemn group and fear made her throat close up for a moment. 'How's Dad?' she managed in a hoarse whisper.

'He's all right. Bruised and a couple of ribs cracked. The doctor said he's to rest for a week or two.'

Kathy appeared at the top of the stairs. Everyone fell silent and watched her walk down.

'Well?' demanded Tom. 'Can we see him now?'

She nodded. 'It's you and Tian he's asking for.'

Annie stepped forward. 'I want to see him, too.'

'And me,' Joanie moved to join her.

Kathy held her step-daughters back. 'He wants to talk to the men first. And I don't want anything to upset him, so you just let them go up alone, Annie. There are times when only men can help one another.'

The three women walked into the kitchen.

'Who have we Gibsons upset so much that they want to harm us?' Annie demanded.

Joanie gasped, 'Oh!' and clapped one hand to her mouth.

They turned to look at her.

'I saw Maddie just before I heard about Dad.'

'That one!' Kathy sniffed scornfully. 'I don't know why you'd even give her the time of day.'

'She stopped me. She wanted to warn me. I think she's still a friend – as much as she can be with a brother like that.'

Annie touched Kathy and shook her head slightly to ask her to be quiet. Kathy had not been able to say a good word about Maddie Pickering since Joanie's troubles with Harry. 'What was she warning you about, then, love?'

'She said Harry is in league with Don and Bill Burns. That he hates me and – and wants to get back at me.' Tears filled Joanie's eyes. 'So it's all my fault that Dad's been hurt.'

'Why is it your fault?' Tom's voice demanded from the doorway.

Joanie explained again while Kathy prepared them all a cup of tea, her usual panacea for times of trouble, then they sat down to discuss the implications.

'I'll tell my friend O'Noonan,' Bartholomew said, cradling his cup in his hands. 'We can't prove anything about Pickering, but if Gerry knows it's a possibility, he can keep an eye open.' But it made sense, it really did. And if it was ever proved, he would personally see that Harry Pickering regretted every rotten, bloody act.

Bartholomew saw his friend the sergeant the following evening, inviting him to go out for a drink, as they still did sometimes. The two men sat in a quiet corner of their favourite pub and went over it all, speaking in low voices and making sure no one overheard them.

'It's getting the proof,' O'Noonan said, chewing on one corner of his lip and tugging at his bushy sidewhiskers. 'That's going to be the difficulty. It all makes sense, though. I knew the Burns lads weren't smart enough to do all this on their own.'

'Pickering is smart, though,' Bartholomew said thoughtfully. 'Too bloody smart. I haven't forgotten what he did to my Joanie, and I never will. He's not the only one with a long memory.' One day he would find some way to pay Pickering back for that.

His friend grabbed his arm. Gerry was the only person outside the family who knew about that incident. 'You're to do nothing about that. I've told you before! I'm not wanting to lock up my best friend.'

'I'll do nothing illegal,' Bartholomew said. 'But I'll find some way to pay him back. And no one will stop me. No one.' John Gibson might not be his father, but he *felt* like a father and the thought of anyone hurting that gentle, old man made fury seethe within him.

While Bartholomew was talking to the sergeant, Tian was talking to a group of unemployed spinners, older men who had not found work on the lake, but who came to some drawing classes he'd been running for unemployed people. It was one of his own contributions to Bilsden in its hour of need. Time hung so heavily on the hands of people who'd been used to working long hours all their lives that a lot of classes had been put on, from simple reading and writing to botany, sewing and drawing.

At the end of his class, he asked a couple of the men to stay behind. 'Would you like to earn a little money?' he asked.

Their faces brightened. 'How?'

'I need someone to keep an eye on my wife and her family.'

They frowned at that, puzzled.

'Someone's trying to hurt them. You'll have heard about John Gibson being beaten up?'

They nodded. Such news spread fast in a small town.

'And then there was the damage done to the Emporium and Bart's house?'

They nodded again.

'Well, if I were to slip you a sovereign a week, do you think you could spread it out among a group of fellows who'd be prepared to keep their eyes open, maybe follow Bart's brothers and Harry Pickering around at night?'

'Aye. We can. And it won't be just for the money, Mester Gilchrist,' one of them said. 'We owe a lot to the Hallams. An' some of us worship with John Gibson. We'll make sure we keep our eyes wide open.'

But before they could start keeping watch, more trouble had arisen, this time of an even more serious nature. Annie and Tian had gone into Manchester to a concert. It had taken him a while to persuade her, but in the end she'd agreed. Not that she was musical, far from it, but he was and she knew he wanted to go. And as he had said, she could do with a change of air, even if only for an evening. He'd wanted Tom and Rosie to come too, make a real outing of it, but Rosie had a cold.

On the way back, when the late train from Manchester got

to the outskirts of Bilsden, they could both see a glow in the vicinity of the River Rows.

'Something's on fire,' Tian said. Annie put her hand in his. She didn't say anything, but he knew what she was thinking – pray God it wasn't one of the Hallam properties.

They could smell smoke as soon as they got out of the train.

'What's burning?' Tian cut short the fulsome greeting of the station master, who had come over to welcome them back in person.

'Just a warehouse down in the River Rows.'

'Do you know which one?' Annie asked.

'I'm afraid not, Mrs Gilchrist.'

But as they left the station, they saw William came hurrying across the square towards them, his face covered in sooty marks and anxiety radiating from him.

'It's one of ours,' Annie whispered, clutching Tian's arm. 'Heaven help us all, I hope no one's been injured.'

'One of our warehouses is on fire,' her son said without preamble.

'Which one?' Annie's voice was so curt it didn't sound like hers.

Tian could feel her fingers digging into his arm. When William told them, those fingers spasmed on him and she moaned in her throat.

'Is it a bad fire?' he asked, when she didn't speak.

William nodded. 'I'm afraid so. I think it's going to be completely gutted. But they've kept the flames from spreading to nearby properties, at least. What was in it? It wasn't—'

'It held the rest of the cotton goods,' Annie said through the tears building up in her throat, 'the ones we were going to sell next month.'

By her side, Tian was cursing softly.

'I want to see it,' she said, setting off in the direction of the River Rows.

'You'll get your evening clothes dirty, Mother,' William protested, trying to hold her back. 'And you can't do anything to help now.'

'What does that matter? I have to see for myself.'

William turned to Tian. 'Can't you stop her? There's nothing to see.'

'I doubt anyone could stop her.'

Both men hurried after her.

When they got there, she was standing on the corner opposite, her face lit up by the glow from the parts of the warehouse which were still burning and tears rolling openly down her cheeks. 'The cotton goods were worth so much,' she whispered. 'The money would have gone a long way towards helping our people. What'll I do now if the war goes on and on?'

Tian put one arm around her shoulders. 'Come away, love. You can do no good here now.'

But she hadn't even heard him. She had darted off to catch the chief fireman, whom she had spotted in the distance and who had been looking anxiously in her direction as he gave a series of instructions to some smoke-blackened men.

'How did it start, Mr Ronsley?' she demanded.

He hesitated, looking at William for guidance.

'She has to know,' he said.

'It was set deliberate, Mrs Gilchrist. Deliberate.'

'How do you know?'

'Well, for one thing, they'd knocked out the night watchman and tied him up.'

She went white. 'Is he all right?'

'Yes. They put him round the corner away from the fire, thank God.'

'Who could have done it?' she wondered aloud.

'I can't say, but we've called in Sergeant O'Noonan. If anyone can find out, it's him. I'm sorry we couldn't save it for you. It'd taken hold before we were called. They'd set fire to several points at once, you see, to make sure it caught.'

'How can you possibly tell that?' Tian asked.

Ronsley shrugged. 'There's signs. You get to understand what an accidental fire looks like. And there was no reason for a warehouse that was just used to store cotton goods to go up, was there? I mean, you didn't have a boiler going in there, and there was no storm, so it wasn't a lightning strike. What else could it be but deliberate?'

Through the numbness that seemed to afflict her, Annie managed to force out a few words. 'I'm sure you and your men did your best and I thank you for that. And will you please tell the sergeant when you see him that I'd like to talk to him, as well?'

'Yes, Mrs Gilchrist.'

Annie was looking round, frowning. 'Hasn't someone sent for Mr Peters?'

Mr Ronsley nodded. 'Aye. We sent for him as soon as we knew it were alight, but his wife sent back word that he's out of town, visiting his father. And he's not expected back till tomorrow.'

Whoever it was had chosen their time well. Matt didn't often go to stay with his father. Once his wife died, Sam Peters had found backers to help him set up a house in the country as a place where the insane could be cared for. Matt hated to go there, for it reminded him of his own mother and how she had needed the same care when she grew strange towards the end of her life. And yet, his father seemed happy in his work. Dr Lewis supervised the way patients were treated, and the house was always full.

'The Lord called me to this work,' Sam always said, for he was as deeply religious as John Gibson, and his care of the deranged patients was tender and thorough.

When they got back to Ridge House, Annie made for the library like a blind woman feeling her way. Tian would have followed her, but she turned and said in a cool, distant voice, 'Could you leave me alone for a bit, please? I want to think.'

'I want to be with you, help you.'

Her voice took on a sharper edge. 'I *need* to be alone.'

'Annie, let me stay with you,' he begged.

She shook her head, walking on and closing the door as if his words had not really registered.

Behind Tian, Winnie was shaking her head. The garden lad had come running to tell them about the fire, so they all knew what was wrong. The mistress was taking it badly, by her expression. And you couldn't move her when she got that look on her face. Even Mr Hallam had known that. She had seen him sometimes snap his mouth shut and sigh.

When Winnie turned and saw the misery on Mr Gilchrist's face, however, she forgot her place, going up to him and touching his sleeve to gain his attention.

'It's one of the warehouses, isn't it, sir? We heard one was on fire.'

He nodded. 'It's a complete ruin.'

Winnie tutted. 'What started it?'

'Someone set it deliberately.'

She stared at him in horror, then her gaze went to the library doors. No wonder the mistress was taking on so. 'Best just to leave her alone then, sir,' she offered. 'She's one to hold her hurts inside herself, the mistress is.'

Tian looked at her for a moment. 'Yes. So it seems. Thank you, Winnie.' He turned on his heel and strode up the stairs two at a time.

Annie didn't come upstairs to join him until well after midnight, and when she did she was abstracted, giving him only half her attention.

'Tell me what you're thinking?' he demanded, pulling her round to face him.

'I'm thinking that I need to get these clothes off. They're filthy. I didn't realise how much mess a fire makes.'

'Don't fob me off! What's brought that look to your face? What are you taking on your shoulders now?'

She pulled away from him. 'It's my fault we've lost so much, Tian. Matt wanted to sell all the cotton goods at the end of last year, when prices were so high. And I wouldn't. In my pride, I felt sure I knew better, felt sure that the prices would go up more.'

'And they have gone up.'

'But I haven't got anything to sell now. I should have sold them. And,' she added in a low voice, 'there's worse.'

'What?'

'Matt wanted to increase the insurance and I wouldn't. It's such a solid warehouse and we had a night watchman. I didn't think—'

'No one is omniscient, not even you.'

'I keep wondering who hated me so much that they would do this. Surely it's not Pickering?'

He could not answer that. He had been wondering the same thing. And he could not seem to offer her any real comfort that night.

As they were sitting down to breakfast the next morning, there was a loud, urgent knocking on the front door. 'What the hell next?' Tian demanded, making no apology for his language.

No one answered, but all eyes turned towards the door.

A voice could be heard saying, 'I must see her at once!'

Annie put down her napkin and stood up. 'It's Matt.'

Tian stood up, too. 'Shall we see him in the library or do you want him to come in here?'

She frowned. 'There's no need for you to—'

He just walked round the table and offered her his arm, his face determined. After a moment's hesitation, she took it.

In the hall, Matt took a step towards them. 'Annie! Mrs Gilchrist! I came as soon as they told me.' He didn't even nod to Tian.

'Will you come into the library, Matt?' She tried to pull her arm away from her husband's, but Tian held on to it firmly and walked across the hall with her.

'You heard about the fire?' she asked Matt as Tian closed the library doors behind them.

Matt nodded. 'I was out of town at my father's. It's too far to walk home. I only just got back on the early carrier's cart.'

What did she care about how he'd got back? 'Sit down.'

He did so, staring at her black-shadowed eyes and tense body. 'I – I think I have some good news for you.'

'That'll make a change.' Her voice was bitter.

'Tell us, Matt,' Tian said softly, putting his arm round his wife's shoulders.

He took a deep breath. 'Annie, you know you didn't want to increase our insurance? You said the goods would be quite safe in a warehouse that was watched night and day, and there was no need to pay a higher premium?'

'I was wrong.' Then she came out of her misery to stare at him, for there was something in his face, a sort of pride.

'Well, I increased the insurance cover anyway. And,' Matt hesitated, 'I did something else – I moved half the stock out of the warehouse. I just – I couldn't feel happy with it all in one place.'

She sat like a frozen creature, her whole face still, as if she could not take in what he was saying. 'Tell me that again, Matt.'

'We've only lost half the stock and it's well insured. I know you think I'm a worrier, but when the prices kept rising, I couldn't help thinking how much money those goods represented. So I moved them. Bit by bit. I didn't want people to realise what I was doing. There was just me and a couple of our operatives involved, and I swore them to silence.'

'Well, done, man!' Tian said, but neither of the others seemed to notice his remark.

'You didn't realise what I was doing, either, did you?' Matt continued, nodding. 'I know the fire is still a blow, but what with the extra insurance and half the goods being in the raw cotton stores at the mill, I think—'

Annie let out a long sobbing breath. 'Oh, Matt! Matt, I—' She buried her face in her hands for a moment, then looked up. 'Thank heavens! Oh, Matt, you've done so well. Thank you.'

Tian could feel her shaking, feel the effort she was making to control herself. 'Leave her now,' he said. 'Annie's exhausted. She didn't sleep much last night.'

She turned on him, her eyes flashing. 'I'll tell Matt when to leave. I don't wish to be treated like a child who needs a nap, thank you.' She went across to the desk and picked up a pen, dipping it into the ink and shaking off the excess impatiently, so that it spattered all over the polished surface. 'Give me that insurance total again, Matt. How much extra did you take out?'

Tian got up and strode out, not returning to the dining-room but walking upstairs to the room he used as a studio. He went to stand by the window, staring out, his face set in bitter lines. He hated it when Annie wouldn't let him look after her, was furious at being spoken to like that in front of Matt Peters, and worried sick at the way she ran herself ragged. He had heard of people working themselves to death and it seemed to him that Annie was trying to do just that. Why wouldn't she share her burdens? The Lord only knew, they were heavy ones.

There was a tap on the door and William came in, sent up by Elizabeth who'd seen Tian crossing the hall from her seat at the great dining table and realised from his expression that something else had upset him.

William hesitated in the doorway, then cleared his throat.

No answer. Tian might have been a figure carved from wood.

William went across to touch his step-father on the arm. 'Tian—'

The other man looked at him, misery in his eyes. 'She always shuts me out.'

'She doesn't mean to hurt you. She's just so used to dealing with everything herself.'

Tian suddenly crashed his clenched fist on the table, sending paint brushes scattering. 'Well, she can just get unused to it. I'm her husband, not a plaything to be picked up and put down.' He sighed and tried to set his anger aside. 'Thank you for taking the trouble to come and speak to me, William, but it's something Annie and I have to resolve together. I thought we were making progress then today, she – I might just as well not have existed.'

'I know she loves you.'

'In her own way.' But would that way be enough? For he

would not be left sitting at the periphery of her life like that. That was why he sometimes allowed himself to show his temper, sometimes created scenes. Anything to shake her out of her obsession with doing everything herself, anything to make her take notice of him. No other millowner in Bilsden had done more than her. Not even Simon Darrington, still busy renovating his estate, could equal Annie's devotion to her people. And Tian did truly admire her for it. But he also worried about her quite desperately at times.

34

Summer 1863

It seemed a year for 'firsts' in England. In London the first underground railway had opened in January, carrying people beneath the busy streets and ancient buildings.

'We'll go down to London and have a ride on that Metropolitan Line,' Tom told Rosie as summer approached.

'Will you ever grow up, Tom Gibson?'

He pulled her close. 'No,' he breathed in her ear and chuckled as she blushed bright red.

In another first, the Co-operative Wholesale Society was formed in Manchester, to provide sound goods for sale in a more organised way – for every town, in the North at least, now seemed to have its Co-operative Society and they had all been buying goods for themselves. John Gibson took a great interest in this, for he was a firm believer in the Co-operative movement, even though this sometimes gave him a conflict of interest between Tom's shops and the local co-op.

The Football Association was formed in London, as well, and definite rules were drawn up for the game. William waxed enthusiastic about the prospects for the sport. 'You'll see,' he told his mother, 'this will lead to better competitions between teams, and will give working people something to do with themselves apart from going into pubs.' And he promptly went out and started the Bilsden Football Club, gathering a group of like-minded men together and holding meetings in the 'Stute to work out the details, then presenting the idea to several local businessmen.

But best of all was the information trickling in from America that the North seemed to be gaining the upper hand in the war. Again, it was Tian people turned to for an authoritative interpretation of each piece of news.

'Will the war be over by the end of the year?' folk always wanted to know.

He would shake his head. 'I don't think so. But maybe by next year.'

And they would brighten, these gaunt, unhappy people, who continued to suffer for that faraway war, a war in which England as a whole wasn't really involved but which was crushing the cotton workers of Lancashire.

In Bilsden, after the warehouse fire, the Gibson family's troubles seemed to die down for a while. What with the extra insurance money and the stock they still had, Hallam's found itself with reasonable reserves to tide it through another year of want for its operatives, and Annie lost that desperate care-worn appearance.

But she still worried about who had set the fire and whether they would try again.

The Burns brothers were furious when they found out that they had not done as much damage as they hoped.

'Bloody Gibsons!' Don growled. 'They allus manage to win.'

'They won't win for ever,' Harry Pickering said, leaning forward and tapping his nose. 'I've got another little plan—'

'What?' Don demanded.

'Give me time to work it out, lad. We want to make sure we succeed this time, don't we?'

At least in Bilsden there was more work now, for the lake had provided over a hundred jobs and even Hervey Bamforth admitted that the operatives had persevered, built up their muscles and were now making a reasonable effort at digging out the requisite hollow. Not like real navvies would have, but better than he'd expected.

On fine weekends that summer and autumn, many folk from Bilsden made the trip out to the lake to see how it was coming on, and Tom and Annie lent money to a few enterprising women who had the happy idea of providing refreshments for the sightseers.

Other minor entrepreneurs managed without Tom's help. They knocked up some benches and tables for picnicking, rough furniture made from scavenged materials. Hervey allowed them to store the pieces with the digging equipment in an area watched carefully at night, then, on fine days, they pulled the things out and washed them down at dawn, charging a small sum for their use.

The engineer, who seemed to regard the lake as his personal territory, grew annoyed at the way sightseers just wandered across the workings, slowing down progress and putting themselves in danger, so he got the men to set up plank walkways across the muddy bits, with ropes tied to stakes, to keep folk away from the rest of the chaos. He even hired a few lads to guide them across from point to point and tell them what was happening.

'I'm glad to be part of this,' Hervey said abruptly to Tian one day.

'So am I.'

'Your wife's an amazing woman.'

'Mmm.'

'And I like your ideas for landscaping the area round the lake. It'll cost a bit more, of course, but it feels right.' He looked sideways at Tian, cleared his throat and added, 'How about coming in with me on a bit of landscaping now and then?'

Tian looked across the slopes which were beginning to show the shapes he had envisaged. 'Why not? I've enjoyed it.' And so a long-term collaboration was born.

'It's going well, isn't it?' Annie asked him as they stood looking down upon the hive of furious activity one day.

'It is.'

She looked sideways at him. He had been cooler towards her since the warehouse fire and she had been feeling guilty about how she had behaved towards him ever since. But whenever she tried to apologise for shutting him out, she could not seem to find the words. And if more trouble came to them, could she share her worries with him, change the way she instinctively thought and reacted? She was not sure, only sure that if she didn't try, she would alienate him completely. Already he was talking of going over to Ireland to see his family: 'With or without you. I can't leave it too long. My mother's been ill this year.'

And that had made her realise how much she enjoyed being married to him. 'Tian, I—' she began, but Tom and his family strolled up just then and the moment was lost.

As summer moved towards autumn, Tian still received letters from his friends in America, especially from Thaddeus Brownsby, who seemed to have little trouble getting mail through. He didn't show these letters to Annie and was very vague about their contents. She was beginning to wonder about them and the investments he refused to discuss in detail. What news did they contain to make him frown and grow tetchy?

One of the letters had brought news that the South had been badly defeated at places called Vicksburg and Gettysburg. It arrived at the same time as the news was being reported in the newspapers, but it gave a lot more information. 'It can't be long now,' Thaddeus wrote. 'If those stubborn fools in the South would only face up to it, they're defeated already.'

There was general rejoicing in Bilsden at the news. Surely now the war would end?

But it didn't. So the hope that had flared brightly for a time died down again and folk turned back to their own concerns. Apart from the ongoing question of getting enough to eat, the thing in which everyone took an interest, whether they lived in fine houses up on Ridge Hill or in one room down in the River Rows, was the lake. Spinners Lake. The name was firmly entrenched now, a source of pride for the whole town.

After another letter from America in late August, Tian seemed more on edge than ever. It was his turn to retreat into himself and sit worrying in corners of rooms, or staring blindly out of the window.

'Is something wrong?' Annie asked him one day.

He jerked out of his reverie. 'Wrong? What should be wrong?'

'I don't know. But since you got that last letter – is it your investments? Has something gone wrong with them?'

'Not yet.' He got up to leave the room. 'I think I'll just go and play with my paints.'

Annie grabbed his arm. 'Tian, wait! Won't you tell me about it? Share your troubles?'

He grinned at her, not a nice grin. 'Why? Do you tell me everything?'

She flushed and drew back.

'Tit for tat, my pet. Tit for tat.' He strolled out, leaving her staring.

But by the time he got to his studio, the worry lines were back. Thaddeus wrote that the *Night Wraith* , as their blockade-running ship was called, was over two weeks late returning from its latest voyage. Tian was now bitterly regretting that he had gone against his original intention of not investing every-thing he owned in this risky venture. He was not, he decided gloomily, the stuff of which gamblers were made. But the two early voyages had been so profitable that when another backer had dropped dead and his more cautious widow pulled out of the enterprise, Tian had used his profits to take up another share.

Two more weeks seemed to crawl past. Why had he done it? he wondered as he lay awake fretting. Why had he risked so much? He must have been mad. Painters could be dropped by the public as quickly as they became fashionable. Without his American money, he might end up dependent upon Annie, and he did not think he could bear that.

Then news came that his mother was ill.

'I have to go and see her,' he told Annie. 'Will you come with me?'

'How can I?'

'How can you, indeed? I'm only your husband, not important enough to deserve your support and time.'

When she came home from the mill to say that she had changed her mind and would come with him, he had left for Ireland. And the house seemed empty.

'You should have gone with him,' William told her bluntly.

'Eh, lass, he needed you with him,' John said more gently to his daughter.

'You're not treating him fairly,' Tom said.

So it was Annie's turn to lie awake and worry. And it was Annie who wrote the first letter, a long epistle explaining that she had changed her mind and would have come with him if he had not left so precipitately. The letter lightened Tian's misery a little, but he still felt resentful that she had not agreed to come when he had first broached the matter.

He returned to Bilsden as suddenly as he'd left. Annie, when she saw through the window who was getting out of the station cab, dropped her papers on the library floor to run across the hall and throw herself into his arms, heedless of everyone else.

Winnie stood there, smiling fondly at her employers. When she saw Mrs Gilchrist covering Mr Gilchrist's face with kisses, her delicate sense of timing made her withdraw to the back of the hall and leave the front door standing open, with all the luggage piled messily nearby.

'Oh, Tian, I missed you,' Annie kissed him again. 'Don't go anywhere without me again! Promise!'

'I promise.' He pulled her close and just held her. He had missed her, too.

'How's your mother?'

'Better. But looking older.' He breathed in the clean smell of Annie's hair and the light eau de cologne she sometimes used. This was the way he'd hoped she'd greet him, the way she never had before.

Something hard and angry inside him softened a little. He was glad she'd missed him. But would she turn to him if there were trouble in her concerns? If she didn't, if she still held him at arm's length, then he didn't know what he'd do. For he did not intend to spend his life waiting for her attention – or forgiving her when she failed to give it at his need. She had to want him, turn to him, walk with him every day, or the marriage would be a failure as far as he was concerned.

Two days later, with Tian busy painting in his room, Annie decided that she felt like a walk. She had not seen her younger sister for a while, so in the afternoon left everything at the mill to Matt's tender care, told Robert to go home without her – to their coachman's obvious disapproval – and set off walking through the Rows. It was such a fine day that you could not help feeling cheer ful and the people she met seemed similarly uplifted by the weather.

On a sudden whim, she took a short cut to Joanie's house, smiling to remember her childhood when she had played in back alleys like these. As she opened the high wooden gate of the back yard, someone pushed her hard, making her stumble forward. She would have fallen but for a large hand, which stretched out to catch her and which kept hold of her.

'Harry Pickering!' she gasped, then turned her head and saw Bill Burns. His brother Don was holding her.

'Mrs Bloody Gilchrist. Two pretty birds in one snare.'

Annie stared. What was Pickering doing here?

'Hold her till we get the other one.'

Don Burns pulled Annie aside, one hand covering her mouth, and the other two men crept along to the kitchen door. Harry risked a peep inside and nodded to Bill, then he opened the door very quietly.

Annie strained against her captor, but she might as well have tried to move a rock, so she tried to kick him.

After a moment, Don gave her a shake and growled, 'Stop that!'

The minutes seemed to crawl past as Annie stood there, with the late-afternoon sunlight mocking the fear that now set chills running through her. What was happening? What mischief was Harry Pickering stirring up now? She had no hope of getting away from a man so strong, but she tried a sudden jerk, to see if she could catch Don off guard. If she could only call for help, surely someone would hear her?

He simply shook her like a rag doll. 'Stand still or I'll knock you out.'

She stood still. You could do nothing to help yourself if you were unconscious and she didn't doubt that he'd carry out his threat.

It seemed a very long time before the kitchen door opened again, and when it did, Harry pushed Joanie out in front of him. Her hands were bound behind her and there was a gag in her mouth. When she saw her sister, she stopped dead in her tracks.

Harry shoved her forward so hard that she fell. 'Oh, dear,' he mocked. 'I do hope you haven't hurt yourself, Mrs Burns. Your husband would be that upset.'

'No need to hurt her,' Bill protested.

'That's the best way to treat women.' Harry dragged Joanie to her feet, banging her against the wall. 'Roughly. It makes sure they do as they're told. Now, you hold her still and I'll deal with the other one.'

He grinned at Annie and reached out to grab her from Don. His hands were far from gentle as he put a gag in her mouth. 'Now get those bloody hoops off.'

She panicked and tried to kick out at him.

He banged her against the wall and when she stopped struggling, pushed his face close to hers. 'I'm not going to rape you, you silly bitch, but those damned hoops will be in the way where we're going. Now, either you can take them off, or I will.'

Annie fumbled for her skirt, untying the tapes that held her hoops in place. As the whole contraption fell to the ground, she was dragged aside and Harry kicked it out of the way. Then he pulled out another piece of rope and tied her hands together behind her.

'Go an' get that cart,' he ordered Don. 'And look sharp. We don't know how long your ma will be out shopping.'

Don slipped out of the back gate and Harry pulled Annie and Joanie to stand beneath the overhang of the coal house, where someone looking out from one of the back bedroom windows of the other houses wouldn't notice them. He and Bill stood in front of them, Harry smiling and nodding to himself, his body very close to theirs.

Standing pressed against the wall behind the two men, Annie felt sick with fear. She looked sideways, seeing how white Joanie's face was, and the two sisters exchanged glances. What did these men intend doing with them? Surely – surely they didn't plan to murder them?

'Hurry up, Don!' Bill muttered beneath his breath, jigging to and fro.

Harry just smiled. 'Don't be so nervous, lad. We've got every detail planned. Nothing's going to go wrong now.' Hadn't he planned all the other troubles they'd caused, so that no one could pin anything on them? And hadn't his planning worked every single time?

There was a clopping sound from the alley and Bill opened the back gate slightly. 'It's him.'

Don came through into the yard. 'All clear.'

'Right. Quick as you can.' Harry grasped Joanie's arm and began to drag her towards the gate, and although she tried to resist, he just laughed and jerked her along, his fingers biting into the soft flesh of her upper arm.

Annie found it just as impossible to stop Bill pulling her after the others.

At the gate, the two men paused again.

'Still clear,' Don said quietly.

'Quick!' Harry whispered.

The two women were pushed outside and tumbled into the back of a cart. Old sacks and rags were then piled over them and jammed well down until Annie felt as if she were suffocating in a dark tunnel. Beside her, she thought she could hear Joanie moaning in her throat, but the sound was so faint that she could not be sure.

A heavy weight settled on top of them, pressing Annie's cheek into the rough wood of the plank floor, and the cart set off, jerking and jolting down the back lane.

'Hey, are you collecting rags now?' a voice called. 'Because if so, I've got some.'

'Aye,' Don called back. 'But I've got a full load now. I'll be back tomorrow. Have your stuff ready then.'

'I won't give you owt unless you give me a soap stone.'

'I'll give you twice what the Gibsons give you.'

Underneath the pile of rags, Annie desperately tried to call out, but could only gurgle faintly in the back of her throat. It was terrifying to lie there, so close to help and so powerless to make her presence known. She could not believe this was happening to her in the centre of Bilsden.

The cart continued to rumble along, but Annie, straining her ears to listen, decided they must be using the back streets because the going was so rough. There was not much other traffic and not many voices called out greetings. Another stop and a long pause, then suddenly the heavy weight was lifted, the sacks and rags were tossed aside and the two women were pulled out and shoved hurriedly through yet another back gate. A man walked past at the end of the alley, where it met the next street, but didn't turn his head.

'Phew!' Don wiped his forehead. 'Thought we were caught then, for sure.'

'He didn't even look down the alley. Stop worriting and take that cart back!'

When they were all inside, Harry fastened the gate carefully with a padlock. 'Don't want anyone interrupting us, do we?' he asked. He didn't wait for an answer but led the way briskly into the house, dragging Joanie and leaving Annie to Bill Bur ns.

Inside, Maddie was waiting for them.

'Get us summat to eat an' drink,' Harry ordered. 'An' be quick about it.'

Maddie looked sideways at Joanie, who glared at her erstwhile friend, though the gag prevented her from speaking.

Maddie flushed and went over to the fire. Harry threw Joanie into a chair and fastened her bound hands to it behind her. 'I'll pull the gag out if you promise not to scream,' he said. Then he pushed his face right next to hers to add, 'And if you do try to call out, I'll throttle you till you're senseless.' He smiled to see the fear in her eyes. 'Now, nod if you agree to keep quiet.'

Joanie nodded. He took the gag out and said to Bill, 'You stand next to her while I see to the other. Thump her if she so much as squeaks.' Without waiting for an answer, he leaned over Annie. 'Same thing goes for you, Mrs Bloody Gilchrist. Do you want the gag out?'

She nodded.

'And will you keep quiet?'

She nodded again. If there seemed any chance of rescue, she would cry out and risk him thumping her. But there was no use crying out now, for no one would pay much attention to a shout or two, even if someone heard them from outside the house.

'What do you want with us?' she asked, when he pulled out the gag.

'What I wanted was some ransom money for Joanie here from her loving family.' The way he said the words was an insult. 'And my two dear friends simply wanted the rest of their father's property back from their mother. I'm sure Mrs Burns will pay up to save her precious daughter-in-law. But,' he stared at Annie thoughtfully, 'maybe I want more now.'

She stared right back at him. 'They'll be looking for us. They'll search all the houses. You'll never get away with it.'

He smiled. 'By the time they get round to a search, you'll be out of here. You don't think we're stupid enough to keep you in town, do you? And since you did decide to join the party, my dear Mrs Gilchrist, I feel we can ask for a lot more in ransom. Your fine new husband will pay to get you back safely, I'm sure. They say he's besotted with you.'

She didn't reply, just sat there, feeling sick with disgust and fear. He was right. If they were got out of Bilsden that night, it'd be too late for anyone to find them. Knowing Harry's cunning, she was sure he'd have a safe hiding place planned.

Time crawled by. The three men ate a hearty meal, but offered nothing to their two prisoners. Every time Maddie came near her, Joanie moved away, as if she didn't want even Maddie's skirt to touch her. And Maddie flushed when that happened, flushed and looked even more miserable.

She had a badly bruised face and Annie saw how careful she was to do as Harry told her, and do it quickly. She was clearly terrified of him,

As the sun sank lower and the little room grew stuffier, Annie realised that she was desperately thirsty. She cleared her throat and looked at Harry.

'Want something?' he asked.

She nodded.

'Well, make sure you speak quiet an' ask nicely.'

'Could we have something to drink?'

Maddie, who had been sitting in a corner, jerked to her feet as if ready to get it, but Harry gestured her back. 'No. Let 'em suffer.'

Annie shut her mouth. She wasn't going to beg.

'When we get to our little hiding place,' he said in a conversational tone, 'I'm going to have a bit of fun with you, Joanie.'

Bill jerked forward. 'You said you wouldn't—'

'Don't be so soft! Are you going to sit there for days with two nice soft pieces available and not lay a finger on them?' He leaned forward and his smile chilled Annie's blood. 'I'm not. I'll have 'em both before we give 'em back.'

Bill looked upset, but said nothing.

Maddie had made a sound of distress in her throat and Harry turned round to glare at her. 'You keep quiet!'

She lowered her eyes and tried to hide her fear that he would hurt Joanie. When she'd seen that Annie, too, was a prisoner, she had nearly fainted. For Annie was a rich woman and there would be worse trouble about this whole affair now.

439

Maddie sat trying not to fidget, trying not to draw Harry's attention to herself. She had begged him not to do this, but he had insisted that it was the only way left to him to get a bit of comfort in life. He didn't intend to slave for the Bilsden Gas Company until he was too old to stagger down to the office and scratch pen to paper. Marrying Joanie would have gained him what he wanted, but the bitch had married Bart Burns instead, so now he had to take any chance that offered. A rich family like the Gibsons would pay well to get their precious womenfolk back.

Joanie sat as quietly as her erstwhile friend, trying not to let panic overwhelm her. Annie had kept her face calm and the only expression to pass across it had been scorn. Joanie tried to do the same, but when she glanced sideways at Harry, he smiled knowingly and she knew she had failed to hide her fear of him.

Don, who had been out to check everything, came back and they settled down to wait again. It was a long time until dusk at this time of year and each hour seemed slower than the last. The men ate another meal prepared by Maddie, who joined them in a cup of tea, but didn't eat anything herself.

When they had finished, Harry smiled at Annie and Joanie. 'If you beg me nicely, I'll let you have a mouthful of water.'

Annie looked out of the window. She had no intention of begging him for anything. Joanie followed suit. He shrugged and made no attempt to give them anything.

One by one the men went to relieve themselves and Annie wished she could, too, but again she wouldn't ask, wouldn't give Harry Pickering a chance to mock her.

As dusk fell, Don went off to get the cart. It was completely dark outside by the time he returned.

'Let's go, then!' Harry said abruptly, jerked Joanie to her feet and stuffed a gag in her mouth again.

It was so easy. No one saw them take the two prisoners out to the cart. The same smelly sacks and cloths were piled on top of Annie and Joanie, and again somebody sat on the back of the cart, pressing down heavily on Annie's legs.

As it jolted off down the back lane, despair filled her. How would Tian ever find them if they left Bilsden? Who would have thought that Harry Pickering would be so filled with hate that he would do this? And would he let them go again, even if he did get the ransom he intended to demand? Somehow, she doubted it.

None of the conspirators saw the man pressed into the darkness just inside a gateless yard near the end of the alley, a man who had waited patiently for hours, watching the back of the house, not daring to move away in case he lost sight of his prey. He had tried to find a lad to carry a message, but it was a quiet street and at this time of day folk were busy feeding their faces.

35

Upper Hey End

When the cart at last came to a halt, Annie and Joanie were hauled off it, with pieces of cloth wrapped loosely around their heads to prevent them from seeing where they were. As they were hustled through the darkness into another building, Annie tried desperately to squint through a gap at the bottom of the cloth to gain some clues as to where they were. There were no sounds and the ground was grassy, so she guessed that they were out in the countryside now, for there were no signs of lights or sounds of people passing by.

Numb with despair, she dragged against Bill Burns as he tried to push her inside after the others. 'He'll kill us,' she whispered, feeling that this man was the least hostile of their captors. 'He won't dare leave us alive afterwards. Will you become a murderer?'

'Bring that bitch in, will you?' roared Harry.

'He's promised not to hurt you,' Bill whispered back to her. 'And afterwards, we'll be so far away, there'll be nothing you can do.'

But Annie didn't believe that Harry would leave any witnesses behind.

Inside, the cloths were taken off their heads and tossed into a corner. Annie stared around. It was a small place, roughly furnished, perhaps one of the little farmhouses on the edge of the moors, she decided, for it was so quiet outside. Where were the owners? Were they part of this conspiracy? Then she frowned as she realised that there were none of the touches which showed people were living there. No pottery except a few pieces on the table, no ornaments or curtains or cushions.

Just rough, wooden furniture and sacking across the windows. Despair flooded through her.

Pickering was standing in front of a small, banked fire, giving orders, clearly enjoying himself. 'Get this fire poked up, Maddie, an' look sharp about it. We all need a nice cup of tea.'

He flicked Joanie's cheek with one fingertip and thumb, leaving a red mark there. 'At least, some of us do. Some of us don't deserve anything.' He shoved her over to a bench by the wall, pushing her down so roughly she banged her head against the wall and yelped. 'Oh dear, did you bang your little head?' he asked with mock solicitousness, then promptly banged her head on the wall again, on purpose, hard. This time she managed not to cry out.

Annie turned to look reproachfully at Bill. He dropped his eyes, but she thought he didn't like what Harry was doing. Bill seemed the only hope, the gentlest of the three, the most reluctant conspirator if she guessed aright. Joanie was again staring at Maddie, who was pretending not to notice.

'They'll need to relieve themselves now,' Don said abruptly. 'I don't want this place smelling of piss if they wet themselves. I promised my friend we'd leave it all neat and tidy. He still uses it now an' then.'

Harry scowled. 'All right, then. One at a time. An' blindfold them again.' He turned to jerk his head at Maddie. 'You go out with them, an' if they escape I'll slice your tits to pieces.'

Maddie's hand went to her breast in an instinctive gesture and Annie realised in horror that Harry's sister didn't consider this an empty threat.

Again, Bill Burns winced.

When Maddie took Joanie outside to the privy, Harry sent Bill to keep an eye on the two women. But once inside the privy, Joanie pulled off the blindfold and said desperately, 'You've got to help us, Maddie.'

'Shh!'

'You've got to. He'll kill us if you don't.'

'He's promised not to.'

'Well, he isn't known for keeping his promises, is he? An' he's going to rape me again, isn't he? Will you stand by and watch it?'

Maddie gulped back a sob. 'I can't help you, Joanie. Don't ask me. I can't. You don't know what he's like. An' if you don't put that blindfold on again, he'll thump us both.'

When Annie was taken out to the privy, she said much the same thing to Maddie.

'I told Joanie, I can't help you.'

'He's going to kill us.'

'No, he's not! He promised!'

Annie's voice was low. 'He won't dare keep that promise. Think about that, Maddie. Are you going to stand by and watch Joanie die?'

She just shook her head helplessly and refused to speak again.

Once back inside the cottage, the two prisoners sat and watched the others.

A couple of times during the night Annie thought she heard a faint scraping noise outside, but in the end decided it must just have been an animal, a sheep probably. She leaned her head back against the wall, wishing she could fall asleep, as Joanie had, leaning against her. But her throat was too dry, the ropes were hurting her wrists too much and her head was thumping.

Across the room, Harry sat watching them. 'Don't even think about trying to escape,' he said softly.

Annie just stared back at him.

The faint call of birds heralded the dawn even before the sky turned light. Bill was watching them now, while Harry slept in the only armchair.

Annie looked across at him, trying to look pleading. When Maddie stirred, she turned her attention on her. She didn't have much hope. Maddie had surely not been so thin before? Her shoulders sagged and she walked like a defeated person, while her eyes looked absolutely haunted. What had Harry been doing to her, to make her so afraid of him?

When Bill got up and walked over to the window, Annie mouthed the word 'Please' but Maddie shook her head, shooting a scared glance at the recumbent Harry.

Suddenly there was a sound outside, surely a footstep? Annie jerked upright, hope shooting through her. Had someone found them? Were they to be rescued?

'Wake up, Harry!' Bill shouted. 'There's someone outside.'

He was out of the chair and over by the window in an instant. 'Are you sure?'

They listened, but the sound wasn't repeated.

'I did hear something,' Bill said. 'I did.'

Annie felt as if her whole body was strung taut with tension. She had heard it, too, and it had sounded like someone stumbling.

Then Harry chuckled and turned round. As he saw Annie, sitting forward as if listening, he threw back his head and laughed. 'It were a sheep,' he said. 'A bloody sheep, that's all. It's just walked away. Did you think your precious artist was coming to rescue you? Sorry, missus. No one knows you're here and no one's going to know.'

'How will you ask for a ransom, then?' She was beginning to hope that the noises during the night had meant something. It might be nothing, but just in case it wouldn't hurt to keep him talking, to cover any more sounds.

'I'm going into Manchester today. They'll not be able to trace a letter posted in Manchester.'

'Won't you be missed from work?'

'No. I'm ill. Pneumonia. Not expected to recover.' He smiled. 'I've thought of everything, you stupid bitch. When the warehouse fire didn't harm you, we decided to be a lot more choosy about what we did next time.'

She felt no surprise. 'We guessed you'd set the fire.'

He became rigid and gaped at her. 'How could you know?'

'We just did. You'd been seen with Bill and Don. But we couldn't prove it.'

He relaxed again. 'Nor you won't prove it. No one saw us do it.'

'There's definitely someone out there!' Bill yelled suddenly, in a high, hysterical voice. He rushed to slam the door shut and bar it with the rough piece of wood that slotted into two sockets.

Harry ran back to the window. A man was standing on the path outside. Sergeant O'Noonan.

'It's the police. We're lost,' Bill moaned.

Harry punched him in the arm. 'Shut up and let me think.'

'You inside there! We know you've got the women. You can't get away, but it'll go easier on you if you surrender!' the sergeant called, furious with the man who had slipped on the muddy ground and given them away before they could get close enough.

'Don't come any nearer!' yelled Harry. 'If you do, we'll kill them.'

The sergeant stopped moving forward.

Round the side of the house, Tian froze and tried to control the agony of his fear for Annie. They were lucky to know where she was. One of the out-of-work operatives he'd asked to keep an eye out had followed Annie to Joanie's house, then been surprised when she didn't come out again. He had heard her say quite clearly to the coachman that she was going to take her sister for a walk.

'I don't know why I felt so worried,' the man had said. 'I just did. So I thought I'd knock an' see they were all right. Only they didn't answer. So I went round t'back an' saw that cart pull away. It were Harry Pickering and them other Burns brothers an' I couldn't see as Mester Bartholomew's wife would want to have them comin' to visit. They're a right nasty pair. I followed 'em an' by the time I were sure summat were up, I didn't dare get back to warn you, or I'd've lost them. An' the one time you're desperate to see a lad as could carry a message, there has to be no one around. Too busy playing football. They're all football mad nowadays, the young 'uns.'

Tian had cut him short and called in Sergeant O'Noonan. A hastily organised search party had found Annie's petticoat and hoops, but little else. They had also proved that Harry Pickering was not lying on his sick bed.

Inside the cottage, the conspirators were beginning to fall out among themselves. 'We'll never get away.' Bill's face was white and fear was written all over it. 'Best give ourselves up quietly like he said.'

'I'm not giving myself up,' Harry said through his teeth. 'And anyone who tries to make me will have to get past this.' He pulled out a sharp knife and brandished it. 'They won't dare risk us hurting their precious women.'

There was silence in the stuffy little room. Maddie stifled a sob and Bill looked at the crazy light in Pickering's eyes and changed his mind about rushing him.

'D'you think it'll work, though?' Don asked hoarsely. 'Do you think they'll really let us get away?'

'Only one way to find out.' Harry raised his voice. 'I meant what I said. If you try anything, Sergeant, they'll be killed.'

O'Noonan's face and voice were as calm as ever. 'What exactly do you want, then?'

'We want the cart. Get someone to harness the donkey an' then bring the cart out front. After that, stand back where we can see you. We'll be holding knives at your women's throats. It's not a pretty sight, a throat as has been slashed open.'

To the side of the hut, Bartholomew bent suddenly, as if pain had struck his belly. If they killed her, he'd kill them, too. He wouldn't care if they hanged him for it afterwards. It wouldn't matter what happened to him if he lost Joanie.

The sergeant took a few steps sideways and conferred with one of his men in a low voice.

Harry called out, 'No tricks, you! If we see anyone leaving, we'll kill the women right off. An' we can see right down that track, so don't think you can creep away. Why do you think we chose this place?'

The constable looked at his sergeant, who shrugged and shook his head, muttering quietly, 'Do as he says for now. But be ready to run for help if I tell you.' Then he turned back towards the cottage and shouted, 'We want to see the women first, to make sure they're still alive.'

Harry grinned and grabbed the nearest of his prisoners by the hair. He pulled Annie to the front door. 'Open it!' he ordered Maddie. 'An' you push Joanie forward, Don, but keep a tight hold of her hair, like this. They can't move when you hold them by the hair.'

He shook Annie to demonstrate how helpless she was and tears of pain came into her eyes, but she stubbornly kept her mouth shut. She would not give him the pleasure of hearing her cry out.

Standing so close, she could see Harry's eyes gleaming. He looked wild and desperate. She could see no way of being rescued without one or both of them being hurt or killed. The hand that held the knife so close to her throat was trembling as if twitching to plunge the blade into her flesh.

As the two men and their captives stood just outside the door, Harry yelled, 'Here they are. Take a good look at them. It'll be the last time you see them alive unless you get us that cart ready.' He moved back into the room and threw Annie against the wall. Don let go of Joanie, who rushed to press herself against her sister.

To one side, Maddie was standing with a hand to her mouth, rocking slightly. None of the men was paying any attention to her.

'But they'll follow us,' Don protested. 'We'll just make things worse for ourselves.'

Harry shook his head. 'No, they won't. I'll tell 'em to get inside this cottage an' then I'll lock 'em in and set fire to it. That'll keep 'em busy long enough for us to get to the nearest station and catch a train. If they manage not to get themselves fried, that is.'

'They'll send word by telegraph to stop us in Manchester.'

'No, they won't.' He looked sideways at Annie and added, 'I've been making new plans during the night. I'm good at making plans. She fell into our arms like a ripe plum. Too good an opportunity to resist. An' I'm not lettin' owt stop me now.'

His eyes were so cold and chill that Annie shivered, in spite of her resolve not to show her fear.

'That's right, Mrs Bleedin' Gilchrist,' he said softly. 'You make sure you stay afraid. Pray your husband's afraid for you, too, an' then maybe, just maybe, you'll live to tell your grand-children about this little adventure.'

But Annie knew that neither she nor Joanie would escape alive if he got away. And her main regret was not for herself but a bitter sorrow that she had not shown Tian how much, how very much, she loved him.

As a man walked to the front of the cottage, leading a horse and cart, she stole a quick glance at Bill but he didn't notice her. He seemed almost paralysed with fear. It was Harry Pickering's will that was pushing them all forward now. She glanced sideways at Maddie, who was hunched up into a corner. At that moment, she looked like an old woman, old and worn.

The cart stopped at the front of the house and Harry roared out of the door, 'Now, stand together in a group to the side. All of you. If I see any others lurking around, I'll use the knife.'

'Do as he says, lads,' Sergeant O'Noonan said in a calm, quiet voice. 'We don't want him to hurt the women. And walk slowly.'

A group of six men gathered, coming round the sides of the cottage. One of them, Annie saw, was Tian, and another was Bart.

Tian looked across at her, all his love showing in his face, and Harry laughed loudly. 'There's your bloody fancy man, Annie Gibson. Not doing you much good now, is he?' He grabbed her by the hair again and began to edge out of the house. He seemed to consider Annie the more valuable hostage for it was to her he gestured as he made his threats.

She could do nothing but move as he indicated, for the knife blade was pressed right against her throat.

Bart was standing, like Tian, looking at the woman he loved, the woman whom he was helpless to rescue.

'Look at our little brother,' Don chuckled. 'We'll take very good care of your pretty little wife for you, Bartie boy. As long as you behave yourself, that is.' And the hand that held a knife to Joanie's throat was very steady.

But Bill felt shame shudder through him at the sight of her terror.

When they had edged past to the cart, Harry turned round and ordered the sergeant and his men to get inside the house. 'And move slowly! You put one foot wrong and Annie Gibson dies first.' He seemed to have forgotten that her name was no longer that of the family he hated so much.

Tian twitched, as if barely restraining himself from rushing to his wife's side, but the sergeant put his hand on his friend's shoulder and pulled him towards the house.

'Very sensible, Mr Gilchrist,' Harry called out. He looked as if he were enjoying himself. 'And don't poke your nose outside again.' Keeping his eyes on the door of the little cottage, he said quietly to Don, 'Go and check the outhouse. We don't want anyone left hiding outside to rescue them, do we? If you find someone, don't try to fight, just remind them that we've got the women and put them with the others.'

'Too many to fight,' he muttered as he watched Don go. 'But not too many for me to deal with, not so long as I've got the women and I keep my wits about me.'

After a nerve-racking silence, Don reappeared. 'No one else here!'

'Good, good!' Harry raised his voice. 'Just stand near the front door for now, Don. If you even see a face, shout and I'll cut her throat.' Then he lowered his voice. 'Feel in my pocket, Maddie. I've got the doorkey there. We'll lock them in and set fire to the place. That'll give us time to get away. And I don't care if they fry, especially this whore's fellow.'

Annie forced herself to keep still and quiet, to ignore whatever he said. He seemed almost exalted, his eyes glittering and his breathing quick and shallow. She had seen madness like this once before, when Beatrice Barrence nearly succeeded in killing her. Just let my Tian escape, she was praying to herself, unaware that behind her Joanie was praying the same thing about Bartholomew.

Maddie stepped forward and began fumbling in Harry's trouser pocket.

'Hurry up, you stupid bitch!' he muttered. 'We need to lock them in.'

So quickly that it took them all by surprise, Maddie grabbed the knife handle and jerked the blade away from Annie's throat, surprise allowing her to take the knife from him. 'Run!' she screamed to Annie in a voice so shrill it seemed to echo across the quietness of the early morning. Even as she spoke, Harry tried to take the knife back from her. They struggled for possession and it slashed across her cheek, but she managed to deflect the blade from her to him. It sank deep into his body and came out again. Everything happened so quickly that it took both of them unawares.

He grunted in shock and looked down at himself, seeing blood soaking through his shirt. Then raised one hand slowly as if still seeking to take the knife from her.

In panic, she stabbed at him again and luck, or maybe fate, drove the knife between his ribs and straight into his heart.

For a moment, he just stood there, then slowly he crumpled to the ground.

Maddie took a step backwards, seeming not to notice the blood spurting from the huge gash in her face. She laughed, a high, hysterical sound. 'You won't beat me again, Harry Pickering!' Then, as she stood and watched her brother fall to the ground at her feet, the laughter turned to sobs and she stood there, weeping loudly, one hand covering her bloody face.

As soon as he realised what was happening, Bill took advantage of the moment to drag his brother's hand and the knife in it away from Joanie's throat. He moved between her and

Don. 'Go on!' he muttered, giving her a push towards the cottage. 'Get away quick.'

'You're a bloody fool!' his brother yelled at him.

'But I'm not a murderer,' Bill shouted back.

At that moment, the men inside started to run out, the sergeant first. 'Don't touch those women again!' he roared.

Don looked wildly around, then took off, running across the moors, but Bill held his arms wide in a gesture of surrender and remained where he was, watching Bartholomew gather Joanie into his arms.

While two of his men ran after Don, the sergeant approached Harry Pickering's body and the woman who still held a knife in her hand. 'Give that to me, Maddie,' he said gently.

She looked down at the knife in bewilderment, then gave a loud gulping sob and threw it from her. Tears were still streaming down her bloody face and dripping pink on to her bodice.

'Thank goodness!' the sergeant murmured to himself, before turning to glare at Bill. 'Don't move, you!'

He nodded his head and kept his arms spread wide. 'I won't. I didn't want to do this. I won't give you any more trouble.'

As soon as she saw her husband emerge from the building, Annie ran across the rough ground, stumbling and sobbing under her breath. 'Tian, Tian!' she called and ran straight into his arms, clinging to him as if she never wanted to let him go again.

'Annie. Oh, thank God you're safe.' He clasped her to him so tightly that she found small bruises on her arm the next day from where his fingers had gripped her. He kept an eye on Bill and Maddie, ready to defend Annie from them if he had to.

Together, they watched the sergeant approach Maddie, watched as Bill stood there, watched as the men caught Don and brought him back after a rough-and-tumble fight.

Joanie was in Bartholomew's arms, weeping all over him and clutching at him.

Annie had tears running down her cheeks but was very still

and quiet, wanting only to cling to Tian. She still could not believe she was alive.

The sergeant put his arm round Maddie. 'Come on, lass. It's over now.' He looked across towards Tian and Bart. 'She killed him by accident in a struggle for the knife,' he said flatly. 'You saw that, didn't you?'

Tian nodded. Maddie had been as much a victim of Harry as the hostages had. O'Noonan sat her down on the rough bench near the cottage door then started tying Bill's hands behind his back. Bill made no effort to resist, but the two constables had a struggle to restrain Don in the same way. No one went near the dead body.

Tian let out a long, shuddering breath of relief and then realised that Annie was shivering. He started walking with her towards the cart. 'We need to get the two women back home,' he said to O'Noonan. 'They're exhausted.'

'Good idea. You and Bart get off. We can deal with these two.'

'Come on, love.' Bartholomew swept Joanie into his arms and started carrying her across to the cart.

But Annie stopped and looked up at Tian. She had been given a second chance, and this time she wanted there to be no doubt about how she felt. 'I love you, Tian Gilchrist. I love you so much. All the time, I kept thinking – I haven't shown him, haven't told him often enough.' She gulped, but had to continue, to say it. 'I didn't want to die without telling you how much I love you.'

'Shh now, I know that,' he soothed. And he did know it. She would never be the dependent type, but through the dreadful hours of that long, dark night, he had come to realise that their love was still the most important thing in his life, knowing that if she survived, he would have no further worries about their marriage. She was so much a part of him now that if she had died, something would have shrivelled inside him.

'Come on, darlin'. I love you, too. Let's get you home,' he said gently. And as they walked through the clear, sunlit air, he felt both joy and relief coursing through him.

'I won't – won't ever shut you out again,' she whispered as he helped her on to the cart. 'I've wanted to say I was sorry – ever since.'

He lifted her on to the cart and sat down with her among the rags and old sacks. On the driving seat, Bartholomew shook the reins and the donkey moved off. Joanie was nestled as close to him as Annie was to Tian.

'When this war is over,' Tian said into Annie's hair, 'I'll take you across to Ireland and we'll have a real holiday together.'

'A long holiday,' she agreed.

'With you all dutiful and loving?' he mocked.

She had not thought to be able to laugh again so soon, but found herself chuckling now. 'No. Just loving.' But the laughter turned almost immediately into a gulping sob.

He hugged her to him. 'That's good enough for me, love. That's the main thing I need in the whole world.' And now, he thought, they would both be working hard at building a good marriage. And he was sure they would be able to succeed, too.

'And when the war is over, we'll help Bilsden to prosperity again,' she said softly. 'Together.'

'Together,' he echoed, and was almost sorry when the cart met a group of men led by Tom and they had to stop holding one another close to answer the questions being thrown at them.

1865

Epilogue: June 1865

The day was sunny and the crowd in festive mood. Annie, resplendent in a new gown and glowing with happiness, clung to Tian's arm, not caring nowadays who saw how much she loved him.

Behind her, Tamsin walked along self-consciously beside Edgar, aware, as her mother was not, that everyone in the crowd was staring at them. Well, that was not surprising, was it? Her mother was the one who had had the idea for this lake, and her mother and Tian had made it happen.

'Doesn't the lake look beautiful?' Edgar asked. 'Isn't it a simply splendid day?'

Tamsin inclined her head in gracious agreement.

The crowd moved aside to let the group pass, but many of them called out comments.

'Bless you, Mrs Gilchrist!'

Or, more daringly, from someone who had known Annie when she lived in Salem Street: 'Well done, Annie love!'

As they took their places on the platform and the town band started to play, Annie remembered for a moment another occasion very much like this one, when she and Frederick had been present for the naming of Hallam Square. He would have been just as delighted as she was about what was happening today.

She sat pretending to listen, but her thoughts were far away. It had taken two years for the Civil War to end in America. Even Tian had not expected it to last so much longer once General Grant was called to the chief command of the Union forces in March 1864, but the South had held out stubbornly. Tian, with his vivid memories of a very determined man called

Darcy Langland, a man who was as sure he was in the right as any Northerner could be, had wondered how the people in the South were surviving.

'Civil War hurts everyone,' he had said many times. 'It cannot be worth it. Pray we never see such a thing again.'

When Lincoln was unanimously nominated for a second term at the Republican Convention in June 1864, people had again hoped that this would mean something more than a political event, but it didn't seem to. The war went on, brother still killing brother.

Tian had made a profit from the war, though, a big profit, thanks to Thaddeus Brownsby, though he had pulled out of any more risky investments once he heard the news that their ship had come safely back to port with its load of cotton. He now had his money in a series of more secure investments. His paintings were selling well, too, for he had got back his joy in his work and it showed. And, in partnership with Hervey Bamforth, he was collaborating on another lake project – which would bring in some money, but which would also give Tian immense satisfaction at making the world more beautiful.

And all through 1864, the cotton operatives of Bilsden had continued to labour on their own lake, first digging it out, then, as streams were diverted to fill it, working to shape the land around it. The money had been found to do the job properly, through public subscriptions, through Lord Liverpool's fund, through another penny rate and through Rosie's concerts. But Annie had let Tian manage more and more of the work, as she had let Tom and Matt take some, but not all, of the load from her in the other businesses.

Sitting on the platform, she suddenly remembered a golden holiday in Ireland the previous summer, when the sun had shone nearly every day. Never had she been so lazy, never laughed so much.

'Sure, it's a miracle, so much sun!' Tian had joked.

And it had seemed as much of a miracle to be accepted finally by Tian's family, as they shared with her their joy in

Sarry's engagement to a young man she had met when visiting friends in Dublin. Tian's mother was looking frailer but happy, and his father, sure now that Annie was making his son happy, spent some time getting to know her, asking about her life. He had also told her about Tian as a boy, Tian as a young man: 'So stubborn he was about the painting. Sure, we never had a chance of finding him a respectable occupation.'

'He's more than respectable now,' Annie had said. 'His painting of the emigrants has been hung in the Royal Academy and even Bilsden's new Town Hall – another Cotton Famine project – is to hang one of his paintings of the lake in a prominent position.'

She abandoned her memories, beguiling as they were, and looked sideways at Spinners Lake, feeling very proud of the part she had played in creating it. How beautiful it all was! And would be even more beautiful once the newly planted trees had grown tall and the bushes had spread out to cover the bare ground.

The music ended and she turned to smile at Tian as she applauded politely.

'You weren't even listening,' he whispered.

'No. I was enjoying a few memories.'

'Frederick would have been so happy to see all this,' he said, echoing her own thoughts. He could say his predecessor's name without bitterness now, because the ghost that had stood between them for so long was finally laid to rest.

'He would. And I'm happy, too. Though I'll be even happier once the mills start work again.'

'—so I'll call upon Mrs Gilchrist to name this lake for us and officially declare it open,' the Mayor intoned, turning to Annie.

Tamsin had to give her mother a poke in the ribs, because she and Tian were looking soppy again. Tamsin sighed. Sometimes she felt so embarrassed when people as old as they kissed and hugged.

Annie walked forward, then turned to hold out one hand to

Tian. 'I can't do this alone,' she called out, in a clear, carrying voice, 'for my husband's been a part of it all from start to finish. Indeed, he gave me both the idea and the name.'

There was cheering and whistling and the crowd swayed to and fro as some of them called out, 'Come on, then, Mr Gilchrist! Come out and join her!'

No one noticed the Mayor tut-tutting to himself, for he had wished it to be her day. But he resigned himself to her sharing the ceremony. She always seemed to have one or other of her family with her, Mrs Gilchrist did. They were a close lot, the Gibsons, even the ones who'd married and changed their names. His eyes strayed to Lord and Lady Darrington, then to Mr and Mrs Burns. Funny how marriage had made Joanie Gibson so pretty. He'd never thought much of her looks before.

'You all know the name of our lake,' Annie called out to the crowd, and they cheered and huzzahed again, so that she had to wait a moment, smiling broadly, before she added, 'The name Tian and I gave to it from the first.' How she had had to fight the Council to keep that name officially. Lacking dignity, they had said. No civic pride in a name like that. Some had even wanted to name it after her! And Leaseby, who always opposed her, had pushed hard for Victoria Lake. But she had persevered. And she'd won.

'I name this lake—' she paused, and the whole crowd paused with her. Then she finished with a lump in her throat, but with joy in her voice '—Spinners Lake.'

'Spinners Lake,' Tian echoed loudly. 'And It's rightly named for those of you who dug it out.'

'Spinners Lake!' a thousand voices roared, and then as the brass band struck up, Tian led his wife down to the edge of the water, where Edgar solemnly took off his shoes and socks and paddled in the lake on their behalf. Within minutes, a hundred other children and not a few adults had followed the lad's example on the stretch where seaside sand had been brought in to form a miniature beach.

The civic dignitaries then gathered in a marquee to enjoy a

feast, while the more common folk ate their picnics or bought food from the vendors who were there in full force that day.

John and Kathy had declined places in the marquee. They sat on blankets and ate with their children and grandchildren around them, beaming at the world. And it was not too long before Annie and Tian slipped out to join them.

'I'm very proud of you, lass,' John said quietly to his eldest daughter as she walked by the edge of the water on his arm.

'Thank you, Dad.'

'We all owe you so much, love.'

She flushed and tears came into her eyes. 'I owe you a lot, too. You're the best of fathers.'

Tian sat by Kathy, watching the two of them. Today you could see that they were father and daughter. 'She's a wonderful woman,' he said quietly.

'She is. And you're exactly the right husband for her.' Kathy suddenly saw Faith, trotting after her grandfather. 'Eh, look at that child! Someone go and catch her or she'll be in the water.'

But when Ben rushed to obey her, it was too late. Crowing triumphantly, the child sat in the water fully clothed, splashing and laughing at the droplets that sparkled in the sunlight.

'Her father is missing so much,' John said as he brought Faith back, after trying in vain to pretend to be angry with her.

Kathy patted his arm and pulled him down to sit beside her again. 'Well, our Mark said in his last letter that he was thinking of coming back, didn't he?'

'Aye, but only for a visit.'

'If he's happy there, we have to be happy for him, John. You can't keep your children on a chain.'

'Aye. I suppose so.'

As the long afternoon turned into dusk, people started to tear themselves away from the new lake. Annie and Tian escaped at last from their well-wishers and wandered further down the shore until they were on their own. Then they lingered for a while to enjoy the reflections of the sunset in the water. She sighed and leaned her back against him, safe in the circle of his arms. 'Spinners Lake,' she said softly.

'You should have let them name it for you.'

'No. It wouldn't have been right. We've all created this. Me, you, and the operatives, Rosie and Tom – even the Town Council.' And they stood there until the glorious sunset had faded into a clear, starry night, reluctant to end this wonderful day, at peace with themselves and their world.

The two children came searching for them and stood nearby, hesitating to interrupt them.

'You go and tell them we're waiting to leave,' Tamsin whispered, poking Edgar in the ribs.

'No! They're being all soppy.' But a smile curved his lips. He rather liked to see his mother and Tian kissing like that – though he'd have died rather than admit it.

CONTACT ANNA

Anna is always delighted to hear from readers and can be contacted via the internet.

Anna has her own web page, with details of her books, some behind-the-scenes information that is available nowhere else and the first chapters of her books to try out, as well as a picture gallery. You can also buy some of her ebooks from the 'shop' on the web page. Go to:
www.annajacobs.com

Anna can be contacted by email at
anna@annajacobs.com

You can also find Anna on Facebook at
www.facebook.com/AnnaJacobsBooks

If you'd like to receive an email newsletter about Anna and her books every month or two, you are cordially invited to join her announcements list. Just email her and ask to be added to the list, or follow the link from her web page.

Beautiful new editions of the Gibson family saga now available